LAURA ENGLISH

LAURA ENGLISH

Lynn Arias Bornstein

Stillpoint Digital Press

Stillpoint Digital Press
Mill Valley, California
http://stillpointidigitalpress.com

Published in the United States of America

Print ISBN 978-1-938808-13-5
Ebook ISBN 978-1-938808-14-2

Book, ebook, and cover designed by David Kudler

Cover art: "Swept in a Bubbly Dream" by Gun Legler (gun-legler.artistwebsites.com). Copyright © 2012, Gun Legler. Used with permission.

10 9 8 7 6 5 4 3 2

STILLPOINTDIGITALPRESS.COM

FOR ISI

PROLOGUE

LONDON, 1979

R obin Landau emerged from the South Kensington tube station straight into a downpour. Back from the Middle East over three years, he was still not re-accustomed to the Londoner's habit of carrying an umbrella, even on such a cloudless morning as this had been. Head lowered, he shouldered his way through the homeward-bound throng moving along the Old Brompton Road. The foot traffic thinned toward Onslow Gardens, and he was able to trot the rest of the way: left around the corner at Cranley Gardens and up the three white marble steps at No. 12.

He paused for a moment to catch his breath before turning the key in the lock and pushing open the heavy door. He switched on the hall light, flung his wet jacket on the coat rack and glanced at his watch. Half past six. His dinner date with Gwen wasn't until eight. Plenty of time for a long shower. Maybe even a quick nap. Yanking his tie to loosen the knot, he climbed the stairs, remembering when, as a boy, he had taken them two at a time. Rain was pelting hard against his bedroom windows. He tossed his clothes on the bed and, naked, crossed the hall to the bathroom. Shivering, he reached into the shower and pulled the circular knob just as doorbell rang. He paused for a second, debating whether to ignore it, when it rang again.

"Blast," he murmured under his breath and, grabbing the blue terrycloth robe that hung on the back of the door, padded barefoot down the hall.

A tall man stood under the portico, water dripping off the low brim of his hat, his rain-soaked trench coat glistening in the light from the hall.

"Mr. Landau?"

"Yes?"

"I have a letter for you."

"A letter?"

"Yes."

"Won't you come in, Mr. . . . ?"

The man stepped over the threshold but came no farther into the hall. He pulled a thick white envelope from the inner pocket of his coat and handed it to Robin.

Turning it over in his hand, he noticed that it was double sealed with heavy tape. On the front were printed the words: *IN THE EVENT OF MY DEATH.*

Robin felt a throb at his temples as a momentary darkness clouded his vision. "Who gave this to you?"

"I'm sorry, Mr. Landau. I am not at liberty to name the sender. I can only tell you that it has been in my possession for several years."

"I see." Robin swallowed over the dry lump in his throat.

"Now that I have delivered it, I will be taking my leave." The man held out his hand.

Robin stared at the envelope for a second, then took the stranger's hand into his own. "Goodbye, Mr. . . ."

The man turned without a word and walked swiftly down the white steps and into the driving rain.

Robin ran his fingertip along the heavy tape that sealed the bulging envelope. It must contain several pages, he thought. Sticking it deep in the pocket of his robe, he walked into the living room. Rain lashed the dark windowpanes, a driving wind rattling bare tree branches against their streaked surfaces. The room was freezing. Opening the door of the small cabinet that served as a bar, he found his father's Glenfiddich and poured a generous measure into a Waterford tumbler. He took a deep swallow. Instantly, a warm tingling sensation traveled down his arms to his fingertips. He switched on the tall floor lamp by the hearth and, squatting on his haunches, lit the twisted papers that stuck out under a small pile of kindling. As he stood, his eye caught his mottled reflection in the large antique mirror that hung over the mantelpiece. He smiled at the leprous face in the age-splotched glass. The grotesque image looked exactly as he felt — like something sitting at the back of Dorian Gray's closet.

Sighing deeply, he plopped into one of the wing chairs facing the fireplace and watched the flames as they rose through the kindling, finally enveloping the oak logs. He felt bone weary, worn out like some grizzled pensioner slumped in his favorite chair by the electric fire in an old people's home. As far as the world outside was concerned, Robin Landau was an enviable young man with no money worries and a bright future. But his friends and work acquaintances, even the Paxtons, weren't aware that under the deceptively vigorous facade there beat a heart that might not see him through many more years.

Robin had been concerned by the fatigue that had plagued him since returning to London, but reasoned that once he put the past behind him and settled into a new life, his energy would return. Months passed, but the fatigue persisted. Finally, he made an appointment with Dr. Daniel Sullivan.

"Now, what's all this nonsense about fatigue? You know, young Robin, I brought you into this world, and a healthier specimen I'd never seen." The aging family doctor's familiar gap-toothed grin hadn't changed since the days when Robin's mother took him to this same office for his annual checkup. "Come on. Let's have a look at you."

Dr. Sullivan spent an especially long time listening to Robin's heart. "I'd like to run an electrocardiogram on you."

As Robin lay on the examining table, electrodes pasted to his body, he watched Dr. Sullivan's smile fade as he read the ink trails on the long sheet of narrow graph paper. "Robin, it looks like you are going to need more tests. I'm ordering an echocardiogram and an angiocardiogram."

"Sounds serious."

"Could be nothing, but better to be on the safe side."

A few days later, Robin was back in Dr. Sullivan's office.

"The tests indicate an abnormal structure of the heart muscle. You were probably born with it. Sometimes these abnormalities do not become evident for many years. Have you ever had any symptoms? Weakness, maybe tightness in the chest, or pain in your arm or jaw?"

Robin remembered several such episodes with exactly those symptoms.

"Well," continued Sullivan, "as I said, often these conditions go on unnoticed until an episode of severe anxiety or shock puts undue stress on the muscle. Nothing much to be done about it, at least not immediately. Put simply, you need a new heart. A South African doctor, Christiaan Barnard, performed a successful heart transplant six years ago. Now they are being done in other medical centers all over the world. What I would like to do is put you on the list for such a procedure."

"In South Africa?"

"No. Dr. Norman Shumway at Stanford Medical Center, in California, is doing these surgeries with great success. I'm going to get your name on the list today. Your age is a big advantage, so I'm optimistic. Meantime, take light exercise, cut out rich food, not too much alcohol. Do you smoke?"

"No." answered Robin emphatically, thinking of his father.

"Good. I know this isn't the best news, but try not to obsess about it. The main thing is to avoid putting stress on your heart. What about work?"

"I like my job. No stress there."

"Good. I want you to have another cardiogram in six months. Hopefully, by that time we'll have some news about where you are on the transplant list. Until then, try to relax as much as possible."

Robin wondered if this condition might be a result of the incident, three years ago, when a piece of his heart went missing. It was the tender part, deep inside, the part that had made him feel safe when Mrs. Morley rocked him to sleep, or happy when he heard the voice of his father in the evening as he opened the front door and called to him — or the rapture when he looked deep into Michaela's eyes. But on that morning in Dov Perez's office at the Institute in Tel Aviv, the essential little fragment vanished — leaving a played-out muscle that beat on borrowed time.

He drew the thick envelope out of his pocket. And what about his mother? For this letter must be from her. In all his life had she ever said or done anything to touch that tender spot in what he used to think of as his heart?

Last night, sitting in this same chair, he had read in the Clarion that this latest play of hers was being held over yet again for another three months. Aunt Kit had tried to coerce him into flying to New York with her for the opening two years ago, but of course he hadn't gone. And now it seems his mother had dropped dead, on stage no doubt, or maybe during her fifth curtain call, leaving instructions to deliver this letter posthumously — how typically dramatic — by way of one of her toadies, the mysterious man who had failed to give his name.

But how could she be dead? Wouldn't Aunt Kit have called? No. They were in Portugal until next month. Wouldn't he have seen it in the evening papers? Her death would have rated major headlines. He had been in such a rush to get home that he hadn't thought to buy, or even look at, a newspaper in one of the kiosks in the Underground. And what about this letter? The man said it had been in his possession for a long time. Was it something she wrote years ago because she was feeling depressed when his father died, or was it when that other . . . no, he wouldn't think about that.

He should throw the wretched thing on the fire and have his shower, but he continued to stare at the leaping copper flames as they curled around the logs. He remembered when he was a little boy, living in this same house, sitting on his mother's lap and touching her bright coppery curls with his fingers. Maybe that was wishful thinking, and it wasn't his mother's lap on which he sat but his father's. Maybe he only gazed at his mother, sitting as she usually did in the matching wing chair on the opposite side of the hearth, her face achingly beautiful in the firelight. Maybe he only imagined what those soft masses of red curls would feel like to touch. His mother. Always just out of reach. He pressed the heels of his hands into his eyes. He wanted to cry, but nothing came. Not a single tear. It's a very sad thing when you can't shed even one tear for your own mother, but, then, he had never really known her — only a woman called Laura English.

CHAPTER 1

BOURNEMOUTH, 1940

Bournemouth Central Station was filled with noise, smoke, and a swarm of people — many in uniform, all in a hurry. Like a small island in the rushing stream of humanity, a child stood alone, bare knees drawn together against the gusts of wind howling down the platform, teeth clenched hard against the chill.

"Remember, when you get to Bournemouth, stay put and Aunt Rose will be there to meet you." Her mother's voice, as she settled her on the train that morning, was tinny to the child's ears, and the kiss that followed so brief she hardly felt its cool touch on her cheek before the tall figure in belted gray serge turned and made her way swiftly down the narrow aisle of the crowded car.

Heart racing, the child rose to her knees and, pressing her hands against the smudged window, watched as her mother carefully made her way down the steps from the train to the platform, where, pausing for a single heartbeat, she squared her shoulders and strode resolutely through the double doors and into the terminal.

As the train pulled out of Waterloo Station, the child's hand automatically felt for the stiff identification card pinned to the lapel of her blue plaid coat. More and more, these past months, she had seen the same sort of tag attached to the clothing of children who waited in silent clusters outside Paddington grammar school or St Mary's Church, from there to be sorted and sent, like parcels, out of London, as far as possible from the war.

Jane Parks remembered the day the war started, as it had for many other children in Britain, with Mr. Chamberlain's reedy voice breaking into a broadcast of *The Children's Hour*. It was a warm Sunday in early September, and after morning service at St. Mary's, the family had wandered over to Paddington

Green. As always on Sunday, shouting children raced over the lawns, still spongy from morning dew, and into thick privet hedges to hide from captors or ambush enemies. Their games were complicated and played by a set of constantly changing rules only they understood.

Jane's friends Brian and Sally Wallace ran over, each grabbing one of her arms. "Jane!" said Brian, his beet-red face looking as if it were going to burst. "It's Pirate's Booty, and I'm captain. You're late, so I have a first mate, but you can be second mate of the bridge or first mate of the main topsail."

"Maintop," answered Jane, and off they went.

"Oh God, this means they'll be at it for an hour at least." sighed Gladys Parks.

"And what else have we got planned?" said her husband, tucking her arm under his. "Come along, let's find some chairs and relax for awhile. Look, there are two under that tree." He led her in the direction of a large willow on the other side of the lawn. Squinting against the sun in the direction of the children, he smiled. "It seems like yesterday I was playing games just like that. Where does the time go?"

"I don't know, Frank. When I was a girl in Bournemouth, only boys played those kinds of games. We had to stay home and sew or bake on Sundays."

"And sometimes take a walk?" he smiled into her eyes. "I'll never forget the day I first laid eyes on you, strolling on the pier with your brother."

"And you were with your mother and sister."

"You were the loveliest girl I had ever seen. It was the last day of my holiday and I had to go back to university. I had no idea how I was going to manage it, but somehow, I was determined to meet you before leaving Bournemouth. You see, I knew right then that you were for me."

"And you did manage it." She smiled into his eyes.

"A bit awkwardly but yes, I did. Mum and Sissy went back to the hotel to pack, and I told them I wanted one more look at the sea. You were leaning over the rail and I stood right next to you and said . . ."

"Pardon me, miss, but have you seen a little white dog?"

He threw his head back and laughed. "That was the first thing that came into my mind."

"We went searching for that nonexistent little white dog for over an hour!"

"And we got to know each other pretty well in that hour, didn't we?"

"Enough for you to ask if you could call on me if you ever came back to Bournemouth."

"And I did come back. All through university and medical school, every chance I got, I came back."

"Frank." She grasped his arm, eyes turned up to his. "You do still feel the same, don't you?"

"Of course, I do. What a question."

"It's just that sometimes you're ... oh, I don't know ... distracted. You do mean so much to me. Everything, really."

"Sweetheart." He turned toward her. You know I always have a lot on my mind. Patients I'm worried about. But of course I feel the same, and you gave me our Janie. What more could anyone one ask?"

Yes, your precious Janie. It's she who runs to you every night and gets the first kiss. It's she who puts the light in your eyes. "Frank, if you ever stopped caring for me. I don't know what I'd . . . "

"Gladys. Now, enough of this nonsense." He glanced at his wrist watch. "It's almost half past one. I don't know about you but I'm hungry. I'll get Jane."

Dr. Parks walked across the lawn and, spotting his daughter with the other children, waved her in. He turned to look back at his wife. She was staring into space, a sad expression on her face. Monday hospital rounds couldn't come soon enough.

By teatime, Dr. Parks was settled down in his wing chair with the Times, while Jane, on the floor at his feet, listened to her favorite program on the wireless. She thought it very rude of Mr. Chamberlain to interrupt *The Children's Hour* and the adventures of Uncle Mac and Auntie Doris. Surely he could have waited until the program was over and the musical presentation that always followed came on.

At the sound of the prime minister's voice, Dr. Parks sprang out of his chair, unaware that his newspaper had fallen onto the floor.

"Gladys!"

She came from the kitchen, wiping her hands of a towel. "What is it, Frank? I'm right in the middle of getting tea."

"It's Chamberlain. On the wireless."

"What?"

"Shh. Listen."

All three stared at the radio as Arthur Chamberlain regretfully declared that a state of war now existed between Great Britain and Germany.

Gladys Parks tucked a loose strand of copper hair into its heavy knot at the back of her neck and, without a word, returned to the kitchen.

"What will happen now, Daddy?"

"Oh, I should think very little at first." Dr. Parks sat down again but made no move to retrieve the Times, which lay scattered on the rug.

"A girl at school said that if war comes, her dad is going to enlist." Jane looked up into her father's eyes, her own filled with apprehension. "Does that mean he'll go off to France, Daddy?" She had heard stories of the Great War when the men went off to France.

"Don't worry, sweetheart, I'm not going to enlist."

"No," said Gladys, setting out the last of the tea things, "you won't have to go to all the trouble. If the army wants doctors, they'll simply come and take you. Tea's ready."

"Don't worry, my Janie, they'll have to go through a lot of younger, fitter men before they get to me." He smiled at his daughter and smoothed the worried frown between her eyes with the tip of his finger. "And, besides, the war will likely be over by the time they do. Now, let's see what Mum has for our tea."

Despite his assurances, Frank Parks was inducted into the Royal Army Medical Corps the following month and posted to a military hospital near Liverpool. Gladys, without Frank to deal with her moods, turned stagnant. She went about her daily chores with mechanical thoroughness, leaving the house only for necessary trips to the neighborhood shops and spending most of the time sitting in her husband's chair, her large gray eyes fixed on the empty grate.

Jane's friends, whose fathers were now also away, had little time for weekend games, keeping instead close to home and their families, but Jane, who had no brothers and sisters to play with or talk to after the lights went out at night, remained stranded in the house with her silent mother.

"Mum, it's such a lovely day. After church, may we go to the zoo?"

"No, we may not. Your father may have enjoyed walking you around to look at a lot of caged animals, but I never did."

"I just thought we might get out in the sun, because once the rain starts . . ."

"Don't you have anyone you can play with?"

"No, Mummy. Sally and Brian have gone to their gran's today, and Gwen and Evan went to Wales to live with their mum's family."

"Well, find yourself a book then."

That afternoon, Jane took her worn copy of *East of the Sun and West of the Moon* from the bookshelf. Settling down in her father's upholstered wing chair, legs tucked under her, she opened to the first page. As Jane turned over the leaves, she was conscious of the faint scent of tobacco and bay rum that, after so many years, had permeated the faded brown and blue paisley-patterned fabric. It was almost as good as having Daddy right there beside her.

The following Sunday, with two dolls and her teddy bear, Jane acted out the story of The Princesses in the Blue Mountain. In the weeks that followed, she went through all her storybooks, acting out every tale, and so forgot, for a little while, how lonely she was and how much she missed her father.

Almost a year to the day of Mr. Chamberlain's speech, the so-called phony war turned real, and the Germans began nightly bombing raids on London. As she lay in bed waiting for the inevitable sirens, Jane created elaborate theatricals behind her closed lids until her mind drifted into nothingness, only to be jolted awake in the middle of the night by the dreaded whine. Groping her way out of bed, she struggled into her shoes and coat, grabbed the square brown box that held her gas mask, and trailed her mother out of the house and around the corner into the shelter that was, as always, filled with the sounds of crying children and the smell of too many bodies crammed too tightly together.

The noise from above that night seemed more terrifying than usual. All about them, women were comforting crying children. Jane ached for a warm arm around her thin shoulders. Tentatively, she moved her fingers along the folds of her mother's skirt, careful not to crease the pleated woolen fabric. Slowly, she placed her small hand over her mother's, but Gladys Parks, whose thoughts were miles away in Liverpool, remained oblivious to her daughter's touch.

As Jane sat through the suffocating night, waiting for the all clear, she studied the faces of the people in the shelter. Apart from a few old men, huddled against the sloping wall, it seemed to be occupied solely by women and children.

All the men are off fighting, she thought, and whispered to some long-ago imagined guardian angel, *Please keep my Daddy safe.* Her glance fell on a young woman who sat caressing her daughter's dark curls while rhythmically stroking the tiny back of an infant who lay sleeping across her knees. Suddenly, Jane felt as she once had, sprawled on the ground after falling out of a swing, with all the breath knocked out of her. As she watched the young mother gently soothe her children, a thought, which until that moment had only been the hint of a suspicion, took shape. Turning to look at her mother's face, pale and beautiful in the half-light, she knew with stinging clarity and utter certainly that her own mother did not, could not, love her. Shivering, Jane closed her eyes and once again turned her mind to the stage behind her eyes where the performance, which had been interrupted by the shrieking sirens, continued.

Music played in her mind, and dancers floated across a pink-lit stage. Jane hummed the tune. Eyes now opened, she stared to sway. It was an old-fashioned, much-loved, song. Softly, she began to sing the words and, as she did, felt a budding lightness in her body as if, by simply willing it, she could lift herself off the ground and fly. Without thinking, she was on her feet dancing in the spaces between the huddled bodies. A feeling of total bliss welled inside her as, all around, she saw smiling faces. Broadening her gestures, she sang the chorus again.

"Another, sing another!" voices shouted when it was over.

Jane glanced in the direction of her mother. She was smiling — a smile that reached all the way to her eyes.

"Yes, Jane," she breathed, "do sing another."

Jane sang and danced until the all-clear siren finally sounded.

Everyday life in London had moved underground. Jane's grammar school was now used as an evacuation center, and classes were held in the shelter under St. Mary's Church. There were no windows in the cellar at St. Mary's, and the dim light, provided by low-watt bulbs that swayed from the ceiling, did little to lessen the gloom.

Gladys Parks had signed on as a volunteer at Paddington Green Children's Hospital and now spent most of her days there, while Jane was cared for after school by Dora Brodie, a neighbor woman. Mrs. Brodie was terrified of the bombings.

"I'll tell you this, I'm not waiting for the Germans to fly over our street and flatten my house one of these fine nights. My sister in Folkstone wants me to come to her, and I'm going. I'm not keen on her husband — table manners like a pig at the trough — but needs must. I'll be sorry to let your mother down and I will miss you, Janie, but war is war."

Jane wondered how long it would be before they, too, would move out of the city.

A few weeks later, she had the answer. "I've had a letter from your Uncle Matthew," said Gladys as they were finishing their breakfast. "He tells me that one of the big hotels in Bournemouth has been taken over as a school for evacuated children. That means it must be safe there for now. He and Rose have offered to take you for as long as need be."

"Me? Wouldn't you be going too?" said Jane, looking up into the clear gray eyes.

"Not right away. I have to stay here because I'm needed at Paddington Green. Besides, I'll have a better chance of hearing news of your father if I'm in London. Christmas is only a month away, and he might get a few days' leave."

"But if Daddy comes home for Christmas, I want to be here, too."

"Don't you see, Jane? With the bombing getting worse every night, it's not safe in London. Most of your friends have already been evacuated. Your father would never forgive me if I let you stay. There'll be other Christmases after the war, but for now, you are going."

"I hardly know Uncle Matthew and Aunt Rose. What if they don't like me?"

"Don't talk nonsense. Most evacuated children are living with strangers.

They're your auntie and uncle, aren't they? Of course they'll like you. In any event, it's all settled. By next week you'll be away from all this racket and by the sea. Now, finish that porridge before it turns to glue."

"But Mum, if I'm not here to sing for you, you'll be so sad."

"Life is sad, Jane. I discovered that a long time ago. You have a gift to make people forget their sadness. It's not just the singing and the dancing. It's the way you hold your head and use your eyes."

"Yes, go on," said Jane excitedly.

"Nothing. Now, mind that porridge."

Once again, Jane rose up on her toes and peered down the length of the platform. The crowd had thinned, and except for a small knot of passengers waiting for the next train, she had an unobstructed view. Still, to her dismay, not a single person seemed to be looking for her.

She wondered what her mother was doing. At this hour she would be at the hospital tending to the people who had been hurt in last night's bombing. Although Jane had never been inside Paddington Green, she had framed a picture in her mind of the wards with rows of beds where her mother, tall and silent, ministered to the injured.

Another scud of cold air whipped against Jane's legs. She shivered. An icy knot of fear had settled in her chest. *What happens if no one comes to get me?* Teeth chattering, she looked down the platform for what seemed the hundredth time. A plump woman was striding purposefully in her direction, one gloved hand holding a funny-looking hat on her head, the other waving furiously. As the woman drew closer, Jane could see that a smile creased her broad face — a face that was suddenly familiar, soft and warm against her own as Aunt Rose bent to hug her.

"There you are, sweetheart!" Aunt Rose exhaled a long breath that smelled of butterscotch. "I was looking for you on Platform one instead of Platform two. Your Uncle Matthew always says I couldn't find my way out of a broom cupboard with a map, and of course, he's right."

She held the child at arm's length. "Look at what a tall girl you've grown into! But then, if I'm not mistaken, you'll be eight years old come spring. And bless me if you're not the very image of your beautiful mother. Well, sweetheart, we can't spend all day on this drafty platform, can we? Let's be getting on home."

Rose took hold of Jane's hand, gripping the small suitcase with her other hand. "My, what cold fingers. We'll have to see about finding you some mittens."

"I have a pair at home, Auntie Rose, but I forgot them."

The earnest expression in the child's voice made Rose smile. "Well, it's not an earth-shattering event, sweetheart. I was just worried about your poor cold little hands." She smiled down into the small face framed in a mass of red curls. It was a strangely adult face, finely modeled and devoid of color except for delicate tracings of lavender veins at the temples. A sudden tear glistened on the rim of the child's eyelid. Trembling, it clung for an instant to the tip of a golden lash before sliding down the pale high-boned cheek. She struggled against the tears, her small body rigid with the effort, but others followed, spilling out of her eyes and wetting her face. She clasped her aunt's hand with both of hers and held it awkwardly to her mouth.

Rose dropped the suitcase, sank to her knees, and took the little girl into her arms. "Ah, sweetheart," she crooned softly, "this must have been quite a day for you, and then me being late on top of it. Just go ahead and cry all the tears out of your eyes, and then we'll go home and see about supper."

Jane stood very still, her face pressed against the softness of her aunt's coat. The tiny hairs of its fur collar tickled her nose, but she did not move. It was a pleasant sensation. The sick feeling was gone from inside her and another one, quite different, was taking its place. She never wanted to move again.

"Better now, dear?" Rose smoothed back the tangle of curls and smiled.

Jane nodded.

"How about a sweet?" She dug in her purse and produced a piece of wrapped butterscotch.

Jane looked into her aunt's bright blue eyes, which had nice little lines at their corners. A shaky smile touched her lips and she took the candy. "Thank you, Aunt Rose."

Again, the woman picked up the small suitcase and they started to walk down the platform. "You're to have your cousin Ned's room. It's right at the top of the house, and it has a nice little fireplace so that it's always cozy and warm, even in winter. And there's a dormer window with a seat where you can look right out to the sea. I'm sure it was staring out that window for so many years that gave Ned the idea of joining the Navy as soon as war was declared." She chuckled and then sighed as they made their way out of the terminal and on to the sidewalk. "Ah, dear, this war is such an inconvenience. Ned was doing so well in engineering school. He only had one more year, and now this. Who knows how long it's all going to last and what will become of the young men and their careers. Oh my, look at the time. We'd better hurry. The bus will be along any minute."

Jane, who had never heard a West Country accent before, found the hard r's and sing-song of her aunt's words comforting to her ears. For the first time in a year, the terrors of war were forgotten.

CHAPTER 2

The house sat high on a chalk cliff above the ocean. Filled with a collection of fascinating objects, it differed in every way from the fanatically neat home her mother kept in London. Small boxes of silver, carved ivory and inlaid wood crowded the top of a crescent shaped table near a window in the living room. A wax doll with a delicately painted face and real hair, a treasured gift to Aunt Rose from her father on her fifth birthday, nestled on a cushion in the corner of the faded green velvet sofa. Ned's prized shell collection shared space on the mantel with a small porcelain monkey, tasseled fez cocked at a jaunty angle over one eye. Dog-eared volumes on every subject from Greek philosophy to practical gardening filled the bookshelves, and a variety of containers — silver bowls and crystal vases, jam jars and marmalade pots — held small bouquets of sweet peas and roses, bringing the freshness of the garden into the house.

Uncle Matthew's Victory Garden, on the leeward side of the house, away from the salty ocean wind, was a delight to the city-bred child. Within a week of her arrival, he put Jane to work helping him pull weeds in the rows of vegetables he had planted since war was declared. One afternoon, he showed her an ancient wishing well tucked away in a corner of the garden near a low creeper-covered wall. Spellbound, she watched as he taught her how to make a wish in the old way by cupping her hands under the water and sipping a bit from each hand as the wish was made.

It was hard to believe that her silent mother and short stocky Uncle Matthew, with his high spirits and ready grin, were really brother and sister.

True, they both had the Stokes family red hair and their eyes were the same hazel-gray color but mother's always looked so dreamy and sad, while Uncle Matt's danced with merriment and all but disappeared in puffy creases when he laughed. Jane's mother was like a queen in a story book, beautiful and untouchable. Uncle Matthew was a jolly elf who was always ready for fun.

Soon after she arrived in Bournemouth, her uncle took Jane for a walk down the Grand Promenade and into the public gardens not far from the house. "Nice, isn't it?" he asked, his eyes crinkling in a smile. "All the children in our neighborhood play here."

"Is it safe?" Jane asked, her eyes turning skyward.

"Yes, sweetheart," he said squeezing her thin hand, "perfectly safe."

Jane knew that her mother's family had been ironmongers in Bournemouth for generations, and she asked Uncle Matthew if she might see the hardware store. They hopped on a bus to the center of town, where he took her around the store and showed her the other shops along the High Street. They visited the Bournemouth Pier with its amusement arcades and famous railway museum, which Uncle Matt swore was the finest of its kind in the world. The winter gardens had been taken over by the Royal Air Force, but he promised that as soon as the war was over he would teach her to bowl on the indoor greens. They went to the Cliff House to see the exhibition of Japanese and Burmese art that had been donated by Sir Merton Russell-Cotes, a great uncle of Aunt Rose, who had been lord mayor of Bournemouth.

"Oh yes, the Mertons and the Easleys and the Russell-Coteses go back as far as anyone can remember in this part of the world. Not that your auntie is one to put on airs, but her family is an old one and, in its day, very grand indeed."

Aunt Rose served delicious meals, hungrily devoured with much chat and laughter, at a small round table in front of the stone fireplace in the kitchen. Supper was always a lively affair, for Uncle Matthew had an opinion on every aspect of Bournemouth life, be it the city government, the local football team, or his regular customers in the store. The Stokes' easy ways and sense of humor soon softened the watchfulness that had been in Jane's eyes since the nightly bombing of London had started.

As the months passed, Jane's old life in Paddington faded into a faintly remembered dream. Bournemouth had became her reality. The seaside town was different in every way possible from London. For one thing, the streets were intact. Destruction did not fall out of the sky at night, and there were no buildings with their façades blown away and their bedrooms and bathrooms grotesquely exposed for all to see. Instead of acrid smoke reeking from the remains of smoldering buildings, the pungent scent of salt filled the air. Best of all, there were no shelters and no sirens. Each night, Jane dozed off to the soft sound of the hissing sea.

At the age of eight, friendships are often sealed in an hour, and so it was the day Betsy Dwyer, a girl Jane's age who lived at the end of the street, said hello to her. Before long, the girls were inseparable. They walked to school together every morning and joined the other neighborhood children in their games after the last class was dismissed. To Jane's surprise, Aunt Rose told her that she could invite anyone she liked to the house — something that was never allowed at home in London.

"I don't want a gang of brats playing hell with my things," her mother had always said. "Go to the square to play. That's what it's for."

In Bournemouth, Jane was learning about freedom. Freedom from noise and smoke and gas masks. Freedom to go to a real school, above ground, with windows thrown open to the sweet, fresh air. Freedom to attend the cinema on a Saturday afternoon, after Uncle Matthew closed the store, and freedom to explore the promenades and the cliffs above the sea.

Best of all was the freedom to run down the dizzying walkway leading from the Stokeses' house to the beach. On Sundays, Jane and Uncle Matt rambled along the sheltered shore, counting the waves as they rolled in stronger and stronger, up to the ninth, which Matthew said was always the mightiest of all. Together, they scampered in and out of the hissing surf, chasing after the tiny gray birds that poked into the sand with their long needle-thin beaks. Diligently, Jane and her uncle searched for shells in the coarse sand, and later, when Jane's pail was filled with treasures, they played with long whips of kelp, which they dragged along the beach and up the zigzag walk home.

Jane was fascinated by the slow-talking townspeople, as different from Londoners as Bournemouth was from the city. Soon, she was making Rose and Matthew roar with laughter at her hilarious imitations of the town's more colorful characters as well as the holiday-makers who, despite the war, still trickled in when the weather turned warm.

"You've got those folks down at the Gull to the life!" shouted Matthew. "How do you remember all that patter of theirs? You're better than that program on the wireless — what's it called, Rosie?"

Her Aunt Rose laughed "Your uncle's right, sweetheart. I've known Elsie Fox since we were schoolgirls, and I would swear it was herself sashaying down the high street with that walk. You surely have a gift for miming."

Something inside Jane's heart popped, and a warm feeling spread through her body, making the tips of her fingers tingle.

"Mark my words, I shouldn't be at all surprised if she goes on the stage someday, Matthew. She's just like Bertie was at her age." Aunt Rose's younger brother, Albert Easley, was an actor who lived in London and was now touring military bases all over England. One of Jane's favorite after-dinner treats was poring over the pages of the thick scrapbooks of clippings and photographs from Bertie's life in the theater that Rose kept on the bottom shelf of the bookcase.

Jane and her friend Betsy sat next to each other in school. Betsy found everything Jane said or did uproariously funny and spent most of her time suppressing the giggles that always exploded no matter how hard she pinched herself. Jane only had to look Betsy's way and she was in fits of laughter. Their teacher tried separating them, but the back of Jane's head, when held at a certain angle, was the height of hilarity to Betsy, and finally the woman gave up, simply ignoring the occasional eruptions. The girls spent hours playing in the gardens near the Grand Promenade or splashing in the waves down at the shore or, when the weather was wet, playing with their dolls. The best fun of all was dressing up and putting on plays with Betsy's mother and Aunt Rose as audience. Betsy's round cheeks, pug nose, long blond hair, and china blue eyes were Jane's idea of perfection.

"I wish I had nice straight hair like yours. It never gets in tangles like mine."

"You're daft," said Betsy. "Mum's taking me into Miss Ethel's for a permanent wave next Saturday so I can get some beautiful curls just like yours."

A few months after Jane's arrival, her cousin Ned came home on leave. He looked exactly as Uncle Matt must have thirty years before, and he had his father's same sense of fun, teasing Jane about pinching his room and telling uproarious stories of life at sea. When she listened to Ned, the war sounded like an exciting adventure, and Jane wondered why Aunt Rose didn't laugh along with the rest of them at his stories. On his last evening, Ned took Jane for a walk while his father read the *Bournemouth Evening Echo* and Rose got supper ready.

"I'm glad you're here, Jane, for Mum's sake especially. I know she misses me, and it makes me feel easier knowing she has you for company while I'm at sea."

"When will you come home, Ned?"

"When the war is over."

"Will it be over soon?"

"Oh, sure, Janie. We'll have Jerry licked in no time. Then you can go back to your parents. You must miss them."

She said nothing but kept on walking. They stopped when they came to the end of the lane. "Ned?"

"Yes, what is it?"

"When the war is over, how soon will it be before I go back?"

"Oh, fairly soon, I should think." He looked at her. "Don't you like it here with Mum and Dad? They're that fond of you." His eyes twinkled just like Uncle Matt's when he smiled.

"Oh, yes! I like it here very much!"

"Good. Because I want you to keep Mum cheerful while I'm away. Will you do that for me?"

"Oh, yes! I promise, Ned."

"Good. Now, we'd better go back or she'll be coming after us." Ned took hold of Jane's hand, and together they walked home in the fading light.

After Ned had returned to his ship, Aunt Rose became unusually preoccupied, going about the house with blank eyes and seeming not to hear when Jane or Uncle Matt spoke. Sometimes, she took Ned's picture off the mantel, gazed at it for a long while, then, with a ragged sigh, returned it to its place and went on with her dusting. She spent long hours in the kitchen, replacing shelving paper and cleaning cabinets. Jane asked Uncle Matt what he thought was wrong with her aunt.

"She's afraid Ned won't come back to us."

"You mean that he'll be killed in the war?" Jane's large gray eyes looked into his.

"Yes."

"Aren't you worried too, Uncle Matt?" She put her small hand on the sleeve of his jacket.

"Well, Janie, I look at it this way. If it's his time then it's his time, and fretting about it isn't going to change anything."

"What do you mean 'his time'?" she asked.

They were in the garden cutting chives for an omelet Rose would soon be preparing for their tea. Uncle Matt put down the long scissors and wiped his forehead with the back of his hand. He took his pipe out of his jacket pocket and began the ritual of lighting it, which Jane found comforting because it reminded her of her father.

"Sweetheart, I believe that all our lives are planned for us: when we're born, who our parents will be, and who we marry, even our children. Just like it was planned that I should have Rosie for my life's companion and that we should have no more babies after Ned. I just don't believe things happen by accident. Everything is meant to be. Now, it may be written that our Ned won't come home, but fretting about it won't change things one way or the other. The trouble with your Aunt Rose is that she has made us, Ned and me, and now you, her whole life. It's too bad she didn't have more children. She has so much love to give."

"Uncle Matt, was it meant that I should come and live with you and Aunt

Rose?"

"Yes, my darling girl, I believe it was."

Summer 1944. The papers were full of the allied landings at Normandy and the beaches along the southern coast, followed by the news of the march up the Rhine Valley into occupied France. By August, Paris had been liberated. There was nothing but hopeful reports all the rest of that year until the Germans launched a surprise attack on Patton's Third Army in the Ardennes Forest, resulting in what turned out to be one of the longest and bloodiest encounters of the war, known as the Battle of the Bulge. By January 1945, the Americans had prevailed, and the allies began the push into Germany.

"It's only a matter of time until we advance all the way into Germany and finish off the Nazis for good and all," said Matthew "Yes, we'll soon have old Schicklgruber on the run!" Jane giggled as she pictured a red-nosed clown, holding up a pair of baggy pants, running away.

The war, however, still raged on the other side of the world. Ned was now with the 457th Task Force on the battleship HMS *Indefatigable* in the South Pacific.

APRIL 4, 1945
DUTY TO INFORM YOU HMS INDEFATIGABLE HIT
IN KAMIKAZE STRIKE 3 APRIL 1945 NORTH ISLAND
FORMOSA. LIEUTENANT EDWARD E. STOKES
KILLED IN ACTION. LETTER TO FOLLOW.
VICE ADMIRAL C. W. M. RAWLINGS R.N.

The pale yellow paper fluttered to the floor and Rose sank to her knees, hands over her face. "No, no, no, no," she wailed as Matthew took the paper from where it had lodged under her knee.

The young boy at the door, one hand steadying his bicycle, was clearly distressed. This was the first such cable he had delivered, although many others who worked at the telegraph office had done so. "May I do anything to help, sir?" he said to Matthew, who was looking at the telegram.

"What? Oh, no, thank you very much." The boy turned and walked his bike down the path. Matthew bent to his wife and gently pulled her to her feet. "Come along, Rosie, let me get you to the couch."

"Jane? Where's Jane?" asked Rose.

"She's gone to the Dwyer girl's for supper. Don't you remember?"

"I knew it. I had such a feeling. Mathew . . . our boy!" she howled. He held her in his arms and stared out the window at the sun setting over the sea. A sea like the one on the other side of the world that had swallowed their Ned.

Spring passed into summer, and grief, like a tattered gray shawl, had settled over Rose's shoulders. On August 6, the Americans dropped an atomic bomb on Hiroshima, effectively ending the war in the Pacific.

"Four months, Matthew! Four months! Tell me, why couldn't they have dropped that bomb four months ago? Just tell me that. Our boy would be alive. He's down there in the ocean, and we don't even have his body to . . . to bury."

Matthew, who used his own anger to lay out a whole new section of garden, flowers in celebration of the end of the war, bore Rose's fury in the first days after the news and what evolved into inconsolable sadness in the days that followed with his usual patience.

Jane devoted herself to Rose, bringing her aunt trays of small, appetizing meals and talking about things she thought might amuse her, but try as she might, the veil of melancholy remained down. Rose's silences, caused as they were by the loss of her son, were not like those of her mother's, and Jane sensed that, in her own good time, Aunt Rose would be herself again.

It was high summer. Jane spent long days at the beach splashing in the waves with her friends and collecting bucketfuls of shells, which she and Betsy Dwyer sorted and re-sorted. Matthew's new garden flourished. Long stems heavy with scarlet gladioli blooms and bright bunches of yellow and purple dahlias filled every corner of the house. Friends came to call. Their gifts of seed cakes and pots of jam lined the pantry shelves. Every Monday, Mary Pennmanix, the librarian from Bournemouth, came by with three or four mysteries for Rose, replacing the ones she had brought the previous week. Matthew thanked her, never letting on that the books went unread from one week to the next. Summer finally drew to a close, and the warm afternoons of early autumn turned chilly. Darkness fell earlier each day.

At the end of September, Bertie wrote to say he was returning home to Bournemouth, and for the first time since the dreadful telegram, Rose smiled.

Forty years old when war was declared and exempt from active duty, Albert Easley toured armed services camps through the war years, playing a wide-ranging repertoire that included Shakespeare, Shaw, and music hall skits. Two years ago, on a brief visit home, he discovered that the house he and Rose had lived in as children was for sale. It was a large half-timbered place with some outbuildings including stables and a large barn, situated in the pine woods of the Bourne Valley. Bertie had always dreamed of managing his own company, and the first thing he did on returning to Bournemouth was to contact the estate agent and inquire about his old home. There had been very little buying and selling of properties during the war, and the old place was still available. The purchase and renovation would take almost all of his savings, but Bertie spent the money gladly, and as soon as the final papers were signed, set about transforming the barn into a theater. Eight months after his return, with a company of venerable London actors and young West Country talent, Albert Easley launched the Bournemouth Players.

Short and squat, with a large head, bulging eyes, frizzy gray hair, and long arms that dangled awkwardly from his broad, rounded shoulders, Bertie on stage transformed his bullfrog form into that of a young adventurer, a sophisticated man about town, or a riotous comic.

Rose liked nothing better than the evenings when Bertie joined them for supper. Sitting at the round table in front of the stone fireplace, he talked of his years in the theater, telling stories of the people he had known and occasionally even doing a turn.

Jane was completely entranced with Bertie and, much to Betsy Dwyer's chagrin, was soon spending most of her free time at the playhouse. Bertie gave her odd jobs painting bits of scenery and sewing buttons on costumes. She watched rehearsals from backstage, and within a few days had every part memorized. Bertie noticed that she was saying the lines along with the actors and made her company prompter. It was a real job in the theater!

More than anything in the world, Jane wanted to be an actress. She idolized Betty Frazier and Patricia Marks, the Bournemouth Players' two leading ladies. Betty had blonde curls, large blue eyes, and a bouncy personality. Patricia was tall and slim, with glossy dark hair, smooth olive skin, and full lips, which she painted bright scarlet. As for herself, Jane doubted that she would ever be a leading lady. For one thing, though some of her friends were ready for brassieres, at twelve she was still as flat-chested as a boy. Her hair was impossibly red, her skin white as chalk, and the tip of what Uncle Bertie called her "aristocratic Russell-Cotes aquiline nose" did not turn fetchingly up, as did Betsy Dwyer's saucy one. She told herself that none of that was really important, because as Bertie often remarked, there were plenty of actresses who were not beautiful but played the challenging character parts, which were always more interesting than leading roles. After all, what mattered most was performing.

Bertie recognized, in Jane, all the symptoms he had suffered long ago as a stage-struck youth, but rather than discourage these ambitions, as his own parents had done, he carefully cultivated her love of the theater.

Despite the contentment of her life in Bournemouth, there were times Jane suffered spells of crushing anxiety. She knew she should be glad that the war over but her heart was filled with dread, for surely her mother would write soon to say that it was time she returned to London. Gladys visited Bournemouth whenever she could get a few days away from the hospital where she was now working on staff as a licensed vocational nurse. Each time she came, the gulf between mother and child had seemed to grow wider. Dr. Parks, who had been stationed in India for most of the war, finally returned home in late November. Jane had looked forward to spending as much time as possible with her father at Christmas but, during her parent's visit to Bournemouth, she was confused and not a little dismayed at the marked change in the man who had once been the center of her world. So preoccupied was her father that he barely said two words to her. It was then she realized that Rose and Matthew Stokes had become her real parents and Gladys and Frank Parks two relative strangers in whose house she had once lived.

As Jane feared, the dreaded letter from her mother came two months before her thirteenth birthday. Jane was frantic. She wrote to her parents asking if she could finish out the school year in Bournemouth. They agreed. Three months' reprieve! The days raced by though, and, as summer neared, Jane was again in a panic at the thought of having to leave the home where she had been so happy. Her life was here. The thought of going back to London was more than she could bear.

And what of her dreams of going on the stage? She remembered how her mother had enjoyed it when she sang and had even smiled sometimes then, but that was long ago and now she might not understand Jane's ambitions the way her aunt and uncle did. What if her mother insisted that Jane attend a secretarial or nursing school to learn a useful skill? Her whole future would be different, drab and plain instead of bright and exciting. Worst of all, how would she endure life without her beloved Bertie?

At mealtimes, she moved the food around on her plate but ate very little. She lost weight. She began waking at three or four every morning and, unable to fall back to sleep, paced the floor of her room until the cold forced her to curl up in the window seat with a blanket, where she watched the sea glimmer like a sheet of black cellophane until, one by one, the stars faded and dawn broke.

When Jane stopped going to the playhouse, Matthew took the situation in hand. One evening late in August. he placed a long distance telephone call to London. The lines were all but impossible, and it was almost an hour before he could get through.

"Gladys, is that you? This is Matthew. Oh, we're fine. Yes, Rose is well. Gladys, the thing is that the girl wants to stay here in Bournemouth over the summer. You know I think the poor thing is afraid of making new acquaintances up in London. She's a regular little country mouse, after these years down here. Thinks she won't know what to say to city folk. You understand, don't you, Gladie?" There was silence on the other end, and Matthew felt a momentary twinge of guilt at telling such an outrageous lie, for Jane possessed remarkable poise and was never at a lack for conversation no matter the age or condition of any person she encountered.

"All right, Matthew. If that's what she wants." Gladys's voice sounded tired and oddly weak through the line. "To tell you the truth, Frank has been strange since he's been back, and with the rationing still on it's hard enough to feed us both properly without worrying about a youngster. Perhaps it would be best if she stayed on for awhile. At least you can get better food down there."

"So, it's settled then?" Matthew asked, holding his breath.

"Yes, it's settled." Her voice was barely a whisper.

"Are you all right, Gladie? You don't sound well."

"I'm fine, Matthew. Say hello to Rose for me and Jane, of course, and from her father too."

"Goodbye then, Gladys." Matthew's mouth was drawn in a hard line. He hung up the receiver and stared at the phone. How could the woman just give up her child like that? For a moment a strange thought flitted through his mind, but he shrugged it off and then he threw his head back and laughed. "Well, if you don't want Jane, we do!"

The second week of September, a collect call came for Matthew from a Mrs. Dora Brodie.

"Is that you, Mr. Stokes?"

"Yes, I'm Matthew Stokes. Who is this?"

"Dora Brodie. I'm a neighbor of your sister's."

"Oh, yes. Is Gladys all right?"

"No, I'm afraid not, Mr. Stokes. Something terrible happened yesterday."

"What . . . what is it?"

"Oh, God. Mr. Stokes, Gladys hadn't been herself at all since Dr. Parks went off to Canada. "

"Canada?"

"Yes. He left two weeks ago . . . with someone."

"What do you mean with someone?"

"A nurse she was . . . you know, an army nurse. They were stationed together out there in Calcutta, and she came back to London at the same time he did. I suppose they had been seeing each other right along. Anyway, about two weeks ago, off they went, and Gladys just shut herself up. Wouldn't answer the door or the telephone. I tried to get her to let me in so I could bring her some food, you know, but . . ."

"Mrs. Brodie, what are you trying to say?"

"Well, yesterday I saw her go out. I sat right by my window so I wouldn't miss her when she came back. She wasn't gone very long. I ran out just as soon as I saw her coming down the street, but she was too fast for me. By the time I got to her house she had already gone inside, and when I rang the bell she wouldn't answer."

"Yes, go on."

"Well, I didn't know what to do. I rang her on the telephone all day and even went down to her house a couple of times and knocked on the door but she wouldn't answer, and then around five o'clock, I went down there again."

Matthew's hand was wet with perspiration. Dropping the receiver, he wiped it on his pants leg before returning it to his ear.

"I rang the doorbell and knocked and shouted for her, and then I went home and called the police. Are you there, Mr. Stokes?"

"Yes, go on."

"They broke in and found her. Oh, Mr. Stokes, I'm so sorry to be the one to tell you, but she . . . she was dead."

"How?"

"Oh, Mr. Stokes, she cut . . . cut her wrists! Oh God, it was a horrible sight. I shall never, never forget it. She still had the razor blade in her hand. Very shiny and bright it was. I think when she went out it was to buy a new one, don't you see? She wanted to make sure it would cut, you know . . . clean. I'll never forgive myself. I should have broken the door down or called the police earlier or . . . something."

"No, I'm sure you did all that you could. I mean, you weren't to know."

"I should have guessed. I think he . . . Dr. Parks, you know . . . was the only person she really cared for in this world, and when he went off so sudden like . . . Thank God Jane wasn't here. Dear child, is she well?"

"Yes, she is very well."

"Well, thank sweet providence she has you and your wife. Mr. Stokes. you will be very gentle when you tell her how . . . how her mother died?"

"Yes, of course. Goodbye, Mrs. Brodie."

Matthew stared at the receiver, deeply ashamed that his tears were not from grief but from the sudden surge that filled his heart.

CHAPTER 3

BOURNEMOUTH, 1951

It was spring. Jane's eighteenth birthday was not far away and in June she would graduate from secondary school. At last, the future she had promised herself since the day Uncle Bertie came into her life six years ago was visible on the horizon. She was going to be an actress.

She had won staring parts in all her school's dramatic productions, and occasionally Bertie cast her in a minor role at the playhouse. During the last four years, she had read the works of nearly every British playwright and many of the Americans as well. She especially liked the plays of Tennessee Williams and spent hours in front of her mirror, acting out speeches from *The Glass Menagerie* and *A Streetcar Named Desire*. Sometimes, she improvised scenes that might have taken place between some of her favorite historical figures: Queen Victoria and Benjamin Disraeli, Queen Elizabeth and Mary, Queen of Scots, or Charles Stuart and Nelly Gwyn. She was especially drawn to Nelly, the sprightly urchin who had been put out on the streets as a child only to become London's reigning actress at seventeen and, two years later, mistress to the king.

With the ear of a natural mimic, Jane had picked up the West Country accent soon after her arrival in Bournemouth, but for the past two years she had been aping Patricia Marks's Royal Academy of Dramatic Arts style of speech. Charles Rockham, the company villain, had given her exercises to help develop a lower register to her voice. These she usually practiced at the beach, sitting in the shelter of a dune or pacing up and down the shoreline.

One Saturday morning, as she sat reading aloud from a worn copy of St. Joan, a group of boys came running down the dunes behind her. Shouting and wrestling, suddenly they lay in a tangled heap at her feet. Embarrassed, the boys took off in the opposite direction — all but one, who stood looking down at her.

"You're getting left behind," said Jane, brushing sand from her skirt.

"I don't mind." His face was wet with perspiration, and bits of sand were caught in his thick blond curls. He looked vaguely familiar but she couldn't place him.

"Are you here on holiday?" She looked up at him, her hand shielding her eyes from the glare of the beach. She was trying to see his eyes more clearly.

"No, I'm with the rugger team from Christchurch. We're to play a match tomorrow."

"Oh, yes, I've heard of little else from my uncle for the past month."

"Well, it's an old rivalry." There was something compelling about his pale green eyes, fringed as they were with thick golden lashes. As they held hers, appraising and gently teasing, Jane felt a warm flush creep up her neck and spread over her cheeks.

"I'm John Keith. Do you mind if I sit here for awhile?"

"No, I don't mind."

She was keenly aware of his bulk beside her in the sand. His scent, a combination of sunshine, salt, and physical exertion, went to her head and made her giddy, as if she had drunk a glass of strong ale. Stealing a glance at his face, she was struck, as if by physical force, with the rugged beauty of his broad forehead, blunt nose, and square chin. It was a craggy profile, like the cliffs that rose behind them from the beach. He turned to face her, and as his eyes met hers, Jane's world tipped slightly.

"Do you know Christchurch at all? It's a nice little town. Of course, not so grand as Bournemouth." His voice was husky, and he spoke in the familiar slow West accent, which always warmed Jane. "I live there with my Gran." He looked up at the cloudless sky. "Fine weather, isn't it, seeing that it's spring? I hope it holds like this for the match. Nothing worse than slogging about in the muck. And what about you? Still in school, are you?"

"Two more months and I'm finished," Jane answered, hugging her knees and watching the light play on his face.

"I've been out a year, thank God. Well, I'd best be off or I'll never catch up to my mates." He rose from his seat in the sand and pulled her up with him. For a moment they stood facing each other. "I hope to see you at the match. I know you will be cheering for Bournemouth, but you might cast a friendly eye in my direction now and then, just to lift my spirits."

Until five minutes ago, attending tomorrow's rugby match had never entered Jane's mind, but if John Keith was going to be at Memorial Field at two o'clock the next day, she would be there too.

"And don't disappear right after." He placed the tip of his finger on the end of her nose.

"No, I won't disappear."

"Say, I don't know your name." His broad smile was dazzling.

"Jane Parks," she whispered.

"Well, then, Jane Parks, I'll be seeing you."

She watched his tall form sprint down the beach until it was out of sight. She laughed out loud. Uncle Matthew is going to faint dead away when I tell him I want to go to a rugby match. She sank back onto the sand and closed her eyes, the sun feeling delightfully warm on her face. His eyes were like the shallows on a sunny day. And the expression in them when he looked at her!

Something about him was familiar. She sat up and stared out at the sea, counting the waves as they washed up on the shoreline. Suddenly, she remembered where she had seen that face! There was a painting of St. Michael the Archangel hanging over a side altar in St. Catherine's Church. She had noticed it last Christmas Eve when the Dwyers had taken her along with them to Mass. All through the service, she had not been able to take her eyes off the beautiful man with broad-winged shoulders and wavy golden hair. The image stayed with her all though the winter, popping into her mind at unexpected moments, touching something deep inside her. And now she had seen the identical face, not as a work of art but living flesh. Smoothing the sand where John Keith's body had left its imprint, Jane let the warm grains sift slowly through her fingers. A deliciously languid feeling coursed through her limbs and, grinning, she whispered to the cloudless sky, "April 20, 1951. My lucky day!"

Despite her classroom antics with Betsy Dwyer, Jane was a good student. Her A-level results were in, and Rose and Matthew took it for granted that she would soon be off to university. But Jane had not sent applications to Exeter or Bristol or, as Uncle Matt had suggested, the University of London. Instead, three days after graduation, she calmly put her school certificate in the top drawer of her bureau and announced that she had taken a job half-days at the Bournemouth Library.

"But Janie, with your brains you could be doing something much more interesting with your life than working part-time in the library." said Matthew.

"Don't worry, Uncle Matt. I have plans for more exciting things to come, but I need to have a job until I'm ready, and the hours at the library won't take up all my time."

"Time for what? What plans? Ready for what?" asked Rose.

"You'll find out." Jane smiled sweetly and kissed her aunt's plump cheek.

Jane liked the idea of earning her own money and felt very much the independent woman as she set out each morning, dressed in a neat skirt and blouse, her unruly hair held off her face with a tight bow at the back of her neck. She was indeed beginning to look like a woman. There were definite curves on her slim frame, and her large eyes were less gamin, more female, with a spark of mischief in their clear grayness.

After she had been working in the library a few months, Jane spoke seriously with Bertie about a permanent place in his company.

"You will have to audition," he said.

"Audition!"

"Now listen, my girl, do you or do you not want to act professionally?" He was unusually serious.

"Of course I do."

"Then you must realize that you are no longer little Jane acting with Uncle Bertie. You must audition for me as managing director and for the rest of the company as well."

She chose a scene from *The Glass Menagerie*. It was the first time any of them had seen her in anything other than the small parts Bertie had given her. Alone on the stage, poised and in full command, Jane went through her scene with a natural presence that claimed the attention of the entire company and inspired their genuine applause. Bertie could hardly contain himself. This child, who had so deeply embedded herself in his heart since she came into his life six years ago, was going to follow in his footsteps on to the stage.

Jane's life was now focused in two directions, the Bournemouth Players and John Keith.

As they got to know each other better, John told Jane more about his life.

"My father was regular army. He served in the near east during the first war and was sent back there again in '41. My mother was from a place in County Durham called Flint Hill. All the family still lives there and, after my father was sent away, her brother wrote and asked us to come and stay with them. Mum always hated that drab little village, and after a few months she packed our things and we came back to our house in Christchurch. Grandfather Keith had died while we were up north and Mum asked my gran to move in with us. They always got on well together, and things were pretty good until word came that my father had been killed in battle at Mersa Matruh. After that, my mother decided she wanted to help with the war effort, so she left me with Gran and went up to London to join the WAAFs.

"When the war ended, Mum showed up in Christchurch with a strange man she introduced to Gran and me as her husband. They wanted to take me to London where my new stepfather had gone back to his job at Lloyd's Insurance, but I decided to stay where I was. I just couldn't leave my old granny. She had no one else in the world, and she's such a sweet lady, if not too attentive. Gran always let me do pretty much as I liked, and by the time I was fifteen, I was missing school as often as going.

"In '47, two older boys let me in on a plan they had to hitchhike in France, and I decided to go with them. It was no problem talking Gran around to the idea. I told her that I would learn as much experiencing real life in foreign parts as in a classroom. She signed the consent to my leaving school a couple of months before term ended and gave me fifty pounds out of her savings on top of it. All she made me promise was to be home in time for the fall term.

"At first, I stayed with my friends traveling in France. We had good luck with rides, and when our money ran out we got jobs in vineyards and on farms. By the end of autumn, the weather had turned cold and wet and the work was scarce, so my pals went back home to England, but I wanted to see Spain. It was warm there and cheap! When converted into pesetas, the money I had was a fortune and I didn't need to find work right away. I roamed around Barcelona spending my days in the Gothic Quarter and my nights in the cafes in the Barrio Chino." He smiled at the memory.

As he spoke, Jane could almost smell the pungent fish markets near the harbor and the sweet flower stalls on the Ramblas. She could hear the raucous voices of old Republican soldiers, sitting in cafes, debating a cause that had been lost more than a decade before. She watched John's face as he spoke, with passion and surprising eloquence, of Granada.

"Janie, someday I'll take you to see the Alhambra! It's an alabaster palace, with walls and ceilings like honeycomb, all bathed in a pale golden light. The terraced gardens overflow with exotic flowers, like nothing you've ever seen back home, and the fountains play into narrow reflecting pools and make a sound so sweet that you think you'll just die from hearing it.

"After Granada I went on to Cordoba. The thing I remember most about that town was never quite knowing where I was. The streets were like a maze, and they had no names. Can you imagine a town with no street names! I'll never forget the glare of those white houses in Cordoba. The kind of white that hurts your eyes. And every house had a patio paved in the most intricate tiles, bright as jewels.

"One day I wandered into the grand mosque. It's called the Mezquita and takes up a whole square block. I didn't think there was much to see in it at first, just a lot of archways painted in red and white stripes. Then I noticed the altars. Christian altars tucked in niches among the arches. I swear to you that as I stood in that ancient mosque I could hear the voices of thousands of dead Muslims crying for revenge against thousands of dead Christians who had violated their holy place. After my experience in the Mezquita, I guess I became kind of captivated with Moorish culture, because after some more time traveling in Andalusía and a week in Seville, I decided I wanted to see Morocco, so I hitched a ride down to Cádiz. As soon as I arrived, I found the port and bought a ticket on a boat leaving for Tangiers the next day. Someday I'll tell you about what happened to me in Marrakesh."

"Oh, John, please tell me now!"

"No, not now. Someday. Anyway, I didn't stay long because by then it was almost Christmas and I decided it was time to get back home to Gran."

The tales of his adventurous life and the strong physical attraction she felt for him made John Keith irresistible to Jane. Her vivid imagination put pictures to his words: images of a golden-haired boy tramping the roads of France and working in the vineyards under the hot sun, the heavy richness of the earth in his nostrils at night as he lay under the stars.

She too, walked the narrow streets and grand boulevards of Barcelona. She listened to the sound of plaintive ballads as they had been sung for hundreds of years in the parks and plazas of Seville. She passed olive trees along the road, planted in pairs from horizon to horizon, over the rolling hills of Andalusía, and in the far distance, silhouetted against the hard blue sky, castles in Spain. Jane had never known anyone who had lived such an exciting life. She was captivated, enchanted, in love.

Jane learned that by the time John returned home from his travels, he had missed most of the school year and had to study hard to catch up. Something in him had changed, and he found he liked the challenge. He had a remarkably retentive memory and was, when he set his mind to it, a fast learner. His grandmother was pleased at his new attitude and was glad that she had helped him to go abroad. Her Johnny had grown up while he had been away and now seemed eager to accept his responsibilities. He finished his last year top of his class but, to his grandmother's dismay, decided against applying to university and now seemed content working in the auto repair shop in Christchurch.

Both she and Jane tried to persuade him to go on with his education, but he became evasive when either of them brought up the subject. "You should try for university, in London maybe. You could go in for the law, Johnny, you're that bright."

"We'll see, Gran."

The old lady finally gave up trying to convince him, but Jane did not.

"I agree with your grandmother. You're wasting yourself tinkering with motors all day."

"You're a great one to talk. You could have your pick of any university in England, and all you care about is acting in your uncle's theater. Look, Jane, there's a big world out there. I'd like to see it. Maybe with you." He smiled into her eyes. "Anyway, the thought of being stuck in London for years and years at university depresses me."

"But you'd have plenty of time to see the world after you get your degree. I think your grandmother is right about the law. It's the perfect career for you. You have a fine mind, John. Just think, in ten years time you could be a famous barrister and I'll be a great actress. What a couple!" She turned to face him, excitement making her eyes sparkle.

It was high summer, and they were sitting side by side on an old stone bench, waiting for Rose to call them in to tea. The morning had been rainy, but now the clouds had parted and the sky was a bright blue, the air heavy with the scents of the garden.

"You're so pretty, Janie." He took her face in his hands and kissed her softly. As always, the touch of his mouth on hers took her breath away. Slowly, he unfastened the top buttons of her blouse. She put her hand over his as if to stop him but, before she could, he undid the next two and slipped his hand inside her bra. The light touch of his fingers was familiar and exciting. He took her hand and put it between his legs. As she felt his hardness rise, he kissed her again, this time with more urgency.

"Aunt Rose will be out here any minute." Her face was flushed and her hair curled damply around her face.

"After tea, let's go to the cottage." His eyes were still hot with passion as he smoothed her hair.

"Yes," she answered.

The cottage was really a decrepit fishing shack they discovered one day while walking on a lonely part of the beach. Peering through the grimy windows, they saw that it was abandoned and pushed open the warped door. A dank smell pervaded the two tiny rooms, and thick cobwebs hung from every corner. It was obvious no one had used the place in years. The following day they returned, this time equipped with a bucket, scouring powder, scrub brushes, and a broom. They worked all day cleaning the shack and, when they were done, claimed it as their own.

John found some old blankets his grandmother had stored in the attic, and he brought them to the cottage along with a kerosene lamp. Jane took some empty milk bottles from Rose's pantry and kept them filled with bunches of pink and yellow wildflowers they collected on the hillocks beyond the dunes. Long summer afternoons were spent at the cottage, lying together on Mrs. Keith's plaid blankets, talking in low voices, kissing and exploring each other's bodies. Jane was deeply in love. Her young body wanted John, but every time she got to the point of complete surrender, something made her stop. She knew that John, as much as he complained, didn't really mind her holding back. He thought she was saving herself for the time when they would be able to marry. But Jane was saving herself for something else.

CHAPTER 4

Early in July of 1952, Sir James Paxton arrived in Bournemouth to scout locations for his next production, *The Heroes of Normandy*. Head of Briarwood Studios and one of Britain's foremost producer-directors, Sir James was famous for molding great stars from raw talent. Albert Easley was one of Paxton's oldest friends and the first thing Sir James did on arrival at the Sea Gull Inn was telephone Bertie to see if they could meet for a drink that evening. Instead, Bertie insisted his chum attend the Bournemouth Players' production of *Major Barbara*.

Paxton had low expectations of anything like a real performance from a troupe of regional players, but he was genuinely fond of Bertie and accepted his friend's invitation with the same note of enthusiasm as if it were an opening night at the Haymarket.

Fortified with two cups of the strongest coffee the Sea Gull had to offer, he settled down in his fifth-row-center house seat just as the curtain rose. The play went much as he expected until Barbara made her entrance. Suddenly, his antennae were up. This girl positively shone! He had seen it before in Marjorie Dunston and Lillian Peters and, of course, in Beryl, but not for years. Funny how the magic hit you right away. She wasn't a bad little actress, either. Not as good as Lillian when he took her out of the Abbey Players in '32, but certainly better than Marjorie when he discovered her playing in two-reel comedies.

What a perfect Valerie she would make! He had been testing actresses for months, but so far no one had quite the quality he was looking for. Just to think, he had almost been desperate enough to sign that grim little creature from Rank. *The Valiant Hours* would start shooting in the middle of October. He would have to get a test on this girl as soon as possible. If she was good on film, he would have plenty of time to prepare her for the role. The part of Valerie was not a large one but pivotal to the story and, if she had the talent he felt she did, it would be an ideal debut with Briarwood.

While Sir James was making plans for her future, Jane was praying that, with such an illustrious person in the audience, she would not make a complete fool of herself. As soon as the final curtain was down, Bertie grabbed her hand and pulled her into the dressing room.

"He wants to meet you!" he wheezed, unscrewing the lid off a jar of cold cream and handing it to her. "He wants to arrange a test!"

She stared at him, clenching the jar, not sure she had heard him correctly. "What did you say?"

"Hurry!" He flung Jane a towel and grinned at her reflection in the mirror as she swiped at her makeup. "My girl, from the day of your audition I knew you had it. That special something. I've tried to develop it as best I could, but there are limits. Now you'll have the very best coaching and the finest in the business will make you up and light you, but it's your own special brightness that is going to take you right to the top." His bulging eyes glistened with tears. "I'm so happy!"

"Bertie, are you saying that . . . that Sir James Paxton liked me?"

"Of course he liked you, my girl. Of course he did."

It was then she saw, framed in the doorway, an enormous man with thick auburn hair, a neatly trimmed beard, and large nose covered with tiny red veins. He wore a tweed suit, Tattersall vest, and a purple and yellow paisley silk tie.

"My dear," he said, surveying her over a pair of wire-rimmed spectacles, "I am Jamie Paxton. Look, I'm not going to dither around. I want you to come up to London as soon as you can and make a test for a part I feel would suit you."

Jane gasped. "Seriously? You really mean it?"

"Of course."

"I don't know what to say!"

"Just say you will be at Briarwood Studios promptly at — let me see." He had taken a small engagement diary out of his jacket pocket and was thumbing through it. "Let us say nine o'clock on the morning of the fifteenth."

Jane nodded her head, the jar of cold cream still grasped in her hand.

"So, sweetheart, all your hard work has paid off, and it looks like you're going to be getting what you've always wanted." Matt grinned over his shoulder as he drove Jane and Rose to the train station. "And according to this Lord Paxton, you're damn good."

"He's a sir, Uncle Matt, not a lord," giggled Jane, "and he only thinks I might be right for this part. It's just a test." Jane had been trying to slow down her racing heart for the past week with thoughts of the very words now voiced by Uncle Matt.

"Well, you've got your old uncle's blessing, for what it's worth."

"It's worth everything to me!" She reached her arms around him from the backseat and hugged him.

"Hey, hey enough of that, or we won't make it to the station in one piece."

Matthew was determined, no matter what the outcome, that this trip to London be special for Jane and Rose. He booked a room for them at the Savoy Hotel, where they would stay the night before the test. He and Rose had gone to a dance at the Savoy before the war, and in Matthew's mind, it remained the utmost in London elegance. Jane, who had never in her life been in a hotel, was awed by the grand dining room with its marble floors and magnificent crystal chandelier. She sipped a few spoonfuls of the savory mushroom soup and left the rest of her meal untouched. Aunt Rose enjoyed all four courses of the delicious dinner, followed by a demitasse and tiny glass of cherry brandy.

Luxuriously comfortable as her bed was, Jane did not sleep that night. Her mind buzzed with the lines Sir James had sent by special delivery post over a week ago. A thrill passed through her body. *Her lines.* This was real! She was used to the distant murmur of the sea at night and the London traffic was like a roar beneath her window.

My whole future depends on how I look on the screen, she thought as she finally slid off to sleep just twenty minutes before their wake-up call.

"Oh, what a good night's sleep I had," yawned Aunt Rose "Just to be away from your uncle's snoring is pure heaven. How about you, my love, did you have a good night?"

"Yes," she said smiling across the night table at her aunt.

They ordered breakfast from room service, and twenty minutes later a cheerful waiter was standing at the entrance to their room. He wheeled in a cart laden with covered silver platters. Rose watched him, fascinated, as he went about the business of setting up a small round table and laying it with a snowy cloth, oversized linen napkins, and heavy gleaming silver. In the center of the table, he placed a slender crystal vase containing a single pink rose. Scrambled eggs and sausages were portioned onto blue and white plates, an intertwined *S H* emblazoned on their rims. There was a rack of toast and a silver basket filled with fragrant muffins. Small cut-crystal bowls held marmalade and jam. Tea was poured.

"Will that be all, madam?" the waiter addressed Aunt Rose.

"Oh, yes, thank you." She handed him some coins. As soon as the door behind closed him, Rose clapped her hands together. "Oh, isn't this posh!"

"Yes, Auntie, very posh."

Jane could get down only a few bites of toast. "I know it's such a sinful waste, but I can't seem to eat anything in this hotel."

"Don't worry, it won't go to waste. If your tummy's full of butterflies, mine isn't." She exchanged Jane's plate for her own, grinning. "Why don't you have your bath first, since I'm going to be occupied here for a while longer?"

The bathroom was tiled in white. Jane leaned over the tub and turned on the taps. The water came out in a rush. She watched the tub fill and, once again, went over her lines. The room was misty with clouds of steam. She glanced at the large mirror over the sink but could see only a hazy image through the vapor. She wiped the damp steam from the surface with the heel of her hand and peered at the streaked reflection in the mirror. At nineteen, Jane looked exactly like her mother. Suddenly, her throat filled with tears. How could her father have left his Gladys when he always said she meant the world to him? She wondered about the woman he had gone away with, if he was happy with her in Canada and if he ever thought of his little girl. She wondered what her mother felt the day she killed herself. *Oh, Mum, if I had come home instead of staying on with Rose and Matt, maybe you wouldn't have done that terrible thing. If I had come home would you still be alive?*

She stepped into the steaming tub and sank into the water. Running her lines for the thousandth time, all thoughts of her father, the woman with whom he fled to Canada, and her mother's suicide cleared from her mind as she repeated Valerie's words into the steam.

That evening, Sir James Paxton watched Jane's test in the screening room at Briarwood Studios. When it was over, he called to the projectionist to run it again. As the screen flickered and went dark, he took off his glasses, pressing his thumb and forefinger over the bridge of his nose. Eyes closed, he sat unmoving for several minutes.

"Should I run it again, Sir James?" the projectionist called down from his booth above Paxton's chair.

"No, thanks, Harry." He heaved himself out of the chair, and strode down the hall to his office. Once at his desk, he lifted the telephone receiver from its cradle and dialed a number.

"Good evening. Savoy Hotel."

"Room 305, please." He fitted a cigarette into the end of a tortoise shell holder, lit it, and waited. "Hello, James Paxton, here. I just ran your test. Miss Parks, you are going to be a very famous woman."

The following day Jane and Aunt Rose were seated in James Paxton's office at Briarwood Studios.

"Your potential is enormous, but it will take hard work, more than you can imagine, in order to realize it." Paxton leaned forward over the desk, pointing a pencil at her. "You must have ballet classes and riding lessons and a voice coach. I want you to be able to recite 'the quality of mercy' speech while swimming the backstroke. You see, I am not just giving you an acting job, I am going to teach you a trade. You'll think me an impossible taskmaster, and at times you might even hate me, but you are going to get the kind of training that will see you through the years, that will make you endurable and indestructible."

"I am prepared to work hard, Sir James."

"Good. Today is Friday. You begin on Monday. You can move in with us until suitable digs can be found for you. There is plenty of room in our house up in Hampstead. It's quite convenient to the studio, and you'll find my wife, Kitty, easy to know. In fact, if you can put up with our noisy brood, you are welcome to stay as long as you wish. Even so, I don't want you to get too homesick for Bournemouth. We will arrange for you to have some weekends off. *Valiant Hours* starts shooting immediately after Jack Baines finishes *The Lady in Grey*. That should be in eight weeks. By the way, do you have a young man?"

"Well, yes, there is someone special. There is a chance that he might be coming up to the University of London, but he understands that my work comes first at the moment."

"Sounds like a fine fellow. I just wanted to make sure you were not engaged or anything of that sort. Nothing worse than a husband and babies to shut down a promising career. Now, I am offering you a three-year exclusive contract. You will want your own solicitor to go over it, and if all meets with his and your uncle's approval, you can start immediately."

The next two months were the most exciting of Jane's life. Facing each new challenge with determination, she soon discovered that Sir James's description of a grueling schedule had been no exaggeration.

Unlike the sprawling movie studios of America, which resembled self-contained cities, Briarwood was more of a repertory theater with sound stages and cameras. Directors and actors worked together closely with writers and technicians to create what was fast becoming the preferred film fare of discriminating film patrons on both sides of the Atlantic. Leaving Technicolor extravaganzas to Hollywood, British studios such as J. Arthur Rank and Briarwood produced well-crafted scripts, intelligently directed and preformed. Briarwood was famous for its adaptation of historic novels and classics, and since the war, a series of zany comedies that featured a group of seasoned stage performers headed by Jasper Quigly.

It was Quigly who spotted Jane sitting in a far corner of the studio dining room, a script open on the table in front of her. "Pardon me, young lady, may I join you?"

Jane started at the familiar voice. She was not quite used to coming in contact with people she had seen since childhood on the screen at the Empire Cinema in Bournemouth. She closed the script and put it down beside her untouched plate. "Yes, please do." She looked up into his round, light-lashed blue eyes.

"My name is Jasper Quigly." He offered her his hand.

"Yes, I know," she said, blushing slightly. "I am Jane Parks, at least for the moment. I think they want to give me a new name."

"That can be awfully frightening." His voice was soft and deep and of a special timbre that gave ordinary words a quality all his own. "You feel rather mucked with at the start. They want to change so many things, one begins to wonder what they saw in the first place."

"Yes, that's exactly how I feel."

"One thing they certainly won't want to alter is that lovely smile."

"Oh, but they do. They want to straighten my front tooth. You see it sticks out a bit." They both laughed.

"Well, let them change the things that don't matter too much and then stand firm on the rest."

"That sounds like a good plan. I am just so grateful being here at all that I don't want to make any trouble."

"Listen to me, my dear, Jamie Paxton is no fool. If he put you under contract, it is because you are going to be very valuable to Briarwood someday."

"I just can't believe all this is really happening to me. You see, I've wanted to be an actress all of my life."

"Ah, yes, of course you have," he said reflectively. "Tell me, why is it you always sit alone in this corner? I've noticed you here before. Don't you want to meet the fellow inmates of this asylum?"

"I spend my breaks studying and, well, I don't like to intrude."

"Jane, would you feel that you were intruding in your own home? Wouldn't you come right in and sit down at the table with your family and chat? Sometimes you must put away the studies and relax for awhile."

"You are very kind."

"Not at all. You must think of us as your family away from home. Sir James is the father and you are, at the moment, the youngest child. The others want to get acquainted. Now why don't you take that plate and let us go and meet some of them?"

Quigly took Jane's arm and led her over to a round table where he introduced her to Robert Gordon and Francis Alexander, who, clad in knee-length tunics, were taking a short break from the *Julius Caesar* set. Maud Jeffries, a character actress best known for playing mother roles, was eating from a plate piled high with a double helping of shepherd's pie. She wore a faded housecoat over what Jane perceived to be some sort of Scottish costume. A tightly curled gray wig sat slightly askew on her head, giving her comfortable face a rakish air. Between large forkfuls of lunch, she was engaged in earnest conversation with a thin young man. As she pointed out some lines of dialogue from her gravy-stained script, she glanced over at Jane.

"Greetings, dearie," she said, saluting the girl with a queen-mother wave of her hand.

"And this is Derick Lindsey," said Quigly.

A dark-haired boy pulled out an empty chair next to him, motioning for her to sit. He wore a black turtleneck sweater and narrow corduroy slacks, which accentuated the thinness of his body. A cigarette dangled out of the corner of his mouth, and he squinted at Maud Jeffries through the smoke.

"I'm sorry, Maud. It still doesn't sound right. It should read this way." He spoke several lines of dialogue in a perfect Scottish accent. His voice was beautiful. "You see, with the emphasis on the last sentence, not the first." He put out his cigarette, pulled another from the pack on the table, and lit it. He glanced at Jane as if seeing her for the first time and smiled. He had white, even teeth, and his eyes were dark and brilliant.

"Very well, I'll try it your way this afternoon. but in the end. you know, it will be up to Freddie which way I say it. After all, he sits in the director's chair for this epic, not you, dearie."

"Squabbles," Quigly whispered in her ear.

Jane accepted Sir James's offer to stay with his family while she looked for digs of her own. Uncle Bertie told her that his old friend had married a girl somewhat younger than he, but she was astonished, when Lady Kitty opened the front door, to discover that her hostess was much closer to Jane's own age than her husband's. Her body moved with the grace of a dancer as she led Jane across the gleaming foyer and into her home. The wide blue eyes, delicately tilt-tipped nose and feathery blond curls framing her heart-shaped face, made a very pretty picture, but Jane soon discovered genuine warmth behind the chiseled perfection of Kitty Paxton's features.

"Jamie's talked of nothing but you since he came back from Bournemouth. Truth be told, the subject was becoming rather tiresome but, now that we've met, I see you are nothing like the insufferable little prima donna I pictured waltzing into our lives. In fact, contrary to all expectation, I have a feeling you and I are going to be great chums."

It took Jane less than a week to settle in with the Paxtons. Lady Kitty, with a unique style of her own, had managed to create an atmosphere of casual elegance in the enormous red brick house. The Paxtons' two boys, Simon and Jamie, clamored for Jane the moment she came home in the evening, and the eldest, a girl named Sarah, found in Jane a willing audience for school intrigues, usually involving her two best friends, Lavender and Henrietta. Unlike her mother or her nurse, Jane treated Sarah as a contemporary, and the child grew to love her. Lady Kitty was making only a half-hearted effort at finding a suitable living situation for Jane. She enjoyed having the young actress as a guest and, as she had predicted the first day they met, a close friendship developed between the two. Soon the search for a flat was abandoned and Jane became a permanent part of the household.

Jane loved the days of hard work at Briarwood. The tenacity that drove her passionate desire to learn the craft of acting surprised even her. She put in half an hour of barre work followed by forty minutes of dance every day. Twice a week, she took a bus to a riding academy in Kensington, where she posted around and around the ring with three tiresome fourth-form girls whom she could hear sniggering contemptuously behind her back as she led the way around the circuit. As much as she hated the riding lessons, she looked forward to the classes at the Royal Academy of Dramatic Arts, which she took several times a week. Unlike the snobbish Kensington equestrians, her fellow students at RADA treated her with casual acceptance, even though she was bound for work in films and not the stage. By autumn, she could, indeed, swim the backstroke and jump a fence on the back of a hunter, as well as speak passable French with an excellent accent.

One rainy afternoon in late September, as she was on her way to voice class, Sir James came up alongside her.

"I hear very satisfactory reports from your instructors. You have learned a great deal, it seems."

"I think I have, Sir James."

"Glad you think so. I can't abide false modesty. Will you come to my office after your class?"

It was the first time she had been in his office since the day in July when Uncle Matt had signed her contract. She was still awed by the room: the richness of the Persian carpet, the softness of the cracked leather chairs, and the gleam of the dark wood paneling. Sir James was seated behind his large double desk. Jack Baines, the director of *The Valiant Hours*, occupied one of two chairs placed in front of the desk. Sir James motioned Jane to sit in the other.

"My dear, we have been discussing the matter of your name. Now, I'm sure you are very attached to it but it simply has to go."

"It's a very easy name to say," she said with a weak smile.

"And just as easy to forget," said Baines.

Paxton, ignoring his comment, continued. "We need a name that reflects what you are and, more importantly, what you will become. In this picture, you play a young nurse. You are soft and yielding but with great inner courage. In the end, you sacrifice the man you love by helping him regain his memory and return to his wife. You are going to cause people you have never met to shed tears. In the future, I want you to be able to play a variety of women, some sympathetic, others not so. As you progress as an artist, you will develop the power to manipulate the emotions of an audience. I want that audience to think of you in multidimensional terms: passionate and judicious, vulnerable and indestructible. Your name must be an essential part of that image. I'm sorry, my dear, but neither Jane nor Parks projects those qualities. You are a clean canvas. The first strokes are vital to the rest of the picture."

Jane listened, spellbound.

"We have talked to everyone who has worked with you over these past six weeks and asked them to suggest names for you. Jack Baines is here today because he has come up with one I like very much."

Jane turned to her director. "What is it?"

"Laura Standish."

Jane burst out laughing, then reddened. "I do think Laura is a very nice name, but I don't know if I'd want to be identified with such an awful stick for the rest of my life."

"What are you talking about?" said Baines.

"Laura Standish." Jane was blushing furiously now. "She was, um, a character in the . . . you know ... the Parliament novels? Anthony Trollope?"

Sir James laughed. "Well, Jack boy, I suppose that's what we get for taking on such a well educated young lady," He paused for a minute to go through the machinations of fitting a cigarette into its holder and lighting it. "Tell me some of your family names. Maybe we can find something there."

"Stokes is my aunt and uncle's name. I would very much like having that."

"Ye gods, it's worse than Parks!" said Baines.

Frowning at the remark, Jane continued "My grandmother's maiden name was Forester and her mother's name was, let me think, oh yes, Maud Baker, and I have an uncle named Tom Collier. I remember my father used to talk about two maiden aunts in Australia by the name of Georgina and Justina Cooper."

"It's like the whole damned English race in one family," said Baines.

"So it is," said Sir James. He looked at Jane through a haze of cigarette smoke. "By God, I've just had a brain wave! Since you are undoubtedly English to the core, that will be your name. Laura English."

"I like it!" said Baines, standing. I'll notify the publicity department." He turned to Jane "See you at rehearsal on Monday. I want everything down cold as far as timing and blocking." He grasped Sir James's hand over the desk. "Well done, Jamie."

When the director was gone, James Paxton got up and came around the desk. He sat on its edge in front of Jane. " 'A rose by any other'."

She looked up at him. "It's just hard to get used to so many changes."

"I know, my dear, but it is worth it, isn't it?"

"Yes," said Jane, straightening her back, "it is. I love this part. I feel I really know Valerie. The words she speaks don't seem to come from the script. I've learned how to make them my own."

"So I have heard from our friend Baines. I know he can seem unreasonably exacting at times, but he's the best director we've had at Briarwood since Teddy Giles went to Hollywood. You can learn a great deal from him."

"I know that. I want to learn all I can from whoever will teach me." She leaned forward in her chair. "I still can't believe my luck in being here when others struggle for years and years and sometimes never get a chance."

"The luck was all on my side, because I was the one who saw you first. It's true that most young actors have had to struggle harder than you to get their chance, but that is because their talent is usually buried under layers of bad training. Few had the benefit of Alfred Easley as a teacher."

Jane smiled, settling back in the chair.

"Listen to me, my dear, you are destined for certain things."

"Destined!" she laughed. "For what things? All I want to do is be the best actress I can."

"Yes, I know, and that is all very commendable, but like it or not, you do have a destiny. A destiny to thrill thousands of people who sit in the dark. Alfred saw it, Jack Baines sees it, and so do I. And next spring, when *Valiant Hours* is released, the world is going to see it."

She shivered.

"Now, I know you have a few days off before shooting starts next week. Will you be going home to Bournemouth?"

"Yes," she said.

"I'm sure you will be as happy to see your family as they will be to see you. And your young man, you must miss him."

"I am looking forward to spending some time with Aunt Rose and Uncle Matt. . . and John . . . but I am very happy here in London."

"I am delighted to hear you say that. I want you to do me a favor while you are at home in Bournemouth."

"If it's studying my lines, I already plan to ..."

"On the contrary. You are word perfect now. What I want is for you to relax and enjoy yourself. Spend as much time as possible with that beau of yours. Let all your feelings for him come to the surface. Do you follow me? Then when you get back it will be fresh in your mind as well as the sadness you will feel at being separated from him and we will get it all on film."

"Oh!" Understand his meaning, she blurted out: "You are an awful old scoundrel!" She clapped her hand over her mouth and gasped, but he was laughing.

"I rather like being pegged as a scoundrel, just not an old one. Off with you now, Miss Laura English."

"I'll see you at home . . . Sir Jamie."

In two months filled with wonders, the greatest of all was her friendship with Derick Lindsey. One day. to her surprise, he appeared at her RADA class, sitting at the back of the room, his lanky figure slouched deep in a chair, a cigarette between his fingers. After class, he walked over and casually put his arm around her shoulder.

"You know, I didn't believe all the hoopla about you, so I had to come see for myself."

"And," she said, her eyes looking straight into his, "what do you think?"

"Good. So good, in fact, that I'm going to give you some of my precious time tonight to go over a few of your scenes in *Valiant Hours*."

It was the first of many evenings spent in the pubs of Chelsea and South Kensington. Derick, the inevitable cigarette between his fingers, delved into the character of Valerie until Jane was acting with a dimension she had not thought possible. Over frothy mugs of golden ale and thick slices of pork pie, they would argue over a gesture or a word. At times, they parted less than cordially, but he always apologized the next day and they went on meeting. Jane realized that, even counting some of her best school chums, Derick was the closest friend she had ever had.

After Sir James Paxton and Jack Baines renamed her, she rushed to the set of *Bonnie Prince Charlie*, where she knew they would be shutting down for the day. Derick, out of costume, was waiting for her. It was raining, and they ran for the underground. When they emerged in Chelsea, they found the rain had stopped but the air was still humid. They stepped into a cafe, a tiny place with red and white checked tablecloths and candles stuck in waxy bottles.

"Oh, I remember this. We liked it, didn't we?" she said.

"Yes. Terrific Bolognese, and I'm famished. Freddie was a real pig today, but we're nearly done. We should wrap early next week."

They sat down and smiled at each other across the table. He lit a cigarette and she told him about the name change.

"Laura English." He exhaled a long stream of smoke at looked up at it reflectively. "Laura English," he repeated drawing out the syllables. "Not bad. You look like a Laura English."

"It's going to be a hell of a note breaking it to my family." She was beginning to pick up some of his phrases, and it amused him.

"Not as hard as mine was, I warrant you."

"What do you mean? Oh, Derick, they did it to you too. What is your real name?"

"David Landau."

"That's not a bad name," she said in surprise.

"My parents didn't think so either, but don't you find anything at all wrong with it?"

"No, I don't. It's not a plain name like Jane Parks. That's why they changed mine, because it's a little too ordinary."

"Well, mine was a little too Jewish."

"Oh, I see." She reddened. "I didn't realize."

"Didn't realize! Don't tell me you are that rare creature, a gentile who is not just the least little bit anti-Semitic? Even my mother . . ."

"Well, I lived a rather sheltered life in Bournemouth, and my aunt and uncle tend to take people for what they are, so I guess I never learned to be anti anything. Naturally, I know anti-Semitism exists; I've just never had any direct experience with it."

"Tell me, Jane love, is there anything unpleasant about you?"

"You had better start calling me Laura or I'll never get used to it and, yes, there are plenty of perfectly horrid things about me. You just haven't discovered them yet."

"I don't want to discover them. I've never known a person as sweet as you. Please let me keep my illusions."

She looked at him seriously. "Tell me, have you suffered much from being Jewish?"

"During the war, my school was evacuated to Wales and I got my fair share of nastiness there. Privileged Jewish boys set down in a poor Welsh village. Every time we went into town, there was a battle. You know, in some parts of this great land Jewish bankers are used as scapegoats to explain away much of the misery people have to endure. The funny part of it is, my father really is a banker in the City. My parents live in a rather grand house in Cleveland Square. My mother is a very elegant lady who never lifts her finger to do anything much more than hold a bridge hand or arrange a bowl of flowers, both of which she does to perfection. Fortunately, I had a very loving nanny." He looked thoughtful. "Before the war, my parents gave enormous parties. I used to watch them from the head of the stairs when I was supposed to be asleep, but it was worth the scolding from Nanny Smithson to see all the guests in their finery. The next day, I would stand in front of the mirror and act out the whole party. I could imitate all the voices and gestures of their friends, and I used to make up plays about them and act them out for my sisters."

"Oh, Derick, that's just what I used to do! I don't have brothers or sisters, but I used to act out everything for my aunt and uncle."

"Of course, darling, we're performers."

"When the time came for me to go to school, my mother, who is not Jewish, wanted me to go Harrow where her brothers, Stephen and Peter, had been, but my father had a bee in his bonnet about another school, a Jewish one called Shelbourne. Sounds deceptively un-Jewish, eh? Anyway, the headmaster's father and my grandfather grew up together in the same town in Poland, and they used to see a great deal of one another when they first came to England. My grandfather prospered, but his friend, Jacobs, did not and so they lost touch.

"One day out of the blue, his son, Benjamin Jacobs, rang my father and asked if he could come 'round and chat with him about the possibility of sending me to his school. My dad had no intention of doing any such thing. but after an hour in his study with Benjamin Jacobs, he was all for me going to Shelbourne. Evidently, Jacobs explained that his was equal to any first-rate public school in England but that I would also grow to understand my heritage. I guess he held it out as a chance to expose me to a painless, if belated, indoctrination. I think he hit a nerve, because down deep my father felt a little guilty about being such a bad Jew. You see, with my mother Church of England, most of their friends are gentiles. I guess when they married, my father was taken with the idea of broadened social possibilities and happily adopted her way of life, but now that I was growing up, he was feeling pangs. As for me, I had never thought one way or another about being Jewish. Davy Landau was British through and through.

"You want to know something funny? After a year in that school I felt 100 percent Jewish. I read everything I could lay my hands on about the history of the Jews. I talked to my classmates, especially the ones from Germany and Poland, about what it meant to be Jewish. I even took to calling myself Daveed, with the accent on the last syllable." He laughed at the memory. "I was determined to go on from Shelbourne to rabbinical school. Mr. Jacobs suggested I join the drama club to help develop my ability to speak in public. I read for a part in a production of *The Merchant of Venice*. Naturally, I wanted to play Shylock, but that wasn't very likely since it was my first tryout. I was cast as

Nerissa!"

"You must have made a charming lady-in-waiting," she laughed.

"I did. What's more, I went totally into the role. During the six weeks of rehearsals and the two weekends of performances, I was a woman. I had submerged myself into playing that part just as I had submerged myself into being Jewish. After that, my Jewishness was just a fact, not a compulsion. By the time I was fourteen, I was a permanent fixture in the drama department and had made up my mind to become an actor. Anyway, when Jamie wanted to change my name I fought it, but in the end he won. You see, acting comes before scruples."

"And do you still consider yourself a Jew?"

"Well, not religious, but there's definitely something still there. You see, Benjamin Jacobs had lived a pretty adventurous life before settling down to run a boy's school. When his father's business failed in London, he was sent to stay with an uncle in Palestine. He lived on a kibbutz and toughened up and made friends with the likes of Ben Gurion and Moses Shertok. During the First World War, he joined the Zion Mule Corps, a Palestinian regiment that fought in the desert against the Turks. I sometimes got invited to his special gatherings on Friday afternoons. There were usually about ten or twelve of us. We would listen to his war stories and he would tell us about Palestine. I guess he made good Zionists out of all of us."

"That's fascinating." She was looking at him intently, elbows resting on the table and her chin cupped in her hands.

"God, I've told you my whole life story. What time is it, anyway?"

"I love listening to you talk. How did you come to work in films?"

"I was at RADA, and Jamie saw me two years ago and offered me a contract."

"Simple as that?"

"Oh, I guess word had got around about the brilliant new boy there." His eyes smiled, and he took her hand across the table. "So, you're almost ready to start shooting. Excited?"

"Very. And nervous."

"You're going to be great, don't worry. It's the waiting around that's the worst."

"I'll be going home to Bournemouth on Friday. Sir James has given me nearly a week off before shooting. He told me, in so many words, to make wild passionate love to John so as to get myself up for the part. Can you imagine?"

The stunned look on Derick's face passed before she noticed. "He's an idiot."

"I called him an old scoundrel."

"I'll bet he loved that," he said, lighting a cigarette.

"As a matter of fact, I think he did." She sat staring out the window for a few minutes. "Derick, I don't know what's the matter with me. I do love John but something keeps holding me back from, you know, going all the way." She looked down into her cup.

"Good God, you're only nineteen years old. Give it some time."

Yes, but what if he gets tired of waiting and finds someone else?"

"What if? As a famous old rogue, my uncle Stephen, said to me when I was just a lad, 'Davy, a girl is like a tram. If one goes by, another will be along in twenty minutes.' I'm giving you the same advice, darling. You'll likely have men dropping at your feet from now on, but the performing is what counts, what lasts. All that really matters is the work."

"I know you're right, about the performing, anyway."

"I'm right about everything."

CHAPTER 5

LONDON, 1952

Living in London, Laura was witnessing the miracle of a great city rebuilding itself from wartime shambles. While James Paxton and Maud Jefferies lamented the loss of elegance and grace that defined prewar London, Laura, who remembered little of her childhood there, found the 1952 version of the city she now called home irresistible — offering and promising everything.

The seeds of the future were being sewn, and Laura, responding to its driving force, passionately desired to be a part of it. With Derick Lindsey as her guide, she was becoming acquainted with the avant-garde of the city. Together, they frequented the small back-alley galleries that exhibited the work of Francis Bacon, Nicolas de Staël, and Lucien Freud. They haunted dusty bookshops, where Derick encouraged her to venture out of the safe world of her beloved Victorians into that of the mind-stretching existentialists: Albert Camus, Simone de Beauvoir, Jean-Paul Sartre — and beyond to Pascal, Heidegger, and Kierkegaard.

Together, they sat in the back row of rundown cinema houses that featured what critic Nico Frank called "film noir." Derick was fascinated by the stories of petty gangsters, truck drivers, waitresses, and nightclub singers who lived in a world of perpetual night. In his opinion, directors such as Robert Siodmak, Jacques Tourneur, Raoul Walsh, and John Huston were pioneering a genre that someday would be recognized as a true art form. Sitting in the back row of these tiny art houses, Derick whispered a running commentary in Laura's ear, pointing out the directing and editing techniques that lent these films their own particular style. Eventually, Laura began to recognize the fine points of camera work, dialogue, and especially lighting, which deepened her appreciation of film.

They had been to a screening of *I Walk Alone*. As the lights came on, Derick breathed a long sigh and ran his fingers through his hair. "If I were ever given the chance to direct, that is the look I'd like to get on film. What Leo Tover did with Lizbeth Scott's face in the taxi scene . . ."

"She is stunning."

"Yes, and in the hands of another art director that's all she would be, another beautiful starlet. Tover goes past prettiness. He brings out the architecture of a face. Did you notice how much Scott and Lancaster look alike? Same brow and jaw. Even their eyes are similar. When they do a scene, the dialogue plays because there is that male-female mirror image thing going on. Granted, that's lighting, but it takes a director like Byron Haskins to recognize it in the first place".

They walked out of the movie house and through the raindrops to a café, where they ate eggs and chips, drank ale and talked until the place closed.

Most of Derick's friends were involved in some aspect of the arts. Writers, painters, and actors, they were creative young men and women who, like Laura and Derick, were intensely involved in their work. His flat in Barkston Gardens off Earl's Court Road was a popular meeting place for the group. Lounging around his fireplace, they ate spaghetti off mismatched plates and drank cheap Spanish rioja, while Bessie Smith and Billy Holiday records played on the phonograph and clouds of acrid smoke from Gauloise cigarettes hung in a blue haze over their heads. On these evenings, Laura curled up in the corner of an old velvet couch and listened to their intense discussions on art, music, and theater. Contributing little to the conversation, she was content enough just to be part of Derick Lindsey's charmed circle.

The best times were those they spent together. A pub crawl through South Kensington, an evening at the theater, or a Sunday afternoon at the Institute of Contemporary Art — whatever they did took on the excitement of a great adventure. Laura was aware of Derick's stark good looks, the fine nose, large expressive eyes, and well-defined mouth yet, though they often held hands and sometimes Derick kissed her, she felt no leap in her pulse or rapid throb to the beat of her heart. Derick was her closest friend and most trusted confident, but Laura remained deeply in love with John Keith.

During those exciting first months, Kitty Paxton was exposing Laura to another side of London: the world of Piccadilly and Bond Street, of Regent Street galleries and William Darby's Cork Street auction rooms. While Derick was introducing her to spicy Bengal curries and Moroccan couscous, Lady Kitty took Laura to the Pheasantry and the Ritz Grille and told her that regulars at Quaglino's knew that the best dishes were not listed on the menu.

Early on, Sir James realized that Laura would require help with clothes. She always looked presentable in her tidy skirts and jumpers, but she desperately needed a signature style to set her apart from the new crop of actresses that seemed to be blossoming from every studio. Since James could think of no one with a better sense of style than his own wife, he recruited Kitty to remake his protégée. They set aside an afternoon when Laura had no classes to tackle her wardrobe. Helplessly, Laura stood by the open armoire as her new friend removed favorite dresses and skirts from hangers and tossed them into a large carton destined for the neighborhood parish house.

"But Kitty, you can't take that! I saved for two months to buy it," she cried as her most beautiful blouse went into the box.

"Darling, you obviously grew up with the idea that ladies with red hair should wear robin's egg blue."

Taking her by the hand, she lead Laura to the full-length mirror. "Now, let's take a good look at you." Kitty's moved around the tall girl like a fairy fluttering around the willowy stem of a lily. "Of course, your hair is simply marvelous, but we're going to get it trimmed just a bit so that it sets off the shape of your face. Do you know that there are models having their back teeth pulled to get cheekbones like yours?"

"I don't believe you, Kitty." Laura had always hated the way her bones stuck out, and as for her hair, she had assumed the studio would want to change the color, perhaps turn her into a blonde. "Imagine anyone thinking bony cheeks and red hair were assets!"

"Well, they definitely are. You act as though you don't even think you are very pretty."

"I don't."

"That's not an affectation, is it? You really mean it."

"Look, Kitty. I don't care about anything but becoming the best actress I possibly can. I'll play the oldest ugliest hag with a false nose and warts if it's a good part. Before Sir James saw me in *Major Barbara*, my ambition reached only as far as the Bournemouth Players, and if it turns out I'm not suited to films I'll try for the stage. I am happy here because I am learning so much, but you must understand that I'm not interested in turning into a glamour girl."

"Jamie's right, you certainly are an original! But want it or not, glamorous is what you're going to be. Trust me, it's in there, just waiting to come out."

Ignoring Laura's protests, Kitty made an appointment for the following week with a seamstress who had a studio in St. John's Wood. Madame Chloé's clients were women of taste who wanted the latest French designs but could not pay for originals. Kitty traveled to Paris twice a year for the autumn and spring shows at Balmain, Dior, and Balenciaga, but found Chloé useful for the odd fill-in dress, and thought she would be perfect for providing Laura with a new wardrobe.

Laura's heart sank as the blue door, bearing the legend *Madame Chloe, Modiste* in faded gold script, opened and a woman of a certain age with badly dyed auburn hair and dingy skin stood before them. Laura, standing a good head taller than the diminutive Madame Chloé, noticed a fine sprinkling of dandruff on the shoulders of the modiste's rumpled dark gray smock and a dark yellow nicotine stain on her index finger.

"*Bonjour*, Lady Kitty," the woman said in a mournful voice.

"*Bonjour*, Madam Chloé. May I present my friend Miss English who is in desperate need of some things right away."

The woman gave Laura a swift upward glance. "Right away is impossible, Lady Kitty." Her accent was half French, half something slightly guttural that Laura couldn't make out. Madame Chloé showed the two women into an adjoining workroom and led Laura to a far corner, where a three-way mirror reflected the surrounding chaos.

"Please take off the dress."

Laura looked around at Kitty, who was sitting on a sagging day bed littered with magazines and swatches of fabric. "Go ahead, dear, Chloé needs to take your measurements."

For the next several minutes, Madame Chloé's yellow tape girded every measurable part of Laura's body. She wrote each number carefully in a small black notebook and slipped it into the pocket of her smock. "*Voilà*. And what does mademoiselle need?" she said, tilting her head to one side.

"Everything," said Kitty before Laura could answer. "Day dresses, skirts, at least three cocktail dresses, and one really good suit."

"Very well, we will look at some pictures." She lifted a large portfolio, containing the latest designs from Paris, off a work table in the center of the room and sat down next to Kitty.

Madame Chloé and Kitty examined page after page of beautiful clothes, arguing over proportions, colors, and textures. At last, Madame Chloe drew the black notebook out of her pocket and began writing. "So, we will make the Balenciaga suit, the two Dior dresses, and the Schiaparelli coat."

"And don't forget, we also want the two Jacques Fath cocktail dresses." Kitty smiled at Laura, who was long past belief.

"Now, we choose the fabrics," said Madame Chloé. She led Kitty and Laura into an adjacent room, which was lined with shelves containing bolts of cloth and sample books of fabrics.

"We had better select from what you have available, since we are in a rush for these," said Kitty, scanning the shelves. "This tweed for the suit. What do you think, Laura, dear?" she held out a bolt of textured fabric in tones of rich tobacco, shot through with green, gold, and tiny threads of pink.

"Oh, it's lovely."

"Good. This for the suit, Chloé. Make her a second skirt out of it as well. Now, for the dresses." She pulled down bolt after bolt, discarding some, putting others aside. At last, she was down to a soft sage green wool and a golden yellow cashmere for the day dresses and a textured fabric in a rich oatmeal shade for the coat. She chose black crepe and emerald green taffeta for the cocktail outfits and some navy merino and a dark gray flannel for the skirts.

As Madame Chloé clipped the pictures of the models they had selected with a corresponding swatch of fabric for each garment, Laura noticed with astonishment that her grimace had turned into something that looked almost like a smile.

"Lady Kitty, you still have the best eye of any of my clients." Turning to Laura, she continued, "She has chosen the perfect fabric for each dress in colors that will suit you perfectly."

Kitty turned to Laura, taking hold of her hand. "I hope you don't mind my charging right in, but for the time being I think I am a better judge of what goes well on you. You know, it is the hardest thing in the world to see oneself objectively."

She turned with a sharp look at Madame Chloé. "We need the skirts, two of the wool dresses, and one cocktail dress right away, and the rest just as soon as possible. And remember, waists as tight as you can and skirts that fit her like a second skin. Smooth but not suggestive. Her body must look refined, and narrow as a blade. You see, my dear Chloé, with the help of your art, Miss English is going to make big bosoms falling out of their décolletage as tired as yesterday's soufflé. Mark my words, Miss English is going to make elegance sexy."

Madame Chloé was positively beaming. "*C'est ca*, Lady Kitty. I will put my other work back for the moment."

"Thank you, I thought you might."

Out on the sidewalk, Kitty laughed. "A bit on the quaint side, but unquestionably the best seamstress in London." They climbed into the dark green Jaguar. "I've made an appointment for your hair, but if you're tired we can put it off for another day."

"Oh, no, I'm not tired at all."

"We're off, then." She started the motor, fluffed her blond curls in the rearview mirror, and maneuvered into the stream of traffic.

Laura sat back in the soft leather seat as Kitty steered the car through the knots of midday traffic moving toward Oxford Street. The streets of London were still a constant source of amusement to Laura, and she was happy to watch the passing scene from the car window as they stopped for minutes at a time in the congested traffic.

"Oh, to hell with this," cried Kitty as she swung the car around and headed down a side street. "I know another way 'round that will get us there quicker than sitting in this mess."

As Kitty drove from one narrow street to another, Laura began to feel uncomfortably warm. Her forehead was damp, and she was conscious of the waistband of her skirt cutting into her stomach. There was something familiar about these curving streets and oddly unpleasant about the tiny shops and doll-sized houses.

The car made another turn. "Good," said Kitty. "This will bring us out at the Edgeware Road and from there . . ."

Laura knew this street! The cobbler's shop, and yes, there was the green-grocer's stall, and next to it the small gray house with the plaque that read 56 Church Street. Her house! In an instant, she was a small child once again living in that street, in that house, with her father gone and her mother growing more and more silent. How clearly she remembered the beautiful face, the graceful white hands, the large gray eyes. Oh, Mother, if I had come home as soon as the war was over! Laura gripped the seat with stiff, icy fingers and, forcing the painful images out of her mind, concentrated on Sir James Paxton, Briarwood Studios, and her future. The pain in her chest eased, and she sighed as Kitty drove down the Edgeware Road toward the West End.

The only beauty parlor Laura had ever known was Miss Ethel's in Bournemouth: a cramped little storefront with the inevitable row of humming bubble dryers under which sat unlovely housewives shouting gossip to one another amid fumes of permanent wave solution and nail varnish.

This spacious salon, decorated in muted shades of pink and gray, was nothing like Miss Ethel's, and Mr. Paul was like no one Laura had ever seen. He fussed over Kitty and Laura, calling for tea and offering them gold-tipped pink cigarettes. Laura couldn't help but stare at his pink silk shirt and tight black pants.

"Now tell me, Kit darling, what are you doing here? Your day is Friday and this is only Wednesday, although God knows I could be wrong." As he talked, Laura noticed that he wore rings on several unlikely fingers. "I went to the most bizarre party last night . . . at least I think it was last night. I woke up this morning with a frightful head and someone called Peter or Roger rattling around my kitchen coddling eggs and scraping toast. You don't suppose I lost a day or two somewhere? Oh, God, if this is Friday, I've missed my Thursday appointment with the dreadful duchess."

"No, darling," Kitty laughed, "I've just come along with my friend Miss English for her appointment. If you look, you will see her name there in the book." She pointed over at the reception desk to the open appointment book.

"Here it is, Paul, Laura English," said the receptionist, rolling her eyes at Kitty.

"Thank God, darling." He gestured to tall girl with cropped black hair and turned to Laura. "Just go along with Dee. She'll show you where you can change."

To her relief, Laura soon realized that Mr. Paul became entirely focused while wielding his long razor-sharp scissors through her red curls. When he finally stood back, eyes squinting, she could hardly believe her own reflection in the mirror. Not very much had actually been cut, but the once-unruly mane was trimmed and shaped so that her prominent cheekbones looked even more defined. Her eyebrows were now swept up at the ends, and a trace of liner and hint of shadow gave her large gray eyes a new, devilish expression.

"Is this truly me?" she said as she stared at her image.

"You have a fabulous face, darling. Wait until Des Malory at Briarwood gets hold of you. I dabble in makeup for fun, and I just couldn't resist those eyebrows. I knew they had potential." He smiled, taking a long drag on his pink cigarette and gave her left brow one last swipe with a tiny brush.

CHAPTER 6

Each time Laura returned to Bournemouth it was a shock. Compared to London, the seaside town seemed impossibly small. Because Matthew and Rose were there, she knew it would always hold a special place in her heart, but now London was home — the most exciting place on earth, the center of her universe.

Her new look made a sensation. Descending from the train in her Madam Chloé oatmeal tweed coat, to which the clever seamstress had added a stand-up collar of off-white beaver, Laura looked as if she had stepped out of the pages of *L'Officiel*. It wasn't until she was standing directly in front of Rose that her aunt recognized her.

"Heavens, can this really be our Jane? You look like a film star already!"

"It's all a façade, Aunt Rose. I haven't shot a foot of film yet."

"It was nice of Lord James to give you this time off for a visit," said Matt.

Laura laughed and kissed her uncle's cheek. "Come on, Duke Matthew. Let's go home."

The moment they arrived at the house, Laura made a dash for the telephone and dialed John's number. He had recently bought a second-hand Austin Healy from the garage where he worked, and in less than fifteen minutes was standing at the front door with Laura clasped tightly in his arms.

"God, it's good to hold you. It's been weeks and weeks since your last time home. What the hell have you done to your hair?" He kissed her. "Let's go for a drive."

Sitting beside him in the car, she studied his profile: the ridge over his deep-set eyes, the thick lashes, the blunt nose, full lips, and strong jaw line, now in need of a shave. As always, his looks shot a thrill straight through her and, at the same time, left her wondering what thoughts went on behind that handsome face. She had known him for a year and a half, but in many ways, he was still a puzzle to her.

During the first months of their relationship, he told her a great deal about his past. As he revealed each new facet of his life, she imagined that a door was being opened, and that each door, as she passed through it, would finally lead to the deepest core of his being: the hidden place she longed to uncover. After taking possession of the cottage, they spent most of their time there, but oddly enough, the more intimate they became, the more distant John grew. Now, it seemed that the boy she thought she had known through the stories he told her was like a character in a series of adventure novels. It was only when he took her in his arms and she could drink in his beauty with all her senses that her uneasiness faded and she felt momentarily at peace.

When they were apart, she stored away amusing stories about Briarwood and London, but when they were together on her visits home, these anecdotes fell flat. Laura sensed that everything about her new life bored John, and sometimes she was at a loss for conversation. She worried that he would meet someone better suited to him, and with all due respect to Derick's Uncle Stephen, she knew another John Keith wouldn't come along, like a tram, in twenty minutes.

Suddenly, she was aware that John was speaking.

". . . and Tommy says we can drop by anytime. So, what do you feel like?"

"Oh, whatever you want, John."

"Well, then, old Tommy will have to understand that seeing my girl is more important than his birthday. Besides. there'll be a mob there, and he won't even notice whether we come or not."

"I don't want you to miss a party because of me."

"Are you daft, Janie? I want to have you all to myself. Besides, I have a surprise for you."

He turned the car toward the main road. "Where are we going?" she said.

"Christchurch."

"Christchurch? What a good idea. I haven't seen your grandmother in ages."

"Well, as a matter of fact, Gran's not there. She's gone over to Lymington to visit a friend for the week. That's the surprise. We'll have the house to ourselves." He took hold of her hand and squeezed it.

It was dark. The tree outside the bedroom window was now only a shadow against the pane. John lay on his back, eyes closed, a faint smile touching the corners of his mouth. She wondered what he was thinking.

Lying in each other's arms on a real bed had taken their lovemaking to a different level. The shack at the beach belonged to their youth. The bed suddenly made them adults, and when John touched her body in the old familiar way, Laura responded with grown-up passion that gave way to abandonment. She opened herself to him willingly and joyfully, expecting to feel, at long last, completely one with him. Suddenly, there was a barrier, then pain. As he pushed farther and farther inside her, the sexual excitement vanished, and she found herself wishing he would hurry and finish. The thought shocked her. This was the most important moment of her life, the moment she had waited for. She had expected to feel — what? Ecstasy? Rapture? Bliss? Instead, she was feeling the onset of tears.

John opened his eyes.

"Well, at last." He turned towards her and took her in his arms. "I know it hurt you, Janie, but after a bit you'll get used to me."

"I know. Just hold me tight." Laura began to cry silently against his shoulder. For months she had imagined that when they finally came together in this way there would be a tremendous rush of love flowing from his body into hers. She had thought that, with this act, they would be finally and forever united. Instead, she felt strangely alone.

"Janie, what is it?" he said, pulling away to look at her.

"Nothing. I'm just an idiot." She smiled into his eyes and then started laughing. Her hand touched his face. "I love you."

"Jane, I've given it a lot of thought, and I've decided I might as well go to university, you know, in London."

She sat up, hugging her legs, chin resting on her knees. "John, that's wonderful! When will you take the entrance exam?"

"I took it in August and just got the word I've been accepted. I wanted to see more of the world first, but I reckon that can wait."

"You'll see that you made the right choice. I can't wait to show you London! There's so much to see there. I know you and Derick Lindsey will be good friends. He's done so much to help me."

"The only thing I'm interested in seeing in London is you, Janie."

"Oh, I almost forgot. I have a new name."

"The devil you have. Why?"

"Because Jane Parks doesn't sound right for an actress. I don't mind, really. I'm getting quite used to it, in fact. It's a very pretty name."

"Well, I don't want to hear it."

"You have it hear it. I want you to call me by it or it will never become a part of me. Sir James says that's very important."

"And who made up this new name for you, Sir James Paxton?"

"Well, I guess it was sort of a group effort. Anyway, it's Laura English, and

I'm really serious about your calling me that. Aunt Rose and Uncle Matt do."

"Well, I'm not. You're my Jane, and Jane you'll always be. Now, come over here." He pulled her down to him and, as their lips met, he began to stroke her back.

The next few days went by in a blur. Mornings, she and Rose lingered over their teacups chatting about her life in London and catching up on the latest Bournemouth gossip. She wanted to tell her aunt what had happened in Christchurch but every time she looked into Rose's innocent blue eyes, the words would not come. Afternoons, she wandered into town or walked along the cliffs above the beach. The sky was crystal blue, with banks of white clouds on the horizon. The soft breeze blowing in from the sea was rich with salt. Derick kept popping into her thoughts, and she realized that she missed him. Bournemouth certainly wasn't thrilling like London, but it had been her home for most of her life. The smell of the sea in the wind, the tiny flowers on the downs, the laughing faces of the children playing on the beach — all this had been part of her growing up and she longed to share it with him.

She saw Betsy Dwyer a few times. Betsy was married now and had a job half-days at the bank in the high street. One afternoon, Laura picked her up after work and they had a bite to eat before Betsy went home.

"I can't wait to get pregnant," Betsy confided as they sat in the tea shop near the bank. "It's not that I don't like my job, but to tell you the truth, I don't feel properly married without a baby." She smiled into Laura's eyes. "So, has John said anything yet?"

"About what?" said Laura.

"Idiot, getting married, of course!"

"No."

"Oh, I am sorry. Well, he will one of these days, don't you worry. He never takes any other girl out. Even now that you're gone for weeks at a time. He just goes 'round with his mates. He'll probably ask you soon."

"Betsy, I don't know if I want to get married right away. I love John with all my heart, but I want to be an actress with all my heart too. I'm learning so much at Briarwood and . . ."

"But surely you wouldn't refuse him if he did ask!" gasped Betsy, a look of amazement in her doll-like blue eyes. "He's the best-looking boy I've ever seen."

Laura smiled. "I know, and I love him. It's just that I have a chance to do what I've always wanted. Anyway, John said that he is going up to the University of London. So, we will both be there, and we can spend all our free time together."

"Well, I hope you get your fill of this acting and come home. You belong in Bournemouth with us." Betsy reached across the table and gave Laura's arm a little squeeze.

Suddenly, Laura knew why she had not confided to her friend about the change in her relationship with John. She looked at Betsy and saw a stranger. A feeling of sadness and loss washed over her as she realized she no longer had anything in common with this girl who had been her closest friend for most of her life.

Laura visited Bertie several times at the theater. He was eager to learn every detail about her training at Briarwood and listened, eyes bulging more than usual, as she described her classes. When she told him her new name, he was delighted.

"Couldn't be more perfect. And how is the part coming along?"

"We've been in rehearsal for the last two weeks, and one of the actors at Briarwood has been giving me incredible coaching on the side. Why don't I bring the script over tomorrow and go through it for you?"

It was a magic moment. Alfred Easley, the person who opened her to the world of theater, reading the part of Dennis to her Valerie. They were like two old dance partners, each falling into the other's rhythm as naturally as if they had never been apart. All the technique she had learned at the Royal Academy of Dramatic Art and all her sessions with Jack Baines and Derick Lindsey took on new meaning as she went through the scene with Bertie. When it was over, they looked at each other for an instant and then, crying and laughing at the same time, fell into each other's arms.

"Oh, if I were only thirty years younger! You and I would have a touring company together that would set the British Isles on its arse."

"We'd do everything!" she danced around the stage. "*St. Joan* and *Lear*. Oscar and Tennessee! And we'd discover new playwrights and introduce their work. Why don't we, Bertie? Three years isn't so long. When my contract is up, Easley & English Theatrical Productions!"

He took both her hands in his. "As I said before, if only. My time for dreaming has passed. Yours has just started. Make those dreams come true, my dearest child."

Each evening, John arrived at the Stokes' door promptly at six. Uncle Matt came home soon after and the four had supper at the round table in front of the stone hearth. As they ate, Laura kept looking at John's face. She wanted to reach out and run her finger along his lips. She wanted to put her hand on his thigh and feel its warmth through the cloth of his trousers. After the meal, they went off to meet friends, or to the cinema in Bournemouth, or just for a drive along the coast in the Austin Healy. No matter how they spent the evening, they always ended up in Christchurch for an hour or so. Later, tucked up in her own bed, Laura hugged herself with happiness as she remembered the feeling of his lips on her body, his caresses, the exciting sound of his gasp as entered her, and the deep moan of satisfaction at his climax.

It was toward the end of her stay that she realized she and John had spent most of their time this week with other people or in bed. They hadn't done much real talking. He seemed to have no interest at all in hearing about her life in London. Whenever she started telling him about the classes she was taking or her part in the film, he just nodded absently, and if she brought up his plans for university he changed the subject.

It was Sunday afternoon and time to leave. She said goodbye to Aunt Rose and Uncle Matt, promising to come home again as soon as she had some time off. John took her to the station. They drove in silence most of the way. She looked over at him and he, feeling her glance, returned it. She couldn't read the expression in his eyes. Sadness, regret — finality?

"When will you be coming up to London?"

"It's no good, Janie."

"What do you mean *no good?*"

"My going to London."

"But what are you talking about? You said you were accepted at university."

"I was, and when I told you I was coming up I meant it, but I spoke too soon. There are places I need to go, things I have to do."

"What things?"

"Look, you'll be busy most of the time. After this picture. there'll be another. Paxton has you for the length of your contract, and I don't want to sit around wasting time waiting for you to get off the set."

"But that's not the way it would be. You'll be in class during the day, and I'll be at the studio. We'll have evenings and weekends, just like any other couple. We can get a flat together. I'm making very good money, and I've saved quite a bit because I haven't had any living expenses. A painter friend of Derick's needs a bigger place and is looking for someone to take over the lease on his flat in South Kensington. It's really charming, and I know we could get it for not too much."

His hands gripped the steering wheel until the knuckles turned a sickening white. "Has it ever occurred to you that I may not want a charming place in South Kensington, wherever that may be? Has it ever occurred to you that I really never had any desire to go to university? I'm not saying it's definite, just that you'd better not count on anything."

"This is a fine way for us to say goodbye."

"Look, Jane, you have the next three years locked up. Let me decide what I want to do with my time. That's only fair." He pulled into a parking space near the entrance to the railway station and turned off the engine. They sat facing each other. "Give us a kiss," he whispered.

In the train, she sat staring out the window, seeing nothing. She went over John's words in her mind, trying to understand his point of view, but all she could see was his face as he told her he wouldn't be coming to London. She had been so sure that once he was there and they were living together everything would fall into place. Now, after coming so close, had she lost him? The thought sent a cold chill through her body. Never again to see his face, never again to lose herself in his arms. She shivered. The train pulled into Waterloo just after six o'clock. The station was crowded with returning weekenders. She pushed her way through a knot of young people boisterously shouting their last goodbyes before heading in separate directions. She walked out of the station and up the Waterloo Road. A brisk wind stung her flushed cheeks, making her eyes water.

"John," she whispered, a little sob escaping as she said his name.

Then, without conscious effort, her thoughts turned to Derick and she heard his words in the wind that whistled by her ears. Performing is what counts, what lasts. All that really matters is your work.

Running toward the entrance to the underground, she glanced at her watch, calculating how long it would take her to get home and praying that Derick would be in when she called.

CHAPTER 7

From the first day of shooting on *The Valiant Hours*, Laura cast any anxiety concerning John Keith out of her mind and focused entirely on implementing all she had learned about her craft during the past months. Nothing else took precedence. Her sole consideration was to translate the character of Valerie Martin into a living presence on the screen.

As for Sir James Paxton, the moment of truth had come. Would his judgment about Laura's potential prove correct this time as it had so often in the past — including his greatest creation, Beryl Villiers? Would this slender girl, in whom he had invested so many bright expectations, come through for him on the screen?

The first day's rushes exceeded his most optimistic hopes. In Valerie, Laura captured the essence of all women who have loved and lost in war. Through the character of the young nurse, she projected vitality in youth and strength in gentleness. The range of subtle expressions that played across her face conveyed the hidden meaning between the lines of spoken dialogue. Her body, virginal in its slimness and sensuous in its pliant grace, moved with the perfect balance of a dancer while the mischief in her glance was irresistible. There had been no one like her on the screen before. She was indeed an original!

Valiant Hours had been shooting for a week when Jasper Quigly came by the set. He had something in mind. He was scheduled to play Merlin in an upcoming production of *Young King Arthur* and had a notion that Laura might make interesting casting as Morgan le Fey. During a break, he mentioned as much to Sir James. Paxton thought the idea an interesting one but said he needed some time to think about it. He had to be certain that Laura had the depth to play such a demanding part. The nurse in *Valiant Hours* was an admirable young girl, pure-hearted and self-sacrificing. Morgan le Fey was a venomous, sexually aggressive woman. As he viewed that evening's rushes, with Quigly's suggestion in mind, any doubts he may have had as to her abilities were dispelled. After *Young King Arthur*, he would cast her in a comedy. He noticed Laura had a flawless sense of timing; the most important element in comic acting. Indeed, Sir James was certain that her greatest success would be in light comedy.

Laura sat back and closed her eyes as Desmond Malory began to contour her face. It was the last day of shooting. Jack Baines told her she was to stay available for additional dubbing but, after tomorrow, it would be back to her usual routine of classes until she was given a new assignment. For better or worse, Valerie was captured on film, irretrievably and unalterably, a permanent record of Laura's competency as an actress. With the spotlight trained on her face and the camera rolling, she had felt alive in every atom of her body, but now that her work on *Valiant Hours* was nearly completed, a niggling anxiety lurked at the back of her mind. She wondered if there were another film with a suitable part for her. What if the worst happened and Sir James was disappointed with her work? What if he called her in to say he had made a mistake?

The night before, she could not get dinner past the lump in her throat, and this morning just the sight of the toast in its rack made her feel sick to her stomach. Now, as she got up from the makeup chair, she stumbled.

"Watch your step, sweetheart." Desmond Malory caught her by the arm and sat her back in the chair.

She put her hand to her forehead. "Oh, Des, everything went black all of a sudden."

"Let me get you some water." He hurried over to the sink and filled a glass "Here, love, drink this."

"I didn't have any breakfast. Maybe that's it."

"Of course it is. Wait a minute." He rooted in the pocket of his smock and pulled out a half-eaten Cadbury bar. "Here, take a bite of this."

She undid the wrapper and bit off a square of the rich chocolate. The smell produced a wave of nausea but she forced herself to swallow it. She needed quick energy. This was her last day, and after working so hard, she couldn't let a little tummy upset ruin it all now. Tomorrow, she would give in to whatever bug she had, but today she needed all her strength. She smiled gratefully and took another bite of the candy.

"You really saved my life, Des. Thanks a million." Suddenly, the candy was coming up. With a trembling hand clamped over her mouth, Laura ran for the bathroom and slammed the door behind her.

Jack Baines stormed into the makeup room. "What's going on in here!

Laura was due on the set five minutes ago."

"She's in the loo being sick," said Desmond. "Poor kid, she was green as a ..."

At that moment, Laura emerged from the bathroom. There were faint circles under her eyes but she seemed better. "Slight delay, Jack. I'll be there in three seconds. Just give me a quick comb, Des."

One look at her face as she came through the door that evening, and Kitty insisted Laura go straight to bed. Now she lay, head on the pillow, staring at the bathroom door. She needed to open that door and get to the toilet in time to be sick there and not on the floor by the bed, as she feared might happen at any minute. Taking a deep breath, she got out of bed and made her way into the bathroom. Each time she vomited, she felt better for a short while, but inevitably the nausea, accompanied by a pounding headache, returned. Kitty brought her weak tea and dry toast, but Laura could not get it down. At eight o'clock, Alice, the children's nurse, brought in a tray with some chicken broth and Jacobs crackers.

"Lady Kitty and Sir James have gone out, but said to tell you they wouldn't be late. Please eat one of those crackers, Miss Laura. You'll just keep getting weaker and weaker if you don't put something in your stomach." She put a spoon into the bowl of soup. "Here, now, just take a little sip."

Laura forced herself to take some. Instantly, Alice had another spoonful at her mouth. The liquid splattered in all directions as Laura jumped out of bed.

"Miss Laura!" Alice shouted, but the girl was retching into the toilet and couldn't hear her.

The next morning, Sir James insisted she see a doctor.

"In this matter I am adamant," he said to Kitty in the identical tone he used on the set. "And don't even think of taking her to that man of yours. She goes straight to Laurie Sedgeway. You can do what you like for yourself, but I am responsible for the girl."

"But Jamie, you know Dr. Sullivan is brilliant. He delivered Simon with much less fuss than old Dr. Pell did with Sarah and Jamie."

"Since Simon was your third, that probably would have been the case, anyway. I simply don't trust a man who purports to do everything. Sedgeway is the best, and to Sedgeway she goes."

"Dr. Sullivan diagnosed Letty Fulmer's gall bladder, while all your precious Laurie Sedgeway did was to dose her with bicarbonate of soda. Dr Sullivan feels that a physician should see his patient as a whole and not in bits."

As she turned away from him, he smiled, resisting the urge to kiss the end of her charming nose. "Well, my darling, the bits of Laura that need looking after will be attended to by Laurie Sedgeway. So get to the telephone and make that appointment."

The following day, Kitty took Laura to Harley Street. Tall and lean, with just the right amount of gray at the temples, Dr. Sedgeway listened to Laura as she related her symptoms. After a brief examination he diagnosed intestinal flu, complicated by nervous exhaustion. He prescribed some pills against the nausea, and suggested a bland diet and plenty of rest.

Laura got plenty of rest because she could hardly raise her head from the pillow, but contrary to the doctor's orders, she could keep neither the bland diet nor the pills down for more than a few minutes. Kitty, Alice, and even Sir James coaxed as much clear soup down her as they could and then watched helplessly as it came up. The days passed, and still the constant racking nausea plagued the girl.

"Laura, my dear, just try one or two spoons of this," said Sir James, a small bowl of broth in his hands. "Jasper and I have something very exciting in the works for you, but you won't be up to playing a corpse if you don't take some nourishment."

Laura looked up at him, a tremulous smile on her wan face. "Jasper and you have something . . . for me?"

"Yes, we do." He held out a spoonful of soup. "Take this and I'll tell you what it is."

Laura swallowed the broth.

"Morgan le Fey."

"Oh . . ." Throwing back the covers, Laura staggered passed James and into the bathroom.

"My God," he said, turning to Kitty. "What are we to do? This has been going on for over a week. Do you think we should call her aunt?"

"No. Let's give it a little more time."

The next day, a maid brought Laura a letter. It was probably from Betsy. She would wait to read it when she wasn't feeling so ill. The only person she wanted to hear from was John, and after more than a month with no word, she had given up all expectation of a letter from him. She didn't even know where he was. She gazed listlessly at the photograph that stood on the night table by her bed. It had been taken at the beach, and John was squinting into the sun. She remembered that day so well. They had gone to the shore with a group of friends and had sat on the dunes, apart from the others, to eat their lunch. It was then that he first told her about Spain. At that time she had known John just a little over a month and everything about him fascinated her. It had been a happy time. A falling-in-love time. She reached for the photo just as her head started spinning, and another wave of nausea came crashing down on her. As she got out of bed, the letter slid off the lace-trimmed blanket cover onto the floor.

Telephone calls to Dr. Sedgeway brought repeated advice to force liquids. On the Tuesday of the second week, Kitty bundled the shivering girl into her car and headed for Bloomsbury.

Dr. Daniel Sullivan's consulting rooms were in Bedford Place, near the British Museum. Short and plump, with a warm, gap-toothed smile, Danny Sullivan's casual manner put Laura instantly at ease.

He put his arm around Kitty's waist. "Hallo, my beauty. What brings you in? Don't tell me you're in the family way again." He seated the two women and sat down behind a littered desk, leaning far back in his chair and locking his hands behind his head.

"No, Danny, nothing like that. It's my friend Miss English. She has a frightful case of intestinal flu and can't keep anything down at all."

He looked sharply at Laura. "How long?"

"It started about two weeks ago," said Laura weakly.

His glance took in her pallor and the dark smudges under her eyes. "Why did you wait so long to come in?"

"Well, actually, Jamie insisted I take her to Lawrence Sedgeway," said Kitty. "He's given her some pills, but they haven't done any good. Just look at the poor creature, she's weak as a kitten." Laura reached into her bag, took out the bottle of pills, and placed them on Dr. Sullivan's cluttered desk.

He picked it up and glanced at the label. "Hmmm, yes. Well, let's take a look at you, and then there are a couple of tests I'd like to run."

"Tests?" Laura looked at the doctor anxiously. "What kind of tests?"

"Just routine. As far as the nausea goes, I'm afraid these pills are no good. In order for them to work, you have to be able to keep them down, and since that's the problem in the first place . . . well, you see my point. I'm going to give you an intramuscular injection of vitamin B^{12}. It's going to hurt like hell, but should put things right by morning." He buzzed and a minute later a nurse appeared. "Miss Hudson will take you to an examining room. I'll be there directly."

As she followed the tall, dark-haired nurse out of the doctor's office and down the hall, Laura thought of Dee at Mr. Paul's and wondered if the two were related.

Danny Sullivan leaned back and folded his hands behind his head. He squinted across the desk at Kitty. "Well, my love, you may not be in the family way but by the look of those distended nipples and her other symptoms, I'd say it's a fair guess that your Miss English certainly is."

"My dear, you must see that the most sensible course would be for you to have an abortion." Sir James's tone of voice was soft but carried its usual note of authority. "After all, you have your future to think of. It wasn't as if you and your young man planned to have this child. It was just a mistake, easily remedied." He took her hand "Now, don't you think I am right?"

"I don't know. I'm still in a bit of a daze. Anyway, I couldn't do anything without John knowing. After all, it's his baby, too."

"Yes, of course it is, but don't you see, there will be plenty of time for babies later. Why bother him with this now?"

"I love John. I couldn't get r . . . rid of his child without even telling him."

"She's right, Jamie," said Kitty "She must let the boy know about her condition. Telephone him right now, darling. Go into the study and have some privacy."

Tears filled her eyes. "But I don't even know where he is!"

"Well, then, ring his grandmother. She must know how to find him."

In a house filled with beautiful rooms, Sir James's study was Laura's favorite. Bookcases lined two walls, their shelves filled with histories and plays, some rare first editions, bound in soft faded leather. Typical of the striking contrasts Kitty had created throughout the house was a huge Matisse nude hanging over the elegant white marble Jacobean fireplace. Tall windows at the far end of the room faced out onto the garden which now, at the height of autumn, was ablaze with asters and mums.

Laura curled up in one of the large wing chairs near the hearth, legs tucked under her, the same way she had as a little girl in her father's chair. She lay her head against a wing of the chair. The fabric was a soft rose chintz printed in a floral pattern. She traced the outline of a white peony with her fingertip. Tears stung her eyes. How many times had she and John made love? Four? Five? What difference did it make? It only took once to conceive. Did she think that because she had been a virgin this couldn't happen? John must have assumed that she had been fitted with a diaphragm before coming home that last time. He must have supposed she had made up her mind to sleep with him and had gone to a doctor before coming to Bournemouth. He probably took it for granted that she was a responsible, mature woman. But she wasn't responsible or mature. She had acted with no more sense than a child. The telephone sat on a small table next to her chair. Laura picked up the receiver and dialed the operator.

She got through almost at once. "Mrs. Keith, this is Laur . . . this is Jane. Is John there?"

"Well, no, dearie." Mrs. Keith sounded surprised.

"Do you know where I could reach him? It's rather important."

"Didn't you get a letter from Johnny? He mailed it to your aunt Rose in Bournemouth because he wasn't quite sure of your address in London. Didn't she send it on to you?"

"A letter?" My God, she did have a vague memory of someone handing her a letter but she thought she had dreamed it. It must have been put away somewhere. "Mrs. Keith, I've been ill and . . ."

"You see, Jane dear, the thing is that Johnny's gone. It all happened very sudden like. He got a telephone call from abroad. He said there was a job for him out there in Egypt. He told me he was going to write and tell you about it."

"Egypt! What kind of job? The last time I was in Bournemouth John told me he had been accepted at the university and that he would be coming up to London. Then, on the day I left, he changed his mind. Had he heard about this job before I left for London?"

"I don't know, dearie. He got the call the day I came home from visiting my friend Bertha in Lymington. It caused me no end of worry, him just taking off like that. I asked him what about you? He said you were working in films now, and that you would be very busy the next few years and this was a good chance for him. A week after he went away, I got a postcard from Cairo. It had a picture of the pyramids on it. Johnny said that he was all right and that I shouldn't worry, and that he would write to me again."

"Mrs. Keith, when you hear from him will you please let me know? You can write to me care of Sir James Paxton."

"Just a minute, let me get a pencil."

Very carefully, Laura gave the old woman the address, spelling out the street name for her and going over the postal zone twice.

"All right, I've got it all down now."

"Thank you, Mrs. Keith. "

"He's quite a one, our Johnny, isn't he?" she chuckled. "Mind you, he's been that way ever since he was a boy. You could never tell what he'd be up to next. Just like his dear father, God rest his soul. Fancy him over there seeing the pyramids in the flesh, so to speak." She chuckled again. "It is all very exciting, don't you agree? He'll be home again, Janie. Don't you worry. He'll have his fill, and then he'll come home to us."

"Goodbye, Mrs. Keith." Laura put the receiver back in its cradle. Her hands were trembling and her forehead was covered in little beads of perspiration. The letter! She opened the door to the study and peered into the hall. No one in sight. She ran up the stairs and into her room, her breath coming in short gasps. She looked on the bureau and in the drawers. There it was sitting on top of a pair of gloves! She tore it open. The letter paper had the initials *J.G.K.* printed at the top of the page.

Dear Jane,

I am sorry that we quarreled on our last day but you must see that I can't bury myself for years at a university. To what end? The law? I've heard from a friend of my father's in Jordan. He has offered me an opportunity to do something interesting and worthwhile. I'll be in Cairo to start and after that, probably Jordan. In any case, if everything works out, I'll be in that part of the world for the next several years. Try to understand, my Janie. You have your career. Now I want mine. I want you to know that you are the only girl I have ever loved. If you had stayed Jane Parks, then you would be here with me now, as my wife. But the way things worked out for you. I know you would be miserable keeping house for me and a bunch of kiddies when you could be acting.

I will write as soon as I can. Until then, I'll be thinking of you.

John

P.S. I know you will be a great success in the film.

She read the letter again, folded it carefully and put it back in the envelope. Gone. To Egypt. But why? He had never mentioned any interest in anything that had to do with Egypt. Would things have been different if he had let her know about this sooner? In his letter, he said that he loved her, and that he would have married her and taken her with him. Would she have given up the chance offered her by James Paxton to go with him? Perhaps he had done her a favor in not forcing her to make that choice. He said that he would write soon. No, as soon as I can. But when would that be?

John. Her beautiful John with the pale green eyes and the look in them that always made her melt inside. She might never again feel the coarse texture of his thick curling hair, the smoothness of the skin at the small of his back, the power of his arms, and how his body felt pressed close to hers.

You are the only girl I have ever loved. Would he really come back to her someday? She shut her eyes and saw a little boy with bright golden curls. One thing was certain. She would not kill the only part of John Keith that was left to her.

CHAPTER 8

"I have given this a great deal of thought and . . ." she hesitated, taking a deep breath. "I've decided to have the baby after all." Laura braced herself for, at best, an argument, at worst, a hasty dismissal from Briarwood Studios.

Sir James peered at her over the rims of his glasses and shook his head. "Stubborn girl. Ah, well, nothing to do about it. We'll have to find you a place to stay until summer. Kitty's aunt lives in New York and . . ."

"As I said, Sir James, I've given the situation careful thought, and I think it would be best if I went to Uncle Bertie's."

"Bertie's! That, my dear, is completely out of the question. Bournemouth is the first place a curious reporter would go to find you. We simply cannot take the chance of having this spread all over the scandal sheets."

"Aunt Rose and Uncle Matt won't talk about this to anyone, and Bertie's house is out of town in Bourne Valley."

"But you can't stay there until the baby is born!"

"Why not?"

"Because you will go mad being shut up in the middle of nowhere until next July. Besides, what about his theater? I hear it's a great success. What if someone sees you on the grounds? Please let us send you to Fiona's. She has a really beautiful place in Locust Valley, out on Long Island, and would see to your every comfort, I guarantee."

"Sir James, you have been more than understanding about all of this, but since I must keep out of London until the baby is born, please let me do it my way."

He looked at her and sighed. "Well, I suppose if your mind is made up, it's made up."

"Thank you."

"Now, after . . ."

Here it comes, she thought. *I'm out.*

"You know that we must go on with *Young King Arthur* as scheduled."

"Yes."

"Jasper is very disappointed that you will not be available to play Morgan le Fey, but he's is set to do a romp with his gang later in the year. I could hold off on that one until you are back at Briarwood."

"Oh! Sir Jamie, I can't belie ... " her voice caught for a moment. "I honestly thought you would sack me because of this."

"And lose you to Rank or, God forbid, MGM? Look, I've been managing film careers for more years than I like to think about. If I'm not prepared to overcome a few minor obstacles along the way, then I may as well get out of the business. Just have this baby as quickly as possible and get back to work. Briarwood will be here waiting for the return of its newest star."

"I don't know anything about that," she said, smiling "I've only had a small part in one film."

"And you stole every blessed scene you were in!"

Her mouth fell open. "What do you mean? I never . . ."

He laughed. "Oh, you didn't do it intentionally. You can't help it. You see, Laura, you possess the two essential elements all the truly great ones have: originality and personal magnetism. It's true that you are still a novice, but no matter how hard you study, or how diligently you apply what you learn, without those two basic qualities you can never achieve real star status. Derick Lindsey, for example, is a very fine actor, but he will never be a top star."

"Oh, I disagree. Derick is . . ."

"Your friend, I understand. Look, young Lindsey is a fine actor, and I'm glad to have him under contract. But if he should walk out tomorrow, I could replace him in ten minutes. There are five or six young lads at RADA right now who do the same parts as Derick and just as well. He is replaceable because there is nothing original about him. Jasper Quigly is irreplaceable because he is wholly original. Do you understand what I am getting at?"

"I think so. But I want to be an *actress*, not some freak people chase about in the streets."

"You might not be able to avoid being chased about in the streets, because as soon as *Valiant Hours* is released you will be public property, and once the Hollywood boys see Laura English, I'm afraid they are going to start offering you the moon. You don't seem to understand that there isn't anyone here or in the States like you."

"*Hollywood.*" She said the word with such genuine disgust that Sir James burst out laughing.

"Well, we will cross that bridge when we come to it. After all, you do have a three-year contract with me. We can do a lot of work in three years! So you see, my dear, your stubborn determination to have this baby, while annoyingly sentimental, doesn't mean the end of our association. On the contrary, I'm going to hold on to you for as long as I can."

"You'll have me forever."

"Now, the immediate thing is to get you out of London as soon as possible. Gossip thrives around a film studio. If word gets out you are preggers and unmarried, well . . ."

"That *would* be the end, wouldn't it?"

"Not the end but definitely sticky. You must disappear until next summer. Naturally, there will be a good deal of speculation at the studio as to where you've gone, but we can handle that. *Valiant Hours* isn't scheduled for release until spring. Fortunately, you're not well known to the press yet. A brief absence can easily be explained here at Briarwood. You want to finish up some school credits. We'll think of something. Can you go to Bertie's straight away?"

"Yes, straight away."

Uncle Matthew and Aunt Rose were overjoyed that Laura had decided to have her baby. To them, all children were precious, and a marriage license was not essential when it came to bringing new life into the world. It was agreed that Laura's child should stay with them in Bournemouth after it was born and the prospect of a baby in her keeping had given Rose a new lease on life. She wanted Laura to come to them immediately, but she explained that Sir James wanted her to keep out of public view and that Bertie's, in the Bourne Valley, would be better suited to that end.

By the second month of her pregnancy, the terrible nausea was completely gone and Laura had regained her usual vitality and enthusiasm. All her life, she had been taken care of, first by Aunt Rose and now by Sir James and Lady Kitty. At last, she had the chance to look after someone she cared about: her beloved Bertie. Strictly adhering to Aunt Rose's housekeeping routines, she set to work, cleaning every corner and polishing every surface. She made curtains for the bare window in her bedroom and started a small vegetable garden in a sheltered spot outside the kitchen. She read a great deal and took a nap every afternoon. Each evening was like a special occasion as she and Bertie ate the supper she prepared and talked endlessly about the theater. Christmas came, and Laura and Bertie decorated the house with paper streamers and holly boughs. Laura cooked a goose with all the trimmings, and Matthew and Rose, who brought a plum pudding, joined them for luncheon on the day.

Apart from Kitty and James Paxton, the only person in London who knew Laura's whereabouts was Derick Lindsey. He came down to see her most Sundays, arriving by taxi from the train station, arms laden with phonograph records and treats from Fortnum & Mason. If the weather was dry, they would tramp through the woods on the other side of the hill that marked the boundary of Bertie's property. The cold air colored their cheeks and numbed the tips of their noses. Sometimes, they brought along a bag of stale bread to feed the family of ducks that patrolled the reedy shoreline of a lake about a half-mile from the house. If the day was wet, they lounged on big pillows in front of the fireplace, listening to Dave Brubeck and Lester Young recordings, while Derick amused her with studio gossip and caught her up on the latest goings-on of their London friends.

Between Sunday visits, he kept her spirits high with long late-night telephone conversations. He asked her to call him David, as his family still did. "Every time I hear Derick, I think of oil rigs in the Persian Gulf."

She laughed. "I'm flattered that you've asked me to call you by the name your family uses."

"Well, I feel very close to you."

The huskiness in his voice brought the blood to her cheeks. "And I feel close to you too. It's strange, I hardly think of myself as Jane Parks anymore. I'm completely comfortable with Laura English. Why do you suppose that is?"

"Oh, I don't know. Probably because you're so hardhearted and unsentimental."

"Probably," she laughed.

If, during those mid-week telephone conversations, David sensed that the confines of Bertie's house were finally closing in on Laura, he would hire a car and drive down on Friday afternoon in order to spend the entire weekend with her. Taking advantage of the mobility, they would head east to Portsmouth or Brighton or west as far as Plymouth, stopping for meals in teashops or rustic inns. These excursions were a great tonic to Laura and helped her forget, for a little while at least, how much she was missing London and Briarwood. Whether exploring the coastal villages or taking a walk together, she and David always had more to share than time allowed.

"You are so good to me, David. Trekking all the way down here when I know there must be more exciting things for you to do in London."

"Don't you know by now that I'd rather be here with you than in London or anywhere else?" It was late February. They were walking back from the lake. Pale sunlight made patterns on the ground as it filtered through the bare branches of the trees. The carpet of fallen leaves was soft and spongy under their feet. Except for the sound of their footfalls, it was perfectly quiet. David reached for her hand.

"Don't you know that I'd like to be with you all the time?"

She understood what he meant by the remark but couldn't think of a response.

He stopped walking, put his hands on her shoulders and turned her toward him. His dark eyes were very intense. "I love you." His voice rang out in the silent wood.

"I love you, too. You're the dearest friend I've ever had."

"Will you marry me, Laura?" She noticed that the skin around his mouth had gone white and his body was tense.

"I can't, David. I'm still in love with John."

A tiny muscle at the side of his mouth twitched. "But you haven't heard from him since that one letter."

"I know, but I can't help it. That's the way it is."

"How long are you going to wait for him?"

"I'm not waiting for him."

"Have you told his grandmother that you're pregnant?"

"No. I don't want John to find out about the baby. Anyway, he's probably met someone else. Otherwise, he would have written me by now. If he doesn't care for me anymore, I certainly don't want him to come back out of a sense of duty or guilt."

"Then why don't you marry me? I promise I'll do everything in my power to make you happy. I think your family likes me, and I know mine will love you."

"David, don't you see that it's because I love you that I wouldn't think of marrying you while I still feel the way I do about John?"

He took his hands off her shoulders and shivered. "It's turned cold. We'd better be getting back."

They walked in silence. She groped for something to say that would make things all right between them again, but David, a frown drawing his brows together, trudged along without speaking.

"I guess I won't be seeing so much of you now," she said as the house came into view.

He turned, facing her. "Not unless you don't want to. Anyway," a shaky smile touched his lips, "I'm not giving up as easily as that."

Dr. Sullivan had referred Laura to Dr. Samuel Barton in Plymouth. Following his instructions, she made an appointment for an examination soon after settling in at Bertie's. Dr. Barton assured her that she was in perfect health and should have no trouble delivering the baby.

One evening, early in her fifth month, David called to chat and was surprised to hear Bertie's voice on the other end of the line.

"She can't talk right now, my boy. Her blood pressure went up quite suddenly, and Dr. Barton says she must stay in bed."

David was down on the next train.

"I don't care what Jamie Paxton has to say about your keeping out of London," said David, his dark eyes filled with concern. "I'm taking you to Dr. Sullivan."

"Yes, David, you're right. I'd feel so much better if I could see him. Thank you for coming."

Dr. Sullivan gave her a thorough examination and prescribed something which would bring her blood pressure down without harming the baby. He spoke to David as Laura went to dress. "It was absolutely the right thing for you to bring her to me. Barton's the best man down in that part of the world, but I'm afraid most physicians outside of London don't put a great deal of stock in the new medications. Without the stuff I've given her, Laura could have been in real trouble. Truth be told, I'm still concerned about the baby. I'd like her to stay up in town for a few days so I can keep track on how she's doing. Kitty told me that Sir James wants Laura out of sight until she delivers, but this is a question of her well-being . . ."

"I know a place she can stay. If I might just use your phone?"

David explained to his mother that his friend Laura English was recovering from a recent illness and needed rest and quiet. Thus it was, with much trepidation on her part, that Laura found herself standing at David's side as he rang the bell at 46 Cleveland Square, Bayswater.

Tall and slim, her fair hair swept up in an elegant French twist, Diana Landau's greeting was gracious but Laura detected a definite coolness in her blue eyes. David's mother did not like the idea of her son associating with actors and kept alive the constant hope in her heart that he would one day, in the not-too-distant future, get over what she termed his *show-business phase*. David must return to Cambridge, she felt, where he had spent two terms after Shelbourne. A career in the foreign service or academia would be much more suitable for her only son than, she could hardly bring herself to think of the word, *acting*!

A uniformed maid took Laura's overnight bag.

"Doris will show you to your room," said Mrs. Landau, fingering the single strand of pearls that gleamed against the deep camel color of her cashmere sweater. "If you need anything, don't hesitate to let her know."

The cheerful little housemaid installed Laura in a comfortable third-floor bedroom. Soon, she was propped up in bed, a tea tray by her side, reading the latest issue of *Harpers and Queen*.

Laura encountered Mr. Landau only twice during her stay at Cleveland Square. He introduced himself politely but briefly as she passed him on the stairs on her way up to the room she was to occupy. He was a handsome man with a finely chiseled profile, thick silvery hair, and dark eyes. *This is how David will look in thirty years*, she thought. They met again the following evening.

Laura had just finished her supper when there was a light tapping at her door. "Come in," she called out, putting her book aside, expecting to see David.

"I've come to see if you are comfortable." Aaron Landau stood tentatively just inside the room. He had no accent but spoke precisely, as one might who was raised in another language.

"Oh, yes, Mr. Landau, very comfortable. You have both been so kind having me to stay. After all, I am a complete stranger to you."

"Well, not such a stranger. We have heard about you from David, and I feel that I know you from him. I am sorry for the circumstances that brought us together, but I am glad we have finally met." He came over to the bed, as if to see her at closer range. "You know, you are very dear to my boy."

"Yes, Mr. Landau, we are close friends."

"I think David would like more than just friendship, eh?" His eyes softened and there was a hint of a smile in their blackness. "He would not like it if he knew I mentioned such a thing, but I know my David, and when he talks about you, it sounds as if his feelings are deep." He paused, but she remained silent and he went on. "You are both young. Sometimes that is best. It was for Mrs. Landau and me." He paused again but still she did not speak. "I will leave you now to rest." He moved toward the door.

"Mr. Landau."

"Yes?"

"I wouldn't hurt David for the world."

"I hope not, Laura." He closed the door softly behind him.

After week of complete bed rest at the Landau's, Laura's blood pressure returned to normal, and Danny Sullivan said she could return to her Uncle Bertie's.

Late in April, *The Valiant Hours* opened in theaters throughout Britain. The critics praised it as another in a long line of first-rate productions by Sir James Paxton. The film's stars, Richard Bennet and Felicia Scott, received excellent reviews for their performances as the wounded soldier and his wife. John Carlton Baines received high praise for direction — and the public went absolutely mad for Laura English.

The baby was kicking furiously as Laura tried to read the article in the *London Clarion*.

FILM SENSATION VANISHES

Laura English, who stole the show in Sir James Paxton's latest, Valiant Hours, has disappeared from London. Sources at Briarwood Studios say that Miss English has not been seen for several months. Makeup artist Desmond Malory told this reporter that the stunning young actress fell ill on her last day of filming. He has not seen or heard from her since then. Is Laura English terminally ill? Is she still alive? Letters have been pouring into the studio since The Valiant Hours was released ten days ago. Cinema-goers in every corner of Britain demand to know the whereabouts of the enchanting girl who has so captivated all our hearts.

Laura laughed to herself. Wouldn't they be interested to know that the enchanting Laura English was sitting in Bournemouth, waiting for her bastard child to be born? Odd that the film should have opened on April 20, two years ago to the day that she met John Keith. Her heart turned over as she remembered him, standing before her on the beach, a dark form against the bright spring sky. Where was he now, at this moment? What was he doing? Who was he with? Despite the depressing fact that she still had had no word from him, Laura kept hoping that a letter would arrive in the next post. The ringing of the telephone startled her.

"It's for you, Laura," called Bertie from downstairs.

"I'm coming," she answered over the banister as she carefully descended the staircase. She took the phone from Bertie. "Who?" she whispered to him.

"David," he mouthed.

She took the receiver from his hand. "David, hello!"

"Have you seen the *Clarion*?"

"Yes. I was just reading it."

"Laura, I want to come down this weekend."

"That would be lovely. I've missed you, it's been over two weeks."

"I know. I told you about the chance of directing that project of Hal Raymond's. Well, it looks like it's a go. I talked to Jamie and he's willing to let me have eight weeks. I'm well aware he thinks it will be a disaster, but Hal's a brilliant producer and this thing could be a real sleeper. Anyway, it's a chance to direct, at last."

"David! I'm so happy for you. When do you start?"

"As soon as we wrap *River's End*, probably another week or two. Anyway, I told everyone I was going fishing in Scotland this weekend. I thought you'd enjoy that one."

"Just your cup of tea. You'd probably have a more exciting time in waders up in Glen Whatever than sitting around here with Your Belliness."

"Laura, you are always exciting to me, belly and all."

"Glutton for punishment."

"I'll see you Friday in time for supper, then."

David and Laura sat at the kitchen table drinking a second cup of coffee. It was Friday, and Bertie had gone over to the theater an hour before.

"Would you like another piece of cake?" she asked.

"I couldn't." He let out a deep, satisfied breath. "You know you are really a fantastic cook. Somehow, I never imagined you in the kitchen."

"Aunt Rose taught me a lot of things about keeping house when I was a little girl."

"You've been happy these months in Bournemouth, haven't you?" he said, smiling at her across the table.

"Yes. I love being able to see so much of Rose and Matt, and Uncle Bertie is an incredible companion. But I'll be glad when the little whoseit comes. Aunt Rose can't wait to get her hands on the baby. I'm so lucky that she wants to take care of it. After all, she brought me up, and I know what a marvelous . . ."

"Laura," he broke in.

"Yes, David. What is it?"

"Marry me."

"My God, just from some chocolate cake?"

"You know I'm serious, darling."

"And you know I'm in love with John. I've explained all that . . ."

"And what about your child, doesn't he or she deserve a father?'

"David, I . . ."

"I know, I know, you love me only as a friend. Well, there's nothing wrong with that. Why can't two friends get married?"

"But why short-change yourself? You should have a girl who loves you back in the same way."

"Don't you think I've tried? I've taken out a lot of girls since I met you. Slept with most of them. It's just no good. You are it for me. Look, Aunt Rose might be the greatest mother in the world, but your child belongs with you."

Laura was surprised at the shock she felt when he mentioned taking other girls to bed. "But what would we do with the baby? We'll both be at the studio all day."

"We'll hire a good nanny who will be there while we're at work, and we'll have the baby in the evenings and on weekends. We can take it on walks in its pram and to the zoo and later on I'll take it out on the Serpentine in Hyde Park." He was grinning broadly. "Look, we can say that we were married last year, and you had to go to Canada immediately because your father was seriously ill."

"David, my father's wife wrote me last year to let me know he died."

"Well, we'll just have to resurrect him for the time being until you make your reappearance in London as my wife."

"What if you don't like the baby once it appears?"

David put his hand on Laura's stomach just as the baby kicked. "Not like it? I love it already." He put his hand up to her face and caressed her cheek. "Almost as much as I do you." Gently, he brushed his lips over hers. "Say you will, darling."

She looked into his eyes and saw that they were filled with love — love for her and, amazingly, the unborn child she carried. John's child. She knew that she would never feel about David the way she had and still did for John. No weakness in the knees when he looked into her eyes, no pounding heart when his hand touched hers, no insistent response to his kiss. Still, there was definitely something. They had fun together. She could talk to him about anything, and he always understood. No one else had his special insights or razor-sharp intelligence or perverse sense of humor. She missed him terribly when they were apart. He was her treasured friend, yet she knew that John Keith, at this moment and for the rest of her days, was in her blood.

Laura smiled. "All right, David, if you are sure."

"David! Idiot, they'll hear you in London." She laughed at his loud whoop. He whooped again, louder this time, as he spun her around Bertie's kitchen floor.

CHAPTER 9

CAIRO, 1953

The bar in Shepherd's Hotel, Cairo, was thronged with the usual mix of British businessmen, American tourists, and multinational ladies of the evening. Snatches of conversation echoed in the high dome above the cocktail lounge, and facets of rainbow light spilled from the massive chandelier at its center, splashing rivers of color across the tables and reflecting off the mosaic tiles embedded in the walls.

John Keith sat at a low table across from the circular bar. For several minutes a dark-haired girl with an impressive expanse of olive-skinned décolletage had been trying to catch his attention. Avoiding her obvious attempts to establish eye contact, he put down the week-old *Time* magazine he had been thumbing through and looked around for something else to read. Damn Hassim. Late as usual. After almost a year in Egypt, the one aspect of Arab life to which John would never be reconciled was the casual disregard for anything resembling punctuality.

Someone had left a *London Clarion* at the next table. Reaching for it, he glanced at the date. A miracle. Only three days old. He scanned the first few pages.

Everything in the news section he had already heard on the BBC. He found the sporting news. Ten more minutes passed and still no sight of Hassim. The dark girl had redirected her voluptuous gaze towards a paunchy Egyptian sitting at the bar.

John turned to the entertainment page.

LOST ACTRESS FOUND

Laura English, absent from Briarwood Studios since the release of The Valiant Hours, reappeared in London early this week — with a husband in tow! Actor Derick Lindsey, also under contract to Briarwood, told this reporter that he and Miss English were married last October. Sadly, the new Mrs. Lindsey departed immediately after the ceremony for Toronto, Canada, to be at the bedside of her ailing father. But Dashing Derick must have spent some time with his bride, for the new Mrs. Lindsey definitely appears to be in .

Sudden dampness pricked at John's armpits. There must be a mistake. Hands shaking, he read the short column of print again. No mistake. Crumpling the paper between his hands, he crouched forward as if protecting his body from a blow. He pressed his forehead on his closed fists and tried to digest the meaning of the smug little item. It wasn't too difficult. Without a single word from her, she was married, pregnant — out of his life. He dropped the paper, dashed his hands across his streaming eyes, and raked his hair with trembling fingers.

In a blur, he saw the fat Egyptian moving to an empty seat next to the dark girl. A large ring set with a red stone flashed as his pudgy fingers started stroking her ample thigh.

Dimly, John was aware of his name being spoken. He looked up into the liquid black eyes of Hassim Ibn Faud.

"Are you all right, old man?"

"I'm fine," John said tightly, not trusting his voice. "You're late."

"Traffic was worse than usual, and to tell you the truth, Yasmin and I had a bit of a row before I left the house. Women are the very devil, aren't they?" he laughed.

"Yes," answered John Keith, "the very devil."

CHAPTER 10

LONDON, 1953

Three expectant fathers occupied the second-floor visitor's lounge at Middlesex Hospital. The eldest, wearing the dark pinstripe and sardonic expression of a Chancery Lane solicitor, was seated in a straight-backed chair well away from the younger two. His eyes moved nervously across the pages of a legal journal. Sighing, he drew a thin gold watch out of his vest pocket and glanced at it impatiently. His wife, in labor with their third child, was taking an infernally long time about it. Another quarter of an hour, and he would have to call chambers and tell Miss Thompson to put off his two o'clock appointment. *Caroline had better produce a boy this time. I hope Mother was wrong about girls running in that family.*

The two men on the opposite side of the room were sprawled, rather than seated, on an ancient brown leather couch. The more agitated of the pair, a day laborer by the look of his clothes and state of his fingernails, was alternately eating biscuits out of a round tin emblazoned with garishly colored images of the newly crowned Elizabeth II and taking puffs from the stub end of an evil-smelling cigar. His pudgy face glistened with sweat, and his large, pale blue eyes darted nervously from the contents of the tin to the big clock.

" 'Ere mate, 'ave a biscuit," said the laborer, holding the tin under his neighbor's nose.

"Thank you, but I couldn't eat anything."

"Just like the missus. When she's in a state she can't eat a bite. Not me. Nervous appetite, you might say. Is this your first?"

The other man nodded and smiled.

"Us too! I'm Davy Jenks," he said, extending his hand.

"David Landau. Nice to meet you."

"Two Davids! Fancy that. In the same waiting room and both waiting for our first baby. What do you reckon the odds are on that?" He gave David a broad smile.

The solicitor cleared his throat pointedly, withdrew a box of Dunhills from the inside pocket of his suit jacket, carefully selected a cigarette, and flicking open the top of a gold lighter, touched the flame to its tip.

"Get *'im*," whinnied Davy Jenks, turning his thumb in the direction of the other man. "Too bleedin' grand to mix with the likes of us. And cool as you like, at that. Me, I'm all nerves," he added, lowering his voice somewhat. "Clara, that's the missus, lost a baby last August, and after we'd been tryin' for almost two years. Nearly broke 'er 'art, that did. You see, us coming from such large families the way we do, well, it just don't seem quite natural . . . only the two of us in the 'ouse, if you know what I mean. The doc told her she had no business gettin' in the family way in the first place because of this blood condition she's got, but she wants a little one in the worst way so we kept on trying. I just hope the doc was wrong. See, my Clara, well, she's the world to me and . . ."

A nurse came to the doorway. She peered at the occupants of the room over the top of a clipboard which she held cradled in her arm. "Which one of you is Mr. Jenks?"

"That's me, miss," said Davy Jenks, an expectant grin on his face.

"Please follow me," she said in a toneless voice.

" 'As the baby come?"

"Please follow me, Mr. Jenks. The doctor is waiting to see you."

"Why does the doc want to see me? Is me wife all right? 'As the baby come? I want to see Clara." He dropped the tin of biscuits on the couch.

"Mr. Jenks, please calm yourself. Just follow me." Legs wobbling, Davy Jenks trailed the nurse out of the waiting room and down the hallway.

"Bad news," sniffed the solicitor, re-crossing his leg.

"You can't be sure of that. Sometimes nurses like to act important."

"Trust me, either the child is dead or the wife, or both. That sort never take the proper prenatal care."

"You can't possibly know that. He seems like a good man to me."

"That sort shouldn't have children."

"What do you mean, 'that sort!' " David's fists clenched.

"All they do is breed up a bunch of filthy brats to be put on the dole. We support them in the end."

David, hardly able to contain himself, wanted to punch the supercilious smirk off the bastard's face. He half-rose from the couch when the nurse reappeared.

"Mr. Ferrin?"

"Yes?"

"You may go to the viewing nursery now, sir." She smiled pleasantly. "Another lovely little girl. Your wife should be ready to see you shortly."

The solicitor stood, checked his watch one last time and, with a deep sigh, folded his journal neatly and slipped it under his arm. As he left the room, he turned and gave David a curt nod.

"Sister," David called to the nurse before she could leave.

"Yes," she looked at a paper attached to the clipboard. "Mr. Landau, is it?" She turned the pleasant smile on him. "Mrs. Landau is still in labor. Everything is right on schedule. Be patient for a little while longer, and I will call you when it is over." She turned to go.

"Sister, that man who was here before, Mr. Jenks, is his wife all right?"

"Are you a relative of the gentleman?" asked the nurse.

"No, but . . ."

"I'm sorry, Mr. Landau, in that case I cannot give you any information." She turned and left the room.

David returned to the couch and sat down. The discarded cookie tin lay on cushion next to him. The room seemed very empty without Davy Jenks. He got up and walked to the window. The pane looked as if it hadn't been washed in years and a nagging apprehension crept into his mind about the general cleanliness of the hospital. He stared down at the grubby little courtyard two stories below. Bright July sunshine illuminated a few half-dead geraniums languishing in untended borders and glinted off piles of refuse crammed in the hospital dustbins. David reached into his pocket for his packet of cigarettes. He lit one and looked at his watch. Did babies always take this long to be born? He wanted to get Laura out of here and back home where everything was waiting, clean and fresh, for her and the baby. He thought of Davy Jenks and his "missus," and his heart contracted.

Laura had awakened early that morning with a dull pain in her back. She turned awkwardly in bed, seeking a more comfortable position, careful not to awaken David. She watched him in the dim light as he slept and a smile touched her lips. Great as her doubts had been about marrying David Landau without being in love with him, greater was her surprise in discovering how truly happy she was with him.

Soon after their marriage, David and Laura leased a house at No. 12 Cranley Gardens, South Kensington. The house had a large drawing room, and although the dining room was on the small side, the kitchen was sunny and cheerful. The master bedroom, situated at the back of the house, overlooked a pretty garden bright with birds and flowers. Two small bedrooms and a bath were located on the second floor, perfect for the baby and his or her nurse. The day after they signed the lease, David's mother telephoned Laura to say she would be happy to help in any way she could in getting them settled.

At first Diana Landau had disapproved her son's impending marriage to *the actress*, as she referred to Laura. To begin with, David was much too young for marriage. When the time did arrive for such an important step, she expected him to choose a girl from their own circle of acquaintances. Although Mrs. Landau considered herself quite tolerant in her outlook, she believed, in the end, that David would only be truly happy with someone of his own background and education.

"Tell me, Aaron, what is to be done about David and the actress?" she asked her husband after David had announced his intention to marry Laura.

"Nothing."

"What do you mean nothing? We must do something. A boy like David, with so much to offer, simply wasted on a girl like that. It's all your fault. If you hadn't sent him to that bizarre school he never would have gotten into this acting business in the first place."

"David has chosen his profession, and he has chosen his wife."

"Profession! Do you call acting a profession?"

"Yes. And our boy will benefit people with his talent just as much as he might as a diplomat or Cambridge don. Maybe more. Can't you see how happy he is with Laura? She really has many good qualities. You have to get to know her better and you will see. In any event, you must give her a chance, because she is David's choice and that is that."

"You know why he is going to marry her."

"You mean because she is going to have a baby?"

"Of course."

"Listen, Diana, if David did not want to marry Laura I'm sure they would have done something about the baby. Oh, don't look so shocked. David is not a man to be trapped into anything he doesn't want. So they have a baby a little early, so what?"

"A little early! She's more than halfway gone."

"I say again, so what, and I say again she is David's choice and that's that!"

Deep down, Diana Landau knew that what her husband said was right. She also realized that if she expected to maintain a relationship with her son, she must do as Aaron said and accept his wife. She invited Laura to lunch at her club and was grudgingly impressed when the girl showed up in a smart dark suit cut in such a way so as to camouflage her thickened waist.

In the years before David had widened her literary tastes, Laura had been an avid reader of both A. J. Cronin and Louis Bromfield, two of Mrs. Landau's favorite authors. As they chatted about *Night in Bombay* and *The Citadel*, Mrs. Landau noticed Laura's lovely modulated voice. She had to admit it was very pleasant discussing books with such an intelligent young woman. Laura's manners were faultless, and she certainly knew how to dress. Her looks, while taking some time to get used to, were really quite striking. She would undoubtedly age well. Once she had made up her mind to give the girl a chance, Diana Landau discovered that she liked David's bride-to-be almost as much as Aaron did, and by the time the quiet marriage took place in the Landau's Cleveland Square drawing room, no one in London would have suspected that Laura English had not been her hand-picked choice for David.

The first thing Diana Landau did at No. 12 Cranley Gardens was send over two of her own staff to scour the house from top to bottom. Next came a crew of workmen, who scraped off the faded wallpaper and covered the walls with three coats of fresh white paint. Old carpets were taken up to reveal beautiful parquet floors that, when cleaned and polished, gleamed like satin.

Laura was thrilled with the clean slate. "Oh, Mrs. Landau! The white walls are perfect for all of David's drawings and paintings. And the floors!"

"It was my pleasure, and Laura dear, don't you think it's time you called me Diana?"

"Yes, I do." She smiled into her mother-in-law's pale blue eyes, and Diana Landau smiled back. Evidently, like the walls and floors at Number 12, this was to be a clean slate between the two women.

Kitty Paxton couldn't wait to wade in on the decoration of the new house. As soon as Diana Landau's crew finished with the walls and floors, Kitty took Laura shopping. First stop was a shop in the Portobello Road, where she bought two Afghan rugs in rich shades of red and blue for the living room.

"My first baby present. So he or she won't have to crawl on the cold floor," Kitty beamed.

At Druce in Baker Street, they discovered a Queen Anne table and six chairs, in dire need of refinishing, at a bargain price. Of course, Kitty knew a *little man* who could restore them for practically nothing. In another shop, they found a pair of Chinese pewter lamps, an assortment of odd chairs, and best of all, a fanciful Florentine bed and armoire with harlequins dancing across the headboard and doors of the armoire.

"The bedroom is my wedding present," said Kitty.

"Kitty! What about the Crown Derby dinner set?"

"Well, it's an early first-anniversary present, then. No arguments."

By the end of June, the house was ready and all Laura had to do was wait for the baby to come.

Now, it seemed, it was really on its way.

The pains soon switched from her lower back to her abdomen. At first, they were no worse than menstrual cramps, but by late morning her contractions were much stronger and coming five minutes apart. David insisted they go to the hospital.

By the time they arrived at the Middlesex, Laura's contractions were coming every three minutes and getting harder. While David signed in at the reception desk, Laura was to be taken directly to a labor room by a nurse who was waiting at her elbow. The nurse's hair was covered by a tight cap, but judging from the color of her skin and eyes, Laura suspected that she, too, was a redhead.

"Come along, Mrs. Landau. I'm going to get you settled in the labor room." From the lilt in her voice it was clear that she had originally come from Ireland. The placket pinned to her uniform read "M. Fitzgerald, R.N."

"When may I see my husband?" Laura asked.

"You'll see your husband when you are in your room."

"I'll see you in just a bit, then, David," she called to him.

"No, I'm afraid you misunderstood. Your husband will have to stay in the visitors' lounge while you are in labor. You may see him after you have delivered and are in your own room. Now let's be getting along."

"I'll see you soon, darling," said David, crossing from the reception desk to where she stood. He kissed her lips softly.

The tiny labor room was, except for a bed and an instrument table, bare of furniture. The nurse hung Laura's clothes away in a closet and gave her a soft white cotton gown to put on. It felt warm and smelled wonderfully clean as she slipped it on over her head.

"Now I'm just going to get you prepped," said Nurse Fitzgerald cheerfully.

"The enema, you mean," said Laura. Doctor Sullivan had briefed her on hospital procedure.

"Yes, the dreaded enema. It's not so bad, really. Just lie down on your side and try to relax." She went into the bathroom and emerged, smiling brightly, carrying a bucket of soapy water and some tubing. Laura closed her eyes and kept saying to herself: *It'll be over soon, it'll be over soon.* Surprisingly, it was, and beyond embarrassment, Laura ran awkwardly to the toilet.

"Now, I'm going to give you a shave," said Nurse Fitzgerald as Laura came out of the bathroom.

"I had a contraction during the enema. What if I have one while you are shaving me and I move?"

"All you mothers worry about the same things. I've been doing this a long time. I could open a proper barber shop what with the experience I've had.

Now, just lie back and relax."

Laura smiled as she lay on the table, feeling the sure, even swipes of the straight-edge razor.

She looked at the clock on the wall in front of her. An hour had passed since she had been prepped. She wished desperately that David were here with her. Tears started to well up and streaked across her temples. She felt uncomfortable on the narrow bed. A contraction started.

"David," she called faintly. "David."

She closed her eyes and thought about the baby struggling to emerge from her womb. Over the months, she had grown quite used to the feeling of life inside her. At first there were only a few vague flutters, then real kicking, which grew stronger every month. The last few weeks, the baby had started turning, stretching Laura's ribs until she thought one would surely crack.

"David, I'm going to feel quite empty afterwards."

"What nonsense, you silly girl." He laughed, kissing the tip of her nose. "Afterwards you'll have the baby!"

Another contraction. She tried to recall the breathing Dr. Sullivan had shown her, but it was one thing to practice in his office and quite another to try doing it when she was in hard labor. She couldn't remember when she was supposed to pant and when she was supposed to hold back. What did women do before these breathing routines had been thought up? She was to have a caudal anesthetic, but her cervix had to be dilated at least five or six centimeters before it could be administered. She wondered how far along she was.

Nurse Fitzgerald came into the room. She put her stethoscope to Laura's belly and listened carefully, moving the cold metal end from place to place. She took her pulse and blood pressure. Finally, she reached for Laura's chart and wrote on it.

"How are the contractions?" she asked, as if she were inquiring about something Laura might be enjoying.

Laura didn't answer because another one was starting.

The nurse put her hand on Laura's belly as she was having the contraction. At last, the pain receded. It seemed to have a life of its own, this unrelenting pain, like a wild beast that ravaged her and then retreated for a time in order to regain strength for the next onslaught. The nurse smiled down at her and wiped her forehead with a damp cloth. "You're doing just fine."

"That was very strong, and they're lasting longer every time. When do you think Dr. Sullivan will give me the anesthetic?"

"Oh, not for a while yet. He should be in to see you shortly. I'll stay with you now until he comes. Just be patient, everything is going along fine," she smiled reassuringly.

Fine for you, thought Laura. She couldn't remember ever feeling so helpless. Another twenty minutes went by on the clock. Suddenly, at the end of a contraction, she vomited. In an instant, Nurse Fitzgerald had a basin under her chin. When the episode was over, she sponged off Laura's face with cool water.

"Don't worry, that's to be expected. What with all the activity going on inside, sometimes the uterus bumps up against the tummy." She patted Laura's arm.

"Nurse?"

"Yes?"

"What is your name?"

"Pardon?"

"The M. What does it stand for?" Laura pointed to the placket.

"Oh, I see. It's Mary," she smiled into Laura's tear-stained eyes. "You have done beautifully, Mrs. Landau. I am going to get Doctor now. Will you be all right on your own for a bit?"

"Yes, Mary." said Laura.

"Good girl." Mary Fitzgerald smiled and left the room.

The next contraction started. Now the pain was centered more in her back. It traveled down her legs. She held onto the rungs at the head of the bed. Her legs were quivering. This was a foreign pain, one she had not experienced before. Was it normal? Maybe the baby was in a strange position, pressing on things it shouldn't. She felt completely out of control. "David!" she cried out. If David were there, she was sure the pain would ease up or at least return to normal and the baby would hurry up and be born.

Dr. Sullivan's round face came into view. "How are you, sweetheart?"

"The pain's in my back," she gasped. "Is that normal?

"Yes, perfectly." He squeezed her hand. "You're doing very well. I'm going to measure your cervix now and see if we can anesthetize you." He disappeared at the end of the bed, and she felt the shock of the cold instrument inside her. "Just short. A couple more should do it." He appeared again at her side. "Naughty girl, you forgot all those breathing techniques I showed you." His voice was teasing.

"Oh . . . it's coming again," she gasped.

"Just hang on to me." She felt the dry warmth of his skin and the rough texture of the hairs on the back of his hand.

The pain was attacking her back and legs again. Her legs were shaking, and her teeth chattered together. Her eyes were squeezed tight. Behind her lids, she saw bright flashes in the black. They formed into designs, merging and changing like a kaleidoscope. Suddenly, out of the chaos was John's face. She wanted to ask him why he had gone away. His beautiful pale green eyes peered up at her from what seemed to be the bottom of a deep well. She tried to shout to him, but her voice wouldn't come and he kept fading farther and farther down in the blackness.

She heard voices at the foot of the bed. A strange doctor was in the room. She caught a glimpse of a thin man in faded gray hospital scrubs. He smiled just before tying a mask over his large nose and thick black moustache. Very gently, he turned her onto her side. She closed her eyes just as she felt a needle pick at the base of her spine.

Laura opened her eyes. The pain had gone. Dr. Sullivan was standing next to the bed, still holding on to her hand. His eyes were smiling gently into hers. She felt a contraction beginning. She felt it so clearly that she could visualize the baby's movements perfectly. But there was no pain! Dr. Sullivan laughed at the look of surprise on her face.

"It's all right. The anesthesiologist has just administered your caudal. It's smooth going from now on."

"Thank you, Dr. Sullivan. Thank you." Again she felt the baby bunching up and pushing to get out.

Another half hour passed. She had been moved into a delivery room. Dr. Sullivan was seated on a stool at the foot of the delivery table. The contractions were coming with almost no time between.

"Okay, Laura, now push! Harder. Come on — *harder.* That's it! No, don't stop. Keep pushing. That's right. Good girl. It's crowning. Here comes the head." She heard a muffled cry. It grew louder. "Now, just a bit more. That's it . . . aah, what a lovely baby!"

Laura raised herself up on her elbows and looked toward Dr. Sullivan. He was holding the baby up for her to see. Testicles. It was a boy! This baby, who had lived in her womb and had entered the world through her body, would someday be a man. Like David. No, like John. This was the little person they had created out of their love.

"You did an excellent job, mum." Dr. Sullivan put the baby across her chest. She looked into its tiny face. "May I see my husband?"

"Of course, sweetheart," he said softly. "You don't want him to miss a moment of it, do you? That's how it should be. After all, without him your son and heir wouldn't be here at all, would he?"

"Mr. Landau, you can come along now." The nurse was standing in the doorway.

"Is my wife all right?"

"Perfectly."

"And the baby."

"Both your wife and baby are fine. Now, just follow me and I'll take you to the viewing nursery."

He followed the nurse down the corridor. Her back was very straight ,and the skirt of her perfectly starched uniform stuck out from her hips and swayed stiffly as she walked. He wondered if she had a family waiting for her at home — a husband and children? Would her dry, efficient manner melt away as she sat relaxing at the supper table, telling them about the three men in the waiting room? Again, David's thoughts turned to Davy Jenks and his Clara.

"Here we are, Mr. Landau."

They stopped in front of a glassed-in room. There were three rows of small box-like cribs, some of which contained a baby wrapped in a blanket. Most of them had their eyes tightly shut and their mouths wide open, crying soundless-ly behind the heavy glass. They looked remarkably the same to him. Gesturing for David to wait, the nursed passed through a door to the right of the glass wall and reappeared a few seconds later on the other side, wearing a protective mask. She made her way to the second row, stopped at the fourth crib on the left-hand side, and took a tightly wrapped bundle out of the crib. She came over to the window where David was standing. Loosening its blanket, she held the baby up to the glass. Its features were incredibly small and absolutely perfect. David nodded and smiled. The nurse nodded and smiled back. The baby's nose twitched and it put a tiny fist to its mouth. The fingers opened. They were ex-quisitely delicate. David swallowed hard. The nurse nodded again and turned away. She put the baby back in its crib and left the room. David stood very still and looked at the crib where the nurse had placed the baby. At its head was a card upon which was printed the name *Landau*. The door to the hall opened.

"Lovely little boy, isn't he?"

"A boy?" He hadn't thought about that at all. Not during all those long hours in the waiting room and not standing in front of the glassed-in nursery.

"Yes. It's always so nice if the first is a boy," she said in her complacent way.

"Will he be all right? In the nursery, I mean. There's no one in there."

"Of course he will be, Mr. Landau." She said, a tight smile on her lips. "You may go up to your wife now. Mrs. Landau is on the fourth floor, Room 412. The lift is at the end of the hall near the reception desk."

David looked at the crib where the small bundle was moving slightly. His throat filled. Tears stung behind his eyelids. Again, he swallowed hard. Turning away from the viewing window, he walked swiftly down the corridor.

CHAPTER 11

ACAPULCO, 1960

THE NEWS

Acapulco's Daily English Language Newspaper

Monday, February 15, 1960

FESTIVAL OPENS ON HIGH NOTE

The Acapulco Film Festival opens Thursday night with an 8:00P.M. screening of Billy Wilder's The Apartment, featuring Jack Lemmon, Shirley MacLaine and Fred MacMurray. All three stars and Mr. Wilder will be in attendance.

Satyajit Ray's Devi will be shown Friday at 6:00 P.M., immediately followed by Jules Dassin's Never on Sunday, starring Mme. Dassin, Greek actress Melina Mercouri. The Dassins are staying at Casa Encanta as guests of Marcello Gianni and his wife, legendary film star Beryl Villiers.

Saturday is British night, with an 8:00 P.M. screening of Beggar's Choice directed by David Landau. Mr. Landau is at the Club de Pesca with his wife, actress Laura English, and their seven-year-old son, Edward.

Tiny rivulets of perspiration ran down Laura's forehead and into her eyes, stinging and blurring the print. She let the newspaper fall next to her chair and dabbed at them with the end of her towel. Only half past ten, but the temperature on the hotel terrace must be nearing eighty. It was hard to believe that Acapulco and London, cold and drizzly when they left five days ago, were on the same planet. She longed to submerge herself in the cool aquamarine water of the pool, but had promised Robin to wait for a swim until he and David returned from their morning walk. This was the first holiday they had taken together as a family in two years, and she decided it would be best to humor her son for once.

Their child had been christened Edward Alfred, after cousin Ned and Uncle Bertie, but his little cries were so like those of a newly hatched bird that his nurse, Mrs. Morley, called him her *little robin* and the name stuck.

Robin was an enchanting child, his golden curls and sea green eyes attracting admiring glances everywhere he went. Shy by nature, he was content to play quietly with his toys on the nursery floor or with his pail and shovel in the sandbox at the neighborhood park, but clung to Mrs. Morley's skirts whenever a stranger came into view. The nurse hinted that the companionship of a little brother or sister would do much to alleviate his shyness, but no sibling appeared.

Mrs. Morley was a great help but, from the first, it was Laura who fed, bathed, and took Robin out for walks in his pram. In spite of all the time she spent with him, deep down Laura sensed there was something lacking in her feelings for the baby. During her pregnancy, she was strongly tied to the life growing inside her because it was created partly by John Keith. But once the newborn emerged as a separate being, it was as if all connection with the tiny being had been severed along with the umbilical cord. Now, every time she looked at the infant, the reality of her separation from John hit her anew and with it came the emptiness and longing brought by their long estrangement. Remembering her own mother's coldness, Laura worried that she would not be able to give her child the attention he needed and vowed that Robin would never suffer as she had before going to live with Aunt Rose and Uncle Matthew. Thus, she took on the role of mother with enthusiasm, as she would any other part, but deep in her heart she knew it was just that: a part she was playing.

One late summer day in Kensington Gardens, the reality of her lack of feeling for the baby became all too evident when another young mother confided to Laura that she had never known what real love was until now.

"I love my parents and friends and, of course, my husband," she giggled, "but what I feel for them is selfish, isn't it? In a way, I always expect something in return." The girl looked down at her sleeping baby. "But the love I feel for this little girl is altogether different. But then, you know what I mean, don't you?" She smiled in a cozy mother-to-mother way.

From that day on, Laura put the mask aside. Playing at mother was a hopeless charade that even she was not a good-enough actress to pull off. She began to think about Briarwood.

After Robin's birth, Dr. Sullivan had advised her to take a year off. "You really shouldn't rush it, Laura. You'll end up regretting the time you miss with the baby."

But when Robin turned three months old, Laura decided she had given it as much time as she could. She was desperate to return to work and wasn't going to put it off any longer.

Her first day back at Briarwood, Sir James Paxton handed Laura a script with *Going Native* printed in the center of the blue cover and *Miss English* in the upper right-hand corner. Laura felt her heart would burst with happiness.

"Rehearsals start in two days, and Jasper wants some time with you at three this afternoon for a meeting with Brian Sykes, Barry Filbert, and Johnny Lynch. Oh, by the way, Maud Jeffries will be playing your slightly addled grandmother."

"Oh, Jamie! This is going to be such fun! How can I thank you for letting me come back?"

"Now, now, we've been all through that. I would like to get a few more pictures out of you before you start producing any more babies, so just hold off for a while in that department." The telephone on his desk buzzed. He picked up the receiver and gestured for her to stay.

She thumbed through the pages of the script, waiting for him to finish the call.

At last he rang off. "Like it?"

"What I've read so far very much. It's really funny."

"Must be. You're grinning like the Cheshire Cat." He got up and came around the desk to where she was sitting. She stood, and, taking her hand, Jamie Paxton led her across the room to one of the large windows facing the quadrangle. "Glad to be back?"

"Oh, yes!"

"No pangs?"

"What do you mean?"

"You know, leaving the baby."

She felt her cheeks grow warm. "Well, no. We have an excellent nurse."

"Yes, I'm sure. It's just that Kitty was always so nervous about being sep ... "

Cheeks burning, Laura looked up at him. "Sir Jamie, I feel just fine."

"Ah, well, that's all right then." He cleared his throat. "You are going to enjoy this romp with Quigly and his gang, and after it's finished I have something very exciting to discuss with you."

"Oh, Sir Jamie! What?"

"No, no, first things first. I simply wanted you to know that I have kept you in mind this year. Now, you'd better get a move on if you want lunch. Jasper wants everyone on time, and it's almost two now.

She half skipped, half ran over the quadrangle to the building that housed the dining room. She wanted to sing and cry and laugh out loud. She was back!

Robin remained an introverted child. Shortly after his third birthday, the overly indulgent Mrs. Morely was replaced by a governess called Miss Boxhill, a change Robin found difficult to accept. He got into the habit of standing by the window watching for his beloved nurse to return. When Miss Boxhill explained that Mrs. Morely was a baby nurse and he was too old for her now. Robin cried as though his heart were broken. After these incidents, he became willful and disobedient. By his fourth birthday, he was in desperate need of strong discipline, but Miss Boxhill's scoldings were met with tantrums and Laura's words with stony silences. Only David, with his gentle voice and serene manner, was able to reason with the child.

Robin's feelings for his mother were mainly centered around her beauty. He liked to gaze at her in the same way he did the princesses in his illustrated fairy tale books, but he saw little of her because most of the time she was at the studio or in her room studying lines. Miss Boxhill was there all the time, but she was forever telling him to do this or that. Daddy was different. True, he sometimes corrected him, but never in a tiresome voice. He just told him once and didn't go on and on about it. Then he would smile and say, "You understand now, don't you, Robbie?"

At the end of each day, Robin's ears grew alert for the sound of David's key. As soon as he heard the scraping in the lock he ran to the door, grabbed hold of his father's hand, and pulled him out into the garden. David had shown the boy how to germinate seeds and set out the young plants in neat rows. Together, they inspected the flower beds, Robin squatting down the better to examine a particularly successful bloom.

His excited cries of "Daddy, come here and look at this one!" filled David's heart in a way that nothing else, not even Laura, had ever done.

Their vegetable garden was Robin's pride. He soon learned how to tell when the carrots and radishes were ready to pull and the curly heads of lettuce were just the right size to cut. Best of all, they could eat the results of their labor.

As Robin grew older, Saturday mornings became time spent with his father. While Laura slept later than she could during the week, David and his son explored London. They took boat excursions on the Thames and went rowing on the Serpentine in Hyde Park. There were visits to the Victoria and Albert, and to Robin's favorite place, the Natural History Museum. At the Tower of London, they marveled at Henry VIII's expanding sets of armor, and in the Egyptian Room at the British Museum they examined row upon row of three thousand-year-old mummies.

Sometimes, they took the underground to the Paxtons' house in Hampstead. Simon and young Jamie were enthusiastic model sailboat builders. The brothers introduced Robin to the craft, and soon he was producing models even more intricate than those of the older boys. Robin loved Hampstead days with the Paxtons where, at the sailing pond on the Heath, they spent hours racing their vessels.

But the best Saturdays where those when David and Robin had no definite destination in mind. Careful not to make too much noise, they crept out of the house very early, walked up Cranley Gardens and turned onto the Old Brompton Road. From there they made their way to Queen's Gate and, turning right onto Cromwell Road, caught a red double-decker bus. They always sat on the top of the bus so as to keep watch for a stop that looked interesting. Often, they found themselves in strange Italian, Hungarian, or Indian neighborhoods, where after exploring for an hour or so, they had a meal of spicy curry or rich goulash, which Robbie loved.

From time to time, Uncle Bertie would come for a few days. During these visits, Robin sometimes stood, unnoticed, at the living room door watching the strange-looking man and his mother as they sipped sherry or tea, laughing and chatting about current plays or actors they knew in the theater. His mother always sat, legs tucked under, in a large chair by the window. He studied her carefully. She seemed very happy because her eyes crinkled at the corners when she spoke. Later, in his room, Robin tried to capture in drawings with his color pencils the expression he had seen on his mother's face.

Laura wanted a child with David. They had been trying to conceive since Robin was about two but with no luck. Dr. Sullivan sent her to a specialist who, after much testing, diagnosed the problem as David's low sperm count and advised a regime of abstinence for twenty days and great diligence during Laura's most fertile time. This proved to be of no use, and month after month, her period arrived, like a symbol of failure, right on schedule. Their lovemaking had always been relaxed and spontaneous. Now, when they were in the mood, it invariably was the wrong day, and often, when the time was right, one or both were exhausted and wanted only to sleep.

Laura was the first to suggest abandoning the effort. They were getting ready to go out to a party, and she was sitting at her dressing table combing her hair. David appeared behind her in the mirror. He traced one of the bright waves with his finger. Her dress of soft black velvet marked a vivid contrast to the creamy whiteness of her skin. He placed his hands on her shoulders, running his fingertips along the fine bones. She was like the porcelain figurines on his mother's mantelpiece — delicate and priceless.

Her large gray eyes smiled at his reflection. "Um, very distinguished in your dinner jacket." She rose and turned to face him. Winding her arms around his slim waist, she said, "David, let's chuck it for a bit. It doesn't mean I won't get pregnant anyway. I just can't stand this fucking on schedule."

David threw back his head and laughed. "I'm relieved you said it first. I've wanted to bring it up for months, but I thought it meant so much to you that I could put up with it for a while longer."

"Having your child does mean a lot to me, David. It must be hard for you playing the role of Robin's father. All the more so because he obviously doesn't look like me, which means he's like . . ."

"Laura, I love Robin. I couldn't possibly love him more if he were mine and had black hair and the Landau nose." He kissed her cheek and ran his tongue along its smoothness down to her neck. David was, indeed, relieved by her decision. The idea of a pregnancy unsettled him. What if he didn't love his own child as much as Robin, whom he cherished with all his heart?

She looked up at him, eyes sparkling. "Come here then," she laughed, pulling him toward the bed. "To hell with the schedule — and the party."

Laura could no longer sit still in the sweltering heat of the terrace. She pulled herself out of the lounge chair and, turning down the floppy brim of her soft straw hat, made her way along the flagstone path to the beach. The shoreline of the bay opened before her like the arms of a welcoming lover. She kicked off her sandals and curled her toes into the yielding softness of the cool sand. A tropical beach was just the thing after monotonous months of slate-gray skies and needle-sharp rain. It was the first week in February, and the weather, when they departed London five days ago, had been bitter. She took off her dark glasses and gazed out at the expanse of ocean. In the distance, opalescent waves swelled out of the turquoise water and crashed beyond the line of the bay before coming to rest in a hissing line of foam on the smooth surface of the sand. Graceful palms, impossibly rooted in the sand, caught the ocean breeze in their fronds and rattled riotously above her head. A slight sweetness, blending with tangy ocean salt, drifted past her. She recognized the elusive scent of jacaranda which, now faint, would later permeate the heavy evening air with such intensity it could be tasted on the tongue.

Laura walked on past the end of the hotel beach, her footprints making sharp depressions in the wet sand at the bubbling edge of the surf line. She bent to inspect an exquisite lavender shell that lay half-buried near a tiny branch of white coral. Smiling, she dropped it in the pocket of her thin cover-up. The familiar thrill of discovering half-concealed treasures in the sand came back to her in a rush of childhood memories: she and Uncle Matthew and the countless

Sunday afternoons they spent exploring the beach near the Bournemouth pier. She felt the warmth of the sun on her lips and realized she was smiling. This was what holidays were for, and even though it was really a business trip, she was enjoying it wholeheartedly. During the first years of their marriage, she and David had taken breaks often, but now, with both of them working full bore, they never seemed to have the time. Robin would be seven in July! Where did the years go?

Twelve pictures in eight years. Now, only Jasper Quigly topped her as Briarwood's biggest star. True to Sir Jamie's prediction, attractive offers from Paramount, MGM, and Twentieth Century Fox came every few months, but Laura, happy where she was, refused to consider any of them. Many of her colleagues had left England for the States. Occasionally, one or another of them returned to London to do a play, but as soon as the run ended, they fled back to their swimming pools, convertibles, and perpetual Southern California summer. Even Paul Andrews, her personal hair stylist, had relocated to Beverly Hills. Five years ago, he opened a salon on Rodeo Drive and, according to the latest news from Kitty, had recently launched a second on Union Square in San Francisco.

David Landau had long since outgrown acting. In 1953, he directed *Bitter Tuesday* for independent producer Hal Raymond. David thrived on the responsibility of complete control over a project and handled the pressure with calm good humor. Since then, most of the work that came his way was from independent producers such as Raymond, where David had the freedom to put together his own team of cameramen, lighting technicians, makeup and costume designers who gave his films the look he wanted. Critics on both sides of the Atlantic applauded his work, and soon he became the darling of a clique of British stage and film directors known as *the angry young men.* In his private life, David Landau was anything but angry. He was in love with his wife, devoted to their son, and his latest film had been entered in the 1960 Acapulco Film Festival.

Laura never regretted her decision to marry David. They started as friends and friends they still were, with mutual affection and support lending strength to their life together. She knew that he loved her deeply, with far greater intensity than she felt for him. He was a skilled and considerate lover, always making sure she was satisfied before he gave himself up to his own desire. They had a good time in bed, Laura sharing funny stories from the studio and David telling her about the trials he sometimes had to go through to get a performance out of a temperamental actress or inebriated leading man. His hilarious imitations of some of the divas he had to deal with left Laura screaming with laughter and begging him to stop before she lost her breath.

Often, especially at the end of a demanding day when she was too tired to resist, Laura's thoughts turned to John Keith. Their lovemaking had been an all-encompassing passion that shook her to the depths of her soul and left her physically spent and emotionally frustrated, for no matter how many times he entered her body, Laura never completely connected with him on the deep level she yearned for. Perhaps if they had not been wrenched apart so suddenly, if she had been given just a little more time with him, she would have discovered that hidden core — the unknown John she could never quite reach. Content as her life was with David, not many days passed without John Keith coming into her mind. It was a fact of her life, one she had given up feeling guilty about it long ago.

Laura made her way from the beach back to the terrace by way of the bar. She hopped up onto one of the tall stools and ordered a lemonade. In the shade of the thatched *palapa*, she sipped the cool liquid, savoring its tartness. Their hotel, the Club de Pesca, was located about mid-point on the western side of the Bahia de Acapulco. From her vantage point at the bar, Laura had a view of the entire bay. To the east lay the Playa Icacos and the buildings of the Naval Academy. On the western side, high on a cliff, she could make out several private homes. One, she had been told, was the residence of the natural daughter of the king of Rumania. Another, constructed of blinding white marble, was owned by the American who invented the ballpoint pen. Not the grandest, but by far the most elegant, was a pink villa called Casa Encantada. Photographed in the pages of *Town & Country* and *House Beautiful*, it was the winter home of Beryl Villiers and Marcello Gianni. Squinting into the glare, she focused in on the magnificent fall of orange and pale yellow bougainvillea cascading over the villa's pink walls. Laura and David had been invited to a gala there at the end of the week, as were Jamie and Kitty Paxton, who were due in from London today. Beryl Villiers, Laura mused as she sipped her lemonade, now there was a star in every sense of the word. She hadn't acted in a film for twenty years, yet her name still evoked all the glamour it had when she was Briarwood's top property.

Since their arrival in Acapulco, the Landaus had attended several parties honoring the British contingent to the festival. They were the usual industry affairs involving undulating crowds, popping flash bulbs, and nonstop queries from the press. Laura didn't mind scheduled interviews, but free-lance stringers could be very annoying. As much as she disliked encounters with pushy reporters, she enjoyed meeting her fans. Used now to her modicum of fame, the flattery she had first experienced at being asked to sign an autograph had been replaced by a genuine desire to get to know these people who liked her well enough to stop her in the street, and she would often chat with them while scrawling her name on the odd bit of proffered paper. The fan magazines called her England's most gracious star, but Laura never thought of herself as a star. She had attained her life's ambition. She was a working performer, and that was enough.

At last Laura saw David and Robin coming toward her.

"Guess who we saw, Mummy? Just now in the lobby." Robin's eyes were bright with excitement.

"I haven't the slightest idea, dear."

"Auntie Kit and Uncle Jamie!" squealed Robin "And Jamie and Simon as well. We're all going out in a boat tomorrow."

Laura looked up to see Kitty and Jamie Paxton coming toward them across the terrace followed by their two sons, twelve-year-old Jamie and ten-year-old Simon, still on midwinter holiday from their school. Sarah, now fifteen, was in boarding school on the East Coast of the United States and wouldn't be home again until summer.

"What a trek," said Kitty looking damp and out of sorts. "Two plane changes and this heat! What are you doing with your hair?"

"More or less nothing," laughed Laura. "Take a minute to see this extraordinary view, and then I suggest a cool bath and a siesta."

Sir James Paxton, wearing tan Bermuda shorts; a madras shirt in shades of pink, green, and purple; and a safari jacket slung over his shoulders, looked remarkably comfortable. His hair had faded to sand, and his neatly trimmed chestnut beard was threaded with silver.

"My dear." He bent down and kissed Laura, exuding, as always, a delicious scent of cut lemons.

"Auntie Laura, tomorrow Dad's taking us deep-sea fishing. May Robin come with us in the boat?" It was Simon.

"Yes, Mummy, please can I go?" Robin looked up adoringly at Simon. Since he could first toddle after them, Simon and Jamie Paxton had been Robin's idols, but it was Simon who always saw to it that Robin was included in any of their adventures.

"David, what do you think?"

"Oh, Uncle David's invited as well, isn't he, Dad?" said Simon.

"Everybody is invited," said Sir James. "Now, if you don't mind, I think I will take your advice about the bath and the siesta." He looked over at Kitty. "Coming, darling?"

"Yes, Jamie, I'll be right there. Go along with Dad, boys." Kitty stretched out on the lounge chair next to Laura's and watched James, Jamie, and Simon disappear into the dark coolness of the hotel.

David, playing with Robin in the pool, beckoned to her, and Laura, now thoroughly baked, was desperate to join them. She patted Kitty's arm. "You'd better go up and have a rest. We'll regroup at cocktail time, how does that sound?"

"Yes, you're right, darling." Still, she made no move to go. "Laura, come shopping with me tomorrow while the boys are at their fishing. I have to find something devastating to wear to the Gianni's party." Realizing that Laura had caught the note of anxiety in her voice she gave a little nervous laugh. "You haven't seen Beryl Villiers in person. She's fatal."

"Kitty, you and Jamie have been married for seventeen years, and Beryl is ancient history. I must say I'm excited to be going to one of the famous Gianni parties. I've been reading about them for years. All those glamorous people. Just imagine, Melina Mercouri will be there. What a thrill!"

"My God, does it ever occur to you that people might think it a thrill to see you? Don't you ever read fan magazines? You know, darling, after all these years I think there is still a lot of Jane Parks left in you."

Laura made a face. "I'm an actress, that's all. The most important thing to me is the work. David told me that once and he was so right. If Jamie dropped me tomorrow, I'd go back to the Bournemouth Players." They both laughed.

"I don't think Jamie has any plans to drop you, darling. He says you got another offer from Paramount."

"Yes. They sent me a script for something called *Continental Divide*. Can you imagine me as a saloon keeper in the American West?"

"Actually, yes, I can. Don't they have Tony Garret signed for that one? It wouldn't be too terrible looking at that face for a month or so,"

"Yes, he's signed, and Maria Valdez to play the Mexican girl."

"You know, Laura, Jamie appreciates your loyalty, but I don't think he'd mind too much if you took up one of these American studios on an offer. After all, what's one picture now and then, and the better you're known in the States the better your films for Briarwood will sell all around."

"I know. Jamie has told me that himself. I simply have no desire to go to Hollywood, even for one picture. Maybe I'm just lazy, but staying right where I am seems fine to me."

"Well, I'm off," said Kitty, pulling herself out of the chair. "See you at the bar around eightish." The two women kissed and, at last, Laura joined David and Robin in the cool waters of the swimming pool.

CHAPTER 12

S ocial animal of the first order, no matter where in the world she happened
to find herself, Kitty Paxton was well acquainted with all the people who
counted. A few minutes in a cool bath to recover from her journey, and she was
on the phone to Chucho de la Rocha, ranking member of Acapulco society.
Delighted as he was to hear from her, Chucho could hardly contain his excitement when she told him of her close friendship with Laura English.

"I saw in the *News* that she was here! In fact, I was going to call and invite
her over. I'm having a crowd for lunch tomorrow. Is that too soon? I want to
grab you both before the vultures descend."

Kitty laughed. "Tomorrow will be perfect."

The next morning, Kitty appeared on the terrace of the Club de Pesca
hotel, very smart in a pair of white slacks and a bright yellow shirt tied in a
knot at her waist. As soon as the men and boys had taken off for their fishing
expedition, she steered Laura in the direction of the Mercado Municipal at the
center of town. Laura bought a pair of white pants similar to Kitty's and several
shirts fashioned out of the loosely woven Mexican cotton called *manta*. Kitty
insisted Laura change out of her sun dress and into the pants right there. She
tied the tails of Laura's turquoise shirt tightly at her waist.

"There! Now you look like a real aficionado."

"Of what?" laughed Laura

"The Acapulco *beau monde*, darling."

They snaked their way through the crowded stalls of the market, stopping
at a booth that featured dresses made in the native Guerrero style. "Perfect
for La Beryl's party," said Kitty, holding up a black cotton lace dress, cut way
off the shoulder with yards of ruffled skirt. Laura had no doubt that when

Kitty Paxton made her entrance in that peasant dress, she would be the chicest woman in the room.

Kitty paid for the dress and they wandered on, fingering woven rebozos in vivid colors and pieces of heavy silver jewelry. Laura glanced at her watch. "It's one thirty. What time are we due at Senor de la Rocha's?"

"Chucho said around one."

Laura looked at her wide-eyed. "My God, Kitty, we're terribly late. We have to get a taxi right away."

Kitty laughed, "Don't worry, darling. An hour late is right on time in Mexico."

The house sat on the crest of the highest hill behind Old Town. Laura and Kitty entered a cavernous room tiled in huge squares of gleaming white onyx and starkly furnished with two long white leather couches and a mammoth black onyx coffee table. Wide archways gave out onto an enormous terrace, where Chucho de la Rocha's guests were sipping drinks and admiring the view of the bay far below.

"*Chata*," Chucho purred, hugging Kitty. "How wonderful to see you. It's been too long. And this, I know, is Laura." Chucho took her hand in his and squeezed it warmly. He wore a white silk shirt open to the waist, exposing an expanse of buttery smooth hairless flesh. Everything about him was soft: the tone of his voice in heavily accented English, the sensuality of his mouth, the fullness of his body, and the languid gaze of his doe-like eyes, which peered at her through thick black lashes.

"Thank you so much for asking us, Señor de la Rocha," said Laura.

"Please! The only Señor de la Rocha I know is my grandfather! I'm Chucho. Come in and meet everyone." He placed himself between Laura and Kitty, linking both of their arms with his. "*Chata, mi angelita*," he leaned towards Kitty, as they walked across the slippery tiled floor, "I hope you don't mind, but Beryl might drop by later. I assume all is as friendly between you as ever?" He raised his eyebrows and looked at her inquisitively.

"Yes, we're friends, Chucho." Laura could hear the tenseness in Kitty's voice.

"Good. I think she wants to show off her newest *novio*. She won't be able to do that on Friday. She must watch herself around the Casa Encanta crowd, but here, among ourselves, she can be free to do as she wishes. I hear he's quite a *torito*! British, a journalist of some sort. *En todas maneras*, if she shows up, we will see for ourselves."

They made their way across the large room and through one of the archways. A wide awning stretched down from the side of the house, shading most of the terrace. Low chairs and lounges, covered in yellow and white striped canvas, were occupied by an assortment of attractive people who were sipping sangria or Champagne. A boy approached with a tray of drinks and Laura took a glass of Champagne. It was deliciously cold. Kitty was now in earnest conversation with Chucho, and Laura, feeling relaxed after a few sips of wine, began to walk around the perimeter of the terrace. She wandered over to a long glass-topped buffet table and helped herself to some seafood salad and sliced mango.

A large woman standing nearby was surveying the food, one long red fingernail tapping her chin. Inches taller and several pounds heavier than Laura, she was dressed in a bright green caftan sewn with bits of mirror. Her black hair was teased and lacquered into a wide bouffant style, and a pair of outsized sunglasses, covering the upper part of her face, sat on the bridge of a surprisingly small nose.

"Decisions, decisions," said the woman in a husky American-accented voice.

"Yes, indeed, quite a selection," said Laura.

The brightly lipsticked mouth widened into a broad grin as the woman stuck out her hand. "I'm Glenda Fisher. Say, does everyone tell you how much you look like Laura English?"

"No, this is the first time, actually," answered Laura, with a smile.

"Amazing. But then, I'm told I often see things others miss." She filled her plate with a generous sample of every dish offered on the buffet and led Laura to a table on the edge of the terrace. Plopping heavily into a sling-back chair, she took off her dark glasses and planted them in the seemingly impregnable coiffure. Her black eyes protruded slightly, giving her face an avid expression.

"Do you live here in Acapulco?" asked Laura.

"Good God no! I've seen people with perfectly serviceable brains molder into lumps of quivering inanity in this tropical paradise. You come, in all innocence, for a few weeks' rest, and before you can say *una coco loco mas* and pass the *bain de soleil* — whoosh, negative knee-jerk responses. No, I'm here to cover the festival and then it's back to civilization."

"And that is?" Laura asked, amused.

"Mexico City. Have you been there?"

"No. Like you, I'm only here for the festival, but I must say I am enjoying the moldering process. Both my husband and I have been on rather a treadmill the past year, and a rest is doing us a world of good."

"But you must see the capital before you go back to England. It's beautiful, really Parisian in flavor."

"I wish we could stay long enough to see more of the country, but I start a new picture soon and I haven't even looked at the script yet. How long have you lived in this part of the world?"

"I came here after graduating from UCLA. two years ahead of schedule, if I'm not too immodest to say. I never really got along with my mother, and my stepfather liked me a little too much, if you catch my drift. Mexico City was the farthest from home I could go on the money I had saved. At that point I spoke not a syllable of Spanish so job possibilities were limited and I was relieved, if not to say thrilled, to get hired as a file clerk at the American Embassy. I answered an ad in the English language newspaper for an apartment, complete with roommate. This turned out to be a mousey little woman who wrote articles for a cat magazine in the States. I never did find out what she was doing in Mexico but, now that I think about it, she was probably CIA. Anyway, she had a cunning little VW convertible that she sometimes loaned me on weekends, you know, so I could explore a bit." Glenda Fisher paused to take a large bite of quiche Lorraine. "Mmmm, heaven," she said, rolling her eyes.

At last she put her fork down and took a long drink of her sangria. "Anyway, as I was saying, one Saturday morning I got the urge to see Puebla, so I borrowed the VW and took off. It's an enchanting region of Mexico and I was curious to see more so I kept on going to Fortin de las Flores. By now it was Wednesday and, figuring I couldn't be in much hotter water with the cat lady, I drove on to Vera Cruz. What a town! I hung out there for a couple of months, you know, exploring the jungle, meeting the locals and jotting down my impressions. By the time I got back to Mexico City I had a whole stack of articles."

"The cat lady must have been furious with you," laughed Laura.

"Oh, I smoothed her fur, but the embassy was not as amicable. They fired me. I sent the Vera Cruz articles to every travel magazine in the States. *Holiday* took them, and I landed a job as a stringer. I made a reasonable living and a lot of great contacts. Three years ago, I took up photography. Photographs sell faster and pay better than travel articles. At the moment, I'm putting together a book on Oaxaca. Fabulous place. You must try to get down there."

From her conversation, Laura gathered that Miss Fisher was not only insatiably curious and utterly fearless but also a free spirit whose general attitude toward men was that anyone was fair game. No strings attached.

"I would say, offhand mind you, that close to a hundred men have passed through my life since I arrived here in '55. That's round figures, of course." Her eyes were full of mischief.

"And you've never thought of settling down with just one?" Laura asked, sipping her Champagne.

"Good God. What a thought! With so many appetizing men in the world, I couldn't possibly choose just one. It would be like limiting myself to a single dish at that gorgeous smorgasbord over there." She took another thirsty swallow of her drink. Her eyes narrowed over the rim of the glass. "You're married to David Landau, aren't you?"

"Yes. David's film, *Beggar's Choice*, is being screened at the festival Saturday night. We are very excited about it, because my boss Jamie Paxton is the producer and the film was made at Briarwood Studios where David started out as an actor years ago."

Glenda Fisher raised one eyebrow and said in a confidential tone, "I've heard the film is a stunner."

Laura smiled at the overstatements that seemed to be Glenda's trademark and she wondered if perhaps this most singular lady had also expanded a bit on the number of men she had known.

Glenda went on, "I must tell you that I've loved your movies for years. I remember seeing *Valiant Hours* when I was in college and thinking you were smashing. My unqualified favorite is *The Hidden Heart*.

She looked at Glenda and smiled. "Jamie Paxton likes to cast me in comedies, but I enjoy doing something with more meat, and *The Hidden Heart* was very meaty."

"To say nothing of Peter Goddard! Now that's a rump roast I wouldn't mind sinking my teeth into."

Laura laughed. Peter was one of her closet friends and very happily homosexual. "It's funny, everybody thinks that actors become involved with one another when they do a film. It really doesn't happen that often. Besides, I'm quite content with my husband."

"How long have you been married?"

"Nearly eight years."

"Eight years! Honestly, don't you ever get bored?"

"Honestly," she shook her head and laughed. "Not with David."

"Well, if you do want a little fling, Acapulco's the place. Simply crawling with gorgeous men. There's a new one in town. Beryl Villiers has her claws in him at the moment, but I have dibs on him after her. I saw him last night and, believe me, he's really something." She rolled her eyes in exactly the same way she had savoring the quiche Lorraine.

"An Englishman, I heard," said Laura "A journalist."

"Yes, and that's where I'll get my hook in. You know, colleagues, and all that. We'll know plenty of people in common." She grinned with anticipation.

"Well, I wish you the best of luck." Just then someone called to Glenda from the other side of the terrace. She put her glasses on.

"Oh, there's Carlos Goldstein!" she said waving to a small man who was standing with Chucho. "He's one of my oldest friends in Mexico. Carlos is a fabulous talent. Surely you must have seen his ear table and tongue chair. Pure genius! Well, no doubt we'll run into each other again before the end of the week."

"I hope so. It was nice meeting you." Laura put out her hand but Glenda had already rushed off, the folds of her caftan wafting Femme into the sultry afternoon air.

Several of Chucho's guests now joined Laura. Before long she was at the center of a noisy crowd of people. Just as the chatter was starting to make her head swim, Laura noticed Kitty coming toward her across the terrace.

"Had enough for one day?" she said. "Not anything like your intellectual London friends, are they?"

"No," answered Laura, "but fun."

Chucho telephoned for a taxi and stood with them in the driveway, chatting while they waited for it to arrive. At last, an ancient Chevrolet with "Taxi Tropical" emblazoned on its door and puffs of black smoke belching from its tailpipe came chugging up the hillside. Chucho opened the door and handed Kitty into the back seat.

"I'll be seeing you both at Beryl's party," he said, smiling. A pale blue Mercedes-Benz pulled up behind the taxi. Chucho looked up.

"Let's go, Laura," said Kitty.

Laura was staring at the couple in the Mercedes. The woman's hair was pulled back in a long ponytail. Her face was very tan. She was waiting, motor idling, for their taxi to leave so she could take the space.

"Laura, what's the matter with you? Get in the cab, we're holding up traffic," said Kitty impatiently.

Laura stood frozen, her eyes riveted on the face of the man in the passenger seat. She squinted. The glare made it hard to make out his features clearly. The woman honked.

Laura stepped into the taxi. "I think I've had a bit too much Champagne." They were moving rapidly down the hill away from the house. The breeze felt good on her flushed face, and she leaned towards the open window.

"I was wondering what was the matter with you. That was Beryl Villiers in that car, and I don't feel like meeting her just now. Friday night will be soon enough."

"Kitty, the person with her . . . it must be the Englishman Chucho told us about, the journalist."

"Yes, I suppose so. What about it?"

"I can't be positive, but I think the man I just saw in that car was John Keith."

CHAPTER 13

Laura opened the slats of the louvered door leading to the terrace off their suite. She stood very still for a moment, luxuriating in the slight breeze wafting over her naked body. A cool shower had washed away the effects of Champagne but not the lingering image of the man in the blue Mercedes. She crossed the room and, with a sigh, lay down on the wide bed. Turning onto her side, she studied the large painting which hung on the opposite wall, a reproduction of Diego Rivera's portrait of Natasha Zakolkowa Gelman. When booking their accommodations at the Club de Pesca, David had learned from the manager that most of the rooms were decorated with works of Mexican painters and that a certain portrait in Suite 5 bore a striking resemblance to his wife. Intrigued, David reserved the suite.

He laughed the first time he saw the picture on the wall beside their bed. "This is going to be very strange. You and Natasha could be twins!"

Laura was still unnerved by the resemblance she bore to the thin woman with a mane of long red hair. Now, as she lay on her side in the exact same pose as Natasha Gelman, Laura stared at the narrowed eyes gazing back at her. Surely her own could not be as cold. This woman looked incapable of love. Was that the similarity David saw in the painting? She shivered. David was her best friend, and she had deep feelings for him. But was that love? And what about Robin? What did she honestly feel for Robin? *Why*, she asked herself for the thousandth time, *couldn't he have looked like me?* His blond curls and green eyes, so like John's, were a constant reminder of what she had lost. John, her only love. John, whom she could never have.

Natasha Gelman's husband, Jacques, was a Mexican film producer, famous for the engineering the career of the comedian Cantinflas. According to David, the Gelmans lived in Cuernavaca and would undoubtedly be attending the festival, especially since Cantinflas would be acting as master of ceremonies at many of the screenings. David couldn't wait to meet Natasha and see the two of them side by side but Laura did not share his enthusiasm for, the longer she looked at the painting, the more she realized this woman was the image, not of herself, but of of Gladys Parks. Laura wanted no reminders that, at least where Robin was concerned, she had become her mother.

She turned onto her back, away from the portrait. Her thoughts now focused on Kitty and her dread of Jamie reconnecting with Beryl Villiers. What power did this woman, so many years older than Kitty, have over men that it could reduce her beautiful, self-confident friend to such a state of nerves? Was she such a Lorelei? What about her newest conquest? Had it really been John Keith sitting beside Beryl Villiers in the blue Mercedes, or simply a figment of too much sun and Champagne?

More than eight years had passed since Laura and John had parted at the train station in Bournemouth, yet not a single detail about him had faded from her memory. The rugged profile and pale green eyes, the thick golden hair which, no matter how carefully he combed it, always ended up curling over his forehead. Here, in the normalcy of a hotel bedroom, she reasoned that the man she saw in the car was probably not John. After all, she didn't get a very good look. It was more of an impression. Something about the shape of the head, the line of the jaw.

The door opened. Robin's voice, high and clear, cried out "Mummy, Mummy, I caught a fish!" As usual, after a day spent with the Paxtons, the boy was in high spirits.

"Hush, Robin," David whispered. "Mum's asleep."

"No, I'm not," she said stretching her arms above her head. "Just having a rest. Come here and tell me about it."

Robin sat down on the bed beside Laura and began to tell her about their day. "I helped reel in a really big fish, one called a dorado, and Uncle Jamie is going to have it stuffed! May I put it in my room, Mum? Uncle Jamie says it won't smell once it's stuffed."

"I suppose so."

"Well, it will take awhile to do the stuffing, and then they'll have to send it to London. It really will get there, won't it, Dad?" He turned to David, a small frown on his flushed face.

"Yes, Robin, I'm sure Uncle Jamie will use a very reliable shipper and your fish will arrive at home in one piece."

"I'm glad you two had such an exciting day," said Laura.

"But that's not all," the boy continued. "Before we even started fishing something else happened."

"What?" said Laura.

Robin took a deep breath. "Well, we decided to walk down to the harbor. We were crossing the street in front of the hotel and I almost got run over, but a man saved me."

"What do you mean?" Laura sat up and looked at David. "Is this true?"

"Yes. Robin ran after Simon and young Jamie without looking both ways first."

"Robin! You know better than that. What made you do such a thing?"

"He was just excited, and no harm was done," said David.

"But you said you were nearly run over." She looked at Robin.

"Yes, a taxi. It all happened so fast, but then the man grabbed me and pulled me out of the way."

"You had a close call. You'll be careful from now on, won't you? This isn't England. People drive on the wrong side of the road here."

"The man was very nice. He took us for a lemonade."

"Did he!"

"Yes," said David. "He was going our way and gave us a lift. When we got down to the wharf, he took us to an outdoor bar and bought everyone a drink. Turned out he was English."

"You should have seen his car, Mum!"

"Really. What was it, an enormous red Cadillac convertible, I suppose," she laughed, relieved that nothing had come of Robin's near miss.

"No. Better than that. A Mercedes-Benz! A beautiful light blue one."

For a sickening moment, Laura's heart stopped beating and started up again with a heavy thud. Her eyes met David's.

"Go along and have your bath now, Robbie," he said, looking at Laura. "It's supper up here tonight and early bed. You've had a long day."

"All right, Daddy." He hesitated for a moment before reaching up to kiss Laura's cheek. His hair, damply curling over his forehead, smelled faintly of fish. She watched him go off toward the bathroom.

David lit a cigarette. "I really didn't know quite what to make of that fellow. While were having our drinks, he was very correct but I noticed he kept looking at Robin. To tell you the truth, I thought he might be a bit on the queer side."

"David, when we were at Kitty's friend's this afternoon they were all gossiping about Beryl Villiers' latest lover, a British journalist. And then she pulled in behind our taxi just as we were leaving, and David, she was driving a powder blue Mercedes."

"So, are you saying that you think this fellow is Beryl Villiers's boyfriend?"

"What was the man's name?"

"He never said. In typical British fashion, none of us exchanged much personal information, just the usual polite conversation. Actually, when I thanked him for rescuing my son I did introduce myself, and when I mentioned my name I thought . . . for an instant . . . he . . ."

"Yes?" Laura's stomach tightened and she felt wetness on her upper lip.

". . . reacted." David ran his fingers through his hair. "I remember thinking how funny it was that he should recognize a director's name, so few people do."

"And you say he kept looking at Robin?"

"Yes. It made me nervous. Shades of *Death in Venice*. Seriously, you never know who hangs out in these places, and Robin is such a beautiful child."

"David, what did the man look like?" She held her breath.

"Big bloke with blond hair, very curly like . . ."

"Yes . . . go on. Like what?"

"I was going to say like Robin's. Why are you looking at me like that?"

"David, the man in the car this afternoon, the one with Beryl Villiers, I only caught a glimpse of him, but at the time I was sure it was John . . . John Keith."

David sat down heavily on the bed. "You know, the thought crossed my mind."

"What do you mean?"

"I don't know. It sounds foolish, but looking at them together, I saw how similar their features were, and I thought that Robin would look just like that when he grows up. But if it was Keith, why would he have recognized my name?"

"I used to talk about you to him, what a great friend you were to me and how much I wanted him to meet you." Her voice trailed off.

"Do you think he would remember that far back?"

"Who knows?"

"Maybe he just goes to a lot of movies and recognized my name as a director. I shouldn't worry, my darling. After all, there are many people in the world with blond curly hair."

"But what if it really is John and we run into him? This seems to be a small town. What if we meet?"

"What if we do?" He took hold of her hand and looked into her eyes. "Laura, be honest with me. Do you still have feelings for him?"

The knot in Laura's stomach tightened. "No, of course not! I'm just afraid that he might figure out Robin is his child and . . . you know . . . make trouble. You are Robin's father, the only one he has ever known, and he loves you with all his heart. It would be devastating if he found out about John. Oh, Christ, why couldn't Robin look more like me? You'd think red hair would be dominant!"

David put out his cigarette in the ashtray on the night stand and took her in his arms. "We probably should have made an effort to get in touch with him at the time, but to tell you the truth, I thought that if we did he would come running back and I would lose you. I simply couldn't take the risk. I was happy that you were pregnant. It gave you a reason to marry me."

"David . . ."

"Darling, it's true. You wouldn't have done it otherwise."

"I'm glad I did."

"Would you like to take Robin and leave for London now? I have to stay until the close of the festival but I could leave directly after."

The sun set very fast in the tropics, and suddenly, the room was dark. Laura could only just make out David's face in the shadows. *If I go now*, she thought, *I'll be safe*. She closed her eyes and saw the man in the blue Mercedes. Her heart quivered.

"I'm not going home. Robin is having the time of his life, and besides, I don't intend to cheat myself out of seeing you win the first prize."

He held her close to him. "You seem quite confident."

"Of course I am. The word is out . . . the film is a stunner!" She reached up and touched his face.

"Laura, I'm glad you are going to stay. If you had wanted to escape John Keith, it would tell me that he still means something to you. If anything happens, we'll face it together. I do love you so dearly."

Laura nestled her head in the hollow of his neck. Her heart was racing. If John was truly Beryl Villiers's newest conquest, was there a chance he might be at her party? Again, she asked herself: what kind of sexual power did this Beryl Villiers have? She must indeed be a femme fatale if Kitty Paxton, the epitome of poise and self-confidence, was frightened to have her husband in the same room with her. And John might be this woman's lover.

Beryl Villiers was the most famous of Sir James Paxton's discoveries. He met her in the South of France on what turned out to be a thwarted attempt to obtain the screen rights to Somerset Maugham's *The Narrow Corner*. Paxton had requested a meeting with the reclusive author in order to show him an outline of the screenplay. Maugham, who was staying in his villa at Cap Ferrat, cancelled one appointment after the other, usually by way of a terse message from Gerald Haxton, his companion and secretary. But James Paxton hadn't built a studio by giving in to minor setbacks. He remained on the Cote d'Azur, taking his mind off the elusive Mr. Maugham by amusing himself in the casino at Monte Carlo.

Paxton's first glimpse of Beryl Villiers was at the chemin de fer table. He had just passed the shoe to a powdery dowager on his left when he noticed an extraordinary girl seated on the opposite side of the table. She had the dark wavy hair and bronze skin of a South Sea Islander but, when she looked up from the table, he saw that her eyes were of the palest china blue. As she met his glance, an earthquake shook the foundations of James Paxton's world.

Later, as the girl passed through the bar, he waylaid her and they exchanged a few pleasantries. She turned out to be the daughter of a government official stationed in Ceylon, traveling with her aunt on a European tour of cathedrals, castles, and museums. James wondered what had brought them to Monte Carlo, where relatively few such attractions were available.

He met the aunt the following afternoon in the grand salon of the Hôtel de Paris. Mrs. Montgomery was an attractive, if somewhat overblown widow, whose Mayfair accent, James suspected, had been acquired sometime after her husband's rapid rise in the world of commerce.

"You see, Mr. Paxton, Beryl's mother died a year ago, and my brother, Beryl's father, that is, asked me to come out to Ceylon — a very nasty place, I can tell you — to act as companion for dear Beryl."

The longer they chatted, the more forthcoming she became. After two pink gins, she confided that her real aim was to find a husband for the girl who, by colonial standards, was getting beyond marriageable age.

"We've been to all the fashionable resorts, but so far the only proposals Beryl has received have not been what I would call entirely decent. I'm at the end of my tether, Mr. Paxton," she said, drinking the last of her cocktail, "the absolute end."

"I think, Mrs. Montgomery, the problem lies in your niece's appearance."

"Well, I know she's not your classic English rose but . . ."

"I mean she's simply too beautiful. When it comes to marriage, men sometimes prefer more conventional looks. I have a strong feeling that Beryl's immediate future lies in a different direction than the center aisle of a church. I head up a small film studio in London and would very much like to do a test."

"You mean for the cinema?"

"Exactly."

"Mr. Paxton, I think nothing short of fate has put you in our path."

"I couldn't agree more, dear lady, I couldn't agree more."

From Beryl's first appearance on the screen in 1933, an air of mystery surrounded her. Jamie did nothing to contradict speculation about the possibility of Ceylonese origins, to which her dark skin, huge black-lashed eyes, magnificent body, and sultry voice only added. By the time her second film was released, she was a star.

Beryl was aware that James Paxton was in love with her and teased him in subtle ways until he was mad with desire. Driven by innate wisdom in such matters, when it came to the point of surrender, Beryl always demurred. Obsessed to have her, Paxton divorced his wife, whose father had financed Briarwood Studios, and married his protégée.

Like a charm found by accident, Beryl brought her husband a run of extraordinary good fortune. All his projects were critical and financial successes. He made a second try at the Maugham book and obtained the release. The studio grew, and he leased several acres near Richmond for location use. Established actors from the London stage were put under contract, famous playwrights sent him screenplays and, by 1936, his films were being screened in New York and San Francisco. In 1937, James Paxton's name was listed in the King's Birthday Honours.

Sir James starred his wife in a series of romantic dramas, some adapted from classics, others original works. She usually played opposite Briarwood's newest and most dashing leading man, Robert Gordon. The contrast between Gordon's athletic physique and fair coloring and Beryl's sultry darkness was compelling. Their smoldering chemistry had fans avid with curiosity about their off-screen relationship, and every new film starring the pair opened to long queues, packed houses, and audiences begging for more.

In 1939, at a party in London, Beryl met Marcello Gianni. A financier and broker in *heavy equipment*, Gianni was richer than Sir James and far more knowledgeable in the ways of the world where women were concerned. He had no permanent address, but changed residences as the mood took him, from his villa on the Lago di Lugano to a twelve-room apartment on the Avenue Victor Hugo in Paris, a flat in Cliveden Place in Belgravia, and a New York pied-à-terre on Fifth Avenue and Seventy-ninth Street. His glamour worked like an aphrodisiac on Beryl. After six years, the glow of stardom was beginning to fade, and life at the center of international café society seemed more desirable than the one she was leading as a film actress, no matter how famous. A month after their meeting, she was ensconced in luxury on the Avenue Victor Hugo.

Gianni engineered a quick divorce for Beryl, and they were married in Switzerland the day after the decree absolute was granted. Despite her abrupt defection, James could not bear to cut Beryl entirely out of his life. She behaved as if running off with another man was the most natural thing in the world and, oblivious to the pain her elopement had caused him, often wrote James long newsy letters about her life in New York, where the Giannis had settled.

He always answered in the same cordial tone.

Marcello Gianni took Beryl to New York for their honeymoon. It was a trip they did not return from for seven years. Since the beginning of the rise of Hitler and the Nazi regime, Gianni had been kept informed as to what was happening to Jews in Eastern Europe. He realized it was only a matter of time before the horror moved west to France and even England. He was also aware that, if investigated, his own ancestry could be potentially dangerous. Ever the pragmatist, he left his Rome and Geneva offices in the hands of two trusted managers and transferred most of his operations to New York. Prior to and during the war in Europe, Gianni made his fortune as an agent dealing in armaments. After the armistice was signed in 1945, he continued in the same business — often in far-flung regions of the world.

When the true extent of the Holocaust came to light, Gianni dedicated himself to the idea of a state for the Jewish people. From the time of its establishment in 1948, the most important component of the state of Israel was its military. Marcello Gianni financed numerous arms purchases for the new nation. In 1952, he endowed the Marcello Gianni Institute of Fine Arts in Tel Aviv. Though many talented young musicians and artists were schooled there, some of the classrooms at the Institute were used for the training of other young Israelis — future members of an organization known as Mossad.

A few years after Beryl left him, James Paxton met the Honorable Catherine Railton at a house party in Kent. The daughter of one of his oldest friends, Kit, as she was called, had just turned nineteen. Strongly attracted to the charming and distinguished older man, Kit pursued James with unrelenting vigor until he finally realized that this delightful young woman was truly in love with him. Lively and intelligent, she showered James with a depth of affection and understanding that belied her youth. The twenty-four-year gap in their ages didn't seem to matter, and the marriage was a great success. In addition to her constancy and unfailing good humor, Kitty provided James with something neither of his other wives had: a family.

Despite the happiness he enjoyed in his life with her and his three children, Kitty Paxton was well aware that her Jamie had never completely expunged Beryl Villiers from his heart.

CHAPTER 14

Traffic, which had been moving at a steady pace along the western end of the Avenida Costera Miguel Aleman, suddenly slowed to a crawl as it turned into the Gran Via Tropical. Clouds of noxious fumes spewed from exhaust pipes, and a symphony of horns, strictly forbidden by Mexican law, trumpeted in a crescendo of discordant beeps. The skirt of Laura's yellow silk dress clung damply to her legs, and she could feel moisture where her bare shoulders met the soft leather seat of the Paxtons' rented Lincoln convertible. She wondered how David could look so cool, dressed as he was in a dark linen suit. At last, they pulled into a driveway marked Casa Encantada and joined the line of automobiles that inched up the perilous grade leading to the house.

"By the number of cars, it looks as if this is going to be one hell of a fiesta," Sir James said to no one in particular. They were almost at the entrance, where several white-jacketed attendants were lined up waiting to greet them.

"Oh, look, Jamie," said Kitty, gesturing toward a couple emerging from a black Citroën, "there's Maurice and Francine! You didn't tell me they would be here. Does he have something in the festival, or does she?"

"Didn't I mention it to you? Francine is in *Le Bête Noir*. Maurice rang me just before we left London to say they're looking forward to seeing you. David and Laura, too," he added, looking in the rearview mirror.

"Darling, wake up, you're a million miles away," said David. "Did you hear what Jamie said? Maurice and Francine Brossard are here."

"Yes, I heard. That's lovely."

"We're here." said Sir James. A boy stepped forward to help the ladies out. He took the keys from Sir James and jumped in behind the wheel. "Be careful, that's a rented car. *Caro rentado!*" Jamie shouted as the boy gunned the motor and, tires screeching, drove away.

Standing at the enormous double doors, thrown open to an entrance hall crammed with people, was a short man in a dark blue raw silk jacket and white linen slacks. Silver hair and a mustache accented his deeply tanned face.

"Good evening and welcome. I am Marcello Gianni," he said, addressing himself to the Landaus.

"Good evening, Signore Gianni, I am David Landau. May I present my wife — "

"Laura English!" Gianni said, bringing her hand to his lips and brushing it with his mustache. "You are even more enchanting off the screen."

"Thank you, Signore Gianni."

"Come, come, join the party," he said with a gesture that drew them into the house. "My dear Kit! More lovely each time I see you, *cara*." Now it was Kitty's turn to have her hand brushed by the mustache. "James, *amico mio*." As the two men shook hands Laura thought she saw something like a look of mutual understanding pass between them. "Please go in. Beryl is on the terrace. I shall join you soon." He turned to greet new arrivals and they went into the house.

The first person Laura saw as she entered the large drawing room was John Keith. He stood apart, at the far end of the room, his face the bland mask of a spectator rather than a participant in the festivities around him. As if to accentuate his aloofness, he wore an old pair of tan slacks and a soft blue cotton shirt. He took a long drink from the tall gin and tonic in his hand. Laura's heart thumped unevenly against the walls of her chest as she watched the muscles of his throat work. Her cheeks flushed and her body filled with familiar longing. She ached to look into his eyes, touch his face, feel his body against hers. It was all she could do to keep from flying across the expanse of richly patterned Indian carpet that separated them and pulling him into her arms. If she had ever doubted it, Laura now knew for certain that this man was, at this moment and for all time, deeply embedded in the very core of her being.

A white-coated house boy stood before them holding a tray of drinks. David took a highball and Laura automatically picked up a glass of Champagne. Nearby, she noticed Kitty and Jamie standing with the Brossards, Francois Truffaut, and Claude Charbol. Kitty gestured to them, indicating they should join their circle. David took her arm and led her to the others. Soon he, Charbol, and Truffaut were embroiled in one of their inevitable discussions on the finer points of filmmaking.

"Let's circulate, darling," said Kitty.

"Pardon me, did you say something?" Laura was trying to locate John from her new position in the room.

"Laura, you've been acting in the oddest way. Are you all right?"

"I'm just fine."

"I haven't seen Beryl yet," Kitty said, scanning the room "Oh, there she is! Look at her, will you. She's got to be close to fifty and doesn't look half that age. They say she hasn't had a lift. Of course, she's taken to wearing her hair pulled tight back in that bloody great ponytail. That probably smoothes everything out."

Laura followed the direction of Kitty's glance and saw the same woman who had been behind the wheel of the blue Mercedes on Wednesday afternoon. She was standing very close to John Keith, her slim fingers resting on his arm. She appeared very small and fragile beside his bulky form. He looked down at her and said something that made her laugh. A pang of primeval jealousy stabbed so sharply at Laura's heart that a wave of dizziness swept over her. For one awful moment she thought she was going to be sick. The sensation brought back a vivid memory of the dreadful nausea of her pregnancy. She lowered her eyes.

"Listen, darling, I can't stand any more of this shop talk," whispered Kitty. "I'm going to roam around a bit."

"Of course, go ahead."

Kitty gave her a surprised look. "Don't you want to come with me? Melina Mercouri is over there. I thought you were absolutely dying to meet her."

"I'll be along in a bit," Laura smiled brightly. Kitty headed into the crowd and was immediately caught up in a circle that revolved around the plump figure of Chucho de la Rocha. Laura noticed Jules Dassin and Carlos Saura breaking away to join David's group as Delphine Seyrig kissed Kitty's cheek and introduced her to Melina Mercouri.

Again, Laura's eyes searched out John, but he was no longer with Beryl. She was speaking instead to Ugo Tognazzi, Jean Sorel, and Larry Harvey, each vying the other two for her attention. Despite her age, it was obvious that this woman was, as Kitty put it, *fatal*. Again, she looked over the crowd. John had disappeared.

"We meet again!"

Laura caught the scent of Femme. She jerked her head around. Glenda Fisher was standing at her elbow. As before, she was dressed in a flowing caftan, this one a vivid shade of purple shot through with iridescent metallic threads.

She leaned toward Laura, "I hope you don't mind my saying so, but you look awful. If you have a touch of Montezuma's revenge, I have a bottle of Lomotil in my bag."

Laura couldn't help but laugh, and some of the tightness at the center of her chest eased away. "Oh, no, nothing like that. You're very kind to offer."

"After five years in this country, I'm prepared for anything. By the way,

Beryl's boy is here tonight. Have you met him yet?"

"No, we just arrived a few minutes ago." Laura's mouth was dry. "But I'd like to," she added, the words sticking to the roof of her mouth and coming out a whisper.

"Okay, but remember, I have first dibs." She jabbed Laura lightly in the ribs and laughed.

Suddenly, Laura realized that this woman, with her staggering track record of conquests, was actually thinking of adding John Keith to her list. She imagined Glenda's large hands, several fingers of which bore heavy silver rings, touching his face, feeling the rich texture of his hair.

"You know, I am feeling rather queasy," she said. "Perhaps some fresh air."

"Good idea." Glenda Fisher pushed through the crowd, Laura following in her wake.

They made their way to the edge of the terrace and stood for a moment, leaning their elbows on the railing.

"What are those lights out there in the water?" asked Laura.

"That's Roqueta. It's an island just across from this point of land."

"Oh, yes, now I remember noticing it from the hotel."

Three guitarists were playing a beautiful tune that Laura had heard over and over since coming to Acapulco. They listened for a while in silence. The warm breeze was laden with the sweet heavy scent of the tropics.

"What is the name of that song?" she asked.

"It's called *Tu Me Acostumbraste,*"

"It's such a lovely melody. Do you know what the words mean?"

Glenda Fisher thought a while. "Well, let's see, they go something like this."

> *You arrived at the door to my heart,*
>
> *entered and locked yourself in —*
>
> *there to stay forever.*
>
> *You taught me all about love*
>
> *and accustomed me to its wonder.*
>
> *Now, I ask myself, how am I to exist?*
>
> *For you, who taught me all these things,*
>
> *forgot the most important lesson of all —*
>
> *how to live without you.*

Glenda rolled her eyes as she said the last line. "Pretty schmaltzy, eh? Well, you can't really translate exactly, but that's the general idea. Hey, Laura, what ..."

Tears were streaming down Laura's cheeks. "I'm terribly sorry. I don't know what's the matter with me," she said, digging in her tiny bag for a handkerchief that was eluding her grasp.

"You're probably going to get your period," said Glenda.

Laura burst out laughing through fresh tears.

"Go ahead, have a good cry." She handed Laura a cocktail napkin. "Listen, we all go through it. I'm manic at the moment, but you should see me just before the curse. Songs, movies, babies — it doesn't take much and I'm off on a sobbing jag." Her wide smile was full of warmth. "Oh, God, I almost forgot. The reason I came over to you in the first place. A small favor for a friend. I hope you won't hate me."

"You have been so kind, of course I won't hate you," said Laura, dabbing under her eyes with the napkin. "What is it?"

"Gerry Maddox wants to meet you."

"Gerry Maddox," she said slowly looking out at the dark water. Tiny lights from yachts anchored nearby bobbed up and down on its surface. She had a strong urge to run down the road, find the beach, plunge into the water, and swim to Roqueta. "I know that name."

"Galaxy Studios," said Glenda.

"Oh, yes. I do remember now."

"I met Gerry about three years ago in Oaxaca. He was on location, and I was on a shoot for *Town & Country*. It was lust at first sight. I chased him shamelessly for days until he finally told me, wouldn't you know it, that he plays for the other team."

"The other . . ." Laura looked questioningly at the big woman.

"Guys."

"Oh, I see. Of course." Laura laughed in embarrassment.

"Anyway, it was some letdown, but we've been good friends ever since. The thing is, he owns the rights to a wonderful book that's going to make a fabulous film, and his greatest fantasy is for you to play the lead."

"I remember he contacted me once several years ago. I can't remember what the project was. Plainly nothing that could induce me to go all the way to America."

"Laura, you're in America now!"

"I suppose so. But this is for David. And it isn't Hollywood. I don't want to go there."

"Well, I can understand that. Southern California is pretty crass. I ought to know. I left it as soon as I could, but a lot of the movie people are really brilliant and ..."

"As I told you, the head of Briarwood is one of our best friends, and I think of the studio as home. I truly have no interest ...”

“Will you at least hear what he has to say? He’s here tonight, and he’s really very sweet. Let me just bring him out to you.” Glenda grasped Laura’s hands and looked into her eyes. “I honestly think you’ll be doing yourself a favor.”

“All right,” said Laura with a shaky sigh. She liked Glenda and, in an odd way, trusted her.

Leaning back against the railing, Laura watched the crowd in the drawing room. David, she noticed, was in deep conversation with Grigori Chukhrai. He had been hoping to have some time with the Russian director, whose film, *Ballad of a Soldier*, won the Palme d’Or last year in Cannes. Now, Sergei Gerasimov was joining them. *David must be in his seventh heaven*, thought Laura and smiled. Kitty and Melina Mercouri, seemingly fast friends, were chatting with Irene Papas. It looked like a Technicolor movie of a party. Any minute, she expected to see Lana Turner descending the staircase in a black sequined dress.

Where was John? In some upstairs bedroom, waiting for Beryl to slip away for a few minutes? Why, she wondered after so many years, had Providence chosen this particular time and place to put him in her path? Uncle Matt believed that each life had its own plan and that one should not resist what fate intends, but what about David? Fate had put him in her way at the same time it removed John. She loved David with all the laughter and pain and trust that seven years of marriage could hold, but she still loved John with an overwhelming passion that the years could not diminish.

“Laura,” Glenda Fisher put her hand on Laura’s arm. “I’d like you to meet my friend Gerry Maddox.”

“How do you do, Miss English.” Gerry Maddox did not look anything like Laura’s idea of a Hollywood producer. He was tall and slim, with close-cropped brown hair, well-defined aristocratic features, and a quiet manner.

“How do you do?” She extended her hand.

“Now that I’ve performed my duty, I’m off to the buffet table to gorge on Beryl’s beluga. Check in with me next week at the Golden Door!” Glenda was off in a cloud of fragrance.

Gerry Maddox led Laura to a corner of the terrace where some tables had been arranged for the buffet supper. Cocktail hour was still going strong, and they had the area to themselves. He held out a chair for her to sit down. For a long while he looked into Laura’s face, saying nothing. At last he spoke. “Laura, I want you for the lead in *Royal Player*.

“You mean the book about Nell Gwyn? The one Carolyn Ferrier brought out last year?”

“Yes. Have you read it?”

"Yes."

"And what did you think of it?"

"I tried to get Jamie Paxton to buy it."

"For you?"

Laura nodded. "Yes, but Mrs. Ferrier had already promised the rights to another producer." She laughed. "It must have been you!"

"I talked to Carolyn about an option when she was still in the research stage. You see, Nell Gwyn has always been a passion of mine."

"Oh . . ." Laura breathed.

"Yours too?"

"Yes."

He reached across the table and took both of her hands in his. "We can make Nelly Gwyn live again, Laura."

A wave of intense excitement shot through her. Since she had first discovered Nell Gwyn, while still a Bournemouth schoolgirl, Laura had felt an eerie kinship with the sprightly Restoration player. Nell's spirit and an unaffected charm had not only captured the hearts of jaded seventeenth-century Londoners but that of King Charles himself. Now it seemed a chance was being dropped in her lap by someone who felt exactly as she did, someone who would pay meticulous attention to detail and mount a spectacular production, someone who saw Laura English as the only possible actress to play a part she had dreamed of all her life.

As Gerry Maddox talked about Nell Gwyn and *Royal Player*, Laura's mind turned to John Keith. A dull pain pulled at her heart. Her John, miraculously found after so many years. But he wasn't hers any more than she was his. She belonged to David Landau — and Laura English.

"It looks like you're having quite a little battle with yourself," said Gerry Maddox.

"Yes," she whispered, then cleared her throat. "Sorry, it's just ..."

"There you are, I've been searching everywhere for you." David stood looking down at them. "Hello, Gerry. I had no idea you had a film in the festival."

"I don't," answered Maddox, rising. He shook David's hand. "I've come here on a mission." He glanced over at Laura, and she smiled.

"Let me in on the joke," said David, sitting down in one of the empty chairs near Laura and lighting a cigarette.

"I'm in Acapulco to seduce your wife."

David smiled.

"I want her for a picture that's set to start production next month."

"I'm afraid you're wasting your time. My wife has a blind prejudice about Hollywood." He put his hand over Laura's and took a long pull on his cigarette.

"David," she said in a quiet voice, "believe it or not, Mr. Maddox has just quashed that prejudice." She turned and smiled at the producer. "Thank you for thinking of me, Mr. Maddox. I'd love to do *Royal Player.*"

CHAPTER 15

The 1960 Acapulco Film Festival was held at the old Fuerte de San Diego, a fortress crowning the hill just opposite the docks, east of the Zócalo. Small by European standards, it had been built in 1616 as a defense against English pirate attacks.

Lit up as at was for the evening's festivities, it looked to Laura like a castle out of a fairy tale. Searchlights arced across the evening sky as she and Kitty, teetering precariously on high-heeled sandals, climbed the rutted stairs leading to the entrance. It was British Night, and the Union Jack fluttered in the warm breeze. Holding on to one another and giggling, the two friends made their way upward in the semi-darkness, spindly heels tangling in the hems of their long gowns.

"Jam-ie!" Kitty gasped between fits of laughter. "Come rescue us!"

Sir James, David, and the three boys had reached the entrance hall and were being greeted by Don Emiliano Vargas, the festival chairman. Robin had Simon Paxton's binoculars around his neck and was peering through them at his mother and Kitty.

"Good God," blustered Sir James, "at times you two behave like a pair of three-year-olds. There's a banister on this wall." He walked back down the few steps to where Laura and his wife were stranded and guided Kitty's hand to a wrought-iron railing. "Look, right here."

"Oh, good heavens," Kitty said through a burst of laughter, "he's right! There is a banister!" She placed Laura's hand on the railing and they proceeded upward. "I think I had a wee bit too much Champagne at dinner," she whispered as they mounted the last steps. "It's such a big night for David. I'm frightfully nervous for him."

"I know," said Laura looking up as they passed under the raised portcullis. "He seems calm, but I think he's wound up tight inside."

They passed into the crowded amphitheater where a waiting usher guided them to their assigned seats. David sat between Laura and Robin, and the Paxtons occupied four seats in the row in front of the Landaus. Laura stared down at the enormous screen that had been placed in the pit of the theater. David took hold of her hand. Despite the heat, his fingers were cold. She looked over at him and smiled.

"Soon now." She squeezed his hand.

"Hold a good thought," he said, squeezing back.

The searchlights went off, and Laura saw that the sky was filled with thousands of stars. "Look, David." She pointed above her.

"Makes all of this seem rather a lot of nonsense, doesn't it?"

"I think it's very much in keeping. It's utter magic, and so is your film."

The screen lit up and the familiar Briarwood ivy-clad wall appeared in bright colors. Strains of beautiful music, Joachim Muller's haunting theme from *Beggar's Choice* filled the starry night She watched the credits superimposed across scenes of a deserted street. And there it was.

Director
DAVID LANDAU

She heard David's "Hush" as Robin started to clap. She smiled because she, too, had felt like clapping. The movie began.

Applause drowned the music accompanying the final credits. The audience was on its feet. The three principals, Margot French, Herbert Stanton, and Mark Hilary were on stage, bowing to the standing crowd. Emiliano Vargas was saying something to Cantinflas, who was presiding as master of ceremonies.

Cantinflas bent to the microphone. "Ladies and gentlemen, Miss French, Mr. Stanton, and Mr. Hilary would like to introduce the director of the magnificent film we have just seen. Will Mr. David Landau come to the stage?"

Cries of "Director! Director!" rang out.

David kissed Laura, got out of his seat, and started down the aisle toward the stage. He hesitated for a moment and walked back until he stood in front of Robin's seat. He put out his hand. "Come along, son."

Tears filled Laura's eyes, and she could barely see David and Robin running down the aisle together.

Sir James turned around his seat in front of Laura and faced her. "He's quite a man, your David," he said.

"Yes," she whispered, "he is."

David was speaking now. His voice, the first thing she had noticed about him, was still that of a trained actor: perfect diction and rich tones, with just the right inflections. He was thanking Jamie for the confidence he had shown in producing the film and praising the actors for putting up with his tyranny. As he related a particularly amusing incident that had occurred during filming, Laura looked at the Paxtons. They were sitting up straight in their seats, listening attentively to David's words.

Sensing something at her back, she turned. Leaning forward in the seat directly behind her was John Keith. His face was inches away. His eyes looked straight into hers. He said nothing.

"John!" she gasped.

"I knew you'd be here tonight. Someone said your . . . husband . . . had a film in the festival."

"John," she repeated.

"You look different. Polished. Prettier, I'd say. He must make you happy. Are you happy?"

Her throat had gone dry. "I saw you last night," she whispered.

"Jane, is the boy with you our son?"

She hesitated.

"Is he, Jane? Is he our son?"

There it was. The question she had feared. "David is his father."

"I met the boy the other day. It was pure accident." His eyes looked into hers. "I met David Landau as well. That boy isn't his son." Applause drowned his words, but Laura knew what he was saying. When it was quiet again, he said, "We can't talk here. Meet me tomorrow morning at the Hotel Caleta."

"I'm with my family. I can't just go off."

"Say you have to do some shopping or that you want to go to church. I'm sure that's one place your husband doesn't go." He laughed. A bitter laugh, different from his old one. "I'll be in the bar at the Hotel Caleta from ten until noon."

It was unreal. After seven years of wondering what she would say to him should they meet again, she was actually talking to John Keith. "I can't believe it's you." She put her hand out to his. Their fingers touched.

"The Hotel Caleta. Ten o'clock tomorrow. We'll talk then," he said in a low voice.

"Robin! You were great!" It was Simon and Jamie Paxton shouting. She whirled around. David was following Robin back to their seats, his mouth curved in a broad smile.

"Did you hear me, Mummy?" piped Robin.

"Yes, I did," she lied.

"I'd better get him under contract straight away, eh, Laura?" said Sir James.

"I guess we have another actor in the family," laughed David, a little out of breath. "He really was quite marvelous. When Vargas handed him the microphone, I didn't know what to expect, but he's a real trouper." David ruffled Robin's golden curls.

Laura turned around once again. As she knew it would be, John Keith's seat was empty.

People around them were moving into the aisles. David touched Laura's shoulder. "Darling, we should probably put in an appearance at the Vargas party. Kitty says Robin can spend the night with Simon and Jamie. We'll drop them off at the hotel on the way."

"Sorry, David. What did you say?"

"I know it's a bore, but Vargas seems very keen on the film and . . ."

She turned to face him. "Oh, yes. The party."

"Are you all right, Laura?" he looked into her eyes. " Not coming down with tummy trouble, are you?"

"No, I'm perfectly fine," she smiled up at him. "Don't worry. I'll dazzle Señor Vargas with my best RADA charm."

"Thanks, darling. I think it must be the applause and excitement, but I feel wonderfully high and . . ." Shrill screams coming from the opposite side of the amphitheater drowned David's words. All heads turned toward the disturbance. David leaned over to the Paxtons' seat. "What's going on?" he asked James, who had Simon's binoculars trained in the general area of the commotion.

"I don't know," he said, squinting into the glass. "It looks like . . . yes . . . . I'm sure. It's Beryl! Two men have her. She looks hysterical." David noticed Jamie's hands trembling as he pressed the lenses to his eyes. "There's someone on the ground."

Two uniformed men ran down the aisle, a stretcher wobbling between them. They bent over the fallen man and carefully lifted him onto the narrow pallet. In seconds, they were speeding back up the aisle. Beryl Villiers broke away from the men supporting her and followed the attendants with the stretcher.

"By God, I think that's Marcello they're carrying out!" said Jamie, stepping into the aisle. "I must see what I can do. Go on to the party. I'll catch up to you as soon as I can." He pushed his way through the crowd, leaving Kitty, hand to her mouth, gazing after him.

Laura put her arm around Kitty's shoulder. "Come on, darling, let's get the boys back to the hotel." She turned to David. "Do you think the party will be cancelled?"

"I'll find out," he said, herding the three boys up the aisle.

Kitty's blue stare moved from her departing husband to Laura. "What do you think happened?" Her voice was little more than a whisper.

"I think the poor man has probably had a heart attack or a stroke. It's a good thing the festival committee arranged to have such a well-equipped first aid station here at the fort. Don't worry about Jamie. He's just going to see if he can help. He'll meet us back at the hotel." Laura gave Kitty's shoulder a reassuring pat.

"It's that woman. I told you, Laura. She's fatal. Jamie sees her in distress, and off he goes." Tears glistened at the rim of her eyes.

Laura guided Kitty into the aisle. "Come along now. Let's get out of this mob."

The recent shocks both women had received that evening at the Fuerte de San Diego sobered them. There were no giggles on the narrow steps as they descended to the road where David was waiting for them with a taxi.

"I just spoke to Vargas. They've called for an ambulance to take Gianni to the hospital. It's not far from here. In any case, the party's off."

"Did Señor Vargas say what happened to Marcello?" asked Kitty.

"No, he didn't." He turned to Laura. "Would you mind terribly if I dropped you at the hotel and took a swing by the hospital?"

"Not at all. I think you should go."

As the taxi pulled up at the entrance to the hotel, Kitty put her hand on David's arm. "Do me a big favor, will you."

"Of course, Kit. What is it?"

"Bring Jamie back with you."

"We'll both be back as soon as possible." He smiled into her tear-filled eyes.

Laura noticed that Kitty was trembling as they walked down the hotel corridor to the boys' room. The Paxton boys were fighting over possession of the key until, with one last grab, a triumphant Simon wrestled it away from his older brother and unlocked the door. "Robin is staying with us."

"But there's no need now." said Laura.

"Goodnight, Auntie Laura!" Chorused the boys, pulling Robin into the room and slamming the door shut behind them.

Laura smiled. "Come on, I'll walk you to your room." Kitty, eyes fixed on the patterned carpet, gave no sign of having heard. "Don't worry. David said he would bring Jamie back with him and he will." Laura took Kitty's arm and led her down the hall to the Paxtons' suite. "Key, please," she said, holding out her hand. Kitty drew the key out of her evening bag and, ignoring Laura's up-turned hand, opened the door herself.

"Kitty, may I come in for a moment?"

"Yes, please do. I could use some company just now." She led Laura into the sitting room, turning on lamps as she went. In the sudden brightness, Laura was shocked at what she saw. Kitty was only in her late thirties. Now, with shoulders slumped and mouth drawn in a tight line, she looked closer to Jamie's age.

"Do you want anything to drink? We have some whiskey, but if you'd like something else I can call down for it."

"No, thanks. I don't want anything. I won't stay long, but I have to talk to you."

"Come on, my legs won't hold up a minute longer." She sank into a chair, kicking the off her high-heeled sandals. "What is it?"

"I've just seen John Keith."

"What?" Slowly, Kitty turned her face to Laura's. "Where?"

"Just now. At the festival."

"Are you sure? There were so many people."

"He was sitting in the seat behind me. When David was on the stage with Robin, he spoke to me."

"My God! What did he say?"

"I haven't had a chance to talk to you. It's a long story but the thing is, he actually saw David and Robin the other day. Evidently, he rescued Robin from a near miss with a taxi and, after, spent some time with them. Kitty, he suspects . . . no, he's certain . . . that Robin is his child."

"What did he say?"

"He wants me to meet him tomorrow."

Kitty was silent for a long time. Finally, she spoke. "To discuss Robin?"

"Maybe."

"What did you feel when you saw him?"

"I don't know. Panic, I guess."

"Because Robin might find out that David isn't his father?"

Laura's eyes brimmed with tears. "No."

"What, then?"

"Because when I saw him, spoke to him, it was as if no time had passed. Oh, God, Kitty. I've never stopped loving him! I can't help it. I still love him!"

Kitty looked steadily at Laura, her eyes ringed with fatigue. "And what about David? You seem perfectly happy with him, or are you a better actress than I thought?"

Putting it off to stress about Jamie, Laura ignored the sarcastic note in her friend's voice. "I am happy with David. He is a wonderful husband and you know what he is like with Robin. I love David dearly but . . ."

"You're not in love with him, right?"

"Yes. That's right." Laura threaded her fingers through her red curls. "I thought it didn't matter. In fact, I thought our marriage had a better chance of working because we've always been such good friends. I thought that was more important than being madly in love. I hadn't counted on ever seeing John Keith again. I certainly never imagined that my feelings would stay so strong after all these years."

"But they have?"

"Incredibly so."

Kitty looked at Laura for a long moment. "I had planned to go to the marketplace tomorrow morning but now, with all this, I can't say what I'll be doing or where I'll be, but if . . . if you feel that you have to see him . . . you can say you are going there with me."

"I'm sorry. It was stupid of me to bring this up with you worried about Jamie. David will bring him back tonight. You know that, don't you?"

"You mean because he is my husband. We are a couple. A perfectly happy couple. Just like you and David? The whole idea of Jamie and Beryl Villiers is ridiculous, isn't it? As ridiculous as you and John Keith."

Laura looked down at her hands. She rose from her chair.

Kitty walked with her to the door. "Laura, darling, promise me something."

"What?"

"Think long and hard about this. After all these years, I know you pretty well. If you don't care about David or Robin, think about your career. David told Jamie that Gerry Maddox had a talk with you at Beryl's party and you're going to sign with him for what sounds like the project of your dreams. Don't lose your head and rush into something you'll regret. You have a great deal on the line, darling."

Laura put her arms around Kitty and held her close. "I know." she whispered.

No sooner had Laura fallen asleep when a high-pitched whine jolted her awake. Heart racing, she flicked on the bedside lamp and jumped to her feet. A thorough search of the room failed to reveal anything flying near the bed or perched on the whitewashed walls. She returned to the bed and switched off the light. Immediately, a buzzing insect swooped by her ear. Obviously, the few slats she had left open on the louvered doors were providing easy access to every winged creature in Acapulco — with her pillow as landing strip. She debated whether to get up and shut the louvers. It was a choice between biting insects, oppressive heat, or freezing air conditioning.

The luminous dial of her tiny leather travel clock read twenty after one. A breeze floated over her. It felt delicious on her skin. They would be huddled in robes, heavy socks, and quilts in London, yet here she was, a few hours away by plane, unable to stand even a sheet over her body. She felt very far from home.

She remembered feeling like this years ago on a trip to Spain. David was thinking of shooting a film there and wanted to scout some location sites. Her thoughts had constantly turned to John on that trip, recalling the stories of his Spanish wanderings and wondering what it would be like to have him there with her. One night, in the tiny seaside town of S'Agaró, the sensation of John's presence had been particularly keen. There was a small balcony outside their room where she lingered, just before bed, watching the moon as it slid between the branches of unfamiliar trees. She could hear David singing snatches of a song as he showered, his voice light and happy. She was wearing a nightgown bought especially for the trip: fashioned from the sheerest lawn, with delicate butterflies appliquéd on the bodice. She had paid an absurd price for it in a shop in the Burlington Arcade, but she knew it would please David, who appreciated fine things. From his parents, he had learned not only good manners but taste and discrimination. John Keith had not been raised with such advantages. He wouldn't have known fine linen from ordinary muslin. The nightgown would be an encumbrance to be eliminated as quickly as possible. Standing on that tiny balcony, in the warm Spanish night, she felt a thrill at the thought of John's strong fingers pulling away the cloth of the nightgown. The harsh reality hit her that she would never again feel as intensely as she had all those years ago in Bournemouth when she was a young girl and so deeply in love. The moon, smaller now, had made its way over the trees and was high in the sky. A bright star glimmered near it. Was it Venus? She closed her eyes tight and repeated the old lines Uncle Matt had taught her:

> Star light, star bright
> First star I see tonight'
> I wish I may, I wish I might
> Have the wish I wish tonight.

"Please," she had whispered into the Spanish heaven, "Let me see him . . . just once again."

And now her wish had come true.

How many years had John been a journalist? How long had he lived in Egypt? Was he in Mexico permanently or on an assignment? What was Beryl Villiers to him? Laura had never once seen his name in a newspaper or magazine, but she didn't follow current events as closely as she should. David, who read the international pages of the newspaper and subscribed to several magazines, had never mentioned seeing John Keith's name. And would he have told her if he had come across it? After all, David wanted to protect what he had, and he surely didn't want old memories of her former lover cropping up.

If she went to meet John tomorrow, what would he say to her? Would he want her back? Would he ask her to take Robin and join him in some remote part of the world? Months passed without her thinking of Aunt Rose and Uncle Matt, yet few days went by that she did not think of John Keith. He was the love of her life. It didn't matter that she had more in common with David or that she had given birth to Robin or that Rose and Matthew had given her the love she needed when she was a frightened child. During all the years since that final goodbye at the railway station in Bournemouth, John had remained in her heart.

What if now, out of the blue, she had the chance to make a life with him and their child? Would she grab it? Could she leave everything behind and start out again as if the time between had not existed? It was obvious that he understood little and cared not at all about Laura English. As far as he was concerned, she was still Jane Parks. To him, Laura English was just a film actress — nothing to do with the woman he had asked to meet him tomorrow at the Hotel Caleta. But she was no longer Jane Parks. Jane had died on the day Laura English was born in Jamie Paxton's office at Briarwood Studios. No, Laura English was born in the underground the night she had made her mother smile as she sang and danced while German bombs dropped from the sky.

She sat up. What if all John had in mind was a friendly chat? Maybe he just wanted to know more about Robin — if he was happy in his school and doing well. Maybe he would say that because of the unpredictability of his life, it was better for Robin, after all, that he had David Landau as a father. He might, as he would to any friend he hadn't seen in years, relate a few of his more exciting adventures as a foreign correspondent. He might even confide in her about his affair with Beryl Villiers! Then, just as they were about to part, he would remember to ask Laura about her newest film. She lay down again, eyes wide open in the blackness.

The door opened. Automatically, she glanced at the clock. It was just past two. She listened as David moved quietly around the room. He went into the bathroom and she heard water running. He turned out the light in the bathroom before coming quietly back into the bedroom This gesture of consideration, so typical in him, touched her.

"David," she said softly.

"Hello, darling. I hope I didn't wake you."

"No, I wasn't asleep. I was watching you in the dark."

He sat down on the bed and reached for her hand. "Marcello Gianni is dead."

"My God! What was it, a heart attack?"

"He was shot."

"Shot!"

"At very close range, evidently with a silencer. No one noticed anything until he collapsed."

"But who would want to kill him? He couldn't have had enemies with all his philanthropic work, endowing colleges and hospitals. He was famous for it."

"He was killed by an assassin. The police are sure of it."

"Assassin? But why?"

"No one knows. The Mexico City police have contacted Interpol."

"What about her?"

"Beryl? She's in a state. Jamie's with her." David dug in his pocket and took out a pack of cigarettes. The light from the match made an arc in the darkness. The sulfur of the match blended with the scent of tobacco. It was a smell she always associated with David.

"He didn't come back with you then?"

"No. She couldn't be alone. He said he had to stay with her."

"And what about Kitty? She needs to have Jamie here with her. She's very worried about his feelings for Beryl Villiers."

"There was nothing I could do about it. Jamie insisted. We'll have to nurse-maid Kit until he comes back."

"David, is he going to come back?"

"Of course he is. Beryl needs an old friend right now, someone she can trust. When I left the hospital, he was on his way to call Kit. He is going to take Beryl back to the house and make some calls for her. Gianni's attorney in New York has to be contacted and some friends in the States who will come to her."

"But doesn't Beryl have friends here?" she asked.

"I suppose so but she wants Jamie and, considering the circumstances, how can he refuse?"

"What . . . what about . . . " she could not speak John's name.

"Nowhere to be seen." He got off the bed, crossed over to the bureau and undressed in a square of moonlight that glowed on the tiled floor. When he was finished, he came back to the bed and lay beside her.

"David ..."

"Laura, you must not worry about Kit. It's true that Beryl Villiers was Jamie's great love, and maybe he does still feel something for her, but do you seriously think he would leave Kit? Not in a thousand years. If there's one thing our friend Jamie is, it's pragmatic. Believe me, he appreciates the life Kit has made for him. Secure, well ordered, and without demands. It's a life he can devote to his work. And when all is said and done, that's still the most important thing to Jamie."

"You should talk to Kitty. She was so upset tonight."

"I understand Kitty's feelings more than you realize. You see, she feels about Jamie the same way I do about you." Laura remained silent. He went on quietly. "You and Jamie are both completely devoted to your work. It's the driving force in both your lives. Kit provides Jamie with the sort of comfortable love he can depend on. It's a love that is so constant and unconditional that he doesn't have to worry about it. Now, imagine what his life would be like if Jamie were to give up Kit for Beryl. He wouldn't have a moment's peace worrying about meeting her demands, which I can well imagine are not easily met, to say nothing of fretting over every young man who happens to cross her path. No, I don't think Kit has anything to worry about."

"I must say, you paint a very pretty picture of Jamie. And, from what you just said, of me as well."

"Let's just say that I'm aware that your work comes first and, who knows, maybe if you weren't so serious about it I wouldn't love you as much. In any case, you have a talent that warrants taking care of. I love you the way Kit loves Jamie, but I'm not afraid of losing you because, my darling, I know, down deep, you would never give up a life so conducive to keeping Laura English alive and flourishing." Gently, he traced the line of her nose with the tip of his finger. "Now, no more talk. We both need to get some sleep. Tomorrow may turn out to be a difficult day." He took her hand, and in a few minutes she heard his quiet even breathing.

For Laura, there was no sleep. She stared into the darkness, conscious only of David's hand resting in hers.

CHAPTER 16

South of town, the rustic bungalows of the old Hotel Caleta spread out along the low cliffs above what was known as the morning beach. John Keith sat under a *palapa* at the hotel's Cantina del Sol and squinted at the glittering bay. His eyes stung in the glare and he took a pair of dark glasses out of his shirt pocket and put them on. Most of the hotel guests were at breakfast or still sleeping in their rooms, and the bar, normally filled with a boisterous crowd of young people drinking cervezas and sangrías, was deserted.

A young waiter, linen towel draped over his arm and a tin tray balanced on the palm of his hand, approached his table. *"A sus ordenes, señor."*

"Una Carta Blanca, por favor," said John.

"Y algo de comer? Tengo mariscos frescos."

"No, gracias, solamente la cerveza." The thought of shrimp and mussels made him feel slightly nauseous.

"Muy bien, entonces."

Leaning back in his chair, John closed his eyes.

He had slept very little the night before. His windowless room at the Hotel Misión had been humid as a steam cabinet. The bed sheets were clammy, and the warped blades of an ancient ceiling fan sprinkled dust motes onto his body as it squeaked around. The sound nearly drove him mad until, after a long search, he found a switch behind the dresser and turned the thing off, the rusty machine executing one last half-hearted turn before shuddering to a halt. A heavy silence filled the room. He tried to take a deep breath but there didn't seem to be enough air in the small space to fill his lungs. He stumbled to the bathroom and took a small brown medicine bottle from his shaving kit. He dropped a red pill into the palm of his hand, scooped it into his mouth with his tongue, and washed it down with the remains of a bottle of Peñafiel pineapple soda. He straightened the bed and lay down spread eagle on the damp sheet, concentrating on keeping his body still. At last, he slept.

The dream was short and vivid. He was straddling the back of a bird, a giant Roc straight out of the *Tales of the Arabian Nights*. His hands clung onto the feathers of the creature's neck as they soared over the ocean into the clouds, higher and higher. Suddenly, the clouds cleared, and he saw the great globe of planet Earth beneath him. He could make out the vast deserts of Saudi Arabia and the shape of the Persian Gulf. The water was blood red: a dark viscous fluid oozing out of the gulf, creating many rivers that snaked over the world, until they collected in a pool on the coast of Mexico. The bird flew higher, the air became thinner, and he felt himself struggling for breath. He pounded the thick neck, but the blows fell softly. He screamed for the bird to go down, but his cries were only faint whispers, dissolving in the howling wind. Just as there was nothing left to breathe and he knew he was going to die, the creature turned to look at him. What he saw was not the face of a bird, but his own features, distorted in a grotesque grin.

He woke gasping for air. His watch read 4:20. Deciding the night was over, he heaved himself off the bed and into the bathroom. A tepid shower cooled him only slightly, and the simple exertion of putting on his clothes started him sweating again. Sliding his feet into a pair of huaraches, he went down to the lobby. Ignoring the stares of the night porter, he moved a chair closer to the entrance of the hotel, where the chances of catching a breeze would be best. He leafed through a Spanish-language magazine and did a crossword puzzle on the back page of a week-old Acapulco News. At 5:30, the night porter went off duty and the day porter, who was familiar to him, took his place behind the reception desk.

"*Quieres alguna cosa, señor?*" he said, smiling across the desk at John. "*Un café?*"

"*Sí, muchas gracias.*"

The coffee was hot and strong and helped clear his mind of the dream. He leaned his head onto the back of the chair and thought of Jane. He had expected some changes after all this time, but she was remarkably the same. Features slightly sharper, but that same melting look, just for him, was still there in her eyes. Last night when her fingertips touched his hand, time stood still and he was in Bournemouth again, young and in love. How he had loved her! He thought he would die when that bloody Sir James Paxton came along and took her over. Anger and frustration had pushed him to grab at a chance to escape as far as possible from England and Jane. He never imagined, once in Egypt, he would discover the real purpose of his life.

Before Hassim informed him about the ban on personal mail during training, he was frantic when Jane didn't answer any of his letters, every one of which, he later learned, had been intercepted and destroyed. Knowing Jane as he did, John was certain she would have written him in care of Gran, whom, she expected, would forward his mail. He thought of her writing letter after letter, probably about the baby, and never receiving one from him in return. What must she have imagined? If he had known about the baby, he would have come straight home and married her. In a few months she could have returned to Cairo with him. Hassim and Gregory Parker, head of the organization in London, couldn't have objected once the thing was done. Jane would have understood about his work and accepted it. Of that he was certain. Why had she rushed into a marriage with that man, of all people? He supposed it was to give the baby, his baby, a name. The idea of his child with a Jewish name forced his nails into the palms of his hands. He looked at his watch. Ten to seven. It was a half-hour taxi ride over to the Hotel Caleta. Two more hours to kill. He got up out of the chair and, nodding to the porter, walked out of the hotel.

The sky was pale, and the early-morning air smelled surprisingly fresh. Turning left, he ambled down the deserted sidewalk, crossed over to the other side, and headed toward the Zócalo. His pace picked up, his steps echoing sharply over the cobblestones in the empty street. He reached the Zôcalo and, standing at its northern end, squinted up at the street sign for Calle Adolfo Ruiz Cortines. There was a small placard beneath it that read Hospital Central an arrow underlining the words. He looked down the street in the direction of the arrow.

The sun was up now, and the milky sky had turned a faint blue. An old woman dressed in black, her stubby legs noticeably bowed, waddled toward him. As she passed, he saw that her lips were moving and that her fingers, hideously twisted with arthritis, clutched a worn missal. More people were in the street now, mostly women dressed in black. There must be a church nearby. As if to confirm his thought, a bell sounded. Again, he glanced down the street in the direction of the arrow and began to walk. One block. Another. His steps slowed. The hospital might be in the next block or a mile away. That was the trouble with this bloody country. The street signs never really told you anything. He shouldn't be doing this. Gianni was surely dead by now. He had probably died before reaching hospital.

His thoughts turned to Beryl and he felt a twinge of genuine sympathy for the pain she must be suffering. She was a good sort, really, desperately fending off the inevitable passing of years with the attention of a string of young paramours. Yet he didn't despise her. In fact, he rather admired her spirit. Surely, no one as beautiful as she had been gave in easily to the ravages of time. Most turned to drink or drugs. At least Beryl used love as an antidote to age. And she was passionate and imaginative, giving as good as she got. He had always left her bed feeling content. They had been well matched in that way. Maybe he should call the house. No, just leave it. Better to go back to the hotel and have another shower and some more coffee. The papers would be in by now. He turned, reversing direction back toward the Zócalo.

"*Otra cerveza, señor?*" John started. It was the boy with the tin tray.

He looked at his watch. Eleven forty. "*Sí, otra cerveza. Bien fría.*" The boy hesitated a minute. John thought he was going to ask him if he had changed his mind about the mariscos, but evidently the look on his face forestalled any further conversation. The boy smiled and headed toward the bar.

Where the hell was she? He was positive that, after the way she had looked at him last night, touching his hand in the old way, that she would be there at ten on the dot. Did that husband of her's keep her on such a short leash? The thought of David Landau sent a surge of anger down his spine. He remembered how often Jane had spoken of him when she first went to London. She would go on endlessly about his kindness to her and how much he was helping with her part. Back then, he had not liked the idea of her friendship with a man with whom she had so much in common, and now, the notion that his child actually thought of Landau, a Jew, as his father turned the whole purpose of his life, for the past eight years, into a phenomenal joke.

The waiter was back with the beer. John watched the foam travel up the glass as he poured it out. A feeling he couldn't control was filling his chest. He looked at his watch. The two hands were straight up. His eyes were wet.

"*Señor.*" A different waiter, or perhaps it was the bartender, stood by his table. John put on the dark glasses again and looked up. "*Para usted, señor.*" He held an envelope in his hand.

John stared blankly into the man's thin brown face.

"*Esta mensaje es para el Señor Keith. Usted es el Señor Keith, verdad?*"

"*Sí, yo soy el Señor* Keith." John put out his hand, and the man gave him the envelope. It bore the Club de Pesca insignia in the upper left-hand corner. "*Gracias,*" he said, running his finger under the sealed flap and removing a single piece of hotel notepaper. He was barely able to make out the words, in Jane's neat handwriting, as they swam before him on the white page.

> John, I won't be able to meet you after all.
>
> Jane

With a savage gesture, he tore the paper into bits, flinging them to the ground. He thrust his hand into his pants pocket and drew out a ball of crumpled bills, from which he extracted a dirty twenty-peso note. His face was red and wet with perspiration, and his breath came in short, hard gasps as he tossed it on the table. His watch read seven minutes past noon. There was a daily flight to Mexico City at 2:50 P.M. Time to get out of this rotten sweet-smelling paradise. He had accomplished what had been required. Soon, he would have to focus all his attention on a new assignment, hopefully in another part of the world. With a concentrated effort, he made himself remember how important his work was, how much it meant to so many, and how committed to it he was.

He strode through the cool lobby of the Hotel Caleta, the soles of his sandals slipping over the polished liver-red tiles. Coming out into the sunlight on the street side, he nodded to the doorman, who raised his hand to a taxi parked at the curb. Handing the doorman a peso note, he got into the cab.

"Hotel Mision". The interior of the taxi smelled strongly of the ubiquitous vanilla bean dangling from the passenger-side visor. John rested his head back on the worn leather seat and closed his eyes. By late afternoon he would be at the organization's penthouse on the Avenida Rincón del Bosque. A long shower followed by a very dry martini on the terrace overlooking the Reforma would help put things back in perspective. He'd sip his drink and maybe another and enjoy the view of that elegant tree-lined avenue. It might be a while before Parker contacted him with another assignment. No matter. He was exhausted. A short rest might not be a bad thing, and the city was filled with diversions. He'd call that girl he'd met at Beryl's. What was her name? He put his hand to his forehead and concentrated. Glenda Fisher. That was it. She told him she lived out by the university, in Pedregal, a district he didn't know. She said she'd be going home as soon as the festival ended and printed her telephone number on a cocktail napkin — which he'd promptly lost. He closed his eyes and concentrated on the small square napkin she had held out to him. He smiled as a series of numbers appeared. 45.72.47 The gift for total recall, which had proved such an asset in his profession, was still in working order. Glenda Fisher. A big girl with a wide mouth and a lot of easy chatter. She would make him laugh. Yes, definitely a good girl to pass the time with until he heard from Parker. He hoped she would be in when he called.

The taxi swerved to avoid a woman crossing in the middle of the street, a child clinging to her hand. He thought of the little boy with a head of yellow curls and felt a queer lurch in his chest. He had a son. One useful thing about Jane's celebrity, he would always know where they were, and one day . . . one day, he . . . his head drooped, and he slept.

CHAPTER 17
LOS ANGELES, 1961

Wide bars of California sunshine streamed through the kitchen windows, warming Laura's back and shoulders. She took a last sip of tea, long gone cold and, setting the mug down on a plate next to the remains of a half-eaten muffin, raised her arms high above her head, stretching to relieve the stiffness in her neck.

In order to acquire a solid back story for this project, Gerry Maddox suggested that Laura make use of the studio library. Taking him at his word, she brought home several books on the period and, over past two weeks, had read her way through some fascinating material, starting with John Evelyn's diary right through to Clifford Bax's *Pretty Witty Nell*.

One of the volumes was a rare edition of seventeenth-century paintings, several pages of which were devoted to court painter Peter Lely. Sir Peter had a specific ideal of beauty — plump chin, voluptuous mouth, and heavy bedroom eyes which he superimposed on all of his subjects. Laura knew that lively little Nell Gwyn could not possibly have looked as Mr. Lely portrayed her, but there she was, peering unsmilingly from under drowsy lids. Toward the back of the book, she came upon a portrait by Simon Verelst. The woman in this picture had a lithe body, graceful hands, and a high white forehead. Her delicate brows were arched over clear, faintly amused eyes, and an airy cloud of golden red hair framed her face. This must have been the real face of Nelly Gwyn, a face Laura liked to think resembled her own more than Rivera's icy rendition of Natasha Gelman.

The sound of the telephone jarred her back to the present.

Reluctantly, she took her eyes off the page and walked across the kitchen to the wall phone. "Hello?"

"Were you outside?" It was David.

"No just immersed in the seventeenth century."

"I won't keep you, then. I'm in Murray Feldman's office with Roy Bliss and Harry Fox. I wanted let you know that *Home Land* is a go."

"Oh, David! I can't believe it's finally happened. What did Martin say?"

"I haven't talked to him yet. I wanted to tell you the good news first."

"David, he wants to do it. He said as much after he read the last revision. Ring me back as soon as you've spoken to him."

"It's seven o'clock in London. He probably won't be in. I should wait until morning."

"Ring him now."

"All right."

"And if ... no, when, Martin says yes, put in a call to Jasper."

"Do you really think Jasper would consider it? After all, Lord Balfour is really only a bit part."

"Cameo, David, not bit. And, yes, I do think he'll come over for it. Especially if you bring him first class and put him in one of those bungalows at the Bel Air. He'll love it. Tell him I miss him."

"All right, I'll try them both and let you know what happens tonight."

"I'll keep everything crossed." She hung up the receiver and smiled, hugging herself. At last, David was going to make his film about Israel! She felt certain that Martin Finchly would take the part of Chaim Weizmann. After all, he and David had been discussing the project for years. She was equally as certain that the role of Lord Balfour would be too tempting for Jasper Quigly to pass up. With those two signed, every top actor in London and Hollywood would be calling their agents to get them a part in the film.

After *Beggar's Choice* won first prize in the Acapulco Film Festival, David began receiving proposals from major producers in Britain, France, and Hollywood to direct top properties. John Gielgud wanted him for a season at the Old Vic, and the great diva Maria Callas called from her island in Greece with a proposal to direct her in a film adaptation of *Aida*, to be shot entirely in Egypt.

David rejected all offers and embarked on the project he had been planning for six years: *Home Land: The Story of Israel*. Oscar winner Roy Bliss collaborated with David on a brilliant screenplay, and cinematographer Barry Hayes promised to join the team. The idea was to produce a major work that would incorporate the sweep of an adventure story with the tight camera work and sharp dialogue that had become David Landau trademarks. Color exteriors would be shot on location in Israel, with dramatic scenes filmed in black and white on a sound stage at Galaxy. David had described the concept for the film at length to Marcello Gianni the previous February in Acapulco, and the Italian proposed to finance the entire project. But Gianni was murdered a few days after he had agreed to what was still only a verbal commitment. No one in the vast Gianni organization had been informed of Marcello's intentions, and David could not bring himself to intrude on Beryl's grief by discussing business. Any hope of financing from that quarter was buried with Gianni. But today, David had pulled off a miracle, and it looked as if multimillionaire entrepreneur Murray Feldman would be backing the project.

Laura turned back to the kitchen table and picked up the thick blue-bound *Royal Player* script. Tucking it under her arm, she opened the French doors and stepped out onto the terrace. The apartment Gerry Maddox had rented for the Landaus was in the Westwood neighborhood of Los Angeles and reflected the academic atmosphere of the nearby UCLA campus rather than the glamour of Beverly Hills or the elegance of Bel Air. The apartment was furnished in the very latest Danish modern style, with spare furniture upholstered in neutral shades of raw silk and linen. It had taken Laura several days to become accustomed to the starkness of her new surroundings, but once the adjustment was made from Cranley Gardens chintz to Scandinavian sleek, she realized that the serenity of her new surroundings were ideal for quiet study.

Maddox kept an apartment a few blocks away that he used when shooting at Galaxy but his primary residence was in Belvedere, a small town across the bay from San Francisco. These days, many actors, directors and writers had, as their primary residences, Swiss chalets, Irish castles, or Wyoming cattle ranches rather than mansions in Beverley Hills. As soon as *Royal Player* was completed, Gerry promised to show Laura and David the charming city of San Francisco and Belvedere Island, which he referred to as his personal paradise.

Laura leaned on the balcony overlooking the tree-shaded street and breathed in the sweet scents of honeysuckle and sunshine. Now that she was actually here, she had to laugh at how wrong she had been about California. In fact, she admitted to herself, in many ways she preferred it to London. Who could not help but respond positively to a place where the sun shone every day, and people actually smiled as they passed on the street? The clerk at the market on the corner was friendlier to her than many of the shopkeepers around South Kensington, where she had lived for eight years. The Hollywood movie crowd was welcoming and easy to know. She was aware that David missed their London friends who discussed issues of the day and abstract ideas rather than the latest scandals, but she was having fun!

The Landaus soon discovered that an automobile was essential to California life and, in the spirit of the place, David leased a Jaguar convertible from a Wiltshire Boulevard car dealer. On weekends, they took long drives along the magnificent coast highway, once as far south as San Diego, where they spent two days at the Hotel Del Coronado. It was mid-April and the ocean was still far too cold for swimming, but they took long walks on the beach, listening to the cries of the wheeling gulls and the hiss of the surf, and Laura thought of Bournemouth and her childhood by the sea.

Though not as intimate as Briarwood, Galaxy was a relatively small studio by Hollywood standards, and Laura soon felt completely comfortable working there. Her costar, on loan from Monumental, was British expatriate Gerald Palfrey who, after the war, had carved out a successful career in American films. Palfrey invariably played charmingly disreputable characters: the cynical theater critic, the erudite art collector, or the jaded man about town. His uncanny resemblance to Charles II made him a natural for the role in *Royal Player*. The role of Barbara Palmer, Countess of Castlemaine, was to be played by Veronica Shawn, whose auburn hair and statuesque figure closely resembled Castlemaine's. At the time of the action, Louise, Duchess of Portsmouth, had replaced Barbara Palmer as Charles's favorite. For this important part, Maddox cast Marlene Falcone, a young French actress who was enjoying immense popularity due to a recent film in which she had appeared bare-breasted. As the kittenish Louise, Marlene was the perfect foil to Veronica's flamboyant Castlemaine.

In an inspired casting decision, Maddox signed Broadway musical star Mandy Valentine to play Moll Davis, Nell's chief rival on the stage as well as in the king's bed. Mandy had the slim dancer's body and dark-haired, chocolate-box prettiness that matched every written description of the actress. Moll, who always claimed to be the daughter of a baronet, affected lady-like airs, while Nell remained the consummate cockney. Their ongoing battle of wits would provide most of the film's comic highlights.

The phone was ringing again. Anxious for David's news, she ran into the house and lunged for the receiver.

"Hello," she said.

"Laura."

"Kitty! Is that you?"

"Yes, darling, it's me."

"How wonderful to hear your voice. How are you?"

"I'm fine. We just got in from a party, and everything is so blissful that I had to call and tell you." Her voice bubbled with all its old gaiety. Laura pictured her friend at the other end of the line, her halo of pale blonde hair creating an incandescent glow around her perfectly etched features, her small body poised lightly on out-turned feet, the faint scent of Miss Dior in the air around her.

"I'm so glad that it's all come right."

"Darling, you know I never would have survived those three months when Jamie was away if it hadn't been for you and David. You kept us all going. When I think of the Easter holiday and everything you did for the boys . . . taking them with you to Diana Landau's brother's place in Scotland, I . . ."

Kitty's voice was fading and Laura broke in. "Well, it's all over now, and everything is as it should be."

"Yes it is, and Jamie says nothing whatever happened while he was with her so I've made up my mind to believe him on that point. Let's face it, if I didn't I'd go starkers."

"Well, thank God it only took Beryl three months to pull herself together," laughed Laura.

"By the time he left, she had a new boyfriend installed. She truly is a bitch."

"Still, if Jamie hadn't stayed on with her and she had gone off the deep end or something, he never would have forgiven himself."

"I suppose so. By the way, I didn't get a chance to tell you before, but Beryl told Jamie all about John Keith."

"Oh?" Laura sat down hard on the stool by the phone.

"Yes. It seems he latched on to them in Paris and got himself invited to Acapulco for the film festival. You see, he wasn't only an amour of Beryl's but very much *un ami de famille*. As chummy with Marcello as he was with Beryl! Evidently they used to have long conversations, especially about Marcello's involvement in Israel. It seems your John was also very interested in the details of that arms sales Marcello was putting together. Frankly, I was astonished that someone as savvy as Marcello would talk to a journalist about such a thing. I mean people who orchestrate such deals usually try to keep away from reporters, not sit down over cocktails for friendly chats with them. He must have trusted Keith a great deal. Jamie said Marcello even told him about his interest in financing David's film. Anyway, Beryl was frightfully hurt when he simply took off without a word after Marcello was killed."

"Did he?" Laura's voice was barely audible.

"This is a terrible connection, darling. Yes, he did. Left without so much as a goodbye, and at a time when Beryl certainly could have used some comfort. Come to think of it, if John Keith had stayed, my Jamie wouldn't have been pressed into service."

"Probably not."

"You know the Mexican police and even Interpol were completely stymied about the murder. It seems the man — they assume it was a man — who did it simply vanished off the face of the earth. Maybe he and your friend John left on the same plane," she laughed. "Darling," her voice serious, "you made the absolute right decision not meeting him that day."

Laura's eyes were fixed on a bright red geranium plant that sat on the railing of the balcony. A pulse throbbed in her throat, which kept her from answering.

"Well, I'd better ring off. It's awfully late, and I'm still in all my regalia. I just wanted to hear your voice. I didn't even ask you about the filming. Is it going well?"

"Yes, very well." Laura couldn't seem to catch her breath.

"How much longer will you be there? I miss you."

"Oh, we're more or less on schedule. Kitty, David just rang to let me know he's got financing for *Home Land*, so we may be here for a good while longer. In fact, I'll be sending for Robin as soon as his school is out. I'm sure Aunt Rose and Uncle Matt will have had enough of him by then."

"I spoke to Rose yesterday, and everything is fine. They're enjoying being up in London tremendously. Going about like a pair of Americans, seeing the Tower and the Abbey and God knows what all."

"I can imagine it. They really are quite remarkable. Totally unsophisticated and with such a capacity for enjoying life."

"Yes, simplicity and naiveté. We could both take a page from their book," said Kitty.

Laura had to laugh. "Oh yes. Simplicity and naiveté. Under your fine tutelage I was ruined for that long ago. And as for you! I'm sure you came out of the womb with an unerring instinct as to how to wear your nappy with chic, and which of the other toddlers in the sandbox would be the most amusing playmates."

"Right you are. By the way, Jamie thinks you should find yourself an American agent. He says David knows several."

"We're coming straight back to London after *Home Land*, so I won't be needing an agent."

"Right, darling. I'll tell him. Kisses."

"Kisses." Laura put the receiver softly back in its cradle. The palm of her hand was damp. She wished Kitty hadn't gone on and on about John.

Had she done the right thing not meeting him that morning in Acapulco? Yes, she could honestly say that she had no regrets about that. Especially now that she was involved in this film and could look forward to David's *Home Land* getting under way. Why, then, did she still think of John so often? His constant presence in her mind was like a picture she had once cut out of a fan magazine and pasted on the wall of her bedroom in Bournemouth. It was a clipping of Norma Shearer, whom she had worshiped at the time. Years later, she tried to take it off the wall but, even after rubbing it with a soapy sponge, the image still remained. That faded smiling face had become an integral part of the wall itself. And so it was with John. He would never be completely erased from her memory, but it was her work that made up the solid foundation of her life and it was David, not John, who was the integral part of that.

Royal Player was finished at the end of June, and Robin was due to arrive in Los Angeles the first week in July. Laura still had a few days of dubbing work left to do at Galaxy. Gerry Maddox left for San Francisco after the final editing, and the atmosphere had eased up at the studio. Everyone who worked with him respected Maddox tremendously, but there was a general sense that the wrap party would be a lot more relaxed without him.

Saying goodbye to the people she had worked with the last four months turned out to be much more difficult than Laura had anticipated. She had become especially close to Mandy Valentine, who was going through a painful divorce and had chosen Laura as her confidante. In a few days, Mandy would flying back to New York and Marlene Falcone returning to her villa in St. Tropez. Incurably mischievousness and outright devilish in her pranks, Marlene had been one of the main reasons the *Royal Player* set had been so much fun. The three said goodbye with tears and promises to keep in touch, although each knew that show-business friendships, while intense, were often fleeting.

Laura had also made friends among the technical crew. She knew all of them by name and often spent her breaks chatting with them. These men and women, perched on rafters, or hidden behind cameras or in makeup rooms knew only too well the real people behind the masks movie stars wore in public, and very few of them gained their admiration, let alone affection.

The last bit of dubbing was finished, and the head sound engineer held up his hand to indicate that she should wait. He came out of his booth, walked over to hers, and opened the door.

"Yes, Frank?" she said.

He took a small white box out of his pocket. "Laura, we didn't want to give you this at the wrap party because we usually don't do this kind of thing but, well . . . it's from all of us." He looked both pleased and embarrassed.

"I don't know what to say." Carefully, she opened the box. Resting on a square of white cotton was a small gold heart on a chain. Her eyes filled with tears. "Truly, Frank, I never expected . . ."

"Here, hold it up to the light."

Through a blur she saw some lines of delicate script written across the heart. Blinking away the tears, she read *Our Royal Player*. "I'll never take it off," she said.

"Laura, you're a real pro."

Coming as it did from the crew on a sound stage, she knew that this tribute, more than anything from critics or costars, was the most valued honor she could receive as an actress.

Robin arrived on schedule. The Landaus spent their son's eighth birthday at Disneyland and the rest of the week touring movie studios, Knott's Berry Farm, and playing in the surf at Malibu. Gerald and Rona Palfrey invited Laura and Robin to spend a few days at their summer house on Lake Arrowhead while David was occupied at the studio with some script changes and casting details. David and Barry Hayes were flying to Israel at the end of the month for location scouting, and Robin was going with them. While they were there, David planned to take his son on a visit to Degania, the kibbutz where Benjamin Jacobs, his headmaster at Shelbourne, had lived as a boy.

Robin was thrilled about the trip and the prospect of spending time alone with his father. During the months his parents had been away in California, he hardly missed his mother at all. Rather, he felt her absence in the same way he did certain of his favorite flowers in winter. But life at No. 12 Cranley Gardens, without his father's daily presence, was painfully empty to the heart of Robin Landau. He knew that he should not be missing his dad so much. After all, many boys his age were sent away to school. He also knew that Miss Boxhill would not like it if he behaved in a less than manly fashion. He put on a brave front except when his father telephoned, which he did every few days. He could hardly keep from crying when he heard the familiar voice and felt miserable after these transatlantic conversations. In fact, the only thing that quieted his anxiety was time spent drawing in the garden. He had taken to sketching insects and birds as well as the late-spring blooms, now flourishing in their beds. Each day, he rushed home after school and, with barely a fleeting wave to Uncle Matt and Aunt Rose, raced through the kitchen, ignoring the glass of milk and plate of biscuits left for him by Miss Boxhill, to settle down in a corner of the garden. There he sat, cross-legged on the grass, his full attention centered on a wandering beetle or the leaf of a daffodil twisting on its stem. Thus, with his sketch pad and pencils, he forgot his loneliness until Aunt Rose called him in for tea.

David, Robin, and Barry Hayes departed for Tel Aviv at the end of July, and Laura, feeling at loose ends now that *Royal Player* had wrapped, grew restless with nothing to do but shop and read novels. She was invited to dinner parties and Sunday brunches, but these occasions, without David, lacked something and, when Gerry Maddox telephoned to ask if she would like to spend some time at his home up north, she jumped at the invitation.

"We'll be properly chaperoned by my agent, who is staying with me for a few days."

"Oh, goodness, I hadn't given it a thought."

"Well, thank you very much," he laughed.

"It's just that you know David so well . . . and . . . oh, come on, Gerry, help me out of this!"

"No, miss, I'm going to let you stew in your own juices." Laura detected a note of playfulness in his voice very different from the tone she was used to hearing at the studio.

CHAPTER 18

BELVEDERE, 1962

As Gerry Maddox guided his sleek Facel Vega under the towers of the Golden Gate Bridge, Laura swung around in her seat to look back at the view. She saw a dazzling white city: houses and apartment buildings cresting its famous hills and jaunty white-capped waves speckling a bay teeming with vessels of every description. Billows of dense fog poured out of the Pacific Ocean and through the Golden Gate Bridge, traveling eastward to spread over the Berkeley hills. She gasped with delight as Gerry's car passed through the white barrier into the sunlight.

"It's like driving through a wall!"

"The Sacramento valley is scorching in summer, and hot air currents pull the fog in from the ocean. Actually, we're very lucky today. San Francisco is usually completely blanketed this time of year. July and August are terrible in the city. Of course, summer is when most of the tourists come. Imagine their shock. Suitcases full of light weight clothes with 62-degree weather and gale-force winds whipping around every corner, to say nothing of riding in half-open cable cars in sandals and short-sleeve shirts. Now, over on my side of the bay, the weather is glorious. You'll see."

They drove through a tunnel and started down the Waldo Grade.

Below, Laura could see the quaint village of Sausalito, its marinas crammed with bobbing sailboats and clusters of mismatched houseboats. They crossed a short bridge over Richardson Bay, and Gerry turned off onto Tiburon Boulevard.

"We're almost there," he said, swinging onto San Rafael Avenue.

Not since the day she first looked into the eyes of John Keith, had Laura experienced a sensation similar to the one that came over her as Belvedere

Island came into view. It was love at first sight.

They drove past a low white building with a brass sign on the door which read San Francisco Yacht Club. "We'll go there for cocktails one night. It's a great place to watch the sun go down," Gerry said as they started up a road narrow as any English country lane.

Laura caught glimpses of steep stone steps leading up to brown shingle and dark green batten-board houses, half hidden in groves of oak and eucalyptus. As they climbed higher, she noticed a lagoon far below, its shoreline edged with ultramodern houses, most of which seemed to be constructed entirely of glass.

"That used to be the town dump, but after a little boy had a bad accident sailing his El Toro out in the bay, the town council decided to fill it so the kids could sail in a safer place. When the cost of real estate in the city began going up and Marin County was still a bargain, young married couples moved here in droves. Suddenly, Belvedere became a bedroom community and the lots around the lagoon were sold off."

"Seems a shame, doesn't it?"

"The old-timers think so."

Now that they were well away from the fog, Laura rolled down her window. She was immediately aware of a pungent licorice smell wafting from feathery wild anise plants along the road and another, faintly musty, but not unpleasant scent, coming from clumps of prehistoric tree ferns. Nasturtiums, wisteria, and vivid blue morning glory trailed over stone walls, and bright orange poppies, pink-centered white daisies, and tiny blue forget-me-nots grew out of cracks in the mortar. As they passed close to a low wall, thickly coated with moss, Laura thrust her arm out of the car window and, as a child might, touched its spongy surface with her fingertips.

Up the twisting road they climbed until, at last, they were at the top of the island. Gerry swung the car into a covered carport and came to a stop next to a powder blue Thunderbird.

"We're here." He grabbed her bags out of the back seat, and they started down what seemed like a hundred narrow steps leading to the house.

"Fortunately, these stairs only go downhill," he said, laughing at the confused look on her face. "I put in an elevator contraption for the trip up. It marked me forever as a newcomer, but I notice the fourth-generation natives are happy to use it."

The house, in contrast to its older neighbors, was small and constructed in simple lines from native redwood, with several domed skylights set in the roof. Gerry led her through a sun-flooded foyer into the living room, whose walls were great sheets of glass. Through them, like a gigantic stage set, lay the city of San Francisco.

"Now you understand why I spend as little time as possible in Los Angeles," he said, obviously pleased at her reaction.

"I've never seen anything like it!"

Graceful sailboats sliced through the waves and a huge cargo vessel, sitting low in the water, moved ponderously under the bridge out into the ocean. A small fleet of fishing boats, their decks laden with crab pots, filed under the bridge, and a red and white ferry boat plowed through the water toward the Marin side of the bay. Seated in the center of all the activity was Angel Island, beautiful sister of grim little Alcatraz.

"Well, it's about time! I thought you said the plane got in at 1:20."

A man dressed in a yellow and red striped Egyptian jalabiya, emerged from the shadows of the hallway. He was as tall as Gerry but at least fifty pounds heavier, and the gown, meant to be loose and flowing, stretched tightly over his broad midsection. Thinning ash-blond hair was combed down, Julius Caesar -style, over his domed forehead. His eyes, in contrast to a deeply tanned face, were startlingly blue. As he put out his hand, Laura noticed a wide bangle bracelet clasped around his wrist and a heavy gold ring on his index finger.

"Don't mind me. I'm usually an angel of sweetness and light, but I do get a tad testy when kept waiting hours and hours on end." He shot a look at Gerry and turned back to Laura. "I'm Norm Gillis."

"How do you do." Laura shook his hand. "I'm Laura English."

"Aren't you just. Jaded as I've become playing agent to the stars, this old party's had rumbley tummy all day at the thought of meeting you."

"All right, Norman, let's get Laura settled before we get too out of control."

Ignoring the remark, Norm took Laura's canvas suitcase in one hand and her arm with the other. Suddenly, he staggered. "Christ almighty, what have you got in this thing, rocks?"

"Here, give it to me. I wouldn't want you to rip a seam on my account." She threw Norm an arch look.

"She'll do, Gerry," he called over his shoulder as they started down the stairs leading to the floor below. "She'll do just fine."

They had finished dinner and Gerry and Laura were sitting on the back deck drinking coffee, waiting for Norman to bring out dessert, a creation he claimed had taken him all morning to make.

"Norm was one of the first people I met in the movie business," Gerry said. "I was a raw kid newly arrived from Plymouth, Massachusetts, just starting in the film department at UCLA, and determined to put Andover and Princeton and the East Coast in general as far in the past as possible. Norm, who's from

Omaha, Nebraska, if you can believe it, had only been in town three or four months himself. His client list consisted of a fourteen-year-old girl from the backwoods of Tennessee, an out-of-work band leader whose only hit has been something forgettable from the thirties, and a pretty young boy of seventeen with a face like a Botticelli angel and a score card raunchier than Caligula's. Well, that little girl is Molly Gardner and the boy is Justin Hook."

"God."

"Right. Norm's good."

"What about the band leader?"

Gerry smiled "Vince Figone?"

"I am sorry, but that name is not familiar."

"He drives a cab in L.A," Gerry laughed.

"And so you two have been friends for a long time?"

"Yes. He can be a real pain in the ass, but he's probably the closest thing to family I have."

It was eight o'clock, and the summer sun was just setting. Across the bay, the western half of the city had drawn a heavy quilt of fog around its shoulders and was settling down for the night, while the eastern half, its windows stained deep rose in the twilight, was getting dressed to go out on the town. Soon all traces of the sunset would fade, and the pale blue sky would darken to cobalt, doming the city with twinkling stars. Over the bridge there were restaurants and dance floors and jazz clubs crowded with people. Yet Laura wished to be nowhere else on earth than on this deck, in this perfect place, listening to the rhythmic chirp of a band of crickets.

"Norm and I have never been lovers. I think we're both afraid of anything happening to our friendship." He paused, waiting for her to respond.

She looked over at him in the fading light. He was very handsome, but his looks had never really attracted her. She supposed this might be the reason. Perhaps it also explained why he kept so much to himself in Los Angeles.

"Gerry," she said softly, "I've always known that you are homosexual and I also know that you are a private sort of person. I see now that you are much more relaxed here than in Los Angeles. I imagine this is where your real friends are and where you feel most yourself. I'd like to get to know the Belvedere Gerry better."

He leaned over and kissed her lightly on the cheek. "Bless the terrible Glenda Fisher for bringing us together," he said softly.

"Now, feast your eyes on this, kiddies!" Norm, his bulk framed in the open sliding door, was balancing a cake plate on the outstretched palm of his hand. He threaded his way onto the deck, the plate tilting at a dangerous angle, and set it down on a small table in front of Laura. "Ten thousand calories a slice. I call it cum cake."

"Come cake? What does that mean?" asked Laura.

"What does it mean? Gerry, where did you find this person? In a Carmelite nunnery?" He plunged a long knife into the whipped cream–covered mound. "It means, you unsullied little neophyte, that there's a grinding orgasm in every bite."

Laura giggled and held out her plate. "Gerry, how long may I stay here?"

"As long as you like," answered Gerry, saluting her with a fork full of cake.

Laura did the same, and Norm raised a fork loaded with a huge glob of whipped cream and crammed into his mouth. Body rigid, eyes rolling wildly and moaning in ecstasy, his bulk collapsed into a canvas lounge chair.

Laura started to laugh and Norm, heaving himself out of the chair, turned to face her. "So, you think this cake is funny, do you?" He lisped in a falsetto "Well, let me inform you, it is not a source of merriment or an object of fun or, pardon the expression, butt of a joke. No indeed. This cake, the recipe of which was willed to me by my dear Aunt Lillian, must be given sober and mindful appreciation. Did I ever tell you about Aunt Lil? Tragic story, really. Lillian — Lester before visiting Miss Jorgensen's doctor in Copenhagen — was my mother's beloved brother who, after the operation, became my mother's beloved sister. Following the demise of her second husband, Herb, or maybe it was her third husband, Claude, yes, definitely Claude, Lil entered the facility at Santa Rita and became a beloved incarcerated sister. See, as far as Aunt Lil was concerned, the bloom had started to wear off old Claude. The coroner's report stated it was something in the cake he had eaten for dinner the night he passed over. Poor guy. He just loved that cake."

"Quit it, I'm going to pee!"

Norm stood, hands on hips, staring at her in mock horror. "Get control of yourself, woman! You're a disgrace to your profession and the British Empire! Think of what your public would say if they could see you now. Think of what the queen would say."

"Well, you should know," squealed Laura she hobbled into the house, holding her skirt around her waist.

"Impertinence!" said Norm "Go take a shower and don't return until you can behave like the Laura English we all know and love."

"Well, who would have believed it?" said Norm, settling down to eat a large piece of cake in earnest. "You'd better keep her around."

"I intend to do just that."

CHAPTER 19

"Listen, angel face," said Norm over Sunday waffles, "it's about time that over-paid staff of mine in L.A. got off their Jax pants rear ends and put in some serious hours. I'm extending the weekend into some real time off, and there's nothing I'd rather do than play with you."

So began a time of childlike freedom, the memory of which, even at the lowest points of her life, could always make Laura smile.

There was an entire day spent in Golden Gate Park, where Laura rowed Norm around Stow Lake as he lounged in the stern of what he assured her had been a lifeboat on the Titanic. In fits of giggles, she boosted his considerable derrière over the bow-shaped bridge in the Japanese Tea Garden. After catching their breath on the other side, they strolled down azalea-bordered paths, tossed coins in the lap of an enormous stone Buddha, and shared a plate of deliciously greasy almond cookies while sipping flowery jasmine tea in the pavilion overlooking the koi pond.

There was a morning in Chinatown where, in a musty smelling herb shop, Norm showed Laura a baby deer fetus floating in a bottle of mysterious pale green liquid and, later, in one of the incense-scented bazaars, he bought her an exquisite peacock blue silk Chinese banker's coat. After feasting on plum duck and glazed walnut prawns at Johnny Kan's, they strolled up Grant Avenue into North Beach, where they stopped for thimble-sized cups of espresso at a sidewalk café on Columbus Avenue and, in the stacks at City Lights, a Laura found a book for David on the German Expressionists.

On a foggy Sunday, Norm and Gerry took her to Stern Grove where, bundled in heavy jackets, they sat against the peeling trunk of a fragrant eucalyptus tree, picnicked on chicken sandwiches, and listened to the San Francisco

Symphony perform an all-Beethoven concert.

Norm drove her up and down the hills into every neighborhood. Laura was enchanted by the small jewel of a city settled by Italian, Irish, Chinese, Jewish, and Anglo-Saxon pioneers, some who came overland in covered wagons in search of gold, some by ship around the Horn in search of a new life, still others across the Pacific Ocean from China to work on the railroad. Together, they built a city that was cultured, cosmopolitan, and fiercely unconventional.

One morning, Norm appeared at the breakfast table in a gray pinstripe Brooks Brothers suit. "Get into that smart little Donald Brooks number I saw hanging in your closet. Today we're lunching on steak tartare and green goddess salad with the swells at El Prado."

As they emerged from the elegant Union Square restaurant into the glare of the sidewalk, Norm took Laura's arm. "I know I promised you Gump's third floor and we'll go, but I have to stop off and see a friend first."

"Of course. Look, you have been wonderful spending all your time with me but I know you've been neglecting things you want to do while you're here. Why don't I go shopping for an hour or so and then we can meet at Gump's afterward?"

"Shut up and follow me," he said, grabbing her hand.

They crossed Stockton Street and walked down Post to Grant Avenue, where capricious gusts of afternoon wind played with her skirt, lifting it to expose flashes of long leg and a lacy slip.

At the corner of Grant and Maiden Lane, Norm turned into a narrow building. Laura followed him into the small lobby and postage-sized elevator, which shuddered ominously as it crept upward. The expression on Norm's face started Laura giggling.

"Oh no! Not in a 4-by-4 cubicle!" he shrieked, rolling his eyes and flattening his body against the wall of the elevator.

"Don't worry, I went to the loo before we left the restaurant."

"Thank God!"

The doors opened and they were in the vestibule of a beauty salon with a familiar pink and gray color scheme. Laura turned to look at Norm. He was grinning.

"Norm, what . . ." she began.

"Darling!" A familiar voice, and then Paul Andrews, gray at the temples but looking much the same as when Laura had last seen him in London five years ago, appeared from behind a chair occupied by an extremely thin woman whose entire head was covered with small squares of tinfoil folded around tufts of hair. He took Laura in his arms and they squeezed each other in a tight hug.

"Good God, Paul, what heinous act are you performing on that poor lady!"

said Norm, staring in horror at the woman in the chair. The woman looked up at him with round, heavily mascaraed eyes.

"She's having her hair streaked, you fool," said Paul under his breath.

"Hmm . . . I don't know," said Norm, shaking his head, "looks like those little foil packets are empty." He felt one tentatively. "Are you sure the hair hasn't dissolved in there? I mean what with the chemicals they put into those dyes ..."

"Paul," rasped the woman as she half-rose out of the chair "who is this person?"

"Someone I shouldn't have allowed through the door," said Paul, throwing Norm a warning look, "but he's brought a dear friend so I'm making an exception, and if he promises act like an adult for ten minutes, I won't boot him out. Now, just read your Town & Country, Mrs. Van der Vries. I'll be back in a few minutes." He offered her a cigarette and lit it.

She held the cigarette between stiff fingers, the tips of which were lacquered brilliant magenta, and looked nervously at Norm. Her glance shifted to Laura. "Say, aren't you Laura English?"

"Yes," said Laura, smiling at the woman.

"I saw you in, oh, what was the name of it, with Malcom McLain . . . you know."

" *The Gift.*"

" *The Gift!* Yes, that's the one. I saw it on television just the other night. Absolutely loved it. English movies are so much more real than American ones, if you know what I mean. I think it's because they're mostly in black and white. But with that hair, you should really be in Technicolor."

"Thank you," said Laura.

"Actually," broke in Norm, "Miss English is here to get her hair dyed a new color."

"Really?" said the woman. "Oh, I don't think you ought to do that."

"Yes, she's going chestnut brown with blond streaks. I told her that sometimes the hair breaks off in those little foil wrappers but she's determined to ..."

Paul, steering Norm away with one hand and taking Laura's arm with the other, said "Come on, darling, let's go into my office."

"Good luck, Mrs. Van der Vries," Norm called over his shoulder.

"How do you two know each other?" asked Laura as Paul led them to the back of the salon.

"Mr. Andrews makes it his business to meet every fascinating man who blows into town," said Norm, casting his eyes in the direction of Paul's small, shapely bottom.

"I met him in Los Angeles when I first came over from London," said Paul, ushering them into a comfortable room. "I've forgotten exactly. Where was it, Norm?"

"The men's room on the sixteenth floor of the Wiltshire Towers."

"Witty, very witty." He turned to Laura. "My God, how long has it been?" He ran his hand through her hair. "Who the hell has been hack . . . I mean styling your hair?"

"Charlie Blair at Galaxy."

"Hmm . . . I hear you have a smash of a picture coming out."

"I don't know. It's hard to tell."

"How is Kitty?"

"I spoke to her about a month ago. She's fine. David is in Israel with our son, scouting locations for a film he'll be making there, and I'm unemployed at the moment. Gerry Maddox very kindly invited me to Belvedere for a few days, but I'm afraid I've outstayed my welcome by a week. I have to go back soon before I'm tossed out."

"Are you kidding?" said Norm "He loves you. In fact if you weren't married, he'd probably propose." Laura laughed. "Oh, you think just because he's queer he wouldn't? You'd be surprised how many gentlemen of my acquaintance are married. You know, my sweet, loving and fucking are two very different things."

"My, my," said Paul, "our Norman has become quite the philosopher since he turned forty. How do you like San Francisco, Laura?"

"It's the most livable city I have ever seen, and I adore Belvedere."

"Well then, why don't you buy something there?" asked Paul casually.

"Because London is home," she answered.

"Why can't you have two homes? Most film stars do, you know."

"I am not a film star. I am an actress, little known outside Britain."

"Sweetie," broke in Norm, "don't forget our Mrs. Van der Vries. You're just as well known here as in England, and once *Royal Player* is released you'll be famous. Paul's right. If you like it here, buy yourself a house. Face it, my darling, you are going to be making a lot of movies in the States from now on, and when you're over here you might as well live in a place you like. After all, what good is fame and money if it isn't to satisfy your heart's desire?"

She looked from one to the other. "What do you think, Paul?"

"I think for once Norm's making sense."

Three days later, Gerry and Laura passed through an arbor, wreathed in purple wisteria, and made their way down a shaded path formed of flat moss-edged stones. The house was built of batten-board redwood, which age had weathered to a soft gray. Two dormer windows, hung with planter boxes overflowing with pink petunias, were tucked under the eaves of the shingled roof. The garden was planted in snapdragons, foxgloves, and old-fashioned pale yellow roses. It was like a bit of England hidden away in California. The only jarring note was the red and white real estate sign planted in a border of mauve and yellow pansies.

The front door was open, and they walked into an empty foyer, their footsteps unnaturally loud on the bare planks of dark flooring. The foyer led to a richly paneled room with a vaulted ceiling and large bay windows, through which could be seen a copy of Gerry's own view. At the opposite end of the room were massive double doors opening into the dining room. Here, the walls were covered in dull gold paper with a Chinese motif of delicately tinted flowers and birds.

Gerry smiled at the delighted expression on her face. "Want to see the rest of the house?"

"Oh yes, please!"

Upstairs were three bedrooms. The two on the front side of the house were those with the dormers and window boxes. On the other side of the house, the large master bedroom faced southeast and had a sweeping view of the bay. Laura stood at the window and looked down into the back garden. It was greatly overgrown with tall stalks of weeds choking out perennials and thick blackberry bushes tumbling over the low stone wall.

"What a mess," said Gerry, coming up behind her. I guess the real estate people have been tending the front garden only. My man Ito could clean it up and replant it."

"What's that?" said Laura, her eyes fastened on something in the corner of the garden.

"What's what?" said Gerry trying to follow the direction of her glance.

"That . . . over there . . . I don't believe it!" She ran out of the room and down the stairs. A moment later he saw her below in the garden standing over something. She looked up smiling, beckoning him to come down.

"Look," she said. Covered in moss and trailing vines was a wishing well.

Gerry smiled. "I haven't seen one of these since childhood summers at Grandfather's house in Nantucket."

"According to folklore, or so says my Uncle Matthew, you are supposed to put both your hands into the water up to your wrists, then close your eyes and make a wish. Then you must scoop a little water in each hand and drink it. Imagine having a wishing well of one's own!"

He looked down into the well. "It's dry."

"Well, we'll just have to get your Mr. Ito to fill it."

The expression Gerry Maddox saw on Laura's face as she stood in the overgrown garden was one he had tried for years after to capture on film and never could.

Laura, Norm, and Gerry sat up talking until two the next morning, at which time she put in a call to her banker in London. The following afternoon, the house on Beach Road was hers.

CHAPTER 20

LOS ANGELES, 1962

The plane had reached its cruising altitude and was leveling off. David sat staring at the *No Smoking* sign. The moment it went dark, he lit a cigarette. "Well, Robin, we're off to Los Angeles." He looked down and ran his hand over the thick blond curls. "It's a haircut for both of us when we get back."

"Dad."

"Yes."

"Would you ever want to live in Israel?"

"No, not really. It's a fascinating place to visit, and as a Jew, I'm glad it exists, but I'm afraid I'm much too soft to live away from my comforts."

"Dad."

"Hmm?"

"I could someday."

"What? Live in Israel?" He smiled at his son.

"Yes. I liked it there. Especially the kibbutz."

"Did you?" he asked, surprised. "I would have thought it a bit Spartan for a boy used to life in South Kensington." He coughed and put out his cigarette.

"Did you see the drawings and paintings hanging on the walls? The boys and girls who live there did them."

"I didn't know you were that interested in art."

"I'm going to be an artist when I grow up."

"Are you?"

"Yes, I am. When you were away I did a lot of drawings, mostly of things in the garden. I'll show you when we get home."

"I'd like to see them very much." David lit another cigarette, inhaled and coughed. "This damn air conditioning." He looked toward the vents in the overhead panel. "Robin, I'm really pleased about the drawing." He smiled to himself. His son was growing up.

"When will you start filming, Dad?"

"Well, we'll probably begin shooting interiors in a month. We have a bit more work to do on the script. Did you know that Uncle Jasper's going to come over in a few weeks?"

Robin nodded. "But when will you be filming in Israel?"

"Oh, not until September."

"Unfair! I'll be back at St. Paul's."

"Robin, I know it's hard for you to be in London when we are here in California."

"Yes, I know, Dad. I missed you very much while you were gone, but after seeing those kids on the kibbutz I felt ashamed of the way I acted while you were gone."

"What do you mean?"

"Well," he paused for a moment "sometimes I used to cry after I talked to you on the telephone."

"Oh, my boy, I am so sorry. I hope that we won't have to be separated for so long this time."

"No, the thing is that I think it will be better this time when I go back. I want to be strong like the kibbutzniks are."

"I'm sure you will be, Robin." He turned away for a moment, to look out of the window and brush away the tears that had filled his eyes.

"You've what?"

"Bought a house."

"You mean just now . . . when we were away?" David burst out laughing. "I let you out of my sight for a few weeks and you buy a house! Where is it?"

"In Belvedere."

"Where Gerry Maddox lives?"

"Yes. David, Belvedere is the most beautiful place. An island like a little bit of England with the most glorious weather, and the house . . .overlooking the water . . . I just couldn't resist it. My check from *Royal Player* more than covered the cost. I know you'll love it when you see it."

"You bought it with the money from *Royal Player*?

"Yes," she said, smiling.

"Darling, you didn't need to do that. If you love it that much I would have bought it for you. You know there isn't anything in this world I wouldn't do for you." He took her in his arms, but as he was about to put his lips on hers he started coughing. He broke away and took a handkerchief out of his pocket.

"Did you catch something in Israel?" she asked.

"Oh, it's nothing," he said, smoothing the frown between her eyes with the tip of his finger. "Probably the air conditioning on the plane. So, when do Robin and I get to see this dream house?"

"What is your schedule like?"

"I called a meeting at the studio for Monday. Then I thought I'd give myself a few days to get over the jet lag and have some time with you. We could fly up to San Francisco in a couple of weeks." He put the handkerchief to his mouth and coughed.

"All right. If that cold hasn't developed into pneumonia." She took his hand and led him into the bedroom. "I'm so glad you're back."

"Hey, I may be contagious."

"I'll risk it," she said

"Okay. Let me just wash my face first." He went into the bathroom and turned on the light. As another paroxysm of coughing caught him, he bent over the sink. There was blood-streaked phlegm in the basin. Slowly he took the wadded-up handkerchief out of his pocket. It was covered with red stains.

Jasper Quigly arrived in Hollywood at the end of August. As Laura predicted, he was enjoying his bungalow at the Bel Air Hotel and didn't mind at all that his part in the film was a small one. He had two days' work at the studio and was staying on another week to give his friends, who comprised the exclusive British colony in Beverly Hills, a chance to outdo one another with lavish entertainments in his honor.

"At my age, dear boy," he told David at the Palfrey's party, "one takes what one can get and is glad of it."

"I wouldn't say you've exactly been on the shelf these last few years," said David. "After all, directing and acting in Lear at the National was no small job. And I seem to recall there was a film squeezed in between performances."

"Yes, all very well, but what about next year? Nothing at all on the horizon. No, dear David, your Lord Balfour was truly a kindness to an old man."

David laughed. "Here's the man with our drinks, and let's have some more of these delicious fish eggs."

"Thank you, I don't mind if I do. You know I was quite friendly with Gerald Palfrey when he was at Rank. Such an amusing fellow. Why do all these chaps come over here?"

"For this, I suppose." said David, indicating the luxurious surroundings.

"Oh, heavens, no. Gerald married an heiress. Rona was the only child of some peer or other, Bradford or someone. Oh yes, she had plenty."

"Maybe it was for the sunshine."

"Hmm . . . I can't see it myself. Filthy weather and all, I'll take dear old London any day over this penny arcade. Ah, here comes your darling girl."

Laura advanced toward them, her face lit up in a way David hadn't seen since the completion of *Royal Player*.

She's only really happy when she's working and the Belvedere house is a godsend until a new project comes along. She and Jasper. No matter how many films they've done, they'll always worry there won't be a next one.

David knew that Norm Gillis had just negotiated the rights to a property Gerry Maddox wanted for Laura. Now that she had signed on with Gillis as her representative in the United States, he had a feeling that more offers were going to come in. That meant they would probably be living most of the time in California. It was good that Laura had found the Belvedere house. He had to admit he liked the place. Gerry told him that many writers and artists lived in the area. They could have a interesting circle of friends, but in his heart, he felt much the same way as Jasper Quigly — filthy weather and all, he, too, would take dear old London.

David was in Israel for almost the entire month of September and Laura used the time to work on the house. July had been spent repairing decks and staircases, and August plastering ceilings and painting walls. Now the workmen were gone, and the house stood waiting. Using all she had learned from Kitty Paxton, Laura chose furniture, fabrics, and fixtures that combined elegance with comfort. She worked for hours with Gerry Maddox's gardener, Mr. Ito, to create a garden of subtle color, delicate fragrance, and peaceful serenity. Lawn chairs were placed in the shady spots, and a hammock was strung between the branches of two oak trees. The well was filled.

Laura met David back in Los Angeles at the end of the month. Filming on *Home Land* was completed and it was ready for editing. David spent every day at the studio going over each frame of film. Laura was worried about the long hours he spent in the editing room and made him promise to take a good rest before starting anything new. David was still plagued with the cough he had picked up in Israel during the summer. Dark smudges ringed his eyes, and he looked even thinner than usual.

In the middle of October, Gerry Maddox sent Laura the script, adapted from the book he had optioned especially for her. It was a mystery in which she would play a dual role. She took the thick blue-bound pages to bed with her and read through the night. At eight o'clock the next morning, she dialed Gerry's number in Belvedere, where he was spending the weekend.

"How's my house?"

"I walked by last evening. Everything looked great from the outside. When are you coming up?"

"As soon as David is done with the final editing. I don't like to leave him just now. He's got such a killing schedule these days, and I'm afraid the only food he eats is what I force down him. He swore to me he'd take a rest after the editing on *Home Land* is finished. We'll come up then."

"Did you have a chance to read any of *Mirror Image*?"

"I read it straight through last night. I couldn't put it down."

"So you liked it."

"Very much."

"You'll do it, then."

As she had in the small hours of the morning, she thought of the challenge this film offered. It was an opportunity to reach far down inside herself and see what she was really capable of as an actress. She thought of the thousands of miles that separated California from England. She thought of Briarwood and Jamie Paxton, of Kitty and how much she missed her, of Rose and Matthew and Uncle Bertie, growing older and only a day away by train from London. She thought of Robin.

"Laura?" said Maddox. "Are you still there?"

"Yes."

"Well, what did you decide?"

"Of course I'll do it. Did you think for a minute I would say no?"

CHAPTER 21

BELVEDERE, 1963

BRITISH STAR WINS TOP AWARD

Hollywood newcomer Laura English took top honors as Best Actress of 1962 at last night's twenty-sixth annual Academy Awards presentation. Miss English, formerly under contract to star-maker Sir James Paxton, won the coveted Oscar for her performance in the Gerry Maddox film Mirror Image. Miss English's husband, director David Landau, unable to attend the Oscar ceremony due to his recent hospitalization for lung surgery, watched the festivities on television from the Landaus' Northern California retreat near San Francisco.

Miss English achieved instant superstar status last year with her American film debut as Nell Gwyn in Maddox's Royal Player.

"Mr. Landau, I thought you were taking your nap. Now, put those papers away and lie down. Are you in pain?

David shook his head.

"All right, but if you experience any discomfort your medication is right here on the table by your bed. Now, please try to sleep for awhile before I bring your dinner. You were up much too late last night."

Miss Wallace reminded David of the starched nurse who had taken him to see Robin at Middlesex Hospital so many years ago. The same gray crepe paper complexion, the same unyielding line of a mouth. She even wore the identical steel-rimmed glasses. He lay back and closed his eyes, not because he felt like sleeping but so Miss Wallace would go away and leave him alone. He heard her fold some newspapers and pick up an empty glass from the night stand. At last, the door shut behind her. He opened his eyes. He didn't feel in the least bit tired. On the contrary. Half a lung out, and he felt he could run a mile. He smiled. Well, maybe not quite a mile. Dr. Marcus had warned him to expect periods of fatigue during the slow healing process, and although he had walked the halls of Stanford Medical Center every day after the operation, the car trip home to Belvedere and the switch from hospital to home care had sapped much of his strength.

David reached for the newspaper Miss Wallace had placed in the magazine rack by the bed. He opened the folded sheets. There was Laura's face smiling out at him beneath the headline. He grinned back at her. "Congratulations, darling."

In playing two complex characters, Charlotte and Felice, Laura had placed demands on herself as never before. In the role of Nell Gwyn, Laura was basically playing herself, and the audience adored her. In *Mirror Image* she portrayed two women, one ruthless and the other mad — neither very appealing. It had been a tremendous risk to take. If the audience didn't believe her performance, she might have been finished as an actress, at least in the States. The film was shot in black and white with two sets, very few costume changes, and a cast of five actors. Gerry Maddox drove them like a madman. They worked days, nights, and weekends in order to keep the momentum at fever pitch. The film was finished in twenty-one days, and when it was over Laura was in a state of aggravated exhaustion.

After the final dubbing, the Landaus flew to San Francisco, rented a car at the airport, and drove directly to Belvedere where, twelve hours of uninterrupted sleep and a walk around the island, improved Laura's state of mind miraculously.

The stay in Belvedere lasted only long enough for Laura to regain her energy and, after a week of relaxation, they went home to London. It seemed strange to feel bitter cold weather again after the mild California climate. They dined a few times with the Paxtons and other old friends, but David insisted they spend most of their evenings at home with Robin. The week before Christmas, they packed up the car and drove down to Bournemouth to spend the holiday with Matthew, Rose, and Bertie. Laura brought gifts from San Francisco for all the family: a luxurious cashmere coat from Ransahoff's for Aunt Rose, a paisley silk robe from Bullock & Jones for Uncle Matthew, and a set of Chinese prints from Gump's for Uncle Bertie. She and David had shopped for Robin's presents in London, but David brought him a box of forty-eight colored pencils and some drawing pads from Flax art supply store, so that he would have something from San Francisco as well.

A few days after Christmas, they returned to London to attend the Paxtons' New Year's Eve party, but David's cough, which he had not entirely shaken since summer, was worse and he had a slight fever. They decided, in the end, to celebrate in front of the fireplace at No. 12 Cranley Gardens.

David promised Laura that if his cough was not better in a few days he would see Danny Sullivan. It persisted through the first weeks of the new year, but David procrastinated and it actually eased off a bit for the rest of the month. It returned in February, and finally, David made the appointment.

Dr. Sullivan gave him a thorough examination, including a series of X-rays and a tuberculosis patch test. He sent David down the street to a lab where samples of blood, urine, and sputum were taken. Dr. Sullivan told him to ring the office if a rash appeared on the T.B. test area and said that he would telephone with the results of the X-rays and other tests as soon as they were back. In the meantime, he put him on an antibiotic, reasoning that if it was an infection it would be better to start fighting it as soon as possible. Two days later, Dr. Sullivan's nurse called, asking David to come in and see the doctor the following day. He didn't sleep much that night and left the house early so Laura wouldn't seeing him pacing until it was time to leave for his appointment.

David couldn't quite decipher the look on Danny Sullivan's face as he sat opposite him across the untidy desk, but it was an expression that made his sweat glands react.

"There's a spot on the upper quadrant of your right lung, David," he said at last.

"What does that mean, T.B?"

"No. You had no reaction to the test."

Automatically, David looked down at the inside of his wrist.

"I sent your pictures over to Ron Horsley. He's the foremost pulmonary man in the city. Unfortunately, he confirmed my suspicions."

A sickening cramp gripped David's stomach and a new burst of perspiration beaded his forehead. "What suspicions?" His voice was barely audible.

"There is a mass, a tumor, in your lung that must be removed as soon as possible."

"Are you sure?" asked David.

"Yes, we are. Your sputum tests contained cancer cells. There is no doubt."

"And if . . . when I have it out . . . will that be the end of it? I mean will I be well again?"

"If we get it all and it hasn't spread, then the prognosis should be very good."

"What if . . . it has spread?" He could hardly frame the words.

"Well, let's cross that bridge when we come to it. For now, we must make arrangements for your hospitalization. Horsley suggested Donald Frasier do the surgery, but I have a different proposal to put to you."

"Yes?"

"The top man in the field is in the States, at Stanford University. His name is Sheldon Marcus. Laura tells me you bought a house in California, on the Tiburon peninsula, is that right?"

"Yes."

"I looked at a map of California in my atlas, and your house is about forty miles from the hospital. My recommendation is that you go to Stanford for the surgery."

"This man is good?"

"The best."

"All right, then. Only you said that the operation should be done as soon as possible. What if this Dr. Marcus is not available right away?"

"He is available."

"How do you know?"

"Because I called him as soon as I got off the phone from Horsley. You're scheduled for surgery on March first."

David bowed his head. "Thank you," he said in a low voice. "But March first! That's only two weeks away." How am I going to tell Laura?

As if reading his thoughts, Sullivan said, "Would you like me to speak to Laura? Sometimes it's easier to have a medical man explain things. That way all the questions are answered on the spot."

"Yes, I think that would be best."

"Good, I'll ring her when you go, and David, don't worry about her. She's a strong girl. She'll be fine."

"Danny."

"Yes,"

"What are my chances?"

"If I knew I would tell you, but I honestly can't. You must just take things one at a time. The surgery first. Then your recovery. Try to focus on those two things and let the rest take care of itself."

A sudden sob broke from David's throat. "I don't want to die, Danny."

Sullivan came around the desk and put his hand on David's shoulder. "Have faith, man. This is 1963. Great strides have been made in the field. That is why I want you to go to Stanford, where they are up to the latest."

"You must think me a bloody awful coward, but you see, it's not the idea of death I mind. It's the thought of losing Laura and my boy."

"Yes. I know. If they were mine, I'd fight like hell before I'd let them go. And that's what you must do. Fight."

Laura sat listening to the steady hum of the airplane engine and thought of David. She had not wanted to leave him even for a day to go to down to Los Angeles for the Academy Awards. On the off chance she should win, Gerry Maddox could have appeared for her, but David had insisted she go.

The picture swept the Oscars. Gerry Maddox won for best direction, John Evans for his script, Bernie Frankel for editing, Bart Mitchell for best supporting actor — and Laura English for best actress. They all had their little gold men, which they would display with pride on mantelpieces or in pretended nonchalance as a doorstop. She looked down at the statue clutched in her hand. Indeed, she hadn't let go of it since Maximilian Schell put it into her outstretched hands two hours before. Did she deserve it? For once, she couldn't be objective about her work. This time she had been too involved, too utterly submerged, to make an objective evaluation of her performance. Since they had given it to her, she supposed she did deserve it. She would leave it at that.

Again, her thoughts turned to David. She had spoken to him briefly on the telephone following the ceremonies, but with a boisterous crowd surrounding her, she couldn't hear much. She needed to get home, to see him and hold him. To make sure he was, as she had left him, on the mend.

The mass in his lung had turned out to be a carcinoid tumor, a very slow-growing variety. Laura was told that carcinoids rarely metastasize, and once David's was surgically removed, that should be the end of it. The recovery was usually slow and would probably involve some discomfort. Laura loved the way doctors always euphemized the word pain, but the prognosis was excellent. The operation was performed, as scheduled, on March first. She stayed in a motel near the hospital for the first week in order to spend as much time as possible stationed outside the ICU. Laura was shocked at the way David looked after his surgery, but she soon got used to the tubes that sprouted from all parts of his body and the constant bleep of the monitoring equipment at the head of his bed. The first two days, he seemed to exist by the grace of the machine that breathed for him and the drops of nourishment that flowed, by means of plastic tubing, into his veins. On the third day, she arrived to find he had been transferred to a private room and most of the paraphernalia had been removed. He looked almost human again. As she bent to kiss him, she saw there was a hint of color in his face and his skin had lost its dryness. He opened his eyes and smiled. From that moment, she felt confident that it was only a matter of time.

She lived her days by rote. Each morning, she drove over the Golden Gate Bridge, through the city, and down Highway 101 to Stanford, and each evening she drove up Highway 101, through the city, and over the Golden Gate

Bridge home. The hours she spent at the hospital were a blur. Years later, she came upon two large squares of needlepoint on the top shelf of her closet and remembered that she had done them during those endless days at Stanford.

Laura soon discovered that famous university hospitals are grim places of life and death. Patients, critically ill or afflicted with rare diseases, are there to be treated with the newest equipment and latest drugs. Families are not catered to. There were no cheerfully decorated lounges equipped with stacks of magazines and television sets, no convivial nurses' station dispensing reassurance and moral support. Laura found temporary escape from the sights and smells of the sickroom only in the crowded hallways, where orderlies, pushing gurneys or rattling carts, threw her annoyed glances as they careened by. The only other refuge was the steamy basement cafeteria, where the pervading odor of overcooked vegetables suppressed any desire to linger over a second cup of coffee. Laura became familiar with the other daily visitors who, like herself, patrolled the passageways in search of some undiscovered sanctuary. Their faces, drawn with sleeplessness or stiff with anxiety, resembled her own. Rarely did anyone attempt conversation. She tried her best to focus solely on David's recovery, but without a new project in the offing, she felt like a rudderless ship stuck in the doldrums.

David slept most of the first week, awaking only to take his meals. She sat with him, making lame jokes about the food and holding his hand after he had eaten, until he fell, once again, into an exhausted sleep. The second week he sat up on the edge of his bed, walked to the bathroom, and took showers. These activities tired him tremendously, and he slept for long intervals afterward, while Laura worked on her needlepoint. When he was awake, she read to him or they watched movies on the television set, fixed high on the wall opposite his bed. In a weak voice, he pointed out the flaws in direction and told her how he would have handled the scene differently. By the third week, Laura realized David was getting his strength back as he took longer walks down the corridors outside his room and complained about the food, the noise, and the nurses. They celebrated with cups of tea and sugary hospital cookies on the day Dr. Marcus told them David could go home the following week.

For the first time in almost a month, Laura allowed herself to think about the scripts she knew had been piling up in Norm's Los Angeles office since the Academy Award nominations were announced. She promised herself she would call Norm the day she brought David home to Belvedere.

He came home a month to the day of his surgery. The Academy Awards presentation was the following Monday evening. Gerry Maddox had made plans to escort Laura to the ceremonies but she called him on Sunday night, while David was showering, to say she would not be coming to Los Angeles.

"Gerry, I don't want to leave David. I had no idea he would be this weak. The trip home took a lot out of him, and I know he is in pain. The nurse is a real horror. She scares me to death. I simply can't leave David alone with her."

"You know, flights run every hour between L.A. and San Francisco. You can take an early-afternoon plane and leave right after the ceremonies."

"No, I want to stay in Belvedere. David and I will cheer you on from here. Besides, he's probably feeling depressed about *Home Land*, and that's another reason I don't want him to be alone."

"All right, what do you want me to say for you?"

"Oh, come on, Gerry. You don't really think I have the slimmest hope of winning do you? I was astonished at the nomination and very grateful, but Mary Tremane is sure to get it this year. Maybe another time for me. If I ever get another film like *Mirror Image*, that is."

"Well, just in case, I'm going to prepare something to say and I'll call you when it's over."

"Yes, do that." She hung up the phone and turned to see David standing framed in the bathroom door behind her. A bath sheet was draped around his waist, and large beads of perspiration stood out on his forehead. Slowly, he made his way to the bed and sat down. The livid scar left by his operation was etched with ghastly clarity into the skin of his back and side like a tight strap.

"I'm well enough for you to go."

"No, David. I really don't want to. It's a waste of time. I have no chance of winning, and I truly don't want to leave you."

"Afraid I'll make a pass at the lovely Miss Wallace?" he said with a wan smile.

"David, let's not argue about it."

"Right, we won't. You are going and there's an end to it. Now ring Gerry and tell him to meet the 3:40 plane tomorrow."

She stood staring at him.

"Do it."

She picked up the receiver and dialed the number. "Gerry, it's me. I guess I'm coming after all."

David, his head resting against the pillows, was smiling.

The plane's pitch altered and Laura looked out the window. Darkness. She hoped David didn't mind too much about the Oscar. He had sounded very pleased on the telephone. But of course he must mind, with *Mirror Image* such a success and *Home Land* a disastrous flop. How had that happened? It was such a beautiful film. Maybe a touch too long and a trifle . . . there was no other word for it . . . preachy. Ashamed of her disloyalty to David, she shifted in her seat. The public just wasn't in the mood for such a sober film. That could very well explain it. But *Mirror Image* was nothing if not sober. Again, she looked down at the Oscar cradled in her lap. Oh, well, he'll get over it in time. What he needs is another project to focus on and he'll begin to think of *Home Land* as a noble effort that simply didn't come off. If only he hadn't invested so many years in it. If only he could start on something new right away.

She felt the plane losing altitude and strained her neck to see out of the small, pitted window. She remembered that the approach into San Francisco was made over water at the southern end of the bay, and she would see nothing until they were almost on the ground. The descent seemed interminable. At last, a pathway of lights appeared, and they touched down. As soon as the doors of the plane opened, Laura, with no luggage and dressed in a floor-length evening gown and fox jacket, ran up the ramp through the airport terminal and out into the chilly April night. She raised her hand to call the first taxi that stood in line outside the airport. The cab screeched to a halt in front of her, and the driver got out and came around to open the door. She noticed him looking at her strangely, but it wasn't until they were barreling up Highway 101 that Laura realized it wasn't only her outfit. The hand she raised to hail him was clasped around the gleaming golden statuette.

CHAPTER 22

Spring in Belvedere started out cold and wet. David spent the days quietly ensconced in the living room, reading in front of the fire or working on a gigantic jigsaw puzzle of the Bayeux Tapestry spread out on a table by the window. Sometimes, Laura came upon him ignoring the brightly colored pieces as he starred at the raindrops spilling down the glass, an unreadable look on his face. For the first time in their life together, he was not sharing his thoughts with her. She knew he was depressed, not only about his illness but also the devastating failure of *Home Land*. What he needed was work. She wanted to talk to him about taking on a new project, but the time never seemed right. She was becoming depressed herself as the days drifted by in idleness. Work was her life's blood, and she desperately needed a transfusion.

By the end of April, the skies finally cleared and they were able to spend time out of doors. A few days of sunshine brought out all the wildflowers along the roadside. Tightly folded buds on sycamore and plane trees suddenly burst, freeing tiny leaves of tender green. Overnight, branches of plum and cherry trees were laden with blossoms, delicate as crepe paper. Songbirds, mad with joy at the arrival of spring, set up a racket in the garden. David fed on the sun and fresh air. He and Laura began taking short walks, first around Belvedere Island, then as his stamina grew, to neighboring Corinthian Island and into the town of Tiburon.

It was a glorious afternoon in mid-May. They strolled hand in hand along the breakwater, pausing to watch the gulls wheel and swoop over the narrow strip of gritty beach. Spider crabs popped in and out of tiny holes along the shoreline, and sandpipers picked their way cautiously over the coarse grains, stopping every so often to insert their long, delicate beaks into the sand. The whole bay was alive with activity. Trim sailboats cut neatly through the waves, and ferries chugged back and forth from Angel Island to the Tiburon dock.

David squinted out across the water, enjoying the scene. Bending to pick up a flat stone, he said, "I think I could easily become a beach bum." He brushed the sand from the surface of the stone and took a deep breath, which now caused him only slight discomfort. "Just smell that air. Seaweed and sun! San Francisco Bay with just the slightest trace of diesel oil."

She smiled up at him and squeezed his hand. "I'm glad you're feeling so much better. Dr. Marcus told me you are progressing so well that by autumn you should be able to start working again."

"Hmm." He polished the stone against his pant leg.

"David?"

"Yes."

"Gerry says he has a couple of very good scripts he wants you to look at. And you know that Phil Simon from Paramount has called several times."

He held the stone in the palm of his hand, turning it over and examining it intently. "I'm really not thinking of another project right now. I just want to experience each day I have in this beautiful place" he turned to face her. "and, most of all, every minute I have with you. Life is so damn precious, and it can be stolen from you so quickly by some insidious disease or a plane crash or in a split second by a terrorist. Did you see the *Chronicle* this morning? Ali Ibn Haziz was killed by a car bomb outside the American Embassy in Paris."

"Yes, I saw," she responded. "Evidently, his chauffeur and an aide were blown away with him."

"He was in Paris for meetings with Peter McCall." He shook his head and skipped the stone out over the water. "The tragedy is that he was the last of a few progressive Jordanians trying to pressure King Hussein into working something out with Israel. But now that they've all been eliminated, I'm afraid the chances of that happening are nil. Hussein will be more wary than ever. I doubt there will ever be peace in that part of the world."

The set of David's jaw made her uneasy. "Look, darling," she said softly. "I know how you must feel about *Home Land*, but the best way to get over it is to get involved with something new. Thank God the tumor was contained and they got it all. Now we must put it behind us and get on with our lives."

"I know I've been in a bloody funk since the surgery and it's been no picnic for you, but when you come so close to losing everything it rather reshuffles the deck. I guess I need to wallow in the doldrums for awhile." He smiled and his jaw softened. "Look, filmmaking was what I decided to do with my life, and *Home Land* aside, I've never regretted that choice. It's just that these days it's not my top priority. Since I got the news that I wasn't immortal, I've had a lot of time to think, and I realize now that I probably would have been just as happy as a writer or a Cambridge don . . . or a rabbi." For an instant his eyes twinkled in the old way. "I guess I've come to terms with what's most important in my life. When I was first diagnosed, I had to face the reality of maybe not making it. Always, the worst was losing the people I love. You and Robin most of all, and Jamie and Barry Hayes. You see what I mean, don't you?" He squinted toward the city. The streets laid out in grids against the hills were sharply defined in the clear air. "Laura, I know that you are only really alive when you are performing. It's always been the best part of your life. But you must understand that right now the best part of my life is simply the living of it." He looked down at her. His face perfectly calm.

She listened to his words, each phrase leaving behind a residue of dread in her heart. David was the one person who, on a deep level, understood what performing meant to someone like her. He understood that expressing her art took precedence over everything else and understood that her dedication to that art often excluded all else, yet he loved and approved of her in spite of, or perhaps because of it. Throughout the long period of his convalescence, she had endured his complaints and silences, realizing it was a normal part of the process, but this new attitude chilled her. She had always taken it for granted that their life, working in films, would never change. It was the foundation of all they had built together. Without it would everything come tumbling down?

A fresh gust of wind blew in from the bay, whipping the sails of the sleek boats. *No matter what he says, he's still depressed over Home Land. It was his first failure and now he's afraid to try again. What he needs is a new project.* She looked out across the water and up at the puffy clouds that scudded along the sky. *Who am I kidding? I'm the one who needs a new project.* Her mind turned to the script sitting on her bureau, and she wondered how much longer Norm could stall Paramount before they offered the part to someone else.

David spent most of 1963 wandering around San Francisco. He was drawn to the North Beach section of the city, where he spent mornings browsing through the dusty shelves at City Lights bookstore and afternoons drinking espresso and discussing philosophy with the denizens of Enrico's Sidewalk Café, who, like David, seemed to have no set schedule to their lives. He played pickup games of chess at Vesuvio's Coffee House and watched grizzled Italians at their daily bocce ball games in Washington Square. He went to the Chinese movies at the Pagoda on Columbus Avenue. He argued politics with vagrants who fished for shiners off the pier at Aquatic Park. He enrolled in Dorr Bothwell's design class at the Art Institute and deepened his knowledge of color and space. He reread Kafka and Camus and the plays of Samuel Beckett.

He grew a beard.

Laura went back to work. She made two films for Galaxy: an adaptation of Arthur Miller's *The Crucible*, and *Fog*, a mystery shot in Carmel, a small seaside village on the Monterey Peninsula. During the filming of *The Crucible*, Gerald and Rona Palfrey invited the Landaus to stay with them in Malibu instead going back to the Westwood apartment. Laura accepted with alacrity, thinking David would enjoy a summer at the beach. Instead, he flew to London in order to spend the time with Robin during his school holiday.

The separation made Laura uneasy, but she could hardly expect David to remain with her. He was, after all, going to be with their son. Guilt pricked at her conscience because David was home with Robin, hearing his news, listening to his concerns, appraising his drawings, and driving down to Bournemouth for a few days with the Stokeses. To top it off, David's sister, Camilla, and her husband, Peter MacDonald, invited David and Robin to join their family at their shooting lodge on the river Spey in the Scottish Highlands for the last two weeks of the boy's long vacation.

And all that summer, Laura made movies.

She told herself that it wasn't her fault if filming on both projects happened to take place during Robin's long vacation. She would have been a fool to pass up either part. Robin's birthday slipped her mind, because it fell on a day they shot a particularly difficult scene on *The Crucible* set. By the time she was able to get to a phone, it was well past midnight in London.

"I bought him a gift from you," said David. "A camera. He's so keen on sketching, I thought he could take photographs of subjects he might like to draw later on." Was David's voice a little stilted, or was it her imagination?

"Thank you," she said. "How are you feeling?"

"Fine. I saw Danny Sullivan, and he pronounced me fit. How is everything there?"

"Going very well. We should be finished in another few weeks." She paused for a few seconds. "Why don't you bring Robin back with you? He could have a month in Belvedere before going back to St. Paul's."

"Camilla and Peter have invited Robin and me to Scotland, and he's counting the days. It's better for him to be with the MacDonald's and their brood than over there where he really doesn't have any friends."

"Yes, you're right. How thoughtful of Camilla and Peter. How are they?"

"Very well."

"Give them my love when you see them. And, David, explain to Robin about my not calling. And tell him I love him."

"I already have."

"Good." Again she paused, expecting David to ask how the work was progressing on her film. The pause grew longer. "David, I miss you."

"I miss you, too."

All at once she felt terribly lonely. "David, tell me you understand about my staying here all summer."

"I understand everything. Always have and always will."

On the trip to Scotland, ten-year-old Robin, who had never held a gun, amazed the party with his marksmanship, bringing down more birds than many of the guests who had been shooting most of their lives. From the fine detail of his drawings, David realized that Robin had a keen eye, but he was astounded by the boy's prowess with a gun and somewhat disturbed at his lack of emotion when the dogs retrieved the limp bodies of the bloodied creatures and dropped them at his son's feet. At such gatherings in the past, David habitually opted out of the shooting, and the small pile of dead birds Robin had killed made him feel queasy.

CHAPTER 23

Sir James Paxton was in the planning stages of what would be an epic film based on the nineteenth-century writer, orientalist, and explorer Sir Richard Francis Burton. The story would encompass Burton's life from 1853, when disguised as a Pathan pilgrim, he made his famous journey from Medina to Mecca, and end with his death in Trieste in 1890. Filming would take the crew on location to Saudi Arabia, Brazil, and Africa.

Paxton's vision was of a film that would combine grand scope with personal elements. One that would fire the imagination of the audience with its physical beauty, while respecting their intellect with well-drawn characters and sharp dialogue. Henri Vadney had submitted a first-rate script, and Barry Hayes had signed on as principal cameraman. Costume and set designers were already doing preliminary sketches. Paxton wanted an unknown for the role of the dashing adventurer and cast Brian Rourke, a young actor he had seen in John Osborne's latest production at the Royal Court Theatre. To support Rourke, Paxton chose a group of seasoned actors, among them Felicia Scott as Burton's moralistic wife, Isabel Arundell, and Roger Deacon as the ambitious John Speke. A director had not as yet been signed.

David and Laura sat on either side of the hearth in their Belvedere home sipping David's Glenfiddich and discussing the stunning blow, still raw, of President Kennedy's assassination the month before. Laura sensed David's mood blackening and she changed the conversation to plans for Christmas in London. Darkness came early in December. The evening was chilly, but the bright fire crackling in the grate created a warm glow, accenting the rich colors of the woods and patterned fabrics in the room.

"Why don't we have Rose and Matthew come to us, in London this year?" said David. "Bertie, too. Miss Boxhill will go to her mother's as usual, and we can use her room for the Stokeses. Bertie can bunk in with Robin. It'll be a terrific squeeze, but . . ." The shrill ring of the telephone interrupted David's words. Scowling, he looked at his watch. "Good God, who can that be at this hour? If it's bloody Norman calling from Los Angeles for one of those endless late-night chats . . ."

"I'll get it," said Laura, running to the phone. A moment later, she returned. "It's Jamie. He wants to talk to you. It's five in the morning over there. I wonder what's so important."

Laura could hear David's muffled voice coming from the kitchen, but she couldn't make out what he was saying. He was gone for over twenty minutes. and by the time he returned to the living room she was bursting with curiosity.

"What did he want?" she asked, trying to sound offhand.

"He's about to start a film on the life of Richard Burton . . . the fellow who discovered the source of the Nile, not the actor."

"And?"

"And he wants me to direct it."

She felt herself grow tense. "What did you say?"

"I said yes."

Laura leaped out of her chair and threw herself into his arms. "Oh David, David, I am so glad!" She danced him around the living room carpet. "At last, you'll be back where you belong."

David began work on *Profane Pilgrim* early in 1964. The crew spent five weeks in Saudi Arabia for the first location filming. In March, they traveled from the dry heat of the desert to the suffocating humidity of Brazil, where Burton had been consul. They finished shooting just before the weather became unbearable and returned to London for interiors at Briarwood Studios.

David checked in with Dr. Sullivan, who put him through a battery of tests and informed him that the rigors of location shooting and the stress of working under primitive conditions seemed to agree with him.

In August, they set out once again, this time for Africa, to film what would be the major portion of the movie: Burton's search for the source of the Nile.

Profane Pilgrim was finished late in October and released in New York the week before Christmas. It was a 3 1/2-hour odyssey — a film that transported the audience through the perfumed bazaars of the Near East and the steaming jungles of Brazil to the purple hills of East Africa, culminating with the discovery of Lake Tanganyika. It took the country by storm. People stood in long lines, often in the rain, to see the film three and four times. Albums of Joachim Muller's score sold faster than record shop managers could reorder them. Copies of Burton's *Personal Narrative of a Pilgrimage to El-medinah and Meccah* and *One Thousand and One Nights,* long out of print, suddenly appeared in bookshop windows. A major cosmetic company came out with two new lipstick shades: *Mecca Morning* and *Profane Pink.* Suddenly, Persian carpets, rosy-hued paisley prints, and brass tabletops were appearing in the pages of House & Garden. Sandalwood and patchouli were the most popular scents for bath products, and fashion designers in London and New York incorporated Turkish bazaar and harem motifs in their collections.

In Belvedere, thick manila envelopes carrying the legends Twentieth Century Fox, Paramount Pictures and Galaxy Studios in their upper left-hand corners began arriving in the mail. David did not leave them neglected on the hall table. He read scripts, talked to producers — made movies.

Gerry Maddox was deeply moved by the astounding beauty of *Profane Pilgrim.* It was obvious that David Landau had an extraordinary gift for directing films of epic proportions while imbuing them with the kind of intimacy he had achieved in *Beggar's Choice.* Henri Vadney's lucid script, the sensitive camera work of Barry Hayes, and Joachim Muller's music enabled David to create a vast epic, peopled by multidimensional characters who spoke intelligent, often witty, dialogue. Maddox reunited the formidable team of Landau, Vadney, Hayes and Muller for *The Great Napoleon, The Sepoy Mutiny* and one last film, *Catherine and Rasputin.* It would be the first and only time David Landau directed his wife.

Diverse in subject matter as they were, these films had one common characteristic: sweeping spectacle combined with intimate realism. Oscar statuettes began to line the bookshelves in David's study.

It was the nineteen-sixties. The media was all-powerful, and into homes in every corner of America had come horrifying images of the assassinations of John Kennedy, Martin Luther King and Robert Kennedy — and the faces of their killers, James Earl Ray, Sirhan Sirhan, and Lee Harvey Oswald, who was shot before the nation's eyes by Jack Ruby. The war in Vietnam and the protests at home were staples on television screens in living rooms across the country. In contrast to the nightly fare of televised graphic violence, glossy magazines dished up detailed accounts of the private lives of millionaire jet setters, known as the Beautiful People, and larger-than-life entertainers dubbed superstars: Liz and Dick, Twiggy, Callas, Streisand — and Laura English.

What was called the *Laura Look* was madly in. Pale skin, large eyes, and masses of copper curls were replicated on California coeds and Manhattan cocktail party regulars.

Laura was in constant demand. No sooner was the dubbing completed on one film than she started another. In 1964, she played a jaded socialite in the Hitchcock mystery *Fiona*. In 1965, she teamed with Denny McLean and Rick Howard, Hollywood's two most exciting leading men, in the screwball comedy *The Brass Ring*. In 1966, she starred in David Landau's *Rasputin*. Some critics said her portrayal of the Czarina Alexandria was stiff. Others pronounced it the greatest role of her career.

Michael Kent had begun his career in 1939 as a contract player with the J. Arthur Rank Organization but, along with many of his countrymen, he was lured to California after the war. With his suave manners, powder-blue eyes, and trim mustache, he was still, at fifty-two, one of Paramount's most popular leading men. The Kent's Georgian house on Roxbury drive was headquarters for Hollywood's so-called British Set. In addition to their Bel Air home, Michael and his charming wife, Maureen, also owned houses in Gstaad and London. After visiting Gerry Maddox in Belvedere, they decided that a Marin County retreat should be added to their inventory of residences. It took them a year to find the right house, complete with swimming pool, tennis courts, and stables, in the charming old town of Ross. Now neighbors, the Landaus and the Kents became close friends.

In 1967, Gerry Maddox teamed Laura and Michael in a romantic comedy, *Autumn Dance*. It was the story of a middle-aged diplomat who falls in love with his daughter's bookish friend and turns her into a glamorous woman of the world — *Pygmalion* told against a contemporary background of New York City. The film had everything: dazzling scenes of the city, a witty script, a great supporting cast, and a happy ending.

Dressed by Jean Varon, coiffed by Kenneth, and jeweled by Harry Winston, Laura had never looked more beautiful or sophisticated. She made her first attempt at vocalizing, and the sad little ballad she sang at the start of the film sold well over a million copies and remained in the top ten for nearly a year. High-end copies of Varon's *Autumn Dance* wardrobe were seen in boutiques on Rodeo Drive and Fifth Avenue and, not long after, copies of copies were available off the rack in large department stores across the country. In time for Christmas, 1967, a famous French perfume house introduced a new fragrance called simply *Laura*.

Richard Avedon photographed her for *Vogue* against a stark white background, perched on a high stool, hair pulled back in a long ponytail, wearing a black leotard and tights. Irving Penn's brilliant color layout for *Harper's Bazaar* had Laura swathed in snow leopard, hair cascading loosely over her shoulders, handling the reins of a troika. David Bailey shot her for the cover of *Town &*

Country in a peacock-blue strapless Arnold Scaasi, red curls massed on top of her head, a David Webb diamond and aquamarine choker encircling her white neck. By 1968, Laura's face was as familiar to the American magazine reader as Liz's or Jackie's.

David's schedule, while busy, was not as hectic as Laura's. Between projects he flew to London to be with Robin, who had graduated from St. Paul's, and was now attending Westminster School. As always, they took great pleasure in each other's company and spent many hours discussing David's newest film or Robin's latest work in progress. He was taking drawing classes at the National Gallery on Saturdays, working in charcoal and ink, and eagerly anticipating the time when he would be proficient enough to begin oils. They still took excursions into unknown parts of London, exploring strange neighborhoods, poking around in junk shops and eating meals in exotic restaurants.

On rare breaks from work, Laura fled to Belvedere. Daily walks around the island revitalized her body and spirit. She drew strength from the scent of tiny wildflowers and ancient ferns and took delight in the sight of squirrels scampering through the limbs of her oak trees and mixed pleasure at the gracefulness of deer families as they feasted in her petunia beds. Most of all, she loved walking down by the shore. The salty smell of the bay, the gulls screeching overhead, and the tiny sandpipers poking in the sand evoked memories of her childhood in Bournemouth. Gradually, she and David became acquainted with Gerry Maddox's friends. He knew most of the writers, musicians, artists, and political activists in the area, and David found their company at least as stimulating as that of his friends in London or his cronies in North Beach. Laura liked the informal style of California entertaining, preferring Sunday brunches to sit-down dinners.

Chapter 24

Belvedere, 1969

Most of the guests had arrived, and Laura was beginning to wonder what had become of Gerry. He had called early that morning to ask if he might bring a friend along. She hoped this didn't mean Norman wasn't coming. He was so swamped with new clients these days that he hadn't been able to get up north for a visit in a long time, and she missed him.

She glanced at her watch just as the doorbell rang.

"Okay, kiddies. Norm's here, the party can begin!" He kissed her on both cheeks.

"This may come as a shock to you, but the party's been going strong for over an hour." She turned to Gerry. "What kept you?" He was standing with a tall woman who looked vaguely familiar.

"Norman couldn't decide what outfit to wear," said Gerry.

"Worth the wait, though," said Norm, slowly turning in order to show off his hot pink Moroccan shirt and flared blue velvet pants.

The tall woman moved forward. "Laura," said Gerry "you know my friend."

"You don't recognize me, do you?" she said before Gerry could introduce them. The rich voice was one Laura had heard before, but she couldn't quite place it. "Glenda Fisher. We met in Acapulco. The film festival. Remember?"

"Of course I do! But . . ." Could this slim woman in the skin-tight Pucci jump suit really be the same Glenda Fisher she had met nine years ago?

"Yes, I know. I lost about 150 pounds and threw away every last caftan I owned."

"I couldn't be more delighted that Gerry brought you. Are you in town for long?"

"Sweetie, would it be possible to continue this fascinating conversation at the buffet table?" interrupted Norm. "My blood sugar is at minus three."

Laura grabbed his hand and led all three into the dining room where a long table, spread with a yellow and blue Provençal cloth, was laden with ceramic patters displaying an array of appetizing dishes.

Norman's eyes sparkled. "Oh, goodie! Three kinds of pâté and smoked tongue! God, I've died and gone to heaven. Blintzes!" He took a plate and started filing it.

Noticing the new arrivals, David broke away from a group on the other side of the room and came to join them. "Gerry. I thought you weren't coming."

"Unavoidably detained. David, meet Glenda Fisher."

The two shook hands, and Glenda flashed a toothy smile. "I met your wife years ago in Acapulco. I was thrilled when *Beggar's Choice* won first at the festival. It's still my favorite of all your films. Of course, I adored *Rasputin!* What a stroke of genius, casting a sex symbol bullfighter as the mad priest. I've known Fermin for years, and let me say that you captured his, shall we say, charisma to the nth."

"Thank you," said David with a slight bow. "You know he doesn't speak a word of English. He learned all his lines phonetically, but he is a natural."

"I'll say," she said, rolling her eyes. A maid came around with a tray of drinks. Glenda took a glass of mineral water and Gerry a gin and tonic. "And how did you two enjoy working together?" said Glenda.

"An experience," David laughed, putting his arm around Laura. "We have always felt that the secret of our happy marriage has been that we do not work together. We tried it that once just for fun."

"And with pretty good results," said Gerry "An Oscar for best director wasn't bad."

"How long will you be here?" asked David.

"A few more days. Actually, I'm putting off going down to Los Angeles. My stepfather died last year, and my mother's all alone now so, once in a while, I have to spend a couple of days with her. Believe me, it's never a pleasant experience."

"Do you still live in Mexico City? I'm so sorry we never got to see it," said Laura.

"Well, you must come and stay with us sometime."

"That's very kind of you."

"Not at all. I think you'd like my husband. His name is Hugo Frank. He's Swiss, but really more of a citizen of the world."

"Hugo Frank? But I know him!" said David. "We were at school together. He was senior to me, by three years as I remember, and way out of my league, very suave and sophisticated, and I . . ." David put his hand over his mouth and coughed. "Pardon me. I just got back from shooting on location, and I think I picked up a virus or something. Maybe we can arrange to get together while you're here."

"I'm afraid that will be impossible. Hugo's flying to Amsterdam tomorrow. He would have been here today except that the opportunity to meet with someone he's been after for a long time came up. You see, he's on a fundraising mission for a charitable organization he's been involved with many years. After Amsterdam, he goes to Zurich."

"I'd like very much to see him again. Maybe we will take a trip down to Mexico one of these days. Now, if you will excuse me, I see Michael giving me the high sign. That means a bridge game is about to start. So nice meeting you, Glenda, and, please, give my best to Hugo when you talk to him." He kissed Laura lightly on the cheek and went off to a corner where three men were already seated at a card table.

"He's charming," said Glenda.

"Yes, he is," said Laura, watching David as he arranged the cards in his hand. He lit a cigarette and Laura frowned. He had given up smoking after his surgery six years ago, but this last film had been a difficult one and he had started again while on location in Rome. She must talk to him about it later. He had been coughing since he came back from Italy. Or had it started before?

"You know, I've often thought of you since our meeting that time in Acapulco. You were marvelous in *Royal Player*. I felt I had a small part in making it happen."

"Indeed you did." said Gerry. "I wouldn't have had a chance with Laura if you hadn't brought us together." He put his arm around Glenda's bony shoulder.

"You two must be starving," said Laura, handing Glenda and Gerry plates. Laura noticed that Glenda walked by the smoked salmon and platter of cheeses and took only a small piece of chicken and some green salad.

She turned to Laura. "For the next couple of days I'm going to be wandering around the city, you know, delaying my encounter with my mother, the dragon lady, as long as I can. Maybe we could have lunch together." She still wore her enormous dark glasses thrust up on her head, but the stiff bouffant hair style had been replaced by the very latest Vidal Sasson geometric bob. Her features were much sharper, but the warmth in her voice and the brilliant smile were the same.

"Yes, I would like that very much. Where are you staying?"

"The St. Francis."

"Perfect. Shall we say Tuesday in the Grill at one?"

"It's a date."

After their guests had gone, David told Laura what he remembered about Hugo Frank. He was the youngest son of a wealthy industrialist who had fled with his family from Germany to Switzerland in 1934.

"At Shelbourne, he always seemed so much older than any of us. You know, impeccably correct in dress and manners, not joining in our pranks, and really pretty hopeless at games. He had a remarkable mind, though, and a wickedly cutting sense of humor. After Shelbourne, he disappeared. I heard he had gone to New York and, evidently, made quite a mark both at Columbia and Harvard business school. I guess now he's a big philanthropist. Like our poor friend Gianni."

Laura felt positively piggish biting into her Monte Cristo sandwich as Glenda pushed a few lettuce leaves around on her plate. "You have fantastic willpower," she said.

"I should be hopeless on a diet."

"You'd have willpower if you lost as much weight as I did. The thought of gaining even one pound terrifies me. I also have a little help."

"What do you mean?"

"These." Glenda opened her purse and took out a plastic pill bottle Laura could see contained green and white capsules.

"Dexamyl?"

Glenda nodded.

"A lot of people in Hollywood use them. David says they're very dangerous."

"Nonsense. You just can't abuse them." She put the bottle back in her purse. "I must say it's great fun lunching with a movie star. There are about twenty people in here staring at you."

"Really? I never notice. Thankfully, people rarely rush at me. I think it's because I'm English. I guess the notorious reserve puts them off, but it is rather flattering when people do ask me for an autograph."

"I'd never get used to that."

"And so you are married now. I remember you saying you never would."

Glenda leaned across the table. "Oh, I used to say a lot of things in those days. Big front. Lots of bravado. The truth is, I was lucky to find someone who wanted to take me on, and Hugo is very good to me."

"I'm happy for you."

"We travel a lot of the time. Hugo is involved in projects all over the world. He does a great deal of work with the Marcello Gianni Institute in Tel Aviv."

"Sounds like an interesting life."

"It is. I miss the old excitement at times, but I'm better off with Hugo. He adores me, and there's something pleasant about that." They both laughed.

"What made you decide to settle down?" asked Laura.

"Remember that boyfriend of Beryl Villiers?" She said, lighting a cigarette. Her eyes on the flame, Glenda didn't notice Laura's expression.

"Yes."

"Well, we got together."

"Oh?"

"Yes. In Mexico City. Right after Marcello Gianni was killed. He called right out of the blue."

"Oh," said Laura.

"I had a pile of contact sheets to crop for *Life* and a piece for *Holiday* with a looming deadline but I didn't do a stroke of work for almost two months. I'd done that kind of thing before. You know, shacked up with someone, just fucking all day long, but this was different."

Laura was feeling sick. "Different?"

"I fell in love." She smiled ruefully.

"I see."

"He was really something, Mr. John Keith. More than just beautiful to look at. He had a sort of . . . vitality, like a life force, about him. All he had to do was touch me. Anyway, he got himself well under my skin, and then he just took off."

"Where did he go?"

"I don't know. One night we were at his apartment, well, the one his company owns. A fabulous penthouse near the Reforma. Anyway, he got a call very late. He was on the phone a long time, and when he finally hung up, he said he had to go somewhere on assignment. He put me in a cab and said he'd be in touch. And that was that. I never heard from him again. Talk about cold turkey. Anyway, I had a pretty tough few months. That's really when I started losing weight. I was so depressed that a friend gave me some Dexies. You know, to pep me up, and before I knew it, I was skinny. It was a strange time. I couldn't concentrate on work or anything serious, so I bought some art supplies and started painting. The stuff was pretty terrible, so I ended up buying a block of clay and tried sculpting. I was just getting good at it when I met Hugo and things turned around for me."

"I'm sorry you had such a rough time."

"Hey, those things happen. I was stupid and fell hard for an emotionally dangerous guy. I shouldn't have let myself believe it could ever be anything more than a fling. He was honest with me right from the start, I'll say that for him. It was just such an awful shock . . . his leaving like that."

"Yes, I can imagine."

"All along I kept kidding myself, but I guess deep down knew that one day he would just take off. See, the first night we were together he told me that he was in love with someone else."

"Beryl?"

"Oh, God no. He liked her a lot, but he was never in love with her. No, this was someone from years ago. A girl he'd been with when he was very young. Evidently, he never got over her. She married someone else. One night when we'd had about seventeen Bacardi Carta Oros, he told me all about it. I think there was a kid, although I can't be sure because things were pretty fuzzy by then. But I do remember that there were tears in his eyes when he talked about it. He must have really loved this woman. For a while, I thought I could make him forget her. We had a hell of a good time together. Anyway, as I said, he took off."

"Well, everything worked out for the best in the end."

"Did it?"

"Yes. You said that Hugo loves you, and it sounds as if you have a nice life."

"Oh, yes. I have a very nice life. But you know something?" She leaned toward Laura, her black eyes bright. "I'd give up my floor-length Maximilian sable and my safe full of emeralds and the shopping trips to Paris and the villa in Cap d'Antibes for another chance with John Keith. I wonder if that woman, whoever she is, has any idea what she could have had."

"Maybe she does," whispered Laura.

As Laura drove back across the bridge, the top of her Jaguar coupe down, Glenda Fisher's words echoed in the wind blowing through her hair. *He told me he was in love with someone else. There were tears in his eyes.* But if John truly loved her, why had she never heard from him? Why had he waited until they met by chance in Acapulco to attempt seeing her alone? He could have contacted her in care of Galaxy Studios, but in the nine years since their encounter at the film festival, there hadn't been a single word. She habitually scanned the international section of the newspaper as well as the major news magazines, but had never seen his byline.

Laura swung off the highway at Tiburon Boulevard and drove out the peninsula toward Belvedere. Again, her thoughts turned to Glenda Fisher. Evidently, the gaudy caftans and ethnic jewelry were gone for good. At lunch, Glenda had been wearing a lime green silk Givenchy suit that set off her dark coloring to perfection. The chunky jewelry had been replaced by a wide gold collar around her now-slim throat and a simple, if enormous, diamond solitaire next to her plain gold wedding ring. Even the sweet scent of Femme had been replaced by the more sophisticated Ma Griffe.

Laura came to the Belvedere turnoff and, as always, her mind calmed at the beauty of this place she had made her own. The water was touched with whitecaps, and sailboats were out in number. A large seagull, perched atop a weathered piling, watched the sandpipers digging for microscopic insects with the detached air of one who never stooped to such indignities to get his dinner. Three small boys, pails in hand, trudged along the beach, their nannies close behind. She thought of Bournemouth and the beach and the bright April day she had met John Keith.

Suddenly, the image of John and Glenda Fisher intruded on the peaceful scene. The car swerved. Hands shaking, she stopped at the side of the road and put her head on the steering wheel. Her palms were wet and her head ached. She shut her eyes tight. Was she, for the rest of her life, going to have this violent reaction at the thought of John with another woman? She was David's wife. He was her best friend, and she loved him. Their marriage had weathered frequent separations, David's illness, and the pressures of success, yet it remained intact, stronger than ever. She raised her head and turned the key over in the ignition. She sat, listening to the low hum of the motor for a while. Then, with a sigh, she guided the car back onto the road.

David's black Mercedes was parked on his side of the carport. She took her parcels out of the back seat, closed the car door, and started down the path to the house. He was standing in the open doorway.

"I've been watching for you." His face looked strained.

"What's the matter?" she said, suddenly alert. "Are you all right?"

"Yes," he said, taking two boxes from her and setting them on the hall table. The house was beautifully cool and smelled, as always, of beeswax, fresh flowers, and the tangy breeze off the bay.

"Well, what's all the excitement then?"

"Glenda just called."

"Oh, dear. I just left her." *Was she going to turn into a pest?*

"Hugo Frank is dead."

"What! How?"

"Shot in the bathroom of his hotel suite in Amsterdam. His watch and wallet were taken. Passport, too. The Dutch police think Hugo must have been in the shower and surprised a thief who was there at a time when hotel rooms are usually vacant. He was naked and his hair was still wet when the floor maid found him."

"Oh, my God."

"I told Glenda we would come right over. He had associates in the city, the people he came here to see, but she asked for you and sounded so lost that I think we should go over, you know, to give her some moral support."

Laura thought of the night Marcello Gianni was shot at the film festival and how Jamie had responded to Beryl's need for him at her side. "Of course we'll go."

The murder of Hugo Frank was news, and Glenda was plagued by reporters right up to the moment the Landaus put her on the Aero Mexico flight Wednesday afternoon.

Tears streamed down her face as she said goodbye to them at the gate. "Please come and see me soon. I don't know why," she said, hugging Laura, "but I've always had a very warm spot in my heart for you."

"Are you going to be all right?" said Laura "Are there, you know, people?"

"Plenty of people. I've lived in Mexico City nearly twenty years. Don't worry about me."

Laura took David's hand as they stood at the plate glass window, watching in silence as Glenda's plane took off; oblivious to the people who craned their necks to stare at her, nudging their companions in recognition.

"Darling," he said softly, "I think you are drawing a crowd."

Slowly, Laura turned and caught several pairs of eyes smiling in her direction. She smiled in return.

A young woman came toward her. "Miss English?" She said tentatively, holding out an envelope and a pen. "May I please have your autograph?"

"Certainly. What is your name?"

"Marcia."

Quickly, Laura wrote on the back of the envelope *To Marcia, best wishes, Laura English.* "Here you are" she said, handing it back to the girl, whose face was now very red.

"Oh, thank you so much. I've seen every one of your movies and I . . ."

"It is her! Come on! Before she gets away!" Three teenage girls rushed forward, scraps of paper in their hands. "Laura . . . Laura wait! Don't go!" they shouted. Others in the lounge started digging in purses and pockets for pens and bits of paper. "Laura . . . Laura!" she heard coming from all sides. David gripped her hand and led her quickly out of the boarding area into the wide corridor leading up to the main lobby where it was unlikely any autograph seekers, for fear of missing their flights, would venture.

Once in the terminal, they leaned against the Pan American ticket counter. "Good God!" David gasped, "Why in hell did I have to pick a movie star to marry?" He coughed and reached in his pocket for his handkerchief.

"I don't know," she said, laughing. "Jamie warned me this would happen years ago. I should have stayed in blissful obscurity with the Bournemouth Players."

"Come on now. Just between us, don't you kind of like it?"

She laughed. The exertion of their dash up the long corridor had left her high cheekbones tinted pink and her hair in unruly curls around her face.

"My God, you are beautiful. No wonder they all go insane at the sight of you. I'm absolutely mad about you myself." He kissed her. Several people glanced their way, recognition dawning, but David and Laura did not notice as the escalator carried them under the lobby and down into the airport garage.

Later, Laura remembered that David's kiss had tasted faintly metallic.

The farther they got from the airport the more relieved Laura felt. Sorry as they both were for the traumatized woman, the exertion of spending every moment with Glenda until they saw her off on the plane to Mexico had taken its toll — especially on David, who looked exhausted.

They drove through the city by way of the Financial District, down Kearney Street and Columbus Avenue to Bay Street and finally along Marina Boulevard to the Golden Gate Bridge. As always, Laura felt a surge of elation the closer she came to Marin County. The day was beautifully clear. The Berkeley hills stood out vividly against the blue of the sky and the tower of the campanile at the University of California sparkled in the bright light.

As soon as they got home, she would fix David a stiff whiskey and soda and get him into his flannel robe. She didn't like the tired look he had worn since returning from Italy. There were dark shadows under his eyes, and several times during the last week she had heard him coughing in the night and had felt him get up and go into the bathroom. What he needed was a good night's sleep. As for herself, she wanted a long bath. Maybe they could have a light supper in front of the television and go to bed early.

David had been clear of his cancer for nearly six years, and were it not for the annual checkups at Stanford, they might have forgotten his tumor had ever existed. But now he had developed this cough. Did he have it before Italy? He had had a slight cold in England at Christmas but anyone can get a cold.

They drove passed Richardson Bay. The Tiburon turnoff was just ahead. She glanced over at David behind the wheel. His profile was as distinguished as ever, but he was pale and there was a tightness at the corners of his mouth that tinged the skin slightly blue. She was glad this latest picture was finished. It had been a difficult one, with a temperamental actress in the second lead and the weather not cooperating on location. Now, he could relax. She would see to it that he got in some tennis with Michael. Maybe they should think about buying a small boat. It would be so good for David to get out on the bay. Do a little fishing. She smiled and, as if sensing her eyes upon him, he looked at her.

"What?"

"Nothing. Keep your eyes on the road. I was just thinking how nice it would be if we had a little boat."

"What made you think of that?" He coughed slightly, gasped, and coughed again.

"Oh, I don't know. David, what is it! David!" He was coughing hard, and his face had turned an ugly mottled purple. With a tremendous effort, he reached in his pocket for a handkerchief and held it to his mouth. Laura put her hands on the wheel, and together they managed to steer the car over to the side of the road, where it bumped along the shoulder and came to rest at a small commercial complex consisting of a real estate office, a hardware store, and a hairdressing salon.

"David, I'm going to phone for help." She opened the car door and got out. "I'll be right back." Thank God this didn't happen on the bridge, she thought as she pushed open the glass door of the real estate office.

It took exactly six minutes for the ambulance to come.

Laura sat next to David, holding his hand in hers as they sped, sirens screaming, towards Marin General Hospital.

"Can you tell me what happened, ma'am?" asked the attendant as he worked over David.

"He started coughing and . . . gasping. He couldn't get his breath. It was horrible." Tears stung her eyes and she wiped them away with an impatient gesture. "Is he going to be all right?"

"His airway is obstructed. I've got a breather on him now and he's doing okay." They arrived at the hospital. The ambulance pulled into a driveway marked EMERGENCY in large red lettering.

Laura ran beside the stretcher as David was carried into the emergency room. She was met by a middle-aged black nurse who asked Laura to step into a small cubicle in order to fill out the necessary forms.

"Please call Dr. Marcus at Stanford," said Laura as she began filling in the form the nurse had handed to her. She could see David being lifted onto a gurney and then wheeled into a partitioned area. "Doctor Sheldon Marcus," she repeated.

The nurse looked in a directory that listed all Bay Area medical facilities. She ran a long thin index finger down a column of names, stopped when she came to the one she sought, and dialed the number. As it rang, she smiled at Laura. "We'll find your doctor. Good thing it's only just after four. He probably hasn't gone home yet. She became alert. "Page Dr. Sheldon Marcus ... emergency."

Laura sat, straining in her chair, eyes fastened on the other woman's face. "Are they going to get him?" she whispered.

The nurse nodded.

Together, they waited for what seemed like a very long time. "Doctor Marcus? This is Marin General. We have a patient of yours here . . . a Mr. David Landau. Yes, he was brought in by ambulance about twenty minutes ago. Severe bronchial trauma. All right, doctor. Yes, right away." She put the receiver down on the desk and ran into the partitioned area.

It was all Laura could do to keep herself from picking up the phone and demanding that Dr. Marcus come at once.

A moment later, the nurse was back. "He wanted to talk to the attending physician. Don't worry, honey, everything's going to be okay." She put the receiver gently back in its cradle. "How about some coffee?" She said, smiling.

Laura looked up at her and slowly shook her head.

It took just under forty minutes for the ambulance to get from Marin General to Stanford Medical Center. Laura followed in David's Mercedes, which a highway patrolman had retrieved from the roadside at the Tiburon turnoff.

Dr. Marcus ordered a CAT scan. It revealed a tumor lodged in the upper portion of David's trachea. A procedure was performed, under general anesthetic, during which a bronchoscope was inserted into the trachea. As the scope traveled through the trachea, parts of the tumor broke free, thus enlarging the airway enough to relieve David's breathing temporarily until he could undergo surgery.

The operation went well, but Laura sensed a soberness in Dr. Marcus's demeanor, far different from his positive attitude after David's first surgery.

The soaring optimism Laura had felt during David's recovery six years ago was replaced by an icy dread that clung like the morning mists on Mt. Tamalpais. Changes in their life, wrought by David's illness, were soon integrated into the pattern of everyday life and memories of other, better, days faded like a pleasant dream. Recovery from the tracheal surgery was not as rapid as that following the lung operation. For months, David was plagued by a racking cough, alleviated only by large doses of a strong codeine syrup that left him in a dazed stupor. In addition, he suffered chronic shortness of breath and had to limit his activities severely so as not to go into bronchial spasm. He took medication to dilate his bronchial passages and medication to counteract the side effects it caused. A depressing collection of bottles and boxes lined the shelves of the medicine cabinet. An inhaler was kept in easy reach on his bedside table.

They both knew his days of directing were over, but Laura was determined that David should find something, other than reading a book a day, to occupy his time. At last, she hit on the idea of his adapting a novel he had raved about into a screenplay.

"You know you've always fooled around with scripts, even Henri's. I thought he'd have a fit when you practically rewrote my confrontation scene in *Rasputin*, but in the end, he had to admit your version was better. You probably would have done a screenplay eventually, so why not now when you have the time?"

"You mean now that I'm finished."

"Nothing of the sort. You know you have to take things easy for awhile, and I thought you might as well make yourself useful. And we can use the money. Especially if we're going to buy that boat."

His tear-filled eyes glittered like obsidian. "Yes," he said when he could speak. "You're right. As usual."

Her heart contracted at the weakness in his voice, once so strong and vibrant. "I'll get you a pad and some pencils. Now, where did I put that book?" She walked steadily out of the den, which had been converted into a bed-sitting room so David would not have to deal with stairs. Her eyes were blinded with tears as she ran down the hall and into the kitchen. Hands braced against the sink, she gave way to the tears of impotence and rage, which poured down her face. "Damn, damn, damn," she whispered.

Five minutes later, she was back in the den, eyes dry, carrying a yellow legal pad, three freshly sharpened No. 2 pencils, and the book. "Get to work. The kettle's on. I'll be back in an hour, and I expect to see some scribbles on that pad."

"Laura."

She turned from the doorway. "Yes?"

"Thanks."

"You'd better not thank me yet. I hear writing is a mighty demanding profession. Not like standing next to a camera barking out orders." She looked at him, sitting in the bed; face drawn, eyes apologetic. "But I think you're up to it."

"Laura."

"Yes?"

"I love you."

Robin had completed his O-level exams and, at sixteen, his heart was set on attending the Chelsea Art School. Over the past year, he had been working furiously putting together an acceptable portfolio to present as part of the admissions process to the prestigious school. He wanted to apply right away, but Laura was adamant that he stay two more years in order to take his A- levels before deciding between art school and university.

Two nights before David was taken ill, Robin had called him asking to be allowed to leave Westminster at the end of term. "It's not that I don't like it there, but I know what I want to do with my life, and two more years of Latin and Shakespeare will be a waste of time." "Sorry, Robbie. In two years you will be free to do what you like, but sixteen is too young to leave school." David knew that, with the exception of the Paxton brothers, most of Robin's friends were other young artists with whom he could discuss his work. He remembered, when he was sixteen, how powerful the first awakenings of his own creativity were, but with he and Laura living primarily in Belvedere, David wanted the reassurance of knowing Robin was still at home at number 12, Cranley Gardens, with Mrs. Boxhill overseeing things in her new position as housekeeper, and Robin attending Westminster.

"Dad, you're just saying this because it's what Mother wants. I must say, it's strange that suddenly she gives a damn about me."

"Robbie! I won't have you talk that way about your mother."

"But it's true, Dad. Since when has she cared where I am or what I do? I'll agree with whatever you think is best, but please give it some more thought, and promise me, it will be your decision, not hers."

"I will give it some more thought, Robbie, but you are very wrong about your mother. She loves you with all her heart."

"Dad, I'm not five years old anymore, and, whether you think I'm old enough to leave school now or in two years, there's one subject I've become an expert on and that's my mother's so-called heart. How many of my birthdays did she miss because she was shooting somewhere on location? How many of my long vacs did I spend with the Paxtons or with Aunt Camilla and Uncle Peter in Scotland because she was in Los Angeles or her precious Belvedere? You were always there for me, Dad, but where was she? The only thing my mother cares about is her work, and the only person she loves with all her heart is Laura English."

All Robin's thoughts of leaving school were abandoned with the news of his father's recurrent illness and surgery. As soon as he was released from school for the long vacation, he flew to California to be with his father.

During his stay in Belvedere, Robin was more than usually restrained with his mother. She imagined he must be homesick for London, but since he did not open up to her about his feelings, she remained silent on the subject. One day, when he seemed especially downcast, she suggested he explore North Beach.

"Perhaps you could sign up for something at the Art Institute. Your father used to take classes there. He'd spent hours sitting in the coffeehouses around the school and ..."

He stopped her in mid-sentence with a terse "No, thanks."

She winced and said no more.

Laura was aware of the wall that existed between her and Robin. It had gone up slowly, year by year, brick by brick. Now the mortar was set, the wall too high to scale.

The reality of David's second bout with cancer had removed the sugar coating from Laura's life, as she perceived it. Time spent walking the corridors of Stanford Hospital, waiting in doctor's stuffy reception rooms, and sitting by his bed at home had provided her with many hours of solitude in which she had been forced to come to terms with an unvarnished version of her relationship with Robin: her return to Briarwood a few short months after his birth, the inevitable choice of yet another project too good to pass up over his needs, and worst of all, the self-delusion that it was the pain of Robin's resemblance to John that excused her own neglect. In her heart, she knew that her son's blond curls and green eyes did not evoke memories too painful to bear. The reality was that she had given up Robin, as she had John — for Laura English.

Robin spent most of his time in Belvedere reading or sketching while David worked on his screenplay. In the late afternoons, they sat at a table Laura set up in the den and played endless games of chess and talked about Robin's plans for the future.

The night before he left, Robin sat for a long time by David's bed. He did most of the talking, as it still winded David to use his voice. Robin reminisced about his childhood and all their adventures roaming around London together when he was a boy. "I'm going to miss you, Dad, but I'll be back as soon as I can, and I don't want you to worry about me. I've decided to give it two more years at Westminster."

"I'm glad, son. And, remember, when the time comes to start art school, Chelsea isn't the only place in the world. I think it would be good for you to travel a bit. Maybe spend a year in Paris or Rome."

"I know, Dad. I've a feeling that someday I might even go to Israel. What do you think of that?"

David chuckled weakly and coughed. "I don't know. Maybe I shouldn't have taken you on that trip at such an impressionable age, but if that's what you want, then you should do it. Life is short son," he wheezed. "Go with your gut and you won't have regrets."

The next morning, Robin left for London.

David's writing went well. He finished two scripts, using the pseudonym David Parks. The second was picked up by 20th Century Fox.

"It seems the name Parks is going to be famous after all," laughed Laura.

Once word was out that David Parks was actually David Landau, the first script was optioned by an independent producer. Encouraged by the success of the two adaptations, David hired Norm as his agent and started on an original screenplay. As Laura had hoped, the work wasn't merely a time-filler between regular appointments with Dr. Marcus at Stanford and Stephen Lubich, the pulmonary specialist at Mr. Zion in the city. It had become a vocation that was giving meaning to David's life.

Norm called frequently about offers for Laura. One in particular, *Morgan le Fey,* seemed sent from the gods. David knew that Laura, because of her pregnancy, had missed playing Morgan in Jasper Quigly's *Young King Arthur.* Now, she had been given a second chance.

"I want you to promise me you'll take this," David said. "The last report from Lubich indicated I'm stable. Look, you'll be a short plane ride away, and I'll be working on this new thing nonstop for the next couple of months, anyway. Only one favor."

"Anything," she said, her eyes sparkling in a way he hadn't seen in months.

"When you come up here on weekends, no practicing spells on me. In my condition, I may not be able to cast them off and I don't want to live the rest of my life as a rabbit."

"I love you, David."

"Me too. Now go call Norm."

David had never lost his fascination for film noir. The plot of his first original screenplay involved a second-rate actress who never makes it in movies but marries a series of rich men, each of whom she contrives to eliminate by a different method.

Norm called David with the news that he had sold it to Universal. "If it's a hit, Robert Evans and Alan Pakula will be fighting over the rights to the next one, which, by the way, I promised to Gerry. So, get to work."

"Am I allowed a week off?" he laughed. "I thought maybe Laura and I might drive down to Carmel and spend a few days. Her next one doesn't start shooting for another month, and we've talked about a little holiday before she leaves for Los Angeles."

"She was some Morgan le Fey, wasn't she? You know, Academy nominations are out next month. I wouldn't be surprised if our gal copped another one of those fancy bookends."

As Norm predicted, Laura was nominated, but on that night Jane Fonda accepted the Oscar for *Klute,* and Laura's concerns were far from the Dorothy Chandler Pavilion. David had taken a turn for the worse.

CHAPTER 25

SAN FRANCISCO, 1972

Kitty Paxton scanned the wall monitor listing BOAC departures. She glanced at her wristwatch. Seven thirty-five. Twenty-five minutes before boarding. She wondered how Robin had managed, at such short notice, to get them on the first flight out this morning. She looked at him slumped in the chair next to hers. It seemed only yesterday he was a chubby child, romping in the garden with Simon and Jamie and now, inches taller and a good deal huskier than either of her sons, he was verging on manhood. Could it really be 1972? Where do the years go?

She dabbed at the corners of her red-rimmed eyes with a handkerchief and asked herself the question all the Paxtons had asked themselves since the terrible news came. What if he doesn't make it this time? What will we do without David Landau in the world?

She would never forget the sound of Robin's voice on the telephone the night before. "I wanted you and Uncle Jamie to know that Dad has been taken to Mt. Zion Hospital in San Francisco. It's very bad this time. I'm flying to California tomorrow morning."

Without hesitating, Kitty said, "Get me a seat on that flight. I'm going with you."

Robin and Kitty landed just after ten in the morning, San Francisco time, and took a cab directly to the hospital. They stood at David's bedside, Robin's face haggard with strain and Kitty, alert with nervous energy, clutching Laura's hand. Whether David was aware of their presence, no one could tell. He lay on the raised bed, eyes half open, tubes attached to various parts of his body, the inevitable monitoring equipment relentlessly beeping at his head. Kitty was allowed only a few minutes in the ICU. Shortly after she was ushered out, the nurse asked Robin to leave.

"You can come back tomorrow but, for today, I'm afraid the doctor's orders were explicit. Only one family member at a time."

Laura grabbed her purse from a chair and took a ring of keys out of it. "Get the house key off this, will you, Robin. You can call a taxi from the lobby. I have no idea when I'll be home. I left some smoked salmon and cheese in the refrigerator and there's a baguette in the bread box. Well, you know where to find everything."

Robin detached the house key from the ring in his mother's purse and handed it back to her. He turned to look down at his father's ashen face. "I'll be back in the morning, Dad." Without a word to his mother, he left the room.

Laura remained by David's bed until the duty nurse put her hand on Laura's arm. "Mrs. Landau, your husband is stable for now, and you've been here since yesterday. You need to go home and get yourself some sleep. We'll call you if there's any change."

Laura smiled at the brogue. "You're Irish," she said.

"Yes, I'm from Tramore, near Waterford."

"What is your name?"

"Mary . . . Mary Donovan."

"I knew another nurse named Mary once. It was a happier time when I knew Mary Fitzgerald. You won't leave my husband, will you?"

"I'll be right here all day." The nurse took Laura's hand.

"And if there's even the slightest change you will call?"

"Right away."

Laura found Kitty and Robin sitting at the kitchen table drinking tea. She noticed two plates with the remains of some half eaten sandwiches. "It doesn't look as if you made much progress with those. I don't blame you. I can't eat anything either. But I do insist you must get some sleep or you'll collapse. Now, both of you, up to your rooms and to bed."

"Do you promise to wake me if there's any change with Dad?" said Robin

"Yes, I promise."

Neither Kitty not Robin had closed their eyes on the long flight from London and, when Laura check an hour later, she found both tucked up in their rooms, fast asleep.

So it was, when the telephone rang at five thirty that evening, Laura, alert for the sound, was the only one in the house who heard it

Laura was all too familiar with hospital smells, but it wasn't the odor of disinfectants or bodily fluids that enveloped her as the elevator doors opened to the intensive care floor at Mt. Zion. It was the smell of dread. Dr. Stephen Lubich was standing at the nurse's station, flipping the pages of a chart in his hands.

"Ah, Laura. I'd like a word with you." She didn't like the somber look on his face as he led her down the hall into a small visitors' lounge. "Please, sit."

"I don't need to sit."

"Laura, I've just gone over David's latest lab results."

"Yes?"

"I think it would be better if we sat down." He led her to a bank of chairs along the wall and took her hand. "I'm afraid this time there is nothing to be done."

"What do you mean? Aren't you going to operate?"

"Surgery is not indicated. He's had two cardiac episodes in the last hour, and he's in renal failure. It's hard to be exact, but he will most likely slip into a coma within the next hour. It may take some time after that. David signed a DNR order when I saw him in my office last year, so apart from basic oxygen, he will go naturally. I've ordered him moved to a private room. He isn't in any pain. It should be very peaceful."

"Are you saying that David is dying? Right now? Today?"

"Yes."

Laura shot out of the chair. "Please take me to wherever you've moved him."

David's bed was next to a window. The thought crossed her mind that this time he would not be there long enough for the ledge to accumulate, as it had during other stays in other hospitals, an array of flowers and cards. It was dark outside. Yellowish fog shrouded the streetlamp at the end of the block, spilling an eerie light onto the roof of a parked car. She hoisted herself up onto the empty ledge so as to be able to sit level with the bed. The skin of David's face, now a dull putty color, was drawn back so that his cheekbones stood out in relief against the stark whiteness of the pillow. His eyes were blank under half-opened lids, and she could not be sure if he knew she was there. She held his hand in hers, stroking the fingers, kissing them now and again.

Laura hoped that Robin and Kitty were still in the upstairs bedrooms sleeping off their jet lag and had not, as yet, seen the scribbled note she left on the kitchen table. She wanted David to herself. The old-fashioned school-room clock on the wall opposite the bed read six twenty. It clicked over. Six twenty-one.

She felt a light touch on her shoulder. A young man in green scrubs, David's chart cradled in his arm, stood by the bed. His checks and jaw were covered with dark bristles and mauve shadows smudged the deep sockets under his large brown eyes.

"I'm Dr. Fredricks. I'm just going to examine your husband. It won't take long. You can stay where you are if you like, although a little break might do you some good."

"I would prefer to stay."

"All right," he said, and proceeded with his examination. Countless times before, Laura had seen other doctors go through the same routine but never with such grace. This man's blunt fingers moved over David's chest and abdomen, exerting pressure at certain points, tapping at others, as if the body under his touch were a fine instrument. He placed his stethoscope on David's chest, listened intently and moved it to a new position. When he was done, he made several notations on the chart and clipped it to the end of the bed.

"You are a real artist," said Laura.

He looked up. "Excuse me?"

"Nothing. You look as if you've been on a long shift."

"I have. I'm just going off. I thought I'd look in before I went home."

"Are you an intern?"

"Resident."

"Oh."

"Mrs. Landau, if you don't mind my saying so, you should really get a little fresh air. At least take a walk down the hall."

"I would prefer to stay here."

"Well, then, could I get you something? Coffee . . . or maybe some water?"

"No, thank you."

"If it wouldn't be an intrusion, would you mind if I sat with you for a while?"

Laura looked at David again and suddenly a chill of comprehension went through her. "Dr. Fredricks?"

"Yes."

"Is David dying? I mean, right now?"

"Yes, he is."

"Is that why you asked to stay with me?"

The young man pulled himself up on the ledge and propped one foot up on the metal frame of the bed. "It may take a while, and I don't think it would be a good idea for you to be alone."

"You are absolutely sure. I mean about David."

"Yes. His vital organs are functioning at an extremely low level now."

Her throat filled with tears and she clenched her teeth together to keep from screaming. Somewhere, in the recesses of her mind, she had a dim memory of feeling exactly this way once before.

The young man put his arm around her. She buried her face in the shoulder of his green tunic and sobbed against the soft, clean-smelling fabric.

"That's right. Go ahead and cry it all out."

All at once, she remembered exactly when she had felt this way before. It was on the day she arrived in Bournemouth and thought that no one had come to meet her. Then, it had been Aunt Rose who held her as she cried into a soft fur collar. Now, it was this young stranger who was offering her comfort when she felt so completely lost.

"I'm sorry," she said wiping her eyes with a Kleenex.

"Nothing to be sorry about."

Together, they sat on the window ledge, their feet propped up on the bed frame, Laura leaning forward to hold David's hand, the young doctor staring into space. Every sixty seconds, the schoolroom clock clicked ahead: click, click, clicking David's life away.

Suddenly, his back arched. His breath was coming in short, violent rasps and his tongue protruded grotesquely from his mouth. The doctor worked on him for a moment and the breathing eased. "I'm afraid he's going now," he said.

"No!" Laura jumped off the ledge and, standing over the bed, looked into David's gray face. She groped for his hand. It was cold and strangely heavy. "David, please don't go." Tears ran down her face and dripped onto the sheet. "You can't go, darling. I need you. David, I need you." Suddenly, she realized it was very quiet. The labored breathing had ceased. David's chest was still. Gradually, his face and neck turned a mottled bluish gray. She looked at his hand. The wedding ring, grown looser this past year, shone faintly in the dim light over the bed.

The young doctor put his arm around her shoulder and drew her away from the bed. "Mrs. Landau."

Laura's eyes were still fixed on David.

"Mrs. Landau, I want you to listen to me." Very gently, he turned her face toward his. "I am going to take you out for a little walk. You need some fresh air."

"No! I can't . . . I can't leave him alone."

"Mrs. Landau. Please listen to me."

"If I leave him they will take him away. They'll do something . . . to his body." Her cheeks and lips, drained of color, stood out in stark contrast against the copper hair framing her pale face.

"They will take him downstairs, but nothing will be done to his body."

"No!" She turned looking frantically at the body lying in the bed.

"Laura! That is not David." She looked up. "David isn't in his body anymore," he said softly. "He's all around us now. He's part of the whole and,

Laura, he's inside you. Now let's go for that walk and breathe some fresh air."

Without looking back, she let him lead her out of the room.

The air outside was chilly. She felt fog on her face as they walked, block after block, down the dark tree-lined streets. They passed a school, a post office, and a grocery store, all shut for the night. They passed a laughing couple coming out of a small café and an old Chinese man shuffling along, his eyes fixed on the sidewalk.

They stopped walking. They were back at the main entrance of the hospital.

"How are you going to get home?" he asked.

"My car." Her voice was barely audible.

"You really shouldn't drive home alone."

"Yes, I can. I'm all right now, but I should go back inside."

"What for?"

She tried to think. There was something she had to do. "To see Dr. Lubich. I should talk to him."

"You can do that tomorrow. Right now you need to eat something and then sleep. Is there anyone at your house?"

"My son and my friend. Oh, yes, that's it. I must call them. I must go back inside and call them at once."

"All right, and then would you let me drive you home? I can take the bus back."

She smiled. "You are so kind but, no, honestly I . . ."

"There you are!" They both turned toward the sound of the voice coming from the direction of the hospital. Robin's form stood, like a colossus, framed in the entrance.

"Oh, Robin," she said, stunned at seeing him. "I was just going to call you."

"You were, eh?"

"Yes. Dr. Fredricks took me out for some air. Robin, Dad died."

"Yes. I know Dad died. I read your note and called over here and they told me. You promised to wake me if anything happened but, of course, you didn't." His voice was angry and getting louder. "You let me find out that my father died from a fucking nurse over the telephone."

"Robin." She reached out for him.

"No!"

"The doctor took Robin by the arm and tried to lead him back into the hospital where they could sit down. "Young man, your mother has just been through . . ."

"Take your hand off me." Robin's teeth were bared. His face was chalk white. "Who the hell are you anyway to tell me what to do?"

"Robin, Dr. Fredricks has been very kind to me. He was with me when

David . . . died."

"How nice for you. Dr. Fredricks was with you when my father died. And where was I? Asleep! And is Dr. Fredricks one of your fans? Are you, Dr. Fredricks, a great fan of my mother's?"

"Robin, please stop it." begged Laura. "Let's go inside where we can sit down."

"No. I came to see Dad. I have seen him. Now I'm going home — to London." Turning away, he ran to where David's black Mercedes was parked. Fumbling with the key, he unlocked the door and slid behind the wheel. A moment later, motor roaring and tires screeching, Robin sped away down the dark street.

Laura put her hand over her mouth. "Oh, my God. I should have called him. I promised I would. I just wanted David to myself . . . you know . . . at the end."

"His feelings are hurt, but he'll get over it. Now, I insist you let me drive you home."

"No, honestly. I'm fine."

He shook his head. "Will you at least call me when you get home?"

"All right."

He took a small note pad out of his pants pocket and wrote a number on a blank page. He handed it to her. "This is the hospital exchange with my extension. Also my number at home. Please let me know you got home okay. And keep my number. You can call me if you need anything at all." He looked at her with his dark cocker spaniel eyes. "Any hour at all, just call. By the way, my name is Doug. Can you remember that? Doug Fredricks."

"How can I thank you for being so very kind?"

"You don't have to thank me. It was a privilege. You see, your son was right. I am a great fan of his mother's. Not the movie star — the lady."

She put her hand on his arm for a moment, then turned and walked in the direction of the hospital parking lot.

He watched until a silver blue Jaguar convertible emerged from the lot and swung onto Divisadero Street. She wouldn't call. She probably had an army of friends to help her through this. It was laughable to think she'd need him. He only wished to God she did.

CHAPTER 26

LONDON, 1973

The room was suffused with the heady scent of incense. John Keith sat cross-legged among a group of saffron-robed monks. The monks were chanting and ringing small round brass bells. The sound of the bells grew louder. He was going mad with it. He shouted at the monks to stop ringing the bells, but his words died away into the noise.

He woke. The telephone was ringing. He squinted at the clock on the bed-side table. The luminous dial read 3:22. "Keith here."

"Hassim here."

At the sound of the clipped, English accented voice, he was instantly alert. Sitting up, he swung his body out of the sheets and onto the edge of the bed. "Yes, Hassim?"

"Greg Parker just rang from Paris. There is something he needs done right away. In New York."

John Keith lowered his voice. "That's not possible. I met with Parker last month and told him I was staying in London permanently and I wanted out. That decision was a long time in coming and final."

"John, old boy, this is a little job. In and out. A piece of cake."

"If it's so easy, why can't someone else do it?"

"Because for anyone else it would not be so easy."

"I told you, I'm out.

"John, it is important that you do this. As a favor to Parker. They are going to come through very generous for this."

"When was money ever an issue, Hassim? I joined for the cause, and I stayed in twenty years for the cause. Now, I'm burned out. "

"I know, my friend. I know. Just this one last job."

He sighed heavily. "What is it?"

"Good man. You're booked on BOAC flight 212. Departs Thursday from Heathrow at 9:50 A.M. Your ticket is at the counter. Contact MacMillan when you get to New York.

"Right."

"I was hoping you might get to Cairo one of these days. I miss you."

"I'll come sometime . . . on holiday. You can show me the pyramids. On camel back."

Hassim laughed. "Take care, old man."

"Right." He replaced the receiver and lay back on the rumpled sheets, staring into the darkness. The dream was still with him. He wondered what it could possibly mean. He could still smell the trace of something like incense.

"Johnny, what time is it?" The sound of the voice startled him. He had completely forgotten about the girl.

"About three thirty."

"Jesus! Who the hell calls at this hour anyway?"

"An old friend."

"Yes. I can imagine." He heard the girl groping for her lighter. She reached across him for the rumpled pack of Pall Malls which were on his side of the bed. "Want one?"

"What? Oh, no."

"And who, may I ask, is this old friend of yours who calls in the middle of the night?" She blew a long stream of smoke into the air above the bed.

"No one. Now finish that thing and go back to sleep." He was making a mental list of what must be done before leaving for New York in two days.

"I'm not sleepy now." Her drawling Sloane Square accent, so sophisticated last night at the party when he desired her, was, at this hour of the morning, an annoying whine. She put her hand on his stomach and started stroking him. "Come on, Johnny." She turned on her side, pressing her breasts against him. There it was. That trace of Oriental sweetness. Not incense but her perfume. She moved her hand down.

The girl rolled over, annoyed that he had finished without seeing to her, but he didn't care. She should have left him alone. Hassim's call had disturbed him. He had made it clear to Parker that he wanted out. In their line of work, one did not write a letter of resignation to the board of directors. Six months ago, he told Parker, his control for almost twenty years, to notify the organization that he was leaving. Parker had understood that it was definite. And now this call from the one person they knew he would not turn down. Would he ever be completely out? Would there always be one last job? Strange, he hadn't been sent to the States in years, and now, a year after reading David Landau's obituary in the Times, this urgent job comes his way. He sat up. Maybe I should be thanking Greg Parker. New York is only five hours away from California — and Jane.

CHAPTER 27

BELVEDERE, 1973

Somewhere inside the house, the telephone was ringing, its sound intruding on the peace of the garden. Early that morning, Laura, as she often did when she wanted a day of uninterrupted quiet, had pulled the telephone cord out of the jacks in the bedroom and kitchen. Now, the insistent sound of the bell reminded her that she had forgotten to disconnect the extension in the den. Annoyed, she shouted over the piercing ring: "For God's sake, why don't you bloody give up!"

She had gone out into the garden that afternoon with a steaming mug of tea and a copy of Carolyn Ferrier's new book under her arm, but the heavy volume remained closed and the amber liquid grew cold as she sat by the wishing well thinking of David. The unrelenting nature of his disease should have prepared her for the inevitability of his death. The attack on the day he died had been far worse than the others, yet somehow she had believed he would pull through. Now, after a year, she had finally faced the reality that David was truly dead and she must find the strength to go on without her dearest friend. Rousing herself, she roamed about the flowerbeds snapping dead heads off zinnias and late roses. The pyrocantha bushes were full of twittering sparrows, drunk on the plump orange berries. Suddenly, the birds rose up in a frantic mass of quivering feathers and flew away, a few especially intoxicated ones headed for certain disaster against windowpanes.

She found an old campaign chair lying on its side under the oak tree. Setting it right, she plopped into the canvas seat and gazed up at the spreading branches. Of all the trees in her garden, this gnarled oak was her favorite. Its twisting branches and dark hollows made her think of favorite childhood stories, mysterious and comforting. Her lids shut and she dozed, waking to find that the pale February sun had vanished, leaving the garden in deep shadow. She shivered and huddled up in the bucket-like canvas chair, putting off the moment when she would have to go inside.

In the first days following David's death, Laura had experienced a tremendous rush of energy. She attended to every detail of the funeral at St. Stephen's in Belvedere and helped Gerry Maddox and Kitty Paxton organize memorial services in Los Angeles and London. She answered scores of condolence letters and dealt with the distribution of David's clothes and personal belongings. A few special things were given to people who had been particularly close to him; a favorite sweater for Barry Hayes, a gray cashmere scarf for Aaron Landau, and David's prized deerstalker cap for Jamie Paxton. The tweed jackets and wonderfully soft camel hair coat she packed up in a large carton and mailed to Robin at Cranley Gardens, keeping for herself an ancient Shetland sweater and a couple of shirts, which she wore around the house and never washed because they carried his scent.

Robin, giving as his excuse the work he must get done for the Chelsea Art School admissions board, attended only the memorial service in London. Kitty Paxton came to Belvedere, but Jamie, in the midst of a production crisis, could not take the time off. He attended the service in London, where he and his sons supported Robin, who gave a moving eulogy in memory of his father. Kitty remained behind in Belvedere, planning to spend at least a month with Laura, but left after only a week when a frantic call came from Jamie informing her that Simon had become engaged and she was needed at home.

"Good God, I leave them alone for a few days and look what happens. Jamie claims he doesn't even know the girl's name! Can you imagine? I've been racking my brain trying to remember anyone Simon was the least bit serious about in the last year." She was piling clothes in her ancient Louis Vuitton trunk. "There was that waif with the green complexion and hairy legs who worked in a health food shop in Islington, and then the Hungarian exercise instructor who broke my Crown Derby plate. Please God, don't let it be her. Maybe it's the French girl he met in Mallorca last summer, arrogant in that way the frogs are, but a real stunner. It's strange," she said, holding a pink lace-trimmed slip in her hand, "I always thought Jamie would be the one to marry first. He and Sophie Hilliard have been inseparable practically since the cradle, and we all adore her. Ah well, I'll let you know the worst as soon as I find out."

"Yes, please." said Laura.

"Darling, I do so hate leaving you." Kitty turned worried eyes on Laura.

"I'm fine."

"Are you sure? You were so marvelous after . . . after David went, handling everything the way you did, but now you look absolutely drained."

"I am drained. I guess the surge of adrenaline finally ran out. I just need some rest, Kitty."

"Yes, of course you do. Will you promise me to get as much as you can? Maureen Kent is going to check in on you every day, and Gerry Maddox will be back here very soon. At the memorial, he told me he only had to go down to Los Angeles for a week or so and then he was coming straight back to keep an eye on you. I think he said that insane agent of yours . . . I can never remember his name . . . is coming as well. And, darling, you won't forget about Christmas, will you?"

"No. I won't forget."

"Good. And you'll be with us right through the new year? You know you can come as early as you like. Next week if you want. After all, Hampstead used to be your home." Kitty's eyes brimmed with tears.

"Yes. I remember."

With a small sigh, Kitty resumed her packing. She wished that she could stay with Laura for a while longer, but God knew what was going on at home and if Simon was involved with someone unacceptable . . . well, she would have to see what could be done.

"Kitty?"

"Yes, darling?"

"Will you do me a favor?"

"Of course."

"When you get back to London, will you ring Robin? He will be waiting to hear from the Chelsea Art School and if he gets turned down he's going to need a shoulder to cry on."

"Why yes, of course I'll check in with him. Do you think he won't be accepted?"

"Well, David thought his work might not be avant-garde enough for Chelsea."

"But surely there are other schools."

"He's got his heart is set on Chelsea."

"Don't worry, we won't let him feel lonely."

"Thanks."

Kitty took off the next day for London, and surprisingly, Laura felt relieved. With no one else in the house, she got into the habit of staying up late into the night listening to old records and going through boxes filled with photographs that had accumulated over the years and which they had never had the time or inclination to put into albums. She trailed about in a flannel nightgown and purple jersey sweatpants, a pair of heavy socks on her feet for warmth. Before she took off for London, Kitty had stocked the refrigerator and pantry with a tempting array of delicacies, but food could not fill the emptiness that Laura felt deep in her heart.

During the years of David's illness Laura had not given much thought to the possibility of his dying, She had unshakable faith in the ability of his doctors to combat his cancer and in David's own strength of will to fight for his life. Now that he was gone, she realized how much of him she had taken for granted: his sense of humor, his tenderness, his sound advice, his reassuring presence in her life.

So many things reminded her of David: his chess board set up in a corner of the living room, the book he had been reading still on the night table by the bed, his plaid robe hanging on a hook in the bathroom. She missed his voice on the telephone, the furrow between his eyes that appeared when he was concentrating, the jokes they had shared, the single word or imperceptible gesture that telegraphed so much, his profile outlined in the half-light as he lay beside her after making love. She even missed the smell of his cigarettes and, coming across a half-empty pack in the pocket of his robe, took one out and lit it. It made her choke at first, but she smoked it down to the end and finished the rest during the next few days.

The next time she went out to the store for bread and eggs, she bought a pack. The surgeon general had issued severe warnings that smoking was dangerous, but she didn't care.

For as long as she could remember she had done the right thing, the thing that those who knew best had told her to do — or not to do. How obedient she had been; changing her name and the way she dressed, spending hours on the hated barre work every day until she thought she would drop, never swearing or smoking or getting tipsy in public. Except for keeping John Keith's child, she had done it all, for the sake of Laura English.

Now she realized that Laura English was nothing more than a fabrication of Jamie Paxton's imagination and her own driving need to perform. The only true thing in her life was David's unconditional love. Without him, she had come face to face with the woman she really was. A woman who had lived with David Landau for nineteen years, accepting his love and loyalty, relying on his judgment and support, but never returning in full measure the love he deserved. The guilt that now consumed her left little for anything or anyone else — least of all Laura English.

A thick manila envelope, forwarded from Norm's office and bearing the 20th Century Fox insignia, arrived in the mail. It contained a script, to which was attached a note:

Laura dear,

I hope you will forgive the intrusion at this sad time, but the enclosed could have been written for you. If you would like to chat with me about it, please call at any time. Sherrie and I send our love,

Phil Simon

She held the envelope in her hands for a long while, feeling its weight on her palms and remembering how David, after his first operation, put off returning to work. But David had wanted time away from commitments in order to savor the life that had been returned to him. She cared little for whatever years were left to her; meaningless years that would stretch out one after the other. What good would anything be without David?

She heaved the heavy envelope into the waste paper basket.

Others scripts came: producers and directors apologizing for intruding on your grief or bothering you at this sad time. Without hesitation, she threw them all away.

The telephone rang constantly. She knew that friends were being kind, and somewhere in her mind she appreciated their concern, but she was existing in a different reality from the rest of the world. It was all but impossible to respond when she heard Maureen Kent's voice on the other end of the line inviting her to a very small dinner ... *you'll know everybody* or Gerry Maddox asking her to the symphony *you don't have to get dressed up and it's your favorite Mahler* or one of her other friends inviting her to come to a movie with the family or Sunday lunch and dominoes.

Sweetly, she refused them all and soon discovered the trick of disconnecting the phone cords.

Only Norm would not be put off. After two days of trying unsuccessfully to reach Laura by telephone, he went around to the house. He rang the doorbell and banged on the door, calling her name. Getting no response, he investigated until he found an open window, and raising it as high as he could, squeezed his bulk inside. He could hear the sounds of Thelonious Monk's *'Round Midnight*. How many times had he been in this house when David had played that record? A lump caught in his throat.

He found Laura sitting on the living room floor reading a letter. By her feet lay a pile of envelopes.

"How the hell did you get in!" she demanded, eyeing the black raw silk jumpsuit and ankle-high red lizard boots. As usual, wide bangles encircled his wrists and rings glinted on several fingers. In spite of herself, a smile twitched at the corners of her mouth.

"Through a window. Thank God you're still British enough to need fresh air in the middle of November. I'm here to tell you that you're coming to Thanksgiving dinner, and no arguments. I'm making my grandmother's famous stuffing with seven secret ingredients and garlic mashed potatoes and I'm getting a free-range turkey."

"A free-range what?" she said, eyes still on the letter.

"It's a turkey that roams around pecking at worms and beetles instead of being crated up and force fed on, pardon the expression, hormone pellets. Anyway, they're supposed to taste like turkeys did at Thanksgiving when we were kids."

"We didn't have Thanksgiving in England, idiot."

"Well, you're having it now! And I'm not spending a whole day over a hot stove just for Gerry."

"I'm in a terrible mood."

"Well, I didn't expect you'd be entertaining us with jokes and snappy patter right at this particular moment in your life. We just want you there. You can even come in that hideous nightgown and those purple things, whatever they are, if you like."

Once again, a little smile pulled at the corners of her mouth.

"Laura, baby," he said slipping off the couch and settling down next to her on the floor. "you've simply got to start getting out. I know it'll be hard at first, but if you don't you're going to forget how to be around people and you'll turn into a recluse like Barbara Hutton or Howard Hughes and end up living on Coca-Cola and growing thirteen-inch fingernails. Speaking of which, you could really use a manicure, sweetie."

"I need more time by myself."

"Have you thought about work at all?" he asked very gently.

She stared into the distance for a long while before she spoke. "It's funny, David always use to say that the characters I played were like other selves inside me and that no matter what ever happened in my life, they would always struggle to get out."

She paused, seeing into the past. "You know," she continued, "David helped with me with my very first part, night after night, until I got it right. We had such bitter arguments about the back story and the deeper meaning behind the dialogue." Again, she paused, thinking of those early days at Briarwood. "It got very intense at times, but David was always right. It was his insights that made me able to achieve whatever I have done as an actress. There wasn't once in nearly twenty years that he wasn't there for me." Tears filled her eyes and fell, unheeded, down her face.

"He was a very special guy."

"Yes, he was. Look at this." Laura handed him the letter she had been reading.

Dear Mrs. Landau,

I'm writing to say how sorry I was to read about David's death. I worked for your husband on twelve films. Because of his kindness I was never out of a job. After I met David I went through a pretty rough time. My wife died giving birth to our little girl and I was fit for nothing. David tracked me down. How he did it I don't know to this day. I'm a carpenter by trade and he put me to work building sets for Bitter Tuesday. After that he used me on every film he made in Britain. David was like a brother to me, and I loved him as if he were one of my own. If there's anything you ever need, please call on me.

Sincerely, David Jenks

13 Penn Street, Shoreditch, London U.K.

Norm handed her the letter. "Do you know this person?"

"No. David never mentioned him. But that's only one in hundreds I've received, some from strangers and some from very well-known people. She looked through the scattered pile on the floor. "Here." She handed him a few of the letters.

He glanced at the pages:

". . . and your husband financed my training at RADA because he said he had faith that one day I would. . . ." It was signed by a well-known stage actor.

". . . David gave me a part in *The Great Napoleon* when no one else would hire me. I had just come out of an addiction treatment program and no one else would take the chance. . . ." This one was from an actress who won an Academy Award two years earlier.

". . . Mr. Landau put my son through university after my husband died. I will never forget. . . ."

On and on, page after page, he read. Finally, he looked up at Laura. His eyes were wet. "These are a great tribute."

"Yes, they are. You know David always gave so much to Robin and me. I didn't realize that he gave to so many others as well. He was always there, Norm. Through the successes and the disappointments. Everything. He was my best friend and I . . ."

"Don't you see that David wouldn't want you to shut yourself away like this? He'd want you to start your life again. And for you that means work."

"I just don't give a damn about it anymore."

"And what about your public? Don't you give a damn about them? Do you know that hundreds of letters come to Galaxy every day? Gerry told me that they've put on an extra girl just to handle your mail. And those letters all say the same thing. Are you all right, and when are you coming back? Whether you like to or not you're a very famous woman and there are people out there who care about you."

"I know it but . . . look, all I ever wanted to do when I was a girl was perform. First it was on the stage with my Uncle Bertie, and then, after Jamie brought me to London, it was films at Briarwood. David used to say that I was only really alive when I was performing, and maybe that was true — but for now it's gone. I've had a lot of time to think these past weeks. For the first time in my life, I can see myself as I really am, and it scares the hell out of me."

"What do you mean?"

She lit a cigarette and inhaled the smoke. "Well, when I was a girl I was very much in love with a boy . . . someone I knew in Bournemouth. There was a time when I could have been with him, but more than anything, I wanted to be an actress so I went to London instead. He went away about the same time I was making my first film. Then, years later I saw him again and I think . . . no, I'm sure . . . that I could have had a second chance with him. But I stayed with David, not for David's sake or Robin's, but to keep my career intact."

"Laura, don't tell me you've been beating yourself up over an old flame. You did the right thing. No matter what you say, you knew David and Robin were ultimately more important and . . ."

"You don't understand. The man was . . . is . . . Robin's father."

"Oh." Norm was silent for a moment. "Did David know?"

"Oh, yes, David knew."

"And that's why you married him."

"Yes."

"And this other guy. You said you saw him again?"

"Once."

"And what happened?"

"Nothing. That's what I'm trying to tell you. John Keith was the great love of my life. The father of my child, for God's sake. But when I had the chance to be with him, I didn't take it. I was afraid to let myself go with whatever feelings might still have been there, because my career would have derailed, maybe forever. Now, what kind of a monster does that make me?

"Laura, baby, did you ever think that deep inside you knew that you belonged with David after all? Maybe that's why you didn't run off with this John person."

"You're right. Deep inside I knew that I belonged with David, because with him could I maintain the status quo. Because with him would I be able to continue being Laura English. And David knew it, too. He knew that what he was getting from me was a kind of leftover love. Even his son was a leftover from another man. Because of my monumental selfishness, David never got a hundred percent of anything."

"That's not true, Laura. I saw the way you were with him through all his illness. How patient and gentle, and how you got him to start writing. I knew you and David, as a couple, for twelve years and in all that time I never saw anything but love between you."

She laughed. "Yes, we had it all, sweetness and light, never a nasty word, but was that real? Norman, I know that David loved me more than anything, even his work, but that was not true for me. I loved Laura English more than anything. The love I had for David was really based on his understanding of what it meant for me to be a performer. He understood the kind of compulsion performers have that trumps everything else — even passion. I wouldn't allow myself to give in to the real passion I had for John, because I wouldn't have had anything left for Laura English. David understood everything and put up with it. We both shared ourselves with Laura English."

"But sweetie, don't you see that if everything you've just said is true, then what you need most is to get back to being Laura English."

She put her hand on his arm and looked up into his eyes. "But Norm, now that David is gone, I've lost her too. It's as if Laura English died with him."

CHAPTER 28

LONDON, 1973

"What did you say?"

"I'm going to Israel, Auntie Kit."

"But, darling, surely there are other art schools you could apply to. Why are you just giving up this way? So what if Chelsea turned you down? There's St. Martin's in the Tottenham Court Road and ..."

"My mind's made up. I just wanted to say goodbye and also to thank you so much for the very nice time I had at the wedding."

"I'm just sorry that your mother wasn't there. I will never know why Jamie told me it was Simon who was engaged when he called me in California. He was probably thinking about some crisis at the studio. Anyway, if I had known it was young Jamie and Sophie I could have stayed on for another few weeks in Belvedere. And I'm sure I would have convinced Laura to come back with me. As it is, I feel terribly guilty because, from what I've heard from Gerry Maddox, it seems your mother has closed herself off. It's really very upsetting. Have you told her about going to Israel?"

"Yes."

"And what did she say?"

"She said she thought it was a good idea."

"Well, I don't," said Kitty. "You are an Englishman, Robin, as your father was, and your future is here. Your mother told me all about the Chelsea Art School. She said that it was probably too avant-garde for you. I know that your talent lies in finer work. Perhaps you should go in for medical illustration or architecture. In any case, you must pursue your studies here, where you are surrounded by people who love you, Simon and the two Jamies and your grandparents and . . . me." Her voice broke. "You know that you are just like a son to me, and I don't want you losing your head and running off to the ends of the earth just because you were turned down by a school you had your heart set on."

"I'm not going to Israel because I wasn't accepted at Chelsea, Auntie Kit. I'm over that disappointment now. If I wanted to stay in London, as you say, there are several good schools where I could apply. I want to go to Israel because I think it's what Dad would have wanted."

"How can you say that? David never expressed any interest in Israel."

"But you're wrong. When I was a small boy he used to tell me stories about his old headmaster at boarding school. Dad admired him a great deal. He used to say that it is the obligation of every Jew, once in his lifetime, to contribute in some way to his people. He did it with *Home Land*. I went to Israel with Dad when he was scouting location sites for the film. I'll never forgot the visit we made to Degania, the first kibbutz ever established in Israel, and I've never forgotten how brave the kids were who lived there. They all seemed to have a deep sense of commitment. I want to make my own contribution — in Israel, not London."

Kitty sighed deeply. "Well, darling, if your mind is made up, there is nothing more I can say. You will take care of yourself? And don't forget your manners, I hear they're a uncouth bunch over there." She laughed "And write to us now and then?"

"Yes, Auntie Kit, I will."

"Goodbye, then, my dearest boy."

CHAPTER 29

MEXICO CITY, 1973

It was getting dark. Laura huddled down in the canvas chair and thought of how, in the end, she didn't eat Norm's free-range turkey or spend Christmas with the Paxtons. Instead, she flew to Mexico City.

Among the condolence letters that arrived daily after David's death a year ago, was one from Glenda Fisher:

> Dearest Laura,
>
> Gerry says you're holed up in your house crying. Why don't you fly down here instead? I'm swamped with work, so won't have any time to nag you about getting dressed or eating or going out to the local hotspots. You can stay in your room or sit in the garden. The autumn sun is warm, and the swimming pool is divine. There's a chair under a mammoth umbrella waiting for you. My little Oaxacan, Belen, isn't much at conversation, but gives a great massage. Buy yourself a black wig and a ticket on Aero Mexico and come. No need to give me notice. Just arrive.
>
> Mi casa, as they say around here, es tu casa.
>
> Love, as ever, Glenda

And so it was, on Thanksgiving Day, hair hidden under a huge Hermès scarf and a small suitcase her only luggage, Laura arrived at Glenda Fisher's house in the Pedregal district of Mexico City. She stayed until the new year.

For once, Glenda had not exaggerated when she said she would leave Laura alone. She was half way through the process of writing a book on the archeological sites of Yucatán and Oaxaca, and her days were spent working in the little office at the back of the house. Still skinny, Glenda had given up design-er clothes in favor of something Laura assumed must be a Frida Khalo look, consisting of embroidered Mexican blouses, long skirts, heavy silver earrings and huaraches. Her dark hair was braided with colored yarn and coiled into a crown at the top of her head.

The bookshelves in Laura's room were crammed with mysteries and recent bestsellers. Despite the altitude, the autumn weather in Mexico City was still warm and she spent the first two days after her arrival sitting in the promised chair, under the big umbrella, reading. Just as she started to feel hungry, the silent Oaxacan maid brought her a light lunch on a tray. When the day heated up, she dove into the pool. If she felt sleepy, she let herself doze in the chair under the big umbrella.

One morning, after she had been at Glenda's for almost a week, Laura decided it was time to take a walk and explore the neighborhood. She found the Pedrigal district, constructed on an extinct lava bed, like no other she had ever seen. Flowers, whose colors where more vivid than any in Bournemouth or Belvedere, grew everywhere in the rich volcanic soil. Many of the ultra modern houses, including Glenda's, were constructed out of the same black lava rock upon which the district was built. Laura had expected the neighborhoods in Mexico City to be replicas of the picturesque colonial villages she had seen on movie sets but the houses here in Pedrigal looked more like those on the cliffs of the Pacific Palisades.

Curious to see the rest of the city, Laura, in scarf and dark glasses, finally ventured out.

For her first excursion, she took a taxi to the Museo de Antropologia in Chapultepec Park. There she latched onto the tail of a group whose guide pro-vided a running lecture as he herded them into room after room of Aztec, Toltec and Zapotec artifacts. From the museum she wandered up the hill to Maximilian and Carlota's Castle. Filled with magnificent furniture, paintings and tapestries, it was similar to any other nineteenth century European palace — and as different as possible from the ancient Mexican world she had left back at the museum.

Now Laura spent every day exploring the city. She visited the Casa Azul, Frida Khalo's house in Coyoacan and the nearby Leon Trotsky museum, which exhibited his papers and, in pride of place, the ice pick with which he had been murdered. Laura loved Coyoacan, which turned out to be exactly the colonial village of her imagination. For the first time since David's death, she was unshackled by the guilt that had paralyzed her for so many months. As she explored the city, she felt only a wistful nostalgia in wishing David was there to share it with her. She thought of the amusing comments he would have made about the over-the-top restaurants and boutiques in the Colonia Juarez and how he would have loved the continental atmosphere of the Colonia Polanco and the charm of San Angel.

Late every afternoon, Glenda emerged from her office, poured drinks, and put a stack of LP's on the phonograph. Together, they sipped Bacardi highballs and listened to Dave Brubeck and Cal Tjader and Stan Getz. Instead of the overwhelming sadness Laura experienced in Belvedere, listening to these same records from David's collection, she now relaxed into the music. Later, side by side in the blue and yellow tiled kitchen, they chatted comfortably while Glenda broiled a chicken or some giant prawns and Laura tossed a big green salad. Laura was getting to know a different Glenda: one who had not lost her wicked sense of humor but who could be sensitive to a friend's need for time to heal.

As Christmas neared, party invitations piled up on the kitchen counter. Glenda assured Laura her friends would welcome her, but when Laura, still reticent to meet people, said she would rather stay at home, Glenda did not push. The one exception was Christmas Eve.

"Listen, baby, no matter what you say, I am not going to leave you alone on Christmas Eve. Warren and Thea Briggs are two of my oldest friends in Mexico. They're both amazing artists and the guiding force behind the Bazar del Sábado, which showcases the work of so many talented craftsmen. Their house in Coyoacan is a museum of Mexican arte popular, and their Christmas Eve party has been a tradition in the arts community for years. It's very low key, and you have my word of honor that no one is going to ask for your autograph."

"All right."

"What?"

"I said, all right, I'll go."

"Well, what do you know about that?"

Glenda was true to her word. The Briggses were warm and welcoming, and their guests easy to know. Laura felt completely relaxed in the bohemian atmosphere. It was stimulating chatting with the kind of people David had liked best: artists and writers, even a few filmmakers, whose conversations were thought-provoking and witty. The whole scene was eerily reminiscent of David's flat in Earl's Court. Glenda had anticipated that Laura might want to leave early, but she practically had to drag her away at 2:00 A.M.

Now, as Glenda put it, that the first olive was out of the bottle, she had no trouble getting her friend out in the evenings. The next week flew by in a round of parties. For the first time since David's final illness, Laura was having fun.

Reluctantly, on New Year's Day, Glenda put Laura on the Aero Mexico flight back to San Francisco. "I'm going to miss you like crazy."

"I think I rather overstayed my welcome. I can't believe it's been over a month."

"You couldn't possibly overstay. Come back any time, little sister."

"Glenda, you gave me back something I thought I had lost."

"It was there all the time, Laura. Now go make some movies."

"I'll try."

Back in Belvedere, the magic of Mexico stayed with Laura. The scripts, sent weekly from Norm's office, still went unread and her telephones remained unplugged, but the crushing depression, fueled by guilt, was gone. At times she could see, somewhere in the near distance, a faint light shining at the end of what had been a very dark tunnel.

At first, the knocking sounded as if it were coming from next door or down the street. Then she realized it was someone at her own front door. She sighed, got out of the campaign chair, and crept around the side of the house in order to get a glimpse of who the caller might be. Norm, probably. Although he had been angry at her for standing them up on Thanksgiving, he understood her reasons for hiding out with Glenda in Mexico City and still dropped by to see her whenever he was in Belvedere with Gerry.

The ancient streetlight, up on Beach Road, shed a faint amber light down the walkway and into the front garden. It barely illuminated the bulky figure standing at the front door. Laura squinted into the semi-darkness. Her breath caught and she put her hand on the wall of the house to brace herself. The man standing outside her door wasn't Norm.

CHAPTER 30

KEFAR AVIV, ISRAEL, 1973

It took a moment, coming out of the noonday glare into the mess hall, for Robin to adjust to dim filtered light of the large room. When his eyes adapted, he recognized some of the young people crowded, shoulder to shoulder, at the round tables that packed the noisy room. He was late. There wasn't much left on the platters set out on the long table near the kitchen. He took a plate and helped himself to what remained of the dregs of salad and falafel. One lone pita sat in the bread basket. He spooned some hummus onto its center, folded it over, and bit into it hungrily. He turned back toward the room and saw Michaela, in tan shorts and a white camp shirt identical to his own, waving from a table in the corner. He smiled and went to join her.

For the first time in over a year, Robin Landau was happy. Through some friends of his father's in the World Zionist Organization, he had obtained a place in a six-month work/study program at the British kibbutz Kefar Aviv. He arrived in the upper Galilee toward the end of April and started work immediately in the vineyards, planting terraces of new vines. Evenings, he had kitchen detail, and three days a week he coached the boy's cricket team. The study part of the program involved classes in Hebrew, taught out of doors on a hillock behind the mess hall. The kibbutz had a fine arts program, and Robin was studying etching and lithography under Dov Perez, one of Israel's foremost printmakers, who also had a teaching position at the Marcello Gianni Institute in Tel Aviv.

Robin set his tray down where Michaela had saved him a place.

"You're late," she shouted over the noise. Michaela had just finished her second year at the University of Tel Aviv and was spending some of her vacation time at Kefar Aviv with her father, Dov Perez. She was one of the few *sabras*, or native Israelis, in residence at the kibbutz, which, in summer, was inhabited predominately by British students.

"I know," he said, hungrily attacking his lunch. "I had to stay after class." He laughed. "I don't think I'm ever going to learn Hebrew. I'm so far behind everybody else."

"Why is that? You all started at the same time, didn't you?" She had a charming accent that, to Robin's ears, sounded vaguely French.

"I guess it's because they learned Hebrew for their Bar Mitzvahs and I didn't have one, but mostly it's because I can't concentrate."

"And why is that?" she said looking into his eyes.

"My mind is too full of you."

She put her hand over his and smiled.

Sitting close to her as he was, a feeling of intense desire swept over Robin. She was small and exquisitely made, with golden skin and almond-shaped hazel eyes that slanted slightly at the corners. Her small body was delightfully supple and sensuous, attributes he had become aware of the first time they made love. Though most of the girls Robin knew in London were not virgins, they did expect a bit of courting before hopping into bed. The open attitude of this Israeli girl both stunned and excited him.

They had met at the weekly Kefar Aviv dance. He had noticed her right away. She was standing by the phonograph looking through a stack of records. Not much over five feet tall, with a mane of gold streaked hair, she was the most desirable girl Robin had ever seen. He crossed over to her side of the room and, as casually as he could, came up beside her.

"I'm trying to find a Doors record I saw here last week. Do you like them?" she asked.

"Sorry, what did you say?"

"The Doors, do you like them? I'm trying to find 'Light My Fire.' Oh, here it is." Their eyes met as she looked up.

"Here, let me put it on," he said.

She started to move to the music, losing herself completely in the beat. He moved with her and they danced until the side was over. They played more records, and during a slow tune by The Mamas and The Papas, she pressed herself up against him and said, "Let's go somewhere."

Robin laughed.

"You think that's funny?" she said, her raised eyebrows causing her eyes to slant up.

Robin pulled her close to him. "No. I don't think it's funny, just unexpected."

"Don't you like me?"

"Of course I do."

"Well?"

"Where can we go? We both live in dorms with a lot of other people."

"My father lives alone. We can go to his room." She grabbed his hand and led him out of the hall.

"What if your father comes back" Robin said as they lay on Dov Perez's narrow bed."He's going to be gone for another couple of hours at least," she answered, turning on her stomach and resting her chin in her hands. "These chess games always go past midnight, and even if he did come back, so what?"

"Well, I'm sure he wouldn't be too happy to find me in bed with his daughter."

"My father isn't like one of your stuffy Englishmen."

"Maybe not, but when it comes to his own daughter . . ."

"Don't be ridiculous. In Israel we are more natural about sex than you are in England. Here, if you like someone and you want them, you just do it."

"Oh, I see," he said, reaching out for her.

Robin had lost his virginity a year and a half before with one of Simon Paxton's cast-off girlfriends. Since then, he had had a few sexual encounters with various girls, but none of these experiences had done much in the way of exploring any erotic sensibilities he might have possessed, for these partners had, without exception, accepted his lovemaking with a placid equanimity that left Robin feeling as if he had performed the act alone. Michaela was anything but placid, and it wasn't long after their first encounter that he was completely besotted with the girl.

The dining hall was emptying and Robin looked at his watch. He had to be in the vineyard in a little less than fifteen minutes.

"You know, my father thinks you have a great deal of talent," said Michaela, looking reflectively at her bowl of fruit salad. She started picking grapes out of the compote. Very gently, she pushed one between his lips and into his mouth. "He told me you have a remarkable eye for detail. He says it's a gift, like total recall."

"I guess it is. I used to spend a lot of time drawing in our garden when I was a small boy."

"My father is certain, if you apply, you would be accepted into a work study program at the Institute."

"The Institute?"

"The Marcello Gianni Institute. He teaches there. You only have a few more weeks here. Have you given any thought about what you want to do then?"

Since meeting Michaela, Robin had not let himself think about what would come after Kefar Aviv. "I suppose I'll go back to London."

"You don't sound very enthusiastic about it."

"I'm not," he said, looking earnestly into her face.

"Then why not apply to the Institute? I'll be back in Tel Aviv at the university." She ran her fingertip along the back of his hand. "We can see each other often."

"Does he really think I'd be accepted?"

"Absolutely. Work study students are given living accommodations and a stipend. You wouldn't have to think about a thing but perfecting your skills." Her hand dropped under the table and rested on his thigh. A path of heat blazed under her hand as she stroked the bare flesh, and the light cotton fabric of his shorts strained as his penis bulged in its crotch. "Robin, I don't want you to go back to London." Her hand closed over the bulge.

That September, Robin entered the Marcello Gianni Institute of Fine Arts in Tel Aviv.

CHAPTER 31

BELVEDERE, 1973

Laura stood facing John Keith. "My God. John! What are you doing here?"

He laughed. "What else should I be doing here? I came to see you."

"But . . . how did you find out where I live?"

"Jane, the whole world knows where you live. Do you think we might go inside?"

She led him around to the back of the house and into the kitchen. Her legs were like rubber and her heart was beating unevenly against the wall of her chest. With trembling fingers, she groped along the wall for the light switch. In the glare of the overhead kitchen light, she noticed sandy threads mixed in with his blond curls and few faint lines around his mouth and eyes. Otherwise, he looked very much the same as the last time she had seen him sitting in the seat behind hers at the film festival in Acapulco.

"I don't believe this. What are you doing here?"

"You asked me that before. I'm here to see you. I was in New York on business, so I decided to look you up."

"But how did you get my address?"

"It wasn't difficult. The organization I work for is very good at that sort of thing."

"I still can't believe it's really you. I mean, no warning, you didn't call or anything."

"I tried to call, but your phone must be out of order. I couldn't get through."

"I got into the habit of unplugging it a year ago. Too many calls."

"Yes, I can imagine. Say, do you think I could have a drink?"

"Sorry," she said shaking her head "I just still can't believe this. You said a drink?"

"Vodka, if you have it."

She opened the freezer, pulled out the bottle of Stolichnaya, and took two glasses out of a cabinet over the counter.

He poured some of the clear liquid into a glass and drank it off in one gulp. "Hmm, good. Nothing like it for warming the blood." He gestured the bottle toward her. "Have some?"

"Yes, I think I could use something. I'm still in shock." She sat down at the kitchen table and put the glass to her lips. "It's unbelievable. You, here in my house. Where did you come from? I mean where do you live?"

He took a chair opposite her. "Nowhere, really. I mean I travel quite a lot but . . . London." He poured himself some more vodka. "I have a flat in London."

"Are you still working as a journalist?"

"No. I have a job with an organization based in Jordan. In fact, I've just handed in my resignation, so I guess I'm a free agent now."

"I see. And what kind of work did you do over there, in the Middle East, I mean." She took another sip of her drink.

"Oh, this and that. Boring stuff, really. So, all your dreams came true. You're a big film star. I wasn't very nice about that, was I? I mean when we were young, you know, back in Bournemouth."

"Oh, John, that was so long ago."

"You know, Jane, I've never married or even had a serious relationship with a woman. Never came close. It's always been you. That's what I would have told you if you had come to the Hotel Caleta that day. I mean it. I've never stopped loving you." He stood and came around to her side of the table. Looking down, he reached out and gently pulled her to her feet.

"John," she whispered, and walked into his arms.

CHAPTER 32

TEL AVIV, 1974

Completely engrossed in the job at hand, Robin Landau wasn't aware that the door to his office had opened. Not wishing to distract him in his delicate task, Dov Perez waited until Robin finished before he spoke. Looking over his shoulder at the British passport, he smiled. "Flawless, as usual. Robin, in all the time you have been here . . . can it be almost a year? In all that time I have never seen your work anything less than perfect."

Robin looked around. "Thanks," he said, stretching his hands above his head to relieve the tension in his shoulders. He jerked his head in the direction of a small pile of documents sitting at the side of the desk. "These are dry."

"May I look?"

"Sure."

Perez picked up a magnifying glass lying on Robin's desk and examined the slightly worn pages through the heavy lens. After a few minutes, he set the glass down and clicked his tongue against his teeth. "You are a great artist," said Perez, drawing up a chair to sit beside Robin.

"The Pablo Picasso of document forgers."

"Duplicator, my boy, duplicator. Tell me, isn't it exhausting, day after day, doing such precise work?"

"No, I like it. I think I was meant to be a . . ."

"Duplicator."

Robin smiled.

Since coming to Israel a year and a half before, Robin had grown taller and even more broad shouldered. His blunt jaw line and jutting brows were those of a mature man, softened only by a fringe of golden lashes that framed his pale green eyes, and a mop of unruly golden hair that curled down over his forehead.

Due to Robin's remarkable talent as a draftsman, Dov Perez obtained a place for him at the Marcello Gianni Institute of Fine Arts. A period of intensive training followed, during which Robin was exposed to new disciplines, designed to help him better utilize his particular skill, as well as large doses of Israeli propaganda, reinforced by his admiration of Dov Perez and his obsession with Michaela. To please her, Robin applied for Israeli citizenship and entered an army training unit for a period of six months of basic training. To the surprise of his platoon leader, the young Englishman turned out to be the best shot in the unit. At the end of his training, he was put on military reserve for two years.

He wanted desperately to marry Michaela, but she put him off. "The time isn't right for that, Robin. I have to do so much traveling for the Institute. It seems these days I'm away more than I'm here. It would be impossible to settle down and set up housekeeping in a Tel Aviv apartment. Be patient."

Dov Perez set aside the documents he had been examining. "Robin, I want to discuss something with you."

"What is it?" Perez's tone was serious and Robin's face became instantly alert.

"I have just heard that your father's friend Gerald Maddox is going to re-release *Home Land* sometime in the near future. I saw the film in 1963. It was a masterpiece, but it wasn't popular with the masses in the United States. Evidently, Maddox thinks it will be worth another showing. Maybe next year."

"They're reissuing all of Dad's films. The vultures will take advantage of his death to make money."

"Maybe so, but that film of your father's was good for Israel's image in the world. I want you to go to the United States and make yourself available to Mr. Gerald Maddox for television appearances or tours or whatever publicity is needed to help promote this film."

"But I loathe Gerry Maddox. He's just an old queer who hangs around kissing my mother's ass."

"Enough!"

Robin closed his eyes. "I'm sorry. I just despise that whole movie crowd."

"But it was your father's life."

"My father," Robin said, "was never like any of those people."

"Including your mother?"

"Especially my mother."

"Robin, whatever your personal feelings, you need to do this thing for us . . . for Israel. This may not happen for another six months or even a year. They have to completely re-master the original print."

"Yes, Dov. All right." Robin picked up the pen and turned back to the passport. "When the time comes, I'll be ready to do whatever is necessary."

CHAPTER 33

SAN FRANCISCO, 1974

It was 8:00 A.M. Pacific Standard Time and Dr. Doug Fredricks was going off duty. As usual, he stopped at the gift shop in the lobby of Mt. Zion Hospital to pick up the morning *Chronicle* and chat for a minute with Gert Herzog. Gert had been in charge of the shop for over forty years.

"Hi, doc. Any interesting cases come in last night?" Gert's thin brown face broke into a mass of fine smile lines.

"Very quiet, Gert," he said, opening the paper and yawning.

"Looks like rain again," she said, glancing out of the large plate glass windows in the lobby of the hospital. "I hate rain on birthdays."

"Yeah," he said, leaning up against the counter, idly turning the pages of the paper. "Whose party are you putting on this time?"

"My five-year-old great-grandson. If my grandchildren keep having babies, I'm going to have to buy a bigger house just for the parties . . ."

Gert's voice faded into background noise as Doug Fredricks stared at a photo on the page in his hand. It was an ad for Saturday Night at the Movies on Channel 2. The movie this week was *Mirror Image*. The photograph was of Laura English. She hadn't made a movie since her husband died over two years ago. He often thought about the night they sat together, side by side on the window ledge next to her husband's bed, sharing the death watch. He wondered if she still lived across the bay in Belvedere — and if he'd ever see her again.

CHAPTER 34

BELVEDERE, 1975

Once again, the false spring had come and, across the Golden Gate Bridge in Marin County, the air was heady with scents of plum blossom, tender new grass, and salty breezes blowing in from the Pacific over the western hills.

As he had the morning after his startling appearance at her door nearly a year ago, John Keith stood at Laura's living room window, feet apart, staring out at the sparkling bay and the San Francisco skyline beyond. "My God, that view! I'll never get use to it."

Laura came up behind him. "Let's go outside."

She led him into the garden and over to the wishing well. They stood side by side looking into it. "Uncle Matt and Aunt Rose had one in their garden, remember?"

"Yes, I do," he said, smiling at her. "I remember everything."

"So many times, before you came, I used to look into this well wishing…" she hesitated.

"Yes? What did you wish?"

His husky whisper in her ear sent shivers down her spine. "That you were here with me."

"I am now."

She turned to look into his eyes. "I still can't quite get it into my head that you are really standing here. That all these past months aren't all something I've been dreaming."

"This isn't a dream, my Janie." He drew her against him.

It was as if time had been suspended during the years they were separated. These days were all that mattered. Laura's heart was at peace and John felt he was home at last.

He could see why she had made her home in Marin County. He, too, loved the small towns, each with their special character. Ross, San Anselmo, and Mill Valley, nestled in the redwoods. Sausalito, the waterfront village, where he and Laura never tired of strolling along the docks, fantasizing about buying one particular two-masted schooner, with a For Sale sign attached to its stern, and sailing down the coast to Mexico. They took walks on a path next to the overgrown train tracks that traversed the old railroad towns of Larkspur and Corte Madera; marveling at the sudden change, when spring came, and the path was in full bloom with tall banks of brilliant morning glories, horse chestnut, and golden acacia. They spent a Saturday at the Marin City Flea Market, where John bought Laura an antique bangle bracelet studded with tiny emeralds and pearls. One Sunday, they wandered into the old Mission San Rafael and watched the priest baptize a screaming red-faced newborn. Sometimes, on the spur of the moment, Laura tucked a couple of sandwiches in David's old knapsack and they drove to Fairfax or Ross to hike to one of the seven lakes that supplied the drinking water for the county. Because the shore meant Bournemouth and home, often on summer days they drove over the hills of West Marin, past horse farms and grazing cattle and pastures carpeted with bright yellow mustard, to Limantour or Dillon's Beach just for the pleasure of getting their feet wet in the freezing surf.

Happiness sharpened their appetites for food as well as exploration; frothy Ramos fizzes and eggs Benedict on the terrace at the Alta Mira Hotel, juicy hamburgers under a bower of hanging ferns at Davood's, and picnics of Italian salami on crusty French in a grove of giant redwood trees at Old Mill Park.

September came and, with it, Indian summer. The fogs of July and August gave way to clear mornings and hot, windy afternoons which ended in glorious sunsets, each arriving a few minutes earlier than the day before as autumn, lurking in the wings, telegraphed cooler months ahead. One such day in October, they climbed to the top of the headlands at Pt. Reyes.

"Too bad you weren't here last winter," said Laura as they stood high above the ocean. "If this were January, we'd be watching the annual flotilla of whales steam by on their way to the spawning grounds in Baja California."

"It's a date. We'll come out here on New Year's Day, 1975." And they did.

Most evenings Laura and John spent at home in front of the fire, but occasionally they dressed up and drove into the city for a meal at Trader Vic's or Fleur de Lys. After dinner they sometimes went to the Lochinvar Room or the Palace Corner for a dance. Close in his arms on a crowded floor, bodies swaying to some memory-laden ballad out of their youth, Laura knew that, should death come at that very moment, she would have no regrets. The all-consuming love she had felt for John so many years ago in Bournemouth was still alive. Like the morning glories on the walking path, she was in full bloom, focusing on what they had now, at this moment, not thinking about the past and what life with him might have been had not Laura English intervened. Laura English, with her overwhelming need to perform, her compulsion to please an audience that overrode everything and everyone else, including John and, later, her own child.

Who was this creature called Laura English? Was she a monster, without a heart, only alive in front of an audience or a camera? And what about David? How much of herself had she ever given him? True, right from the start, she had never lied to him about John. David understood the way she felt, and still, month after month, had kept on asking her to marry him. And why had she finally given in? Not because her feelings for David had changed, but because she knew he would be exactly right for Laura English. Jamie Paxton might have made Laura English into a star but it was David Landau who, in their years together, had nourished her insatiable hunger to perform. David, the kindest, funniest, most intelligent of men, had cosseted her, indulged her, overlooked her every fault — even her neglect of Robin, whom he loved as his own. Despite the laughs they shared and the romps in bed and the care she had given him throughout his illness, David had always known that she would never be able to return his love in equal measure. It had taken almost a year of paralyzing guilt for Laura to realize that, as far as David had been concerned, whatever she was capable of giving him had been enough.

The happiness John and Laura were experiencing in being together wakened a new openness in him and, one by one, the mysterious layers that so frustrated her as a girl were slowly peeling away. Her dashing boy with teasing sea-green eyes and golden curls and secret thoughts kept hidden from her was finally talking about his life, as he had once started to do when he told her about his travels to France and Spain. One night, lying side by side in bed, he told her the rest of the story.

"I don't know if you ever noticed the initials *JGK* on my letter paper and my brushes. The *G* stands for, don't laugh, Glubb. My father was a lieutenant colonel in the regular army. When war was declared in 1914, he was sent to Cairo, and later he was posted to the region that became, after the war, Trans-Jordan. Shortly after he arrived in Trans-Jordan, he met John Bagot Glubb. He wasn't a flamboyant character like T. E. Lawrence, but John Glubb played just as important a part in support of the Arab uprising. Through Glubb, my father met Ali Ibn Faud, the son of a Hashemite emir. Because of this friendship with Faud, my father developed a deep understanding of Bedouin culture. Like

Glubb and Lawrence before him, he made it his personal mission to help them achieve the universal respect their ancient tradition deserved.

"After the war my father returned to England, met my mother, and settled down to an army desk job in London. But he never lost touch with John Glubb and, when I was born, he insisted I be named for his friend, whom the Hashemites now called Glubb Pasha. My father was never happy in London, and he asked Glubb to pull some strings to get him transferred back to the Near East. Not long after, he got the news there was an important post for him in Constantinople. He took it. When war broke out in '39, he was transferred to Libya. He managed to keep in touch with my mother, but not much could be said in letters so we had no idea where he might be fighting. In June of '42, just after my twelfth birthday, a telegram came that he had been killed at Mersa Matruh.

"I knew nothing about any of my father's history in the Middle East until that trip I told you about in 1947, when I wandered from Spain to Morocco. I was in Marrakech, living off my earnings from France and taking in as much of the local color as I could before all my money ran out. I knew I wouldn't be able to get work there, so I ate the local diet, stayed in a rat trap of an hotel, and saw the sights. One thing I did every few days was check in at the British counsel to get some of the money I had in the safe there and read the English newspaper.

"I was still asleep one morning when a man came knocking at the door of my room. He said his name was Ali Ibn Faud and that he was a friend of my father. His son was with him, a kid about my age called Hassim. Faud told me that the week before, at a reception at the British consulate, he heard about an English boy named Keith who was living in a disreputable part of town. The consul told him he had convinced the boy to leave his money in their safe because he was worried he might be robbed. Faud took me out of that flea bag and drove me up in the hills to an enormous villa, the closest thing to a palace I had ever seen.

"After I had been given a meal, Faud told me there was someone there who had come all the way from Amman, Jordan, especially to see me. He brought me into a room in another part of the house, and standing there was a man Faud said was William Keith. My father."

"You mean he wasn't dead? That must have been a terrible shock!" said Laura.

"Shock is an understatement! As far as I knew, my had father died in 1942. My mother and grandmother had grieved over his death for years. Now it turned out that my mother, who had a new husband, wasn't a widow at all. She was still married to my father, who was standing there — alive! I felt the room start to spin. Faud sat me down, and a servant brought me a glass of mint tea. When I felt better, my father told me his story.

"Obviously, he didn't die at Mersa Matruh. He escaped in the chaos of the battle and made his way to Jordan. He stayed in Amman all through the war, working directly under Ali Ibn Faud. It was sheer luck, or maybe fate, that Faud and I had been in Marrakech at the same time and that the British consul had been worried enough about me to mention my situation to him. Evidently, the palace in Marrakesh was a kind of vacation villa of Faud's wife's family. His primary residence was in Amman, where he headed up an organization whose purpose, since the United Nations had begun debating the issue, was to prevent the partition of Palestine.

"During the five days we spent together in that place up in the hills above Marrakech, my father explained in detail how, because of the universal guilt over what the Nazis did to the Jews during the war, the Zionists were on the verge of convincing the United Nations to rob the Palestinians of their ancient homeland. The work my father had been doing as an agent for the organization both he and Faud and Hassim belonged to was aimed at preventing that catastrophe. By the time he had to return to Amman, I understood what commitment to a cause meant. The last thing my father said to me before he left was that, someday, he wanted me to join him. A year later, he was dead. Killed by a Zionist agent in Cairo after the partition of Palestine.

"In 1953, Ali Ibn Faud contacted me to let me know there was a job for me with his son, Hassim, in Cairo. You were in London being groomed for stardom by James Paxton. So I went.

"Jane, now you see why your marrying a Jew and giving our son the name of a Jew is abhorrent to me." They were lying together in the darkness, her head cradled in his arm. His voice was low as he spoke. "He is my son, isn't he, Jane?"

Several times she had caught him studying photos of Robin, most taken with David at his side, but he had never asked her the question she had been dreading. Now that he had, Laura answered without hesitation. "Yes, he is."

She heard him sigh in the darkness.

"David was a good father to Robin. He . . ."

"I would rather not discuss that. You know, I read about your marriage and the birth of your son sitting in the bar at Shepherd's in Cairo. That was quite a blow, I'll tell you."

"Oh John, I . . ."

"I don't know why, but I always had the feeling your child might be mine. Then, when I saw that boy running across the street in Acapulco, it was like looking at myself, and when I met the man he called Dad, I knew for sure that man was the Jew you married." He paused for a long time and Laura, sensing he had more to say, said nothing.

"Jane, why didn't you meet me when I asked you to? It was just like that time in Marrakech with Faud. The gods put you and me in the same place at the same time. If you had just come to me that morning, I know I could have convinced you to take the boy and leave with me right then. I had a nice apartment in Cairo. We could have had a life together; you, me, and our son." Again, he paused. "I never stopped thinking about him after that time in Acapulco. Once, before I had to go on what might have turned out to be a pretty dangerous mission, I even wrote him a letter. I gave it to my superior, Greg Parker, who is based in London. He promised to get it to him in case anything happened to me. I imagine it's still sitting in Greg's safety deposit box." John said nothing more until a bitter little laugh broke the silence. "I suppose now that our son is no longer a child his values have become deeply rooted and probably differ 180 degrees from mine. Am I right?"

In spite of their new closeness, the one thing she could not bring herself to do was tell John their son was living in Israel. Instead of answering his question, she turned her body toward him and put her arm around his waist "John, why didn't you write to me after that first letter telling me you had gone to Egypt? I didn't even see it right away because I was . . . sick . . . at the time. But there were no other letters after that."

"I did write. Many times. I sent them all to Gran to forward on to you. Before she died she told me that a colleague of mine had contacted her with a warning that it would be putting me at great risk if she forwarded my correspondence. He said it would be best if she destroyed any letters. Instead, as each came, she hid it away. I found them all in a drawer after she died."

"Oh no!"

"She was an old lady, and she loved me very much. She was afraid to do otherwise."

"Everything would have been so different if she had sent your letters on to me."

"Would it?"

"Of course."

"Would you have really given up your film career to come and live in Egypt with me?"

"You know I would."

"Well, it's nice to think it, but the point is that we are together now." He sat up and looked down at her. Laura had never looked more radiant. He touched the red curls that lay in disarray on the pillow. "Jane, I can't discuss exactly what my work was, but I want you to know that the assignment I carried out in

New York before coming here was my last. I notified Cairo that I was taking early retirement, and they knew I meant it." He smiled "I always lived my life from one day to the next, one year to the next. I never cared much about planning any sort of future. What I'm trying to say is, now that I've found you again, I desperately want a future."

"John . . ."

"Let me finish, Jane. For twenty years, I worked for a cause that I believed in, and still believe in, passionately. It's hard to break ties with the organization. Sometimes it's impossible. But Hassim is my friend, and he is very high up in the organization. I put my trust in him, and so far, he's come through. All I want, for however long I have to live, is to be with you." He kissed her softly on her cheeks and eyes and then on her lips. His mouth trailed down her neck to her breasts, the velvet tip of her nipples. She drew him closer and started to caress him.

CHAPTER 35

PORTLAND, OREGON, 1975

Robin Landau tried to focus his attention on the face of the attractive woman sitting in the chair across from him, but the movements of the cameramen beyond her shoulder were distracting and the bright glare from the overhead lights forced his eyes into a squint. How did his mother manage to concentrate on what she was doing with everything else that went on behind the cameras? And this was only a simple interview program — she actually performed under these conditions. For a fleeting moment, a tiny wedge of respect pushed its way under the iron curtain of resentment.

"Tell us, Robin, why do you think *Home Land* was not a success when it was released twelve years ago?" asked the interviewer, smiling brightly.

"Well, Miss Flanders, you have to remember that films have changed drastically in recent years. When *Home Land* was released in 1962, the public was still used to seeing John Wayne westerns and Doris Day comedies at their local movie theaters. They wanted escape in their films rather than realism. My father was simply ahead of his time, that's all."

"And now the public is ready?"

"Definitely."

"Will your mother be attending the premiere next week?"

In every interview in every city across the United States, the same question had been asked, and every time the same sensation of coldness shot through him. He smiled. "I certainly hope she will."

"Is she still in Northern California?"

"Yes, I believe she is at her home there."

"Robin, your mother is still one of the most popular actresses of our time. Do you think she will be making another film in the near future, or has she gone into permanent retirement?"

"I do not have the answer to that question, Miss Flanders. My only hope is that she will attend the premiere showing of *Home Land* as a tribute to my father and as her first step in a reentry back into the world." Acid filled his throat as he recited the pat answer.

"That is a wish I'm sure we all share. Thank you, Robin Landau. Next up, Hollywood's own Don Loper will discusses the latest in spring fashions, but first some messages from the folks who bring you Portland AM."

Robin rose from the modular chair and disconnected the small microphone pinned to his lapel. The interviewer was holding a mirror to her face as a makeup man blotted her forehead and chin. The director approached him. He wore a Hawaiian print shirt and baggy jeans. His grizzled hair was tied back in a ponytail.

"Hey, I just wanted to say that you did all right."

"Thank you. I've been doing a lot of these programs, and I guess I'm getting used to it."

"How many shows you done?" He glanced over his shoulder at the next guest, who was now seated in the chair Robin had just vacated.

"This is the fourteenth."

"Christ. How many more you got?"

"Oh, just a few more. California is my final stop. I will be in Oakland tomorrow."

"Well, we all got our problems, man," he laughed. "Seriously, though, I wanted to tell you that I worked with your mom once on a picture."

"Really."

"Yeah, I was like fifth cameraman. She was a real doll to work with."

"Ah," Robin sighed.

"Yeah, a real doll. Listen, get her to go back to work."

"Well, I don't really . . ."

"Hey, they're starting. Later, man."

Robin took his handkerchief out of his pocket and wiped his upper lip.

"Mr. Landau?" Robin turned. A thin black girl with a clip board cradled in her arm handed him a slip of paper. "This message came for you while you were on camera."

"Thank you." The unfolded the pink paper read "Telephone Miss Perez as soon as possible." He ran out of the main entrance of the television station and hailed a taxi. "Benson Hotel, please, and hurry."

"Is everything all right, Micki?" Robin undid his tie and threw it on the bed.

"Fine. But something urgent just came up."

"God, your message scared me to death. I thought something had happened to you. What is it that is so urgent?" He started undoing the buttons of his shirt.

"There is an agent, a very important one, someone who has been responsible for the deaths of many of our people."

"Yes?"

"He lives in London but has not been seen there, or anywhere else in Europe or the Middle East, for almost a year. A week ago, a contact based in San Francisco spotted him. He's been under surveillance since then, and now we are certain exactly where he has been for the last year. He has been living with a friend north of San Francisco, where your mother lives."

"You mean in Marin County?"

"Yes. In Marin County. This man is a one of the most deadly anti-Israeli agents in the world. Mossad has been trying to eliminate him for nearly twenty years. We have no idea how long he will be in such a vulnerable position. This is an opportunity that may never come again. So you see how important it is."

"Why are you telling this to me?"

"It's been decided that you are to do it."

"Do what?"

"Take the sanction. Eliminate him."

"Me! But Micki, I've never . . . "

"That is what my father keeps saying but I know you can do it! Listen to me, Robin. Not only are you a superior marksman, but you have a unique knowledge of the area."

"But I'm a document forger, not a bloody assassin!"

Ignoring his remark, she went on. "Now listen carefully. It will be arranged for this Englishman to contact you. Tell him that you have been sent by his control, a person named Gregory Parker. Do you have that? Gregory Parker. Tell him that you must see him on a matter of great urgency about some information he has. And this is the most important part. You will ask to meet him in a secluded place out of doors. Only you know of such places in this . . . Marin County. You will be waiting for him, and when he arrives you will shoot him from ambush. It is as simple as that."

"Simple! Micki, I work with Mossad, yes, but as a duplicator. I forge passports and birth certificates. I don't even carry a gun, for Christ's sake!"

"But you were the best marksman in your army unit, and you told me that was because you had been shooting game in Scotland since you were a kid."

"I know, but this is killing a man. I can't do that."

"Yes, you can. You will be shooting through a high-powered lens at a distance. Think of him as an animal. It will be over in a matter of seconds."

Robin's heart was jerking wildly. He felt as if he were going to pass out. He sat down on the bed. "Miki, don't ask me to do this."

"I didn't hear you say that. When you get to San Francisco, you will go directly to 1563 25th Avenue. They will give you the weapon."

"Why can't someone there do it?"

"Robin. You don't understand. For over twenty years, this man has been one of the most lethal agents they have. He's with a pro-Arab organization headquartered in London, but he works mostly as an agent for an anti-Israeli group based in Cairo and, since 1964, he's also been associated to some degree with the PLO. I told you, he's not an Arab, he is an Englishman — an extremely disarming one. With charm and intelligence, this man has infiltrated pro-Israeli groups in Europe and America and has undermined them with disinformation. He has turned agents and sabotaged arms deals. And as far as carrying out assassinations, we are certain he took the Marcello Gianni and Hugo Frank sanctions. He has even murdered pro-peace Arabs. Remember the car bomb that killed the Jordanian Ali Ibn Haziz? Haziz was in the last stages of brokering an agreement with ..."

"Yes, I do remember. My mother told me how distressed my father was about that assassination. He was just out of surgery and she was worried it might affect his recovery. But I still say, why not let these people in San Francisco do it?"

"Because we don't know them well enough to trust them with something this important. There are hundreds of groups in the States like the one at 1563 25th Avenue. All kinds of people get attached to them. Robin, if it's to be done, you're the one to do it."

Robin tried to swallow, but his throat felt as if it was stuffed with cotton. "Michaela, I can't kill another human being."

"This man has killed many, many people . . . good people who wanted to help Israel. Robin, he murdered the man who endowed the Institute where you work! He has been lying low for a year. Mossad has word there is something big in the planning stages. Whatever it is, this man will be involved."

"What if I shoot him and miss?" Robin's hand was shaking.

"You were the best shot in your unit during your army training. You won't miss. Robin, until now this man has never been in such a vulnerable position."

He thought of her as she pleaded with him on the other end of the wire. Tiny and perfect, her eyes full of passion.

"Do you have some paper and something to write with?"

He pulled open the drawer of the bedside table. Except for a Gideon Bible, the drawer was empty. He opened the book, tore out a page, and took his pen out of the pocket of his jacket. "Yes, I have something."

"When you arrive in San Francisco, call this number: 921-4787. Did you get that? 921-4787. It is an office where they take messages for the group at 1563 25th Avenue. Someone there will call the house where he is staying and leave word for him to contact Mr. Brown at your hotel. You will tell the hotel operator to put through any calls for Mr. Brown to your room. When the Englishman calls, tell him you were sent by Gregory Parker. Tell him that Parker sent you and that you need to see him urgently about some crucial information only he has. Have you got all that?"

"Yes."

"Good. When you arrange to meet him, make sure it is somewhere out of the way. Do you know such a place?"

"There are several in Marin County."

"You see? You know the area. That is why you and you alone are best able to do this job. When it is done, just keep on with your schedule."

"You mean go on a television interview program after killing a man?"

"It is most important that there be no variation from your schedule. Yes, you go on a television program."

"God, Micki. I don't know if I can do this."

"Robin. You are a citizen of Israel. You have told me so many times that is it your true home."

"Yes, I know, but . . ."

"Being a citizen of Israel means that you must be always be ready to give of your particular strengths to protect her. In this instance, you have two unique strengths. One is a good eye, and the other is a special knowledge of a particular place."

Again he pictured her, wearing the inevitable tan pants and white shirt. She was the only thing he wanted, the only thing he loved, she was everything. He sighed. "I suppose I should buy myself a pair of gloves while I'm here in Portland."

"Good, now you're getting it. Rubber gloves, the very thin kind. And after you have used the gun, be sure to get rid of it as soon as you can. Get rid of the gloves later. A downtown trash bin is best."

"When do I do this?"

"Today is Monday. You are scheduled to go on the air in Oakland on Wednesday afternoon. Get down to San Francisco this afternoon and make that call as soon as you arrive. Be sure it's from a pay phone. Make the appointment with your man sometime for Tuesday."

"That's tomorrow!"

"I told you, we have no idea how long he will remain in the area. Speed is vital. Take a taxi directly from the airport to the house on 25th Avenue. From there, go to your hotel and tell the switchboard operator to put through any calls for Mr. Brown. Then, wait to hear from him. Robin, I know you can do this, and when you are home in Israel again, we will be married. Just as you want."

Robin's pulse was racing. "You've thought it over, then?"

"Yes."

"And you're sure?"

"How could I say no to a man who shares my dedication? Robin, we are not like other young people in the world who meet and fall in love. We have a duty to Israel, and that duty is part of our commitment to each other."

"Would you have decided not to marry me if I refused to do this . . . this thing you ask."

"But you didn't refuse."

"No, I didn't refuse." He had agreed to this monstrous thing for one reason only, and it wasn't the state of Israel — it was for Michaela. Suddenly he felt a sharp squeezing in his chest and his left arm felt strangely heavy. He flexed it up and down and tried to catch his breath. After several tries, he managed a deep intake of air. "Can you tell me the name of this man I am going to kill?"

"We never use names. It's much too dangerous."

"Maybe it would be easier for me to do this if the man remained anonymous, but I need to know his name."

"All right, but never mention it when you are dealing with the people at the house on 25th Avenue. Just refer to him as the sanction. Can you remember that?"

"I suppose that's a sanitized word for the victim of a contract killing?"

"Exactly."

"What is his name""

She hesitated for several seconds. "It's Keith. John Keith."

Robin wrote the name in the margin of the Bible next to the words *I have finished my course, I have kept the faith.*

Michaela put down the phone. It was done. Robin was taking the sanction and very soon an enemy of Israel would be dead. She prayed, between now and tomorrow, Robin would not somehow discover that his mark, John Keith, was living in his mother's house; that he was, in fact, her lover. On the other hand, from all he had told her, she knew Robin hated his mother. Maybe hurting her would have been an irresistible incentive. No, promising marriage was safer. She turned to look at the thin dark man standing next to her.

"Poor boy" she sighed "poor boy."

CHAPTER 36

BELVEDERE, 1975

Manuevering the unlit road to Bon Tempe Reservoir at 5:20 in the morning was like driving an obstacle course with blinders on. The Jaguar's headlights threw out a steady beam, which spot lit potholes and bumps along the way but did little to illuminate unexpected hairpin turns and overgrown foliage that spilled onto the poorly maintained roadway. A family of raccoons, red eyes reflected in the headlights, crouched on the bank at one of the sharp curves. Another twist in the road cast an eerie glow on an antlered stag, standing in perfect stillness next to the trunk of a gnarled oak. What a magnificent creature! It seemed the height of irony, given his line of work, that he had never killed an animal for sport.

John almost missed the small wooden arrow with the lettering: *Bon Tempe Reservoir 1/2 mile*. He swung the car off Bolinas Road onto a rutted dirt track leading to the deserted parking area below the lake. He cut off the motor and thought of the times last summer when he and Laura had hiked up the grade from this spot to the lake, looking forward to a relaxing picnic by the water. It was a very different place in the pre-dawn gloom. His watch read 5:42. He was more than fifteen minutes early. He noticed another car parked on the far side of the lot, wedged under the low branches of a redwood tree. It was probably left overnight. No one would be back to get it until later that day.

He got out of the car and started trudging up the path to the lake. How the hell would his contact know about Bon Tempe? Parker, of course, the consummate detail man, had chosen the venue. John pictured Greg hunched over his desk in his London office scrutinizing a map of Marin County and finding the exact spot: accessible and, at 6 A.M., deserted.

Hassim had kept his promise. Greg Parker had accepted his resignation from the Cairo station, and John had heard nothing more from him all this year. Until yesterday. What could possibly be so urgent now that Parker had made contact? Crucial information only he had was what Parker's man, Mr. Brown, said. Well, he'd accumulated a great deal of information in twenty years — a lot of it crucial. He wondered what he had that they needed. There was probably something important in the works. He was relieved he was out of it for good. He'd give this man Brown anything he possibly could and hoped it wouldn't take too long. He thought of Jane still asleep in what was now their bed. Suddenly, the image of that car parked so conveniently under those low branches flashed in his mind. An impulse to get out of there nearly overtook him. I'm turning into an old woman, he thought, and continued to climb.

Panting slightly, he reached the top of the grade. The water lay still, like a flat sheet of stainless steel. Somewhere, an owl hooted. The sky was fading from gunmetal to pearl. He stood at the edge of the lake, watching the changing light reflect on its surface. A frog croaked. A minute later, an answer came from across the lake. Again, he shivered, resolving this would be the last time he would ever again be called upon to wait for a contact in a lonely spot at some ungodly hour. He would get in touch with Hassim as soon as he got back to Belvedere and make it clear that he was completely done and they couldn't be calling on him every time they needed a piece of information. Wasn't twenty years of his life enough?

Twenty years. He had gone into the organization with so many illusions: lofty ideals of youth, joining the noble cause, filling the place left by his father. And, one by one, as those illusions shattered, he was left with the reality of his work: treachery, sabotage, assassinations. For twenty years, he had told himself it was all for the greater good. But evil deeds, no matter how great the cause, were still evil deeds. The carapace of denial he had built around himself, while protection from guilt, had barred him from marriage and children and real friendships. His conscience was a tame dog. The part of his brain that housed remorse had long ago been lobotomized. Now, he wanted — what? Absolution? No, absolution came to the repentant. Everything he had done had been done willingly. He had given twenty years to a cause he believed in. Yes, still believed in. He did not repent. It was just that now he wanted, what? A pulse beat in his temple. A peaceful life — and Jane.

He heard a sound and turned toward it. A man stood in the shadow of a large tree. He was holding something in his right hand. Instantly alert, John put his hand inside his jacket and slowly drew his gun from its holster. The man emerged from the shadow. The pale light from the rising sun illuminated a cap of bright yellow curls. John squinted and his breath caught in his throat.

"You!" he cried.

The assassin raised his weapon and John put up his left hand, palm facing out, as if to ward off the thing he knew was coming. He looked into the face that was a reflection of his own, and contrary to twenty years of reflex action, John Keith lowered to his side the hand that held his weapon.

Robin's gun, equipped with a silencer, made only a faint popping sound as he pulled the trigger. Following instructions, he fired a second time. Once more, he heard the popping sound. The man dropped. Robin ran to the body. It was completely still. Again, following the explicit orders he had been given; he held the silencer behind the man's left ear and fired. He stood up. A sudden weakness forced him down on his haunches. He put his head between his knees. As soon as the lightheadedness faded, he walked to the edge of the water and heaved the gun far as he could into the middle of the reservoir. He stripped the rubber gloves from his hands and stuffed them into the pocket of his jacket. His next move should have been to run down the path to his car, but he paused, looking down at the upturned face. There was a bloody mass where an ear had once been. He shuddered but the dizziness did not return. He had the feeling he had seen the man somewhere before but he couldn't remember where. A mop of gray-blond curls fell over the broad forehead. The eyes were half-open. Robin noticed they were fringed with thick gold-tipped lashes. If he had paused to look closer at those dead eyes before fleeing down the dusty path, Robin would have seen they were the same pale green as his own.

CHAPTER 37

Laura rinsed the dish she had used for her sandwich. By one-thirty she had been too hungry to wait lunch any longer and she went ahead and ate without John. He had left the house at 5:30 that morning. To keep an appointment, he said. He told Laura nothing about who he was meeting or why, only that he would probably be back later in the morning but could possibly be gone all day. She understood that he had done some kind of intelligence work for the last twenty years and knew the organization he worked for was engaged in supporting the Palestinian cause but John had not told her anything specific about what his job entailed. She sensed that he would not be able to answer any probing questions honestly and Laura did not want to set up a situation where he might close himself off from her again. Last year at this time, she had still been in the final stages of mourning. Then came the miracle of John at her doorstep. Now, she was celebrating every minute with the man she had loved all her life. She wanted nothing to ruin that.

The first time she was forced to think about Laura English was at Christmas. Gerry Maddox was home in Belvedere, and as usual, Norm was spending the holidays with him.

Gerry called to invite them to Christmas dinner. "I've only met John a few times, and I want to get to know him better."

"That sounds so serious."

"I don't mean it to. It's simply that I care about you very much, and I want to get to know the person you are living with."

There were some muffled sounds in the background, and after a short pause, Norm came on the line. "Now, listen, sweetie, last year you were in your snake-pit phase so I forgave you for not showing up for Thanksgiving and hibernating right through Christmas in Mexico, but this year, no excuses. Be here at six sharp!"

"All right, but go easy on John, okay?"

"What did you think I had in mind? The third degree, or a simple seduction?"

"I mean it, Norm."

"Oh God, don't tell me the man has no sense of humor."

"Yes, he has a sense of humor. It's just that he might not find you as hilarious as I do."

Or as David did, thought Norm. Oh well, if he's what she wants. "So, Laura baby, this is the guy, huh?"

"Yes."

"Well, I'm glad you are having your second chance. Gerry says that *Home Land* is re-releasing in March. I guess you know that Robin has been traveling in the States to promote it. Gerry says he's been booked on every talk show in every major market since December. Have you heard from him? Is John going to see him at all while he's here?"

"No." She paused. "Look, it's just that David had such a tremendous influence on Robin, much more than I ever did. Robin was David's boy. It's better to leave it at that. Besides, John doesn't know that Robin is living in Israel."

"Why not?"

"Oh, nothing. Let's drop it."

"Okay. So, we're on for Christmas?"

"Yes, we're on."

Norm hung up the phone and looked over at Gerry. "Old chum, there's something about it I just don't like."

Christmas at Gerry's couldn't have been more festive. The branches of a ten-foot noble pine were laden with ornaments, some of which dated from Gerry's childhood in Plymouth, others collected on his travels all over the world. The tree made the perfect ice breaker, and before long John and Gerry were sharing travel stories. Michael and Maureen Kent arrived with Rona and Gerald Palfrey, who had flown up from Los Angeles for the occasion and were staying with their old friends in Ross.

Norm, harried but waving off all offers of help, emerged from the kitchen at intervals carrying platters of steaming food. When every inch of space on the sideboard was filled, he wiped his dripping forehead with the corner of his apron and, tossing it through the open kitchen door, announced: "Soup's on, kiddies."

The conversation, which first centered on the magnificent feast, inevitably turned to the movie business.

"Laura, why did we never make another picture together after *Autumn Dance*?" said Michael Kent down the table. He turned to John "Do you remember that one?" Not waiting for a reply, he went on. "Laura was a complete joy to work with, light as a fairy."

Laura's eyes met Norm's and twinkled mischievously. He pursed his lips and raised his eyebrows slightly.

"Michael's right," said Gerald Palfrey "Laura was always a dream to work with, fell right into one's own rhythm, like a good dance partner. How well I remember *Royal Player*," he said to John, who was sitting across the table between Rona and Maureen. "That was Laura's first film at Galaxy. Before that she had worked exclusively for Jamie Paxton at Briarwood." He turned to Laura, seated next to him "Didn't we have fun?"

"Remember Marlene and her tricks?" laughed Laura.

"Pity she died so young," said Gerald. "She was really a pain to work with because she didn't take anything seriously, but when she had a moment, it was something special . . . like no one else."

"How old was she?" said Rona Palfrey.

"Couldn't have been much over thirty-five," said Michael Kent. "Cancer. Bloody rotten luck."

"Yes, rotten," said Laura. They all looked at her and then quickly away.

"Laura, what do you say we find ourselves a little script?" said Michael Kent "As a matter of fact, my agent sent me one the other day that could do very well for us."

"Oh Michael, that's so dear of you, but I'm retired." She looked across the table at John and smiled.

"Surely not! John, you wouldn't mind if Laura did a film once in a while, would you?" asked Gerald Palfrey.

"Of course he wouldn't, Gerald," said Laura. "It isn't that at all. I just don't think I could handle the rigors anymore. For one thing, I'm completely out of shape. I used to do at least forty-five minutes of barre work every day when I was making pictures. I haven't so much as stretched my legs in a year . . ."

"Hmm, I wouldn't say that," murmured Norm.

Laura shot him a glance and went on, ". . . and I'm fat as a pig. You know, everybody expects me to appear in skin-tight Givenchy . . ."

"So, you go on a diet, you'd drop the weight in a month," said Norm "I think Michael's right. At least look at the script."

"I'd really rather not."

"Oh, she's impossible. There's absolutely nothing anyone can do to budge her," said Norm "I must have sent her a dozen scripts in the past year. Nothing. But someday the irresistible project will come along and . . ."

"Enough," said Laura . The subject was clearly closed.

After dinner, they all gathered near the piano while Maureen Kent played Christmas carols, and around 1 A.M., Norm recited his famous version of "'Twas the Night Before Christmas."

"Well, now you've seen it all, John," said Norm. "Your lady love heading for the loo, in full emergency mode." He folded his hands across his belly and sighed. "Is that woman never going to get potty trained?"

John laughed.

"She wet her panties on the occasion of our first encounter," went on Norm, "and I've loved her madly ever since. Here she comes! I hope you are ready to behave now, missy."

Laura looked from Norm to John. "No promises!"

At a quarter to two, Michael Kent had the bright idea of putting in a call to the Paxtons. The telephone traveled around the room as the Kents, the Palfreys, and finally Gerry chatted with Kitty and Jamie. Laura was trying to remember the last time she had spoken to them when the receiver was thrust into her hand.

She put it to her ear. "Hello."

"Laura! Is that you? I say, this is a surprise. No one said you were there. How are you, my dear."

"I'm fine, Jamie." Laura smiled at the sound of his voice.

"You sound it. Oh dear, Kitty's grabbing."

"Laura, Laura . . . are you there?"

"Kitty!"

"How are you, my darling?"

"Wonderful."

"You sound your old self again," said Kitty. "And everything is all right?"

"Yes. Everything is perfect. Listen, Kitty, I know we haven't had a real chat in ages. I'll ring very soon and we'll talk."

"Promise?"

"Absolutely."

As she fell asleep that night, a montage of all the characters she had ever played came into her mind in a muddled but not unpleasant way.

The next day, she and John ate a light breakfast at the kitchen table. In the afternoon, dressed in plaid shirts and jeans, they went for a walk around Belvedere Island. All the while, she could not shake the presence of Laura English. It stayed with her right up to the end of the day when they came home tired and ready for a real meal.

As she took Norm's Christmas dinner leftovers from the refrigerator and arranged them on a platter, the thought came to her that, no matter how deeply she was immersed in her present existence and no matter how wonderful it was, someday she would have to come to terms with Laura English.

Early in the new year, Gerry Maddox called from Los Angeles. "I wanted you to know that the re-release of *Home Land* is set for the first week in March."

"Yes, I know. Norm mentioned it."

"And are you attending the L.A. opening?"

"Oh, Gerry, I don't think so. You see, John . . ."

"I was thinking that we might go together."

"Yes, but . . ."

"Laura, I know that you are in love with John, and I am happy for you, believe me." He paused for a moment "The last thing I intend to do is get maudlin, but I think David would want you there."

Tears stung her eyes. "I know," she whispered.

"Laura, I remember how bad things were for you after David died, and no one is more delighted for you than I am that you've found ..."

"Gerry, you don't understand. John has certain feelings, deep feelings, about Zionism."

"It's not as if I'm asking you to go on a bond tour." His voice was suddenly harsh. "I'm sorry, it's just that if John loves you, he'll understand. That's what love is all about, isn't it?"

She didn't answer.

"Laura. Every filmmaker has one picture that comes straight from his gut. Usually, it's the one that bombs. For David, *Home Land* was that picture. I've always felt that its failure contributed in some way to his illness. You know how he was. Always holding everything inside in that stiff-upper-lip way of his. I think *Home Land* just ate away inside him. I want to give it another chance . . . for David."

"Don't you think I know how David felt about that film? I want it to have a second chance just as much as you do."

"Okay, then come with me and watch it happen."

Almost two months had passed, and Laura had still not told John that she would be going to Los Angeles with Gerry Maddox on the 9th of March to attend the opening of *Home Land*.

She looked at her watch. Twenty to three. This worrying was senseless. John might not be home until late this afternoon. She needed some air. Pulling a jacket out of the hall closet, she ran down Beach Road as far the San Francisco Yacht Club. Panting, she slowed her pace along the sidewalk as she headed toward the seawall. A light sweat broke out on her forehead and she realized, as she took off her jacket, that the day had turned warm. It had come again: the false spring that fooled the fruit trees into sprouting blossoms too soon, only to be knocked off by cold gusts of rain in March. When she reached the granite wall, Laura stopped to look out across the bay at the unobstructed view of San Francisco. She recalled how often, after his first surgery, she and David had walked this same route. He had especially loved this view: the gentle slope of Angel Island, the sailboats bobbing in their slips at the Corinthian Yacht Club, the city streets that ran straight up the hills in neat grids from Cow Hollow to the crest of Pacific Heights, the wisps of fog filtering through the towers of the great bridge, the fishing boats and ferries and tankers going about their business. A seagull swooped down and landed on the beach. It stood for a while preening in the sunlight, then took off over the water. She remembered the frustration she had felt during the months of David's convalescence, when she had longed to get back to work and all he wanted to do was loaf. Laura turned and started home.

A black and white patrol car was parked just past the house. She paused for a moment at her gate, wondering what the Fairfax police were doing in Belvedere. The car door swung open and an officer got out. He walked down the hill to where she was standing.

"Ma'am?"

"Yes"

"I'm Officer Ken Brady, Fairfax PD" He showed her his badge. "May I come in for a minute?"

"What is it?" she said, looking up into his face and seeing only her own distorted reflection in his mirrored sunglasses.

"I think it'd be better if we went inside."

She opened the door and walked ahead of him into the living room. She turned to face him. He took off the glasses. His eyes were very blue.

"Ma'am. Are you acquainted with a person named John G. Keith?"

Her knees started to shake. The police officer led her to the nearest chair.

"Ma'am." He stood above her, his eyes looking down into hers.

"Has something happened to John?"

"I'm afraid so."

"Please tell me."

"He was found forty-five minutes ago up at Bon Tempe Reservoir. A card with your name and address was wedged under his driver's license and a Jaguar registered in your name was in the parking area."

"Found? What do you mean found?" Her teeth were chattering and she was trembling uncontrollably.

"I'm afraid he was not alive."

The officer caught her as she slid off the chair.

The first thing Laura saw when she opened her eyes was a man wearing a white coat. A stethoscope hung loosely around his neck, and he was writing something on a chart cradled in his arm. A doctor. She was lying on a bed in brightly lit room, hooked up to one of those beeping machines just like the ones that had been attached to David during his hospital stays.

"What is this?" she said.

The doctor turned to her and smiled. "You're awake."

"What is this?" she repeated.

"The machine? It's monitoring your heart rate." He glanced at the screen across which a spiky line traveled, faded out, and then reappeared. "Does it bother you?"

"Yes. It reminds me of David." She closed her eyes and shook her head. "I'm sorry. You don't know about David." Her voice was very weak. "David was my husband. He spent a lot of time on those machines."

"Yes, I know."

She turned her head on the pillow and looked at him. His face was familiar, but she couldn't recall where she had seen him before. "What do you mean, you know?"

"My name is Doug Fredricks. I was at Mount Zion Hospital when your husband . . . died."

She looked at him again. The stocky build, the five o'clock shadow, the cocker spaniel eyes. "Yes," she said slowly "I do remember. You took me outside . . . after it was over . . for a walk. Am I at Mt. Zion?"

"No. Marin General. I'm on staff here now."

"Oh," she said.

"And I have a bone to pick with you."

Her head was spinning slightly and she couldn't seem to focus. What was she doing in the hospital? Was she sick? She didn't remember being sick. She realized that the doctor was saying something.

" . . . and you said you'd call me when you got home and you never did."

"Oh."

He smiled. "I guess you made it okay."

"Yes, I guess I did." She smiled faintly. "Doctor, why am I here? I can't seem to remember anything."

She lay, very white against the crisp hospital sheets. He noticed that her eyes were almost devoid of color, like water through a glass. Pale silver and sandy threads mixed with the once-fiery red hair. He thought that she was more beautiful than he remembered.

"Why am I here?" She repeated.

He sat down on the bed and took her hand. "You had a shock. Can you remember what it was?"

"No," she said.

"It had to do with a friend of yours." He paused and gripped her hand a bit tighter. "John Keith?" Again, he paused. "Do you remember now?"

She turned toward the window. The sky was overcast. The false spring had ended. "John is . . ." Her eyes turned from the window to him. "Dead?"

"Yes, Laura, I'm afraid so. I'm so very sorry."

"What happened to him? Did he have an accident?"

Doug Fredricks looked out the window at the gray sky. How do you tell a woman, this woman in particular, that her lover, for that was surely the case, had been shot twice through the chest and a third time through his brain? It had been three years since the night they sat together on the window ledge beside the bed where her husband lay dying. He had known quite a few women since then but none had made him forget the hauntingly beautiful face of this woman with whom he shared those hours. Though he knew his chances of ever meeting her again were slim, when his contract at Mt. Zion came to an end, he applied for an opening at Marin General Hospital. And now, here she was.

"Dr. Fredricks, please tell me the truth. What happened to John?"

He took hold of her hand. "Somebody shot him."

She said nothing for a long time. She looked into the sad brown eyes, remembering that other time, by David's bed. "Thank you for telling me."

"How about a little water?" She nodded and he filled the glass from the pitcher by her bed. He held the glass up to her mouth and she drank.

"Dr. Fredricks . . ."

"Laura, will you please call me Doug?"

"All right, Doug. May I go home now?"

"It would be best if you stayed here overnight. To be on the safe side."

"No thanks, I'll be all right."

"Nothing doing! Listen, I remember your stubborn streak of old. You're staying right here in this bed, and you're going to let us take care of you at least overnight. Okay?"

She turned her head away. Dry sobs shook her body. Very gently he drew her to him. She lay her head against his chest and listened to the comforting rhythm of his heart.

CHAPTER 38

TEL AVIV, 1975

HOME LAND SCORES BIG SECOND TIME AROUND
LATE DIRECTOR'S TRIUMPH

In a career spanning almost two decades, noted director screenwriter and three-time Oscar winner David Landau produced only one flop. Last night, that flop was hailed as one of his greatest achievements.

Home Land is not only the story of the creation of the Jewish state, it is the saga of a people bonded by a common memory and stands as a living memorial to those who share that memory and as a guide for others who wish to understand it.

Among those present at last night's premier was Landau's widow, Academy Award–winning actress Laura English. "In my heart, I feel certain David knows what happened here tonight."

Miss English, who has been in seclusion since the death of her husband, recently suffered another tragic loss when it was revealed that her companion, British journalist John Keith, was the victim of a shooting at a reservoir near her Northern California home. The actress was accompanied to the premiere by Galaxy Studios producer/director Gerald Maddox, her agent, Norman Gillis, and her personal physician.

K itty Paxton took the scissors out of her desk drawer and carefully clipped the article to enclose in the letter she had just written to Robin.

Out of the public eye for nearly three years, Laura had been brave in exposing herself to crowds of adoring fans and clamoring reporters. Kitty sighed thinking of all her darling friend had been through: David's final illness and death, followed by that strange period of limbo, and now, just as she had the chance of a future with the man she had always loved, this final horrific blow. At least Laura had a band of loyal friends surrounding her on the night of the premiere. In fact, among that cadre of loving faces the only one was missing: Robin's. What could have been so urgent that, after all the work he had done to promote the film, he wasn't there to witness David's ultimate triumph? Why did he suddenly have to rush back to Israel? She had hoped that by this time the dear boy would have had his fill of that misguided adventure and returned home to London. Simon had recently been promoted editor in chief at Randolph & Mallory's, a house specializing in botanical and natural history publications. He had mentioned only the other day that one of their top illustrators had announced his retirement and would be leaving in June. If Robin were to come home now, a position ideally suited to his particular gifts would be available. The boys could be working together! A few weeks ago, she had written to him mentioning the job at Randolph's but, as yet, had not received a reply. Kitty Paxton was not one to give up easily when she wanted something badly enough and she wanted Robin home again in London. This letter contained a more detailed description of the job at Randolph's and another plea for him to return home.

Kitty sealed the envelope and addressed it to Robin Landau, c/o the Marcello Gianni Institute. She thought of Marcello's murder and Jamie's instant flight to Beryl's side, but after fifteen years, that momentary defection no longer pained her. In fact, with the passing of time, Kitty discovered, on the rare occasions she and Beryl met, they had a great deal to say to one another. She smiled. There was something to be said about the mellowing process that comes with middle age.

"Well, old thing," she said aloud, pushing herself out of Jamie's chair and away from his desk, "you'd better get a move on or this won't make the morning post. And you, stubborn boy," she said brandishing the letter, "answer this or I will come over there and drag you to London myself!"

Robin slid Aunt Kit's letter back into the thin blue envelope. It was thoughtful of her to send the clipping. Tears filled his eyes and a sob escaped his constricted throat at the sight of his father's handsome face. His emotions were raw. He had slept very little since returning to Israel over a month ago. Each night, flashes of memory intruded just as drowsiness began to draw him into sleep: the soles of his thin leather shoes slipping on the dirt path from the reservoir to the parking area, the shower of needles falling onto the windshield as he backed the rental car out from under the branches of the redwood tree, the pale sun cresting over the Berkeley hills as he sped back over the Golden

Gate Bridge from Marin County to San Francisco, the endless paper work involved in returning the Ford Pinto to the Hertz agency on Post Street, the open suitcase on his bed as he packed his shirts and underwear, the cab ride over the Oakland-Bay bridge to the Channel 2 studios and the smell of stale cigarettes and patchouli in the taxi on the way to the San Francisco airport after that final, nightmarish, interview. And always, the face of the man he killed at the Bon Tempe Reservoir. Night after night, as the vision appeared, Robin struggled to remember the name that went with the face but it continued to elude him, and he awakened to the loneliness and despair that had become, since his arrival back at the Institute, his sole companions.

Only the certainty of Michaela's promise to marry him kept Robin sane on the long flight from San Francisco to Tel Aviv. Picturing her back in his arms helped, if for only a few moments, to blur the images that now seemed permanently etched on his brain: the startled look, the upturned face and a bloody hole where an ear had once been. And the single word: "You!" Why that word? It was as if he recognized him.

The plane finally touched down at Ben Gurion Airport. Robin cleared customs and passed out of the double doors. He searched the waiting area. Michaela was not there.

The icy premonition that chilled Robin on the taxi ride to the Institute was still with him as walked down the hall to the offices he shared with Dov Perez.

After congratulating him on the remarkable efficiency with which he had carried out his assignment, Perez informed him that Michaela had left the country.

"But that can't be, Dov!"

"She left yesterday."

"Where has she gone?" His left arm had suddenly become cold and heavy.

"I am sorry, Robin," said the older man, not unkindly, "that I cannot tell you."

"What do you mean you can't tell me? I talked to her on the phone from the States. We are going to be married. She must have told you."

Again Perez looked into Robin's eyes with something like tenderness. "My boy, that can never be."

"What are you talking about? She told me . . . just four days ago she . . ." There was pain now, radiating down his arm. He needed to sit down.

"I do not know what she said to you, but Michaela could not possibly marry you. She is married already."

Dov Perez took hold of Robin as his knees gave way. "Here, my boy, sit down."

"What in hell do you mean she's married?" His voice was very weak.

Dov Perez was shocked at Robin's deathly pallor. "Michaela has been married to a member of Mossad for two years."

"But we were . . . lovers. Surely you knew," he whispered.

"Yes, I was aware of that."

"I thought you and I were friends. How could you let it go on? Why didn't you say anything to me about . . . about . . ."

"Robin, a few days ago you performed a mission of utmost importance to Israel. In order to accomplish that mission, you had to have the kind of commitment that only comes from a strong attachment to a control."

Robin, his face now a dusky red, bolted to his feet. "Control. Control! What the hell are you talking about?" He fingers gripped onto the back of the chair, his voice ragged and broken.

"Robin! Pull yourself together!"

"Do you mean to say," continued Robin, "that Michaela, your daughter, goddamn it, was my control?"

"Yes, I mean precisely that."

"That everything she did . . . what we did . . . was all just a means to get me to . . . kill . . . that man?"

"Of course not. The opportunity to dispose of the agent was, naturally, not foreseen, but yes, the attachment you had for my daughter was essential in enabling her to persuade you to take on whatever mission was necessary."

"Tell me, Dov, is this standard procedure? Does every new Mossad recruit get a luscious young girl to fuck?"

A muscle at the corner of Perez's eye twitched. "No. But since you are not a *sabra*, we couldn't be certain that your commitment to the state of Israel was strong enough. We knew, from the first day you came to Kefar Aviv, that you were not the usual Jewish boy who comes from England to spend his summer holiday on a kibbutz. We were certain you were there because you were searching for something, something important to give purpose to your life. It was Michaela who suggested that she act as your guide. Your superior ability as a draftsman proved invaluable to us, but it wasn't until your military service that Michaela realized, if the opportunity arose, you could be useful in other ways. At first, I was against her when she suggested you take the sanction. I did not think you capable of such an act, but she said that she could convince you, and she was correct. Sometimes, in our work, we must use extreme measures. Michaela is wholly committed and ..."

"Oh, she used extreme measures, all right. She told me the one thing I wanted to hear. That we would marry. And now you are telling me that all this year, all those times she was in my bed "guiding" me, she had no feelings for me at all? I'll tell you, she's one hell of an actress. Better than my mother!"

"Robin. Please . . ." There was pity in Perez's eyes as he put his hand on Robin's arm.

"And I'll tell you this, your bloody Mossad was absolutely right." Perspiration stood out on Robin's forehead and slid down the sides of his flushed face onto his jaw. "I murdered a man, not in battle or self-defense, but in cold blood because Michaela told me she would marry me. I would have done anything for her after she promised me that. And what about her . . . husband. Did he know that Michaela and I . . . "

"I believe that they have no secrets. They are extremely com ...'"

"Committed? Is that it?"

"Yes"

"Dov, tell me one more thing. What makes a county become so depraved that it demands that kind of commitment?"

"The fact that it must fight every day for its existence."

The following day Robin resumed his job as a document duplicator at the Marcello Gianni Institute, hoping against hope that Michaela would return and tell him that her father was out of his mind, that none of what he had said was true, that she was out of the country for some entirely plausible reason, and that they could be married as soon as he wished. A month passed, and another.

Robin put the clipping into the envelope with Kitty Paxton's letter. A shaky smile touched his dry lips. Good old Aunt Kit. She had always been more of a mother to him than his own. He thought of his mother, most likely accompanied by her entourage of pet poofs, at his father's memorial. Because that is what the premiere was, nothing short of a memorial tribute to his father's genius. She had probably looked her old glamorous self. Evidently, she wasn't in deep mourning for that boyfriend of hers, the one Aunt Kit had said had got himself shot. Suddenly his body stiffened. Aunt Kit had written to him about the incident, but at the time, he had been too preoccupied over the loss of Michaela for anything but the pain of her absence to make an impression. As he remembered, she hadn't given many details in that letter. Or had she?

Oh, Christ! Why hadn't he thought of it before! Had Kit mentioned the man's name? He pulled open the top drawer of his desk. There it was, the blue airmail envelope, in a stack of letters. He unfolded the pages.

" . . . and so, dear boy, please write to your mother as soon as you can. This has been such a great shock to her. You see, she and John Keith knew each other in Bournemouth, many years ago, when they were . . ."

The pages of the letter fluttered out of his hands and onto the floor. He remembered Michaela's voice over the telephone. *We never use names.* But something had made him insist. He remembered the page torn out of the Gideon Bible — and the name he had scrawled in the margin: John G. Keith. He felt a violent urge to vomit. He made an effort to take a deep breath, but his chest seemed to be held in a vise and all he could manage were a few shallow gasps. He slumped over and rested his head on his desk. Again, the face of the man he had killed appeared in the swirling blackness behind his eyes. Slowly, they opened and focused on the French birth certificate he had finished and left to dry.

He pushed himself out of the chair. His knees were still unsteady, but he was able to take a deep breath, then another. He felt better, stronger. *All right, the man I killed knew my mother ... was probably my mother's lover. But she couldn't have known he was a professional assassin. As bad as she is, I have to believe she never knew that. Maybe she didn't really care for him as much as Aunt Kit thinks. After all, they may have known each other once, but that was years ago. What could he possibly have meant to her after so long? In any case, there's nothing I can do now to bring him back. I've got to forget it and get on with ... what?* He bent to retrieve the letter from the floor. There it was, the faintest trace of Miss Dior. He held the pages to his nose. Suddenly all the Paxtons seemed very close.

"So, Simon, you have a job for me if I want it. Well, that's fine, because I'm coming home. You were right all along, Aunt Kit, I never belonged in this bloody place."

CHAPTER 39

LONDON, 1976

Kitty Paxton shook the rain off her umbrella and set it down with her packages under the portico by the front door. Before she could get her key out of her handbag, the door was opened by an elderly housemaid.

"Good afternoon, Lady Kitty. I was just drawing the curtains in the dining room, or I wouldn't have seen you get out of the taxi. Nasty day it turned out to be. Shall I put those packages upstairs?"

"Yes, thank you, Margaret. It certainly is pouring out there." She handed the maid her hat and, glancing in the mirror above the hall table, fluffed out the ash-blond curls framing her face.

"Your messages are on the pad by the telephone in Sir James's study."

"Anything important?"

"Sir James said he would ring again when they finished shooting today. Around seven, he said. And Mrs. Layton called to confirm luncheon tomorrow. Oh, and a gentleman rang. Twice. He said he would like you to call him when you came in."

"Thank you, Margaret. Will you tell Anna I'll need my green silk faille suit for tonight."

"She knows, Lady Kitty. Everything is laid out in your dressing room. Your engagement is for half past seven. Shall I let Anna know you'll be wanting your bath in an hour?"

"Yes, please, Margaret."

Kitty walked down the hall and into to her husband's study. It took her a moment to recognize the name on the message pad. Norman Gillis. Who in the world is Norman Gillis? There were two telephone numbers under the name. Long numbers, each starting with 213. The area code for Los Angeles.

Of course, Norman Gillis. Laura's agent. *Oh my God, Laura!* A frisson of alarm jolted her. Automatically, she looked at her watch. Fifteen minutes past five. It was eight hours earlier in California. She wondered what time he got to the office.

Wishing Jamie wasn't away on location in Spain, Kitty switched on the desk lamp and sat down in his big leather chair. She picked up the receiver and dialed the number.

"Good morning, Gillis Agency."

"Good morning. Mr. Gillis, please."

"May I say who is calling?"

"Catherine Paxton. I am returning his call."

"Just a moment, Ms. Paxton"

Music was playing in her ear. Percy Faith or Montovani. Certainly, Montovani.

There was a click. "Kitty?"

"Yes, Norman. You rang. Is everything all right?"

"Everything is fine."

"Oh, I am relieved. When I got your message naturally the first thing I thought of was Laura. She was in tolerable spirits when I spoke to her last week but . . ."

"Laura is fine. She's loafing. but healthy loafing, if you know what I mean, not like after David."

"Yes, she told me she spends quite a lot of time out of doors and reads a great deal but no scripts, I gather."

"No scripts. As a matter of fact, that's what I called about. Do you know Gerry's friend, Glenda Fisher?"

"Not really. I met her in Acapulco once ages ago. A touch on the flamboyant side, as I remember. I think she and Laura are great chums."

"Yes, they still keep in touch. She was married to a Swiss financier, Hugo Frank. Tremendously rich. Anyway, her husband died several years ago and left her very well fixed."

Kitty wondered if there was going to be a point to this conversation. She hardly knew this man. Why had he contacted her?

"Well, she called me yesterday."

"Pardon me. I'm sorry. Who called you?"

"Glenda Fisher. She called me yesterday. About a friend of hers. A New York producer named Mark Levy."

"I know that name. I believe he is an acquaintance of my husband."

"That's not surprising. Anyway, it seems he is putting together an idea for a musical."

"Yes, I see." Kitty, tapping her fingernails on the desk, wondered again where all this was going.

"An adaptation of *Royal Player.*"

"I see. Wait, did you say *Royal Player*? But that was ..."

"Exactly! Laura's first big hit. It was Glenda who talked Levy into producing it — for Laura."

"A musical?"

"She can sing, you know. Remember that little tune from *Autumn Dance*? It sold a million copies. And Laura was always a wonderful dancer. She'd be sensational."

"Maybe so, but to convince Laura . . ."

"That's where you come in."

"Me?"

"Yes. Right now, Levy is getting together his financing for the show. Glenda told him that if he got Laura English she'd put a chunk of her own money in. Not only did her husband leave her a pile but she's been sculpting the last few years and Gerry says her work is selling like mad."

"With Laura English, it would be a great investment for anyone."

"I agree. Listen, Kitty, I have an idea that if some of Laura's friends put in the money, me included and Gerry Maddox, too, it would be sort of a family venture. See what I mean?"

"Yes, but . . ."

"And I thought of Beryl Villiers."

"Beryl!"

"Sure. She's rolling in the stuff, and it might be fun for her to back a Broadway show. You know, lots of parties and her name in the columns again."

"You know, you are right. These days, Beryl lives a rather secluded life at her villa in Théoule."

"Théoule? Never heard of it."

"Théoule-sur-Mer. It's up the coast on the wrong side of Cannes. Very exclusive, actually. Not a popular destination with the emirs, if you know what I mean."

"Well, can you write her or maybe call?"

"Norman, this must be fate. I received a letter from Beryl two days ago inviting me to come over and spend some time with her. Jamie is filming in Spain, and she thought I could meet up with him after."

"Will you go and talk to her then?"

Kitty thought of the half-finished letter to Beryl she had started this morning declining her invitation. There it was, wedged in the leather frame of blotter in front of her. She slipped out the pages of thin blue paper and slowly tore them in half.

"Norman?"

"Yes."

"I'm on my way!"

CHAPTER 40

CANNES, 1976

Glenda Fisher was late. Beryl Gianni and Kitty Paxton had been waiting for her on the terrace of the Carlton Hotel for almost half an hour, and Kitty was starting to fidget.

"Where do you think she's got to?" she said, checking her watch.

"Who knows, with her," replied Beryl, drinking off the last of her Campari spritzer.

Kitty peered across the palm-lined boulevard to the Croisette. As always, the seaside promenade was crowded with afternoon strollers. Sidestepping a red Ferrari, whose owner blasted a stream of Italian profanities in her direction, a deeply tanned woman in a brief leopard-patterned bikini top and shocking pink hip-hugger pants dashed across the street. Tossing a head of short, frosted curls, she laughed as the man at the wheel made a rude gesture. A wide pink-lipsticked grin still on her face, the woman mounted the steps to the terrace.

"At last!" cried Kitty.

"Hi." Glenda gently drew a trembling toy Maltese terrier from under her arm and set it down next to her chair. "Sorry I'm late."

A waiter appeared. "Madame?"

"A Perrier for me and a Vittel, *sans gaz,* for my dog.

"*À votre service, madame.*"

Glenda sighed, arching her back and putting her face up to the sun. "Hmm, nice."

"How did your meeting go?" asked Beryl.

"Oh, fine. Henri says he'll put in whatever we need."

"Just like that?"

"Oh, sure." The waiter appeared with a tray bearing Glenda's Perrier, a small crystal bowl, and a bottle of Evian water. "Garcon, I ordered Vittel."

"Yes, Madame, I know, but Evian is better for the dogs. Less salt, you understand." He placed the bowl at Glenda's feet and poured some of the Evian water into it. The dog put out its small pink tongue and began to lap at the water, stopped and looked up at the waiter, a perplexed expression in its boot-button eyes.

"As you see, she prefers Vittel."

The waiter shrugged. "As you wish, Madame, but it is on your conscience."

"I must say you sound very offhand about the whole thing," said Beryl, looking narrowly at Glenda. To my recollection, Henri Bergerac was never one to make quick decisions, especially when it came to large sums of money."

"As I said, Henri and I are very old friends." She smiled at Beryl and took a sip of her Perrier.

The older woman's face looked cloudy.

"Well," said Kitty, "that is good news. Mark Levy called me at the crack of dawn this morning to say that Carol Silon and Tommy Baron are hard at work on the score, and what he's heard of it so far is better than *Mercy, Me* and that one ran almost three years. Tony French is doing the dance numbers, and Mark's got Arlene for costumes and Roger Sydney for sets!"

"Fantastic," said Glenda. "Now all we have to do is sell it to Laura."

Beryl turned to Kitty. "I still say we should have talked to her before we went ahead and set so much in motion. Here we are, mounting a Silon-Baron production with a top couture designer doing the costumes and Roger Sydney, no less, designing the sets, and we haven't even spoken to, let alone signed, the star."

"We agreed, did we not," said Kitty "that when we talk to Laura everything has to be in place? She must be shown a finished score and complete portfolios of set and costume sketches, or it won't have the same impact. The show must be there waiting for her to step into."

"I don't see why she must be so mightily coddled," said Beryl.

"Beryl, darling," said Glenda, removing her enormous dark glasses and planting them in the gold-tipped curls, "the whole reason we are backing this production is to get Laura out of retirement. For nearly three years, she's turned down every script that's been offered to her, but Norm Gillis thinks she's really dying to go back to work. She's just scared."

"That's exactly it," said Beryl. "If she's scared to do a film, which is the medium she's used to, what makes you believe she'd ever consider attempting musical comedy? I should think doing live theater would be much more frightening than film."

"As I have explained to you before, it was *Royal Player* that brought Laura to America and made her a star in the first place," said Kitty. "The stage adaptation of that film might be the one project she won't be able to resist."

"Might be is not good enough," said Beryl.

"Beryl," said Glenda "have you forgotten that we are putting together this deal because we care about Laura and want to get her back into the world? Isn't that why we've each put in $300,000, and why I just spent half a day using everything I have on Henri Bergerac to get him to ..."

"I thought you said he did it for old time's sake." Beryl's eyes narrowed and she smirked in Glenda's direction.

"He did. Some old-time knowledge of a few business deals he wouldn't want publicized."

"Ah ha! So it wasn't your charm that made him agree to put in whatever we need."

"Beryl! Shut up!" said Kitty. "And you too," she said turning on Glenda, who was sticking out her tongue. "You are both behaving like a pair of prize-winning bitches."

Glenda clapped her hands over the tiny Maltese's ears. "*S'il te plait! Pas devant l'enfant.*"

"Glenda is right," continued Kitty. "What we all want is to get Laura out of retirement, and to do that we must present this project to her as a *fait accompli*. She can't be allowed the time to mull it over endlessly."

"And if she refuses out of hand?" asked Beryl. "What then? We will have already spent a small fortune on the production."

"She won't refuse," said Kitty, looking at Glenda.

"You mean?" asked Glenda.

"Yes," answered Kitty.

"What is all this?" cried Beryl.

"Our ace in the hole," said Glenda.

"And that is?"

"The one reason she won't turn us down."

"Beryl," Kitty smiled "I didn't mention it to you because it wasn't certain, but I spoke to him last night and — "

"Him? Who is him?" Beryl's face was growing flushed. "I thought we were partners! Why are you two keeping me in the dark?"

"Beryl, we were not keeping you in the dark. It's just that I didn't wish to speak of it until it was definite."

"Well, what is it?" Beryl demanded.

"Uncle Bertie," said Glenda.

"Who in God's name is Uncle Bertie?"

"Albert Easley," said Kitty "He was one of the great character actors of his day and one of Jamie's oldest friends. Bertie's been the director of his own company in Bournemouth for, oh my God, it must be over thirty years now."

"Well, what about him?"

"He has agreed to take the part of Chiffinch."

"How old is this Uncle Bertie?"

"Oh, he must be deep in his seventies, maybe even early eighties."

"Have you gone mad? You've hired some senile scenery chewer from the provinces to play the king's procurer? After all, it's our own money we're risking."

"William Chiffinch was not a young man by the time Nell Gwyn came into King Charles's life. And Albert Easley is neither senile nor, as you so quaintly put it, a scenery chewer. I haven't been the wife of James Paxton for thirty-five years without learning something about casting, and Bertie is perfect for the part. We're lucky to get him."

Beryl's expression softened. "I'm sorry. Kitty, dear. You are right of course. But why do you think that this Uncle Bertie is our ace in the hole?"

"Because Laura is absolutely devoted to him. She told me times without number that her one dream was to work with him again, as she did when she was a young girl. You see, Jamie just happened to be scouting locations on the south coast when he discovered Laura. It was only because of his long friendship with Alfred Easley that he went to see a Bournemouth Players production in the first place — and was completely bowled over by a young actress in the company named Jane Parks."

"And Jane Parks became . . ."

"Laura English!"

"I see. Well then, I suppose your Uncle Bertie news is good."

"Yes," said Kitty, "the very best news."

"Well," said Glenda stretching her hands above her head, "I'm going up for a nap. Henri's taking us to the Coq d'Or and then to the new disco in the Martinez tonight. He's coming by for us here at eight."

"He is?" Beryl's eyes brightened.

"As a matter of fact, he suggested it when I mentioned your name."

"He did?" Beryl's cheeks grew pink.

"Yes, and he asked if you were as beautiful as he remembered."

"And what did you say?" asked Beryl, her eyes narrowing.

"I said that you haven't changed."

"Hmm, well . . ."

Glenda threw her head back and laughed. "Beryl, darling, I told him you were lovelier now than ever and that you had several men in attendance at the moment, but that I was sure I could convince you to break your date for this evening to join his party."

"Did you really, Glenda?"

"Really," she said looking earnestly into the older woman's eyes.

"At times you are almost human."

"At times."

"Well," said Beryl rising, "if we're meeting here at eight, Kitty and I had better get back to the villa to freshen up and change." She summoned the waiter for the bill and gave him instructions to call her driver, who was parked in a side street around the corner from the Carlton.

"We'll see you later, dear." Kitty bent to kiss Glenda. "Well done," she whispered in her ear.

"Just how long does it take her to freshen up?" Glenda whispered. "Three hours?"

"*Salôpe*," Kitty whispered back.

Glenda watched the two perfectly groomed women climb into the back seat of Beryl's enormous black Daimler. The chauffeur shut the door, got in on the driver's side, and sped westward along the Croisette toward Théoule and Beryl's villa.

God, she thought, talk about a couple of well-preserved dames! Kitty, she knew, was past fifty, and Beryl must be close to seventy if she was a day. But, of course, they had taken care of themselves: never ate an unhealthy thing, drank nothing stronger than Champagne, probably purged once a month.

She sighed and looked down at the tiny Maltese, who was gazing up at her mistress expectantly. She had not taken anywhere near that kind of care of herself. Probably in a few years she would look like a hag, but she'd had a hell of a good time. And regrets? Not many. She regretted that she hadn't discovered her talent for sculpting sooner. It was only two years ago that she really began to explore that medium seriously, and her pieces were selling faster than she could turn them out. Maybe if she had been a rich and famous woman when John Keith came into her life . . . no, Keith wasn't after money. He was chasing a memory. A memory he found when Laura English wandered into the Gianni's party that night in Acapulco. After that, there wasn't a chance in hell he'd ever get serious about anyone else. Fun, sure, but as for love, he was lost to anyone but Laura. Well, if she couldn't have John Keith, at least his heart had belonged to the woman she always thought of as a little sister. And now he's dead, and she's grieving a second time. She hoped with all her heart that Gerry and Norman and Kitty were right — that Nelly would get Laura back where she was meant to be: entertaining an audience.

CHAPTER 41

BELVEDERE, 1976

At first, it was little more than the awareness that she was no longer asleep. Then she heard the first sweet, clear notes of a bird singing outside her window. It was, if not the same bird, a cousin of the one she and John used to listen to in those first drowsy moments before full wakefulness. Instead of tears filling her throat at the memory, a smile touched her lips. The year they had together was a sort of miracle, an unexpected gift they had been granted.

After the initial shock of his death, Laura realized it would be ungrateful to grieve for John. Instead she would treasure, in memory, each one of those perfect days. It was odd that the only photograph she had of him was the one she had taken years ago on the beach at Bournemouth. There were hundreds of David, boxes of them that she took down from the top shelf in her closet and looked at often. Those concrete reminders of his striking face, reflecting a fine intellect and sharp wit, made a fact of him — that he had existed in her life as mentor and helpmate and husband. She needed no tangible image of John. The features of the man who had been her one great love were indelibly etched in her heart.

She opened her eyes and glanced at the tiny crystal clock on the night stand. Seven twenty. A pale golden light filtered through the muslin curtains, which billowed out slightly in the breeze coming though the half-opened window. It was mid-week. A good day for Stinson. She would have the whole length of glorious beach to herself.

She sat up. *What in holy hell are you doing? In less than two months you'll be forty-three years old. Do you really want to spend the rest of your life reading and walking on the beach?*

During her last visit to Bournemouth a few months ago, she was shocked to see how frail Aunt Rose had become, but Uncle Matt was as hearty as ever. Longevity ran in her family. She probably had another forty years ahead of her. What was Laura English planning on doing with them? She smiled. She hadn't thought of Laura English for a long time. There was a time, here with John, when she had hated Laura English for having taken first place — to the exclusion of everything and everyone else. Now, she missed her.

Deep down, in the place where she couldn't lie to herself, she knew what she wanted. Every few weeks, Norm called to let her know that another script, written especially with her in mind, had arrived at his office. All it would take was the slightest show of interest on her part, and he would be licking stamps on large manila envelopes and sending screenplays to Belvedere for her approval. Why, then, didn't she simply telephone him? Truth? She was afraid. It had been — how long? Years since she'd made a film. Did she have the energy to keep up the momentum through long days on a set? Did she have the discipline it took to keep going even when she was exhausted? Could she still memorize dialogue? Suddenly, with vivid clarity, she could hear David's voice telling her the only way to rid herself of this burden of fear was simply to take it from her shoulders. She was a performer. Of course she still had the discipline, the energy, and, yes, the talent. If she was past glamorous roles, so be it. Bertie always said the juiciest ones were character parts.

Laura English stretched her arms high above her head, reaching as high as she could, filling her lungs with a satisfying breath.

CHAPTER 42

NEW YORK, 1977

LAURA ENGLISH ENDS RETIREMENT

Laura English, in seclusion since the death of her husband, director David Landau, has signed with producer Mark Levy to star in the new Silon-Baron musical *Nelly*, opening at the Lyceum Theatre on October 7th.

Based on the 1961 film *Royal Player*, which starred Miss English, *Nelly* tells the tale of notorious seventeenth-century actress and courtesan Nell Gwyn.

Cast members will include veteran musical comedy star John Farley as King Charles II and Monica Lacey as Moll Davis. Miss Lacey wowed audiences with her performance as Julie in last year's revival of *Show Boat*.

Miss English's uncle, beloved character actor Albert Easley, will join the cast as Chiffinch, the King's procurer.

The applause was like a roar of thunder. The house lights came on as someone thrust a bouquet of pink roses in her arms. There was Norm, in the fifth-row aisle seat, blowing kisses. In the adjoining seats Gerry Maddox, Paul Andrews and Doug Fredericks were clapping like mad. As she scanned the rows, there didn't seem to be one stranger in the house. Gerald and Rona Palfrey with Maureen and Michael Kent and Glenda Fisher and Beryl Gianni sitting on either side of Henri Bergerac. All the Paxtons were there, including Sarah, who had come for the opening from New York with her American husband and their two small children. Still, the applause went on. Her eyes traveled up to the boxes. For a moment, she thought she saw Aunt Rose and Uncle Matt, but that was not possible because word had come last week that

Rose died and Matthew could not come to the opening. Oh, how she wished he could be here. He and Aunt Rose had believed in her from the time she had made up her mind to be an actress. She had been nothing more than a child, but they had never scoffed at her dreams or thought any less of them because they were the dreams of a child.

David. You would understand better than anyone what this means to me. Please know that you were always the better part of my ambition, my perseverance, and, yes, my triumphs, but the time had to come when I would have to do it without you — and I have!

Suddenly, she realized that not once tonight had her thoughts turned either to John or to Robin. But that was as it should be, because they had no interest in this part of her life. She knew that, for different reasons, it threatened them — and they were right to feel as they did. Still, she wished that Robin had come to New York with the Paxtons. Perhaps if he could see her on the stage, as she was in the beginning, he would understand better. It was sad that there had always been so much bitterness between them. Maybe if she had told him about his father it might have made a difference? She would never know.

Impossibly, the clapping and shouts grew louder, and now the audience was chanting . . . what it was, she could not make out.

"Do you hear that, my girl?" She turned at the sound of Bertie's voice in her ear.

"Yes, can you make out what they are saying?"

"It sounds to me like *Take It in Your Stride*. I guess they want it again." His old eyes were twinkling. "Shall we give it to them?"

"Oh yes, Bertie! Let's give it to them."

The other principals on the stage formed a semi-circle around Laura and Bertie as they sang and danced their duet. The audience went wild.

"Maybe I should have listened to you years ago when you wanted to form a company with me," Bertie gasped in her ear.

"Easley and English! It's still not too late."

"I think that's what we're doing now, my girl."

The audience was calling her name. The others stepped aside to leave her alone at center stage. She looked out onto the sea of faces. Waves of love were coming back at her. Through the tears spilling onto her cheeks, Laura English was laughing.

EPILOGUE

LONDON, 1979

IN THE EVENT OF MY DEATH. Robin turned the envelope over and placed the tip of his finger at the edge of the tape. He hesitated. Why couldn't bring himself to open the thing? If his mother really was dead, maybe he owed, if not to her, then to himself — what? Closure? He went to the drinks cabinet, poured himself more of the Glenfiddich, and returned to the chair. The flames were dying down in the grate. With a sudden movement, he wedged his finger under the tape and ripped the open the flap. Carefully, he smoothed the heavy pages.

June 7, 1967

My dear boy,

This is a difficult letter to begin, but the knowledge that when you read it I shall be dead gives me the courage to put down what needs to be said. I guess that is an advantage to nonexistence — no possible recriminations.

The year is 1967. You are thirteen years old. I met you once when you were just a child, so I have some idea of what you must look like now. Your short, chubby legs have lengthened and there is a coat of down on your cheeks that will be ready for the razor in a year or so. These days your voice might be giving you some trouble, and you wonder if it will ever decide to settle down. You must be curious why a stranger should be thinking about you in this very personal way. The time has come for you to understand who I am and why I have written this letter.

Robin sat up straight and made an effort to take a deep breath but managed only a few shallow gulps of air. It felt as if a steel vise was girding his chest, threatening to shut off the air supply. A sheen of perspiration glistened on his forehead and upper lip as the sickening nausea, that always accompanied these episodes, rose up his throat, leaving a bitter taste of bile in his mouth. Suppressing the impulse to look at the signature, he continued reading.

> Many years ago, in Bournemouth, I fell in love with a young girl. Her name was Jane Parks. The day we met she was sitting on the beach reciting lines out of a book of plays. Her skirt was all bunched up around her legs, and her hair was blowing in the wind. I can still see her face as she looked up at me with those steady Celtic grey eyes of hers. After all this time, the memory of that day is still fresh, and the pain of remembering it raw. Jane and I were very much in love and there was a time when we loved completely. I thought we would marry and be together always, but she had a dream. She wanted to become an actress. One day, a very powerful man discovered her, took her to London, and her dream began to come true. And what became of us? Jane was in London so, when a friend of my father's offered me a job with the organization he worked for, I took it. The job was in Egypt, far away from England, which suited me fine just then. I was hurt and angry but still hoped that, after a year or two, Jane would get acting out of her system and we could get married.
>
> What I have to say now is very important. I had been in Cairo about six months when I happened to see an article in an English newspaper. It said that Jane had married and was going to have a baby. The last time I was with her was in early October, just before she started work on her first film. I was the only man she was seeing. I am absolutely sure of that. I wonder if you remember the day we met in Acapulco. It was like seeing myself at the age of six. There was no question in my mind then and, if your birthday falls in July, there will be none in yours. I am your father.

The vise around his chest squeezed tighter. He thought this must be what it feels like to drown — or to be born. Maybe the struggle through the narrow birth canal is exactly like this. Hours of pressure, unable to breathe. Maybe birth and death are really the same experience. Gasping for breath, he read on.

> I'm sure it must come as a terrible shock to learn that the man you grew up believing to be your father is, in fact, no relation to you. And, given his religious background, it will also come as a shock to learn that the organization I have devoted fifteen years of my life to is one that advocates for the rights of thousands of displaced Palestinians who were removed from

their homeland in order to create a state for European Jews. Your foster father most likely filled your mind with ideas about the Zionist cause but if you could see, as I have, the atrocities perpetrated on innocent women and children, you would understand a great injustice has been inflicted on an ancient and noble people and why I have, as my father did before me, given my life to their cause.

As I write this letter, you are a boy of thirteen. By the time you receive it you may be a man of forty, or you might die before me and never read it at all. But, if you are reading it, I want you to know that not a day has passed, since I knew of your existence, that you have not been in my thoughts.

After that chance encounter in Acapulco, I made up my mind to ask Jane to come back to me. I tried, but things didn't work out. Now that you are a boy on the threshold of manhood, it is important that you know I wanted us to be together. You may wonder why I have never tried to get in touch with you after that one meeting. Because I still love the woman who is the other part of you and I knew that contacting you would have made her extremely distressed. I have done things in my life for which I may have to pay, maybe by a sanction ordered by the Zionists against my life. But while I still have breath in my body, I want to honor the one good thing have known — my love for your mother.

There is nothing more to say. I wanted you to know that you had a father who, although you never knew him, cared for you.

John G. Keith

The Waterford tumbler fell to the floor, spilling the last drops of golden liquid on the patterned rug under Robin's cold, bare feet. A final spasm stiffened his body and blackness closed around him. The muscle with the little missing piece stopped beating.

THE END

ABOUT THE AUTHOR

Lynn Arias Bornstein is a fifth-generation native San Franciscan. She was educated at the Convent of the Sacred Heart and the Katherine Delmar Burke School. Her interest in the arts led her to pursue a degree in graphic design from the San Francisco Art Institute. She continued her studies in Mexico City in the early 1960's, at a time when that city was a world center of culture and new ideas. Soon after her return to San Francisco, she met and married her first husband. The couple settled in Marin County, where they raised their two children in the historic town of Mill Valley. A community volunteer for over forty years, one of Bornstein's main interests is awakening children to an appreciation of literature and the visual arts. In writing Laura English, her goal was to "create a tale in which the characters and settings would provide a pleasurable escape for the reader."

Lynn lives in Marin County, California. She is currently writing a memoir.

Acknowledgements

I wish to thank my editor, Carolyn Miller, whose advice and encourage-
ment kept me on track, and David Kudler, a publisher with the patience of a
saint, for dealing so kindly with a first-time author.

— L.A.B.

STILLPOINT DIGITAL PRESS

Stillpoint Digital Press creates fine ebook, audiobook, and print editions in genres from fiction to literary nonfiction, from memoir to poetry.

In addition to publishing, Stillpoint provides editing and other publishing services to independent publishers, aiming to give a human face to digital publishing, offering a full range of editorial services, from editing, layout and ebook conversion to distribution and marketing.

For more about Stillpoint Digital Press and its books and services, visit us on the web at http://stillpointdigitalpress.com

READ MORE STILLPOINT TITLES:

STILLPOINT/ROMANCE
The Mercenary Major: A Regency Romance by Kate Moore
Sweet Bargain: A Regency Romance by Kate Moore
Sexy Lexy: A Contemporary Romance by Kate Moore

STILLPOINT/MYSTERY
Death in a Fair Place: A Ben Felkin Mystery by W.L. Taylor
Dread in a Fair Place: A Ben Felkin Mystery by W.L. Taylor

STILLPOINT/THOUGHT
Myths to Live By by Joseph Campbell
A Joseph Campbell Companion: Reflections on the Art of Living
by Joseph Campbell
Gods & Games: Toward a New Theology of Play by David L. Miller
Excursions to the Far Side of the Mind: A Book of Memes by Howard Rheingold

STILLPOINT/VERSE
Easing into Dark by Jaqueline Kudler
Sacred Precinct by Jaqueline Kudler
Practice by Dan Belmm
Space/Gap/Interval/Distance by Judy Halebsky
The Stranger Dissolves by Christina Downing

STILLPOINT/MEMORY
Sail Away: Journeys of a Merchant Seaman by Jack Beritzhoff
Pasta in My Bra: a Saga of Cerebral Palsy by Nicole Sykes

AND MORE!

stillpointdigitalpress.com

Made in the USA
San Bernardino, CA
30 March 2014